CANCERQUEEN
and other stories

◇◇◇

Also by Tommaso Landolfi

GOGOL'S WIFE AND OTHER STORIES

CANCERQUEEN
and other stories

TOMMASO LANDOLFI

TRANSLATED BY
Raymond Rosenthal

THE DIAL PRESS · NEW YORK

1971

CONTENTS

✦✦✦

A Note on Landolfi

Tommaso Landolfi is not an easy author; he demands a creative effort from his reader; but he is not gnarled in parable or murky with symbolic meanings that require the laborious services of erudite explicators. His stories mean just what they say on the surface, and a trifle below that surface, though of course like all good stories they spread about them a penumbra of pregnant doubts and uncertainties; they make a long echo within us. The reader who reads this book without undue cultural apprehensions will be on a surer track than the reader, or critic, who searches for mysterious meanings or hidden patterns.

By emphasizing Landolfi's availability to the common yet creative reader, I did not mean to imply that he is flat or ordinary. On the contrary, he is brilliantly original, but his originality is not composed of the usual trappings. There are no flashy milieux, exotic lingoes, or up-to-the-minute references in Landolfi's stories. His ability to think sharply and clearly is always there; and his style is austere yet decora-

tive, with the etched solemnity of a Mannerist façade. Part of his originality derives from this analytical ability, or rather from the conflict
between a deeply sensual nature and a deeply reflective mind. He is
that unique creature in modern writing, an obstinately reasonable and
reasoning writer who has somehow managed to preserve in the depths
of despair a sensual, even romantic, relation to life and its infinite
possibilities.

To put it in a phrase, Landolfi is humble toward the spirit and
high-handed with life and the world. In this sense, he reverses the
customary stance of the Italian writer. He is in fact a metaphysical
writer, the first modern Italian writer since Leopardi with obsessive
metaphysical concerns. He became what he is by a typically modern
form of cross-breeding. Just as French logic precipitated something essential in Samuel Beckett, and English latter-day romanticism released
something quirky in Jorge Luis Borges, so Russian literature, both
classic and modern, gave Landolfi that particular form and accent, that
special approach to his material, which makes him unique among con-
temporary Italian writers. For even the best Italian writers, such as
Moravia, Gadda and Pavese, regard the metaphysical question as settled; they end their books precisely at the point where Landolfi begins
his.

To be a true metaphysical writer not only means that one raises
what Russian writers of the last century called the "accursed questions"
—what is good and what is evil, why do we live and why do we die,
what is the essence of man and what is the meaning of his destiny on
earth?—but that one questions the very underpinnings of reality and,
what's more, questions them from the standpoint of the spirit. Landolfi in his most characteristic fiction starts from scratch every time he
puts pen to paper. And every one of his stories in this book, whether
trembling with horror or quaking with laughter, attacks an essentially
spiritual problem, not because Landolfi thinks he can solve it by this
means—spiritual problems can't be "solved,"—but because this is the
only way he knows of making a foray into "that unknown which

makes us what we are." To the casual observer Beckett's despair—I mention him because in feeling and obsessiveness he most resembles Landolfi—may seem deeper and more intense than Landolfi's, due to the latter's sprightliness and impeccable good manners, but that casual observer should look more deeply. He would discover that Landolfi, who flees all social and political bandwagons and despises the gyrations of literary fashion, is a writer of the most profound existential anguish, and that his despair is at once more aware of itself and more realistic than anything that can be summarized in a superficial catchword.

If, as Landolfi believes, the spirit is the only reality and so the only all-engrossing subject for literature, this may in turn help us to understand the peculiar role that style plays in his work. It is at one and the same time a way to call up the demons and to exorcize them, as a sensitive Italian critic, Giacomo Debenedetti, has described: "Nobody will miss the singular maneuver of this artist, who presents himself to us with the most well-bred correctness. . . . He uses all of his urbanity to calm us, to put us at our ease. Imagine that you have come as a guest to a castle and the host, accompanying you to the room set aside for you, opens the shutters, shows you the beautiful view and acquaints you with the room's comforts and conveniences. But then when night falls you begin to hear all around you an insidious concert of squeaks and groans. The next morning, after a sleepless night, you learn that this is the room haunted by ghosts. And the host's politeness and exaggerated concern now appear to you in another light." But, Debenedetti hastens to explain, this is not bad faith on Landolfi's part but rather his ceremonious way of involving us, making us his accomplices and witnesses. "Landolfi," Debenedetti declares, "is an impassioned, high-class gambler. He plays on the clarity of the surface, of the invention, in order to eclipse something else. But then he plays on the meaning of the eclipse, to lure us into lifting the veil. But at this point he stops playing. That is the story."

Landolfi treats us with ceremonial politeness and thus lures us into many compromising adventures. Dangerous adventures in which women, madmen, gamblers and animals play the crucial roles. In "The Mute" we shall live in the mind of a child murderer who reminds us of Dostoevsky's Stavrogin and Nabokov's Humbert Humbert and yet is a pure creation of Landolfi's anguish and frightening vision. In "Cancerqueen" we shall fly to the moon with a mad inventor out of the pages of Poe and Céline, an adventure which in the end assumes an emblematic meaning for all those poor souls who can neither live nor die and must continue to exist in a perpetual twilight. In "Week of Sun" we shall inhabit the fantasies of a madman that tell us more of the pain, misery, and self-fulfillment of insanity than a thousand case histories. And in "Night Must Fall" we shall be dragged into the blandishing eloquence of a young poet, whose bitterness at the world's inevitable repetitiveness and banality turns into a cry against all brute suffering. In short it is the world of fantastic reality of the great Russian writers and especially of the modern Russian poets from Blok to Mandelstam. And I can think of no better way to sum up Landolfi's flavor and fascination than by the words Mandelstam wrote to describe Ariosto, another Italian fantast: "A Pushkin sadness mixed charmingly with Mediterranean arrogance."

Raymond Rosenthal

CANCERQUEEN
and other stories

The Mute

◇◇◇
——————
◇◇◇

I

They're here . . . they're coming. No, they're not coming, it's impossible, it's too soon. But if they do not come now they will come later, that is certain, inescapable. But, after all, it is so for everyone, not only for me. Of course, and yet for everyone else it is different. Why different? This is the point I must clarify, not out of idle intellectual curiosity (what do I care about the problem in itself, and how others feel?), but rather in order to become more like them. So, let's see if we can understand all this; it is necessary, urgent, for me to find a way to die. Let's start all over again. Now, this is how my reasoning went: what makes an average man's waiting (for death) different from that of a man sentenced to death, such as myself? Obviously, I replied, after mature reflection, it is the fact that the former is unaware both of the time and manner of his death; so all that I must do is put myself in the condition of being unaware, etc., and all terror will be overcome. Consequently, I have ordered my lawyer to do everything in his power, but without informing me. And in fact, at this very moment, I have no idea whether my appeal for a pardon was rejected, what date has been set for the execution and how, strictly speaking, this is to take place; for if it is true that in this state one dies in the electric chair, my lawyer could still obtain my transfer to another state, in which case I would die by hanging or in some other manner. So all my problems should be solved. And instead, my problems aren't solved at all; for quite some time now I've come to see that my reasoning was naive; I realized that it was, but didn't know exactly why. So then, why was it? Let us think a little more. And straightaway my new line of reasoning leads to this result: my reasoning was naive because I forgot the main proposition, as I'm doing right now. All right then, let us go on to the secondary proposition: it was naive because an average man's life expectancy, the forecast of his life's termination, let us say, is different from that of a man sentenced to death. I mean that while everyone else, following a certain natural course, may hope to die many years hence, I can under no circumstances entertain such a hope: what with postponements, objections and appeals, I might even hang on for a year or two, but then . . . In short, my situation is like that of a cancer patient to whom the doctors have granted a given, approximate yet at any rate very short time to live. . . . Nonsense! Would the possibility to assume that one's death is far removed be enough to achieve tranquility, and, conversely, the assumption of its proximity be enough to cause alarm, anguish, despair? And what about old people then, whom we often see quietly waiting for it? They say old people are helped by nature, which blunts their faculties. But what about those cancer patients I mentioned, and all the other people stricken by some fatal, fast-consuming disease? Actually, I've never been able to understand how they manage to live or, rather, die; and yet they do live and die. But in spite of all my agitation and brain-racking, I too live, and shall end by dying, even without having found a way to do it; the point is that I am desperate, desperate, while they are not, not always; I am overwhelmed by fear, by terror. . . . There was one of them, I remember, in my town: he had a sore on his leg and gangrene set in, but they could not take off the leg because his heart was too weak; it would have amounted to killing him outright. So there he was, with that fire and destruction which kept mounting, mounting and whose progress you could (he could!) measure from day to day, hour to hour. And what do you think he did? Did he go into a frenzy, curse, offer his soul to the devil or, when the worst came to the worst, pray? Oh, it would have been easy, if he had known how to pray. No, he didn't do a thing: he just stayed there, waiting for the evil beast to sink its fangs little by little into his entrails, and at last into his heart. He sent for all his relations a few at a time, and for all the notables in the town, to take his leave of them, he embraced and kissed them and wished them well; during one of these visits he lifted the blankets covering his leg and, almost without anger, without impatience, he said to the gangrene: "Come on, do your job." Well now, how could this happen? I keep asking myself this, I've got to know; although knowing perhaps won't help me. Yes, a moment ago I was tempted to conclude, with regard to my initial argument, that in substance it was naive because it was reasoning, since nobody, no matter what he does, will ever be able to put himself in someone else's situation or even imagine himself in it, so all that I was left with was an argument pure and simple; and it is not by reasoning that one can find a way to die; at best one will find a way to commit suicide, which is a completely different and, by its nature, antithetic matter. So I was tempted to draw that conclusion; but now, suddenly now, a frightful idea has entered my mind. Frightful! Perhaps I will have to evaluate the innermost quality of that kind of waiting for death and my kind. . . . I tremble at the thought of being more precise, and yet I must. I mean, could it be that waiting for death in itself might be different for the innocent and the guilty? God forbid! In that case there would be no salvation for me, because I am guilty: I have killed! There would be no salvation, not from death which is the least of evils and perhaps does not even exist, but from dread and terror which are a definite reality. My nights have grown longer, endless nightmares, I am afraid to fall asleep because they might come at any moment: they will enter surreptitiously, taking advantage of my dozing off for a second (I saw this in a movie); most likely after having spent the previous evening sitting on my bed, telling spicy stories, getting me to talk about my women; they will grab my arms, before telling me the moment has come. . . . My food has turned into poison, the world is disfigured, each emotion, each minute pleasure is threatened, sterilized; a dark shadow weighs on everything, anguish lurks in every thing, each moment brings with it all the tortures of the damned, each moment is a poisonous thing that I must gulp down and can only swallow by rallying all of my strength, light offends me, darkness is solid, suffocating, threatening, every visible thing is alien to me and yet wounds me deeply. A torture without name or end: because I must die, because *I am condemned to death!* Ah, who will ever understand the meaning of these words unless he himself is condemned to death? Yes, torture without end: because if I meet death like this, the torture cannot help but continue beyond it, or death itself will be the eternal continuation of my sufferings. Oh God, how can one live, how can one die like this? Or should I hope for forgiveness and find peace in the hope of a future? Why not? This might be the right path, but the trouble is that no one can show it to me unless it already exists within me. And it does not: I do not hope for forgiveness, because I neither trust nor believe in the one who would have to grant it to me; and it is not with the future that I want or can concern myself, but with the present. It is now and here that I must resolve my situation; right now, immediately. And I have no other way but to . . . It is an absurd, insane way: I have killed, I have killed a fifteen-year-old girl! But it is the only way. In short, I must try to convince myself. . . . But I did kill, I killed a fifteen-year-old girl. I must try to convince myself that I am not guilty. It will be difficult, impossible, I know: nevertheless I must try, or at least I must attempt to understand why I did it, or at least . . . Who can tell? Perhaps remembering how it happened, point by point, I will find . . . ah, find what? an explanation if not a justification, as they say? Well, yes, and if not an explanation of what happened, one of myself, or on one hand where I began from and, on the other, the event itself . . . Oh God (or rather, Oh surviving light of my soul) help me! . . . I hear steps outside; will they leave me enough time?

II

There was a kind of shadow on her brow, or perhaps actually something murky about her eyes. But not murky, it was really as if she looked at you facing the sun or through the shadow of her lashes; something dark, I cannot describe it in any other way. Or (at the third try) at most I could say that it was nocturnal, shadowy. And that look of hers was at once shy and bold; bold in a very specific way, as if she were trying to overcome a feeling of anxiety, or rather it was like . . . like a moan, I find no other word. Ah, why try? I become confused when I try to define it . . . mute, in a way, but mute of something. Is it possible to be mute of something, as one is full or speaking of something? If so, her eyes were mute of voluptuousness, tenderness, but also of sorrow, foreboding. . . . What the devil am I writing? Never mind. And she herself, all of her, was of a beauty that I will not even call perfect: more and different from perfect, a terrible, unconscious beauty. Women who are aware of their power, they say, are the most dangerous: no doubt, but this is for gross spirits, blind senses. Quite tall but not too tall, slim, when I first saw her I decided that she must be fifteen, and that is what she was, as I discovered later. I used to meet her in the morning at eight or a few minutes before, when she was going to school. In the beginning it was by chance, then because I arranged for those encounters, that is, made sure to be there when she passed by. What I could see of her body through her simple little dress drove me crazy; sometimes she rested the weight of her books against her hip which then appeared clearly defined, terrifyingly soft, curved, round; there were moments when the wind molded her loins through the cloth, or, as I faced her, and saw her tender but already firm breasts, quivering, her small belly, her dizzying hollows, I gasped for air. Her legs, perfectly shaped already, slender, determined, moved inside me as a child moves inside her mother; but—a detail that made you want to weep with despair, almost with horror—she still flung out her feet, only her feet, to either side, like a duckling. At first she did not look at me, then she began to do so, indefinably, from her nocturnal aura. Nocturnal was her hair, too, cut in bangs, and so undoubtedly was that other small, just growing tuft. . . . But why continue this raving, this delirium of memory? In short, I realized soon enough that I must have her, that I could not do without her and without having her; I would die otherwise, die of suffocation. Was it love? I don't know, I don't care: it was a flame, a volcano, a fountain of blood inside me.

But how could I have her, how even speak to her without stirring up a hornet's nest, malevolence (the town was small), without running into trouble with the usual parents, perhaps brothers, without having to fight for her, and with scant hope of success, fight against those who unjustly kept her to themselves, against the very world in which she was enmeshed? Her own world, and this larger one through which she undeservedly roamed, a forbidden creature hailing from the limits of time and space. I did not know what to decide. I imagined saying to her point-blank, like Garibaldi to Anita, "You are mine"; but suppose she answered, or kept silent like Anita, I certainly was no Garibaldi, and so how could I sustain that sort of role? I did not know what to decide; and yet there was no doubt that she was there to sustain me, fulfill and fill me, and at the same time to ask for my help and become filled with me, yielding to me half of her celestial virtue in exchange for half of my blood. So how was it possible that anything should stand in the way of the fulfillment of our lofty fate? . . . I am still crazy today, I know; yet how can anyone speak in such terms? So then, in more terrestrial terms, one thing was clear—I needed at least her consent.

I said that she had begun to look at me indefinably; I nevertheless did my best to define those looks, and I won't go into all the possibilities I turned over in my mind. In the end I concluded that they could be interpreted more or less as follows: I like you because I like you and because you like me. Me, a silly little girl who really has no right yet to a man's admiration; but I do have something to hide. This, obviously, was a mere interpretation and a vague one at that, of scarce immediate use; but was it my fault if I had of necessity to proceed by dint of probing? At any rate, that kind of hypothesis seemed reassuring, at least to the extent that it excluded all aversion on her part; in other words, so much seemed certain, I was not confronted by an *a priori* rejection. Having convinced myself of this, nothing prevented me from proceeding like a mathematician who poses a hypothesis in precisely this manner, reserving the right to see what comes of it and to start all over again with another. As for what she might be hiding, that for the time being I would consider an embellishment on my interpretation, an inessential addition as to which the future would enlighten me. There is no need to add that, if there really was some dark flaw in her, it would become my most powerful ally. . . . Oh damned, hideous explanations, in which all is lost! Instead, you have to come to life in these pages, and die again, and be mine as you once were. Useless explanations, too: I was to understand everything sooner than I had hoped.

I studied her habits. I noticed that she used to go for solitary rides on her bicycle. Indeed she was almost always alone, save for the occasional presence of some member of her family: why? Her favorite goal seemed to be a spot at the end of the promenade along the sea, where there was a particular bench on which she sometimes sat briefly to rest. Now as it happens, not far from there, stood a small tennis court, its shorter side protected by straw mats which, as a matter of fact, projected for a couple of feet, forming, at the junction with the court's longer side, a dead angle or small niche. There, a man on watch (me in fact) could comfortably station himself, so that when she arrived she would think she was alone; what's more, the place was usually deserted, at least in the late afternoon, her time. So what I intended to do was clear: take advantage of these favorable circumstances to approach her somehow, if possible to speak to her. And I wasted no time.

The first afternoon she did not come; on the second I saw her from a distance, approaching slowly, almost warily, swaying on her bicycle. I disappeared into my shelter; she came as far as the bench, leaned against it, still astraddle, then got off, glanced all around in her guarded way, and finally sat down. This was the moment, and I came out with an absentminded air; she was looking at the sea and paid no attention to me; or, rather, she must have noticed me somehow and certainly recognized me, but in any case she thought that I would walk past her. Instead, I sat down too, of course at the other end of the bench. But what was I supposed to say to her? Nothing—best to say nothing and just wait. She kept looking at the sea, motionless; yet I noted with pleasure that she was slightly troubled. I could see her small ear twitch a little and now and then her lips close tightly. Because of these imperceptible movements her beautiful profile also appeared singularly and ridiculously altered, regressing, if I can put it so, to its childhood cast. But how I could exploit that tension, whatever its cause, I had not the faintest idea; on the other hand I could tell that in a moment or two she would leave, and that would be that.

I racked my brain furiously; and the scheme I came up with on the spur of the moment could not have been more abstruse, although, in truth, it did follow quite logically from my first impulse, which, on seeing her troubled, had been to reassure and soothe her. But the pretext at my disposal was too weak and uncertain; so now I decided to increase her uneasiness, just enough to justify my intervening. And I started, first, to hum under my breath a series of extemporaneous sounds (I did not want to compromise my chances with a song or a melody that she might dislike, or risk appearing too intelligent or not intelligent enough), then I burst into a brief sinister laugh, all to myself, then, as if commenting on a sudden thought, I gave a few grunts accompanied by appropriate gesticulations—in a word, I did my best to convince her that I was one of those half-demented persons who often haunt park benches (no doubt, in performing that very act, I was more than half demented). And here, as I had foreseen, she turned around and looked at me blankly with feigned indifference, but actually quite dismayed; and she got up with studied slowness, as if preparing not to run away, but simply to leave. The question of how to address her, as a child or a young lady, I had answered a long time ago, recognizing the obvious advantages offered by the first course, so I said:

"What is it, did I frighten you? Relax, don't worry: it's just that sometimes the funniest things pop into my head, and you know . . ."

She kept silent; but I thought I saw her clouded eyes light up with kindness and trust. She looked at me less blankly; and meekly, that's definite. I immediately continued:

"Where do you go to school, do you like school?" The reference to her being a schoolgirl, a child, was intentional.

She kept silent, observing me furtively; she seemed timid but not intimidated.

"You live here all year round, right? Do you have any brothers or sisters?"

She kept silent. Damn it, if she didn't answer pretty soon I wouldn't—in fact I already didn't—know what else to say. And why didn't she answer? Was it a fit of bashfulness, as sometimes happens with small children?

"That's a nice bicycle; is it yours?"

She kept silent. No. Her silence was definitely becoming unnatural; and, I couldn't quite believe it, her eyes looked much brighter now, glistening with unyielding tears. She needed a little shock; I decided to ask her a somewhat more unsettling question.

"What are you doing here all by yourself? Girls your age are supposed to go biking with their little friends from school, aren't they?"

She kept silent. And at last . . . Oh my dear child, may you be blessed for that moment which brought you even closer to me, subjected you to me. May you be blessed for that moment and for this moment too, in which I drown and which completely gives you back to me (but did I ever lose you? Did I not make you mine for eternity?). . . . And at last, as I was saying, she made an eloquent gesture: yes, eloquent.

She was mute. Not mute of something as, with a facile literary effect, I said earlier when describing the look in her eyes: she was mute, period. Of course, here too, to pick that phrase up again and partly distort it, one could say that she was mute of many things—but only because nothing prevents one from stringing together sentences that mean nothing; unless one intended it to mean that her defect had preserved intact and perhaps even heightened all her other faculties (for example, she was not at all deaf, as most aphasics often are). A defect which, I am convinced, was not definitive but rather connected with a specific condition of one of her organs or her system, and so susceptible to elimination with appropriate treatment; for the moment, however, she was mute—and by now she is irremediably so.

She was mute. And I, who had grown used to consider, to see her as utterly perfect, like the Maid of Orleans, what was I to make of this unsuspected handicap? But was it a handicap in the first place? In truth my longings had left me no other choice than to value it as a new perfection; I mean that this was their natural course, though not free from dangers and traps. If perfection by excess is generally oppressive, perfection by default, so help me God, is by its very nature distressing, unbearable. . . . There is no point in my explaining in greater detail or anticipating: we shall see further on, or we shall not, and it is all the same, what decisive role this muteness was to play in our destiny. On the other hand, there on the bench my immediate reaction to her eloquent gesture was not only surprise and lacerating sorrow but also elation: for, in a way, her confession put her at my mercy, both in itself and in myself; besides, her proffering it assured me of her favorable disposition.

With vivacious, childish gestures she continued to point to her mouth, almost making an effort to articulate words; but she did not grunt in a disagreeable or painful way as aphasics generally do. I could see the crown of her small teeth, the wet, gleaming tongue, the vivid red gums; I saw them, that is, I watched spellbound and still did not find anything appropriate to say. Finally I said, or rather stammered:

"I see; but . . . it doesn't matter."

She answered by opening her mouth several times, forcefully: it mattered, it mattered a lot. I plunged:

"I assure you, you're actually better off; what is the good of talking, exchanging empty words with people? Empty, yet through them we lose so much of ourselves. . . ."

She watched me attentively; I felt I could continue.

". . . So much that we could employ more . . . more nobly. It is through words, the so-called gift of speech that man loses his soul, did you ever think of that?"

I was getting carried away; yet her nocturnal eyes were fixed on me with greater intensity, and slowly she nodded yes! But I couldn't count on it; children often act that way, pretending they understand. It was best not to push the test to extremes, return to a more easygoing tone.

"What do you miss? You can hear, you can see, read: do you like to read?"

Yes.

"So there, isn't that like a conversation, like talking with someone, and much more worthwhile?"

Yes, ardently. Fine, I had hit the right tone.

"And even if you can't speak by saying words, you can still write . . ."

A strange agitation which I did not notice right away seized her at this point:

"And writing does not allow us to say things at random or lose ourselves in trivial chatter; when we write we are alone with our conscience . . ."

Her agitation increased; she looked at me imploringly, that is, she implored me to understand her. She made several convulsed gestures that I could not interpret; she repeated them desperately, and I thought I knew what she meant. Could it be true? It was more than I had hoped for.

"What, do you write?"

Yes, with relief and pride.

"Well, of course, you go to school, and you have to write, among other things, more than the others in fact, because they can talk to the teachers, while you . . ."

No, that wasn't it.

"You mean you write for yourself?"

Yes, you've finally understood.

"And what do you write?"

Vague gesture: a little of everything. But then, movement of a slender index finger, pointing to her soft swallow's breast. Does she mean a diary?

"A diary?"

Yes, that too.

But here she seemed to remember something, and made a sign that meant she had to leave in a hurry; she stood up, mounted the bicycle, taking care not to expose her legs, barely nodded her head goodbye and really left. Just as well, since quite unaware, she had begun to lapse into the mute's painful mimicked language, and I certainly did not want that. I watched her leave: the thrust of her loins with which she righted her balance on the point of losing it, made me shiver.

Naturally these encounters continued with a certain regularity, despite the dangers involved, though they were not prearranged. She did not seem to worry about being seen—perhaps her family allowed her a measure of freedom, relied on her good sense. It was all quite easy: having found her to be docile, intelligent and sensitive, and even, albeit in a very general fashion, inclined to the poetic, the rest came of itself. My role was demanding, that is true, since I had to do all the talking, but how incredibly beautiful was the reward I got from her tacit yet eloquent, lively answers, her airy games, if I may call them that. I remember one time: I was reciting to her, as happened very often by now, reciting in a low voice an excruciatingly tender and sad poem, which seemed to tangibly evoke our thousand lives straining toward fulfillment but disillusioned and finally resigned to the fatuous play of the celestial seasons. All the while, her eyes were fixed on me moist with tears. And suddenly she broke or melted into silent weeping, both as bitter and tender as those verses; and the tears streamed, streamed down her face without distorting it; and she swallowed them, unable to check them. Oh supreme confession of the feminine soul to which beauty is pain, oh supreme, unique joy, comparable to no other for the man to whom that confession is offered!

Yes, that is right, I would like to say something about her, exactly, about this her, before going on to that other her. I would like to, but I do not know how. Who was she? I don't know, there is only one thing I can say, and in order to say it I will perhaps have to resort for the third time to that wretched phrase of mine, within whose circle, I don't know why, I am still confined. Yes, I squirm and grope: at least I would like to know whom I killed, whom I made eternally mine, and I certainly will not find out if I go on like this. (Not "at least." Only sometimes I cannot resist the blasphemous temptation to define her, and do it with the cold language of reason.) But let me say it finally! Her gaze was mute of something, I declared at the outset; then I partly contradicted this statement, only to confirm it to some extent immediately afterwards; and now, on the seesaw of an image which is mediocre and above all relative, I would like, wretch that I am, to return to my first formulation. And yet, it is almost exactly so: her soul was, like the look in her eyes, mute of something. Of everything. But perhaps her fifteen years were mute: of everything, just as they were avid of everything. That is all I can say, but perhaps all is already here; and the boiling lake of blood in my heart. Of what mattered most (her love?), she never spoke. Who knows? maybe she could not; and her muteness was crushing, deafening, stunning, like the very voice of silence. How could I not? . . .

Our meetings continued, but I was burning. . . . She lived in a small house, on the ground floor, and my scheme was readily conceived: late at night, when all of her family was fast asleep, she would get out through one of the windows; I would be waiting for her, and my own house was only a short walk from hers. But this turned out to be more difficult: when I felt the right moment had come and I got up the courage to inform her of my plan, presenting, of course, the usual pretexts of books and readings, she listened without showing too much surprise, but shook her head in sign of refusal, nor did she volunteer an excuse. And the same every time from then on, whenever with all due caution I returned to the subject; she seemed immovable and I was starting to despair and become desperate. Then all of a sudden she yielded, in her way, on a day like any other: I cannot imagine what went on in her lovely round little head just at that moment, or what made her decide. We agreed to meet that very night; true enough, her assent as she left was somewhat vague, but I never doubted that she would come.

I spent the intervening time like a salamander or a scorpion in the middle of a fire, and at long last it was two o'clock, the hour we had agreed upon. Opposite her house stood a large building that had gone up quite recently which had a kind of shadowy portico: from there I stared at the window or, more accurately, the slice of window (of the bathroom) through which she was supposed to get out of the house. But the seconds, the minutes passed, and there was no sign of anything; that slice of window looked as though it were sealed, incomparably foolish rather than cruel in its blindness, nor did I perceive any other signs. Apart from my anguish and disappointment, I was beginning to feel ill at ease, for in a small town even the walls have eyes and some insomniac might have noticed my standing there on guard. The bell of the church tower, in the distance, struck a quarter past two. At last, when I no longer felt capable of mastering my agitation and was about to run away, the lower section of the half-shutter moved imperceptibly, slowly began to lift outwards, and from behind it the girl's small black head appeared for an instant; it immediately disappeared, then appeared again, this time protruding a little farther out. She peered round, saw me, then extended a tiny white hand from the darkness and with her index finger repeatedly signaled no—in short, she was telling me that she did not want to or could not come. But whatever her motive, how could I possibly accept a thing like that? I waved my arms desperately, imploring, then it occurred to me that most likely she could not see my movements, and, abandoning all caution, I left my dusky shelter to wave at her in the full light. She seemed to hesitate, again she disappeared; I stepped back into the shadow, feeling as if I had been burnt alive. But an instant later God willed that the entire shutter open without a sound: on the edge of the darkness a small foot appeared and was placed on the windowsill, one of her tiny maddening feet, encased in one of those soft flat shoes that young girls wear around the house. Followed by the leg, it slipped across the sill on its heel, fell off and hung suspended limply in the void, and was joined in the same manner by its twin. . . . Ah, why must I dwell on these details? The reason is obvious; yet now they lacerate me. . . . Having then sat down on the sill, she dropped lightly to the ground. Another lacerating detail: she had gone to the trouble of putting on her slacks, I am sure to avoid showing her legs when climbing out like that.

The short stretch of road to my house ran along the railroad embankment and, except for the men working on two buildings under construction, was deserted even during the day. All the same, we certainly could not walk away together. So I started out ahead, leaving her where she was: she already knew that she was supposed to follow me at a distance, hiding as much as possible. And she did. I reached the hallway inside my building which lacked permanent lighting but was dimly illuminated by the streetlamps outside; she joined me a moment later. She joined me and seized my arm, shaking it and her head too, convulsively, wrinkling her eyes: she was trying to tell me that she had changed her mind, she did not feel up to it, she was scared. I should have foreseen this sort of afterthought, this feminine dodge which after all was natural and perfectly sincere; but my ardor had prevented my doing so. In any event, since I had not foreseen anything, I now felt lost. But there was very little I could have done; she clasped my hand weakly in hers, which was ice cold, and immediately ran away. I went to the door; she was running like a gazelle, nor could I possibly set off in pursuit. She turned the corner, and I was left there, trying to swallow my feelings as best I could.

The following day she did not come to the promenade bench, or the day after. Finally, on the third day, I saw her arrive pedaling fast on her bicycle, and I was already preparing some cleverly insinuating arguments; but she stopped a few paces away without getting off, one foot resting on the ground, and gave me a long look in silence, so to speak. Then, suddenly, with a series of rapid gestures she informed me that she had made up her mind now, that that night at the same hour as last time she would come to my place, that in fact there was no point in coming to get her: she knew the way, it would be enough for me to wait downstairs. How she managed to communicate all this without resorting to deaf and dumb language (which she knew I abhorred) I couldn't say; all I know is that I understood immediately. But she did not give me the time to answer at all; she swung her bicycle around and left quickly without another look.

That night she arrived on the dot, and behaved with complete naturalness, as if the most important matter were over and done with. We read some poetry, drank tea, I avoided even touching her with a finger —in short everything went off in the usual way, as with a mature woman. But not for more than half an hour: there was the danger that somebody at home might wake up (although even in that case we could still hope to get away with it, since she had her own room), and on the other hand she must get some sleep, in the morning she had to go to school. To school! She was after all a child. After that she came quite often, and began to stay a little longer, in spite of all the good reasons not to. Among other things we read a few pages of her diary: in it mention was made, mysteriously and with circumspection, of the meeting with me, and I was described as "an unhappy man."

Anyway, nothing of all this matters. What does matter is that the fire which devoured me did not allow me to fondle my prey for very long or charge her innocence with voluptuous expectation. . . . Fine, now there's a lovely sentence: as if it were possible to translate all this into the terms of vulgar seduction! My prey? I was hers and not hers, the prey of someone or something that overwhelmed and swept away and determined us both within our fates, our mutual and single fate. . . . I may be guilty, but I am pure: is that possible? It is, even if it is not possible. I wanted, I want her happiness: that fire could have no other meaning. It was the living proof of an ineluctable good, even if it were painful to achieve (but is it not so for all that is good?), and at the same time it was the precise sign of a test which, obscure though it may be, must be faced; there could be no other meaning. . . . One night I embraced her, kissed her; and sadly, rejoicing, I saw that she was prepared for it. Yet at that very moment she rushed away: would she, after this, return? She did.

She returned the following night. She did not hesitate: right away, the following night. And here begins that which, I can already see, I want to understand and will not understand. There is nothing I can do but tell everything without pity. And what is the point? Or does my logic, I dare not say my justification, reside in the facts themselves? Am I perhaps saved by the very fact that I have done what I have done? Does perhaps the fact or event justify itself? It might be so: we shall see. Now, I will speak at random, I will keep silent inside and let my pen follow its course; perhaps from my words will spurt a monstrous dazzling truth. Dazzling and monstrous! It makes one laugh. Or does it? Could not, should not what is monstrous be dazzling and what is dazzling be monstrous? Are these two not the two necessary elements of a single image, or, better, the two faces of necessity itself? And is truth not as necessary as necessity is true, are not truth and necessity a single thing? . . . Ah, what an illusion—that anything could come from these pages. Nevertheless I have now reached the point. I have dwelt as long as I could on the irrelevant, I have put it off, I have even tried to convince myself (see above) that someone or something actually overwhelmed us; but now I have reached the point: here I am, I can no longer elude it. The moment always comes when we must face . . . what? whom? ourselves, our deeds, our consciences? At the least, that unknown which makes us what we are.

Her breasts were half-opened buds; as when the imprisoned red flower just begins to show its head, shy, bewildered and already triumphant. And all of her, an ever new miracle, was bursting open like a pomegranate. Her pale belly curved in softly and with supreme defenseless tenderness implied that secret ear; and down there on the soft, yielding ivory, still rather scant yet already jealously tangled at the center, over the lips of the ancient wound, curly, absurdly parted and neatly arranged, shone that small tuft. Nocturnal archetypes of what explodes and scatters its gaudy petals in the light of day, and yields to every passerby in the gutter: the ear, the hair, the mouth . . .

Stunned, breathless, and ridiculously buttoned up in my clothes, I stood before her, silent, bereft of memory, almost without desire: my desire was too great, incommensurable with any other thing, as in the same way this young girl's body was incommensurable, this body which kindled and adorned that desire—beautiful, not lewd, and even more innocent than before. If from the beginning it had been clear to me that she must be mine, now I could readily see that she could not be mine. The shape that was before me throbbing with her soul was a fathomless ocean, a boundless, improbable, blinding desert on which there was no hope of rest, of which there was no hope of possession. What was I to do, penetrate with my foul flesh those eternal limbs, eternal as the light, fecund as the dust of stars, inexhaustible as the hidden fount of life? What could I achieve by such a sordid compromise? This was not what I wanted, this was not how I could possess her. And even granting that I could thereby have for an instant quenched my unnamed thirst, wasn't there and did I not know that inherent in it there was, as an indisputable condemnation, the what then? The afterwards, when compelled by my vulgar, insignificant, insufficient act, she and my very life would gradually withdraw from me, desert me? Can one possess the ocean and the desert? And if so, how? That was the question, as unfathomable as the ocean, which I kept asking myself. Asking is incorrect: I heard it, in spite of myself, resound and vibrate in all of my being. Can one at least partake of these things? enjoy them? But how?

Besides she was mute. A physical peculiarity, of course; which in a moment was to favor me by its very existence and by that alone, since she actually did not even get the chance to speak. But this is not what I am trying to say; I am really asking why was she mute? Nothing happens by chance: why was she mute? What did her silence mean, in so far as it was involuntary and fated? And what did it mean as regards myself? An accusation, a sign, a token of acquiescence? What? An invitation perhaps, a conclusion, a seal? These absurd associations which, in reply to no less absurd questions, formed nevertheless in my head, seemed to become closer and closer approximations, seemed to draw ever closer to grasping a meaning, or rather a word, exactly as when we search for a word that will perfectly fit an idea of ours or a feeling. But the word eluded me, escaped me, in fact it escaped from me contemptuously, with a fiendish hiss, I was about to say. Could it be, once again, Necessity? Necessity in the absolute, an abstract quality beyond determining force or impact, without a mark; an aloof quality, itself waiting for direction, violence. . . . I realize that in talking like this I am as crazy as I was then. Yet someone has said, "Mute as fate." Aloof as this muteness or necessity was, I nevertheless felt its pressure, though I did not know toward what.

I felt lost, whereas she looked at me almost tranquilly, just slightly flushed, hiding certain parts of her body with her hands, more playfully than anything else; she must have thought that I only wanted to look at her and precisely because of her virginal nature she didn't consider it too objectionable. An uncontrollable tremor shook me. And suddenly inside of me began to loom, to swell, something unknown, both monstrous and radiant, sinister, ineffably serene, consuming and ethereal (almost a malignant and vivifying solar orb), which now burst into deafening, compelling clangors, or shattered into infinite, distant echoes. I did not know what that internal *fioritura* was, and yet the anguish of not knowing did not take away that strange peacefulness, that sort of happiness which had sprung up with it in my soul. What could it be if not a mystical answer to my desperate questions, to my unarmed desire? A moment before there had been nothing within me but arid and desolate emptiness, a void: now it was an allness which had only to be given a name. But to do so grew more urgent from one instant to the next, and this anxiety was rapidly sweeping away all peace. A friendly celestial power had given me a sign that it existed, that there could be a way for me to possess that child wholly and eternally; but it would not make itself known. I was suffocating: I had to understand.

And I understood—suddenly. Suddenly everything was clear. And it was like an unfettering, a breaking loose of bells: terror, revulsion, joy, rapture, gratification and a thousand other emotions which lie dormant, which perhaps no one has ever named, mingled in that tolling of the soul, heard by the ear as well. Now I knew what I must do. And I knew I must do it right away. I did not know, that is true, how I must do it: I was sentenced that night, I shall not say to act, but to think, to feel by successive approximations.

She looked at me with her shadowy gaze, through her lashes, somewhat disappointed perhaps, or perhaps lost in a virginal melancholy; certainly she was preparing to rise and leave. I picked up one of her stockings from the chair and caressingly slipped it around her neck.

"Do you realize that I could kill you, like this?" and I pulled it lightly.

She laughed nervously, lifting her hands to her throat; I tightened my grip, she made a movement with her face, or a grimace, which if she had not been mute would have been an "Oh" without any particular intention, or at the most it would have expressed playful irritation, not apprehensiveness. I pulled a little more. . . . Actually I was just testing; and I clearly saw that this was not the right way, that in this manner I would obtain nothing, nothing complete. This was not the desired image, which would move into its resolving position in the turmoil of my mind, placating me and everything; this was not the image of peace (the peace of my soul). But which was the true one? This new problem assailed me with great violence, abolishing all other emotions; I let go of her and looked around in bewilderment, searching for the object with which I would kill her, and could not find it. She sighed, and suddenly she felt cold, or was shaken, unbeknownst to herself, by a shiver that was not of coldness; she closed her eyes and pulled the sheet up to her chin. I saw her already wrapped in her shroud and perhaps that, indirectly, hastened her end. At any rate, that shroud was white and could not, must not, be so. At the same time I suffered for her, for her imminent suffering, I would have liked to spare her from it, I would have liked her not to be aware of . . . How could I ever hope that she, still a child, would joyously accept death as the supreme fulfillment? Or should I hope? Was I slandering her?

And here another mad, puerile idea, which rose from I know not where or by what delirious association, entered my head.

"Look," I said, "would you believe that with this finger, my index finger, I can cut and open a wound? Just with my finger, nothing else. You don't believe me? Now look, give me your hand."

She drew her hand from under the sheet and held out her own index finger, lean, slightly crooked.

"Watch this," I added, taking it with my left, "I will rub your finger with mine and in a moment you'll feel you're being cut. Look, I'm not holding anything in my hand. All right, ready?"

This is a trick kids play all the time but which she was unfamiliar with as I had hoped; while holding the other person's finger with your left hand and rubbing it with the index finger of your right, you exert with your thumbnail (the left thumb which is hidden by the moving index finger) an increasing pressure on the finger you are rubbing, and your victim, whose attention is focused on that rubbing motion, ends up by associating the pain with it, which actually is inflicted by the nail. So I rubbed her index finger in the manner just described, and after a few seconds, twisting her mouth in pain or perhaps admiration, she brusquely withdrew her hand.

"Was I right? Did you see?"

She did not answer and again I felt that she was about to rise and leave; it was very late, dawn could not be far off.

"Look, it's a trick, I'll explain it to you. But now, before you leave, because of course, you've got to leave, or tomorrow in school you won't be able to keep your eyes open, let us lie down here for five minutes, next to each other, without doing anything bad. All right? Let's put out the light, it's nicer, in the dark everyone can see what he likes. Just for five minutes."

As soon as we were in the dark and before joining her on the bed, I reached out toward the chest of drawers. I knew in exactly what spot was the thing I wanted to get, a used razor blade. I had dropped it there in the morning because it's the sort of thing you never know how to get rid of: I was afraid that if I threw it into the garbage, the garbage man might cut himself—how touching! Used and quite dull, but still sharp enough for my purpose . . . A crazy, childish idea, I was already saying to myself: can one imagine anything more maladroit? Did I really believe that she would not notice?

"What do you see? Oh, of course, you can't tell me in the dark. Well, I see . . . I see a fiord. Do you know what a fiord is? Look how high the mountains are that enclose it, they clutch it, choke it, they're all rocks. And the water down there at the bottom is dusky but like steel; not like the lake of your eyes which is dark as the night. No, just look, even from up here, leaning over, we can see our reflected image; tiny, of course . . . Hordes of mice, the mice they have in those places, every so often come here to die, nobody knows why. They fling themselves into the water, they take their own lives. . . . And once, a long time ago, a man flew over this fiord straddling a goat, and perhaps the women riding the celestial horses still come this way; but who can see them now? We will see them, we will be able to, I think; what do you say?"

She trembled, responding, I could feel it—supreme rapture, joy more profound, more mysterious, more desolate than the fiord.

"But tell me, what if we were to jump from up here, what would happen? Just think how we'd be flying, what happiness perhaps, a flight that would do away with time, with sorrow, we would go to meet our images there at the bottom, or it might be like rising, rising at great speed into the sky, for the sky is in that water, there are clouds racing swiftly, even though they look a little flat and tarnished, there is . . ."

Dear God, why all this? I mustn't let myself go like this, I must . . . I must.

"That's enough; now I don't see anything any more. Instead, listen to this: I could actually cut your veins with my finger, do you know that? There she goes again, she doesn't believe me . . ." and I took her wrist.

She let me hold it without suspicion, limply: tiny, fragile in my hand.

"Watch out, watch out!" The same playful warning as before, but also a dreadful warning, shouted by my very bowels, by all the invisible objects surrounding us, against a real and atrocious danger.

I began to rub her wrist: with my finger, as before, but now it wasn't my thumbnail that pressed into her skin. What pressed, cut, was that little blade of mine, and firmly, unhesitatingly, with one stroke, her veins were also severed. She gave a muffled, guttural cry, withdrew her hand, then appeared to quiet down; but a moment later she probably felt wet and sat up with a jerk; she must have been about to turn on the lamp on the night table. Well no, she mustn't: she must not because she must not, for her own sake I mean, and because of the horror she would feel at seeing herself like that. But by now I no longer thought of that, by now all the sinister, shapeless, unknown, ruthless and triumphant feelings that can be contained in a man had been unleashed inside of me; but also all that is free, jubilant, beneficent, just, ineffable and heavenly. My soul was not enslaved by blind instincts, but on the contrary delivered to its necessity; do you understand me, whoever you may be, reading these pages, delivered not from but to its necessity (the same perhaps that guarded her soul?). That which was must be.

In that black room I dealt, with my fragile weapon, furious blows. I began at the throat, which I found and caught first; and then down, further down, at the yielding breasts, the pale belly, the still lively thighs, the arms outstretched in vain, the pearly hands, everywhere. But a surviving will or an obscure force turned my hand from her face; only once it met her humid tongue and could not hold back.

That idolized body must have become a single, acute wound. And she almost without defending herself, cried out, cried out in her way, moaned; but very soon she fell silent, and rested against my arm much heavier than she was when alive. And then, only then was I at peace.

I did not turn on the light right away, I did not want to see her like that; in the dark I pulled the sheet over her up to her chin, as she had done not so long ago. Wet, the sheet, it too was heavy. I lingered longer, perhaps for a long time; did I laugh, cry, or . . . or what? Could there be an expression commensurate with my grief and exultation? Anyhow I don't know what I did. At last I put on the light: there, now her shroud was all red. I had not liked it white; I wanted it like this, exactly like this. And look—her nocturnal and astral face intact, now she belonged to me forever.

But already, with a sucking pull, as the vortex draws the bobbing flotsam, trite and vulgar reality, terror, horror—in short, reality—flowed back, crashed into me with a roar. But this is another story.

III

Well, was I able, by re-imagining these things, to prove my innocence? Certainly not as they understand it; but am I therefore less guilty? It is not the many motives that one might adduce, that they did adduce against me, which worry me; for she was not something separate from me or I from her. Something else perplexes me, and it is precisely what I just mentioned. I'm not perplexed, of course, over my guilt. Let's admit it: if all that one can assume as not mentioned above—and which I do not formulate distinctly, since by now I am convinced of its futility—if all that were true, why did I not die at the very moment of her death? I could have killed myself, of course, and perhaps I did not do it out of cowardice; but that is beside the point. What then kept me alive, why was my destiny not accomplished? Aha! Because even if she were not something apart from me, I was something apart from her—there is no other explanation. But if I was other than she, she must have been other than I. . . . Oh insipid logic, how you acquire unsuspected vigor when you ally yourself with the most secret meanings!

And if she was something other than I, I did not have the right to kill her (could it be that by such a tortuous path we come back to what *they* think because of mere stupidity?). And if I did not have the right to kill her, I am guilty. And if I am guilty, for me there is no way to die.

But I shall die all the same. And here I would like to remark on two or three points at random, for the amusement and edification of whoever will be given these papers after my death (the judge, no doubt).

First: can one prove one's innocence to oneself (I am not interested in somebody else's verdict) without first understanding it? Is not any and all justification obviously conditioned by an understanding, a total understanding? In writing these pages, this, this alone, is what I have attempted to understand. And I have not understood. Nothing, ever, is understood; hence nothing can be justified. So how can anyone establish what is legitimate and what is not? Why, just think: in my case, they would have to understand what I myself do not understand.

Second: is it really necessary to find a way to die, to know how to die, in order to die? She, for instance, surely did not know how to die, and yet she died. It is ridiculous, absurd if you wish, but it is so: one does something one does not know how to do. Shouldn't it be enough, I say, that one does not know how to do it, for that something not to take place? But not at all: so what must we think then? We could discern in this the intervention of some blind and adverse or supremely beneficent force, provided, however, the necessity of death were proven. And who, what unworthy believer or devout person would go so far? To gulp it down is all that is left him. Anyhow, it is almost amusing.

Third: it is, after all, a mere hypothesis of mine that to die is easier for the innocent man, that he alone can find a way to do it. And if that were not at all true? Just think what a light would shine on both the efforts of the allegedly innocent to remain that way, and my efforts here to recognize myself as such: what hilarious maneuvering, what an all-encompassing display of idiocy! On the other hand, this, I mean the fact that it may not be true, is comforting to me . . . or is it? What could it mean: simply that dying is equally difficult for everyone, or that no one is innocent?

Fourth: I forgot to mention (or did I do so deliberately?) that I am fifty years old. Fifty. Is that important? Does that add to my guilt, or doesn't it?

Fifth and I think last: nothing of what I said is true. Not because it is not true but because I said it.

And so I have finished. . . . Or should I put down here the last question, almost an affirmation, the most atrocious, the most secret and searing, the one that is perhaps the most incomprehensible for everyone except myself? But of course, why not? I must go all the way, to the very bottom. Could it be true, I ask, that even death was not enough? If that were so I would be innocent, like a person who has done all that lay in his power; and yet, though it may cost me the salvation of my soul, I do not want it to be so. Even death is not enough to attain life and eternity (if that is what I am trying to say): and so what is required? Or where else shall we find what is true, what is necessary?

I have finished, I have finished—out of pity for myself. And whether there be a way or not, whether I know or do not know how to die, be it just or unjust, sufficient or insufficient . . .

They're coming; they're coming. No, they're not coming yet.
But if they aren't coming now, they will.

Hands

◇◇◇
———————
◇◇◇

Federico was retiring for the night. In the courtyard his old hunting bitch, left behind to guard the house, bounced to meet him with a festive welcome. The courtyard was enclosed on three sides, while the fourth opened onto the orchard below and, beyond a row of low houses, a narrow valley which, rising gently, stopped at the high and faraway horizon, running into a line of rounded hills; over it a hazy moon cast its bland and shadowy light. Federico lived in the large deserted house completely alone and for the sake of convenience he came and went by a service entrance which, if one followed a set path across two damp storage rooms and a pantry, brought one out at last to the kitchen, the first room furnished with an electric bulb. Moaning and groaning over the remorseless boredom of country life, faced by the prospect of an empty, lonely evening and the annoying necessity of the small, inevitable chores still required for his late supper, he fitted the massive ancient key into the lock. The small bitch wanted to get inside too and without giving him the time to open, threw herself against the door

like a ram, scratching at it with her front paws. Since in the semi-dark-
ness she had sat down between his feet, he chased her away and she
suddenly remembered a dry and polished bone she had been saving
there close by, went to pick it up and began turning it over loudly in
her jaws.

As he was groping through the first storage room, a faint scam-
pering sound attracted Federico's attention. "A mouse," he thought,
knowing that some lived there; and indeed, having quickly lit a match,
he caught sight of a big corpulent fellow who, leaning clumsily to right
and left, was precipitously descending along the edge of one of
the room's corners to hide behind the rim of a no longer used cistern.
Federico knew of the bitch's hatred for mice (actually, because when
he was a child he had often taken her to hunt for mice in the attic,
she expressed this dislike more ostentatiously than was called for, in
order to please him) and he decided to amuse himself with a nocturnal
chase. He called her but, outside, her sonorous gnawing rang unperturbed through the silence of the night. At last he managed to infuse
his voice with so urgent and promising a tone that she was induced to
interrupt her activity and rush inside greatly excited. Federico pointed
to the spot where he assumed the mouse had hidden and, still urging
the bitch on, began to pound on the wooden cover of the cistern. The
mouse, frightened, frantically abandoned his shelter and a spasmodic
scrabble of his big claws across the floor marked his passage between
the paws of the dog who failed to snatch him and lost sight of him. Although a man's nose is not worth that of a dog, a human eye is
definitely sharper than a canine one: Federico had reason to believe that
the mouse—it is difficult to understand why he had not escaped upward
—had flattened out beneath a large iron bin that rested not directly on
the floor but on the wooden slats of an old bath mat; he led the bitch
to the spot and, instead of starting to paw and scratch around the
container's base, she halted, her body tensed, at a certain distance, on
the route the mouse would have to take in order to escape. But no matter how hard Federico kicked the bin and rattled the slats, the animal

did not come out; convinced, therefore, that he had been mistaken and already bored with the game, he gave up the idea and went on inside. From the adjacent room, however, he heard the bitch scratch and whine, a clear indication that the mouse was indeed there; up to that point she had attributed her own certainty to her master, albeit leaving him the initiative, but seeing him desert the battlefield without a blow being struck filled her with despair. This revived Federico's interest in the adventure and induced him to retrace his steps, equipped this time with an ancient candlestick.

He set the candlestick on the floor and decisively lifted one side of the bin; the clever animal had indeed squeezed under it and had given no sign of his presence despite the terrific noise they had made all around him. Discovered, he was incapable of deciding immediately which direction he should take, and flitted frenziedly this way and that under the wooden slats; at least that much could be inferred from the movements of the bitch who lacked a free field and so was unable to pounce once and for all on her enemy.

A frantic struggle ensued between the two beasts, dominated by the shrill squeaks of the mouse. He was evidently confronting his enormous opponent in a very nasty way, because the latter, fearing for the moist safety of her muzzle, could not bring herself to make an open-mouthed grab for him, but snapped viciously and then quickly pulled back her head. Probably the mouse, partially protected by the slats, his most vulnerable parts sheltered, fought only with his powerful snout. At last, his situation having become unbearable, he tricked the bitch with an adroit feint and crashed through in the direction of the courtyard.

The bitch, instantly recovering from her bewilderment, took off in furious pursuit and, jumping over the candle, doused it. Two of her bounds were worth several of the mouse's tiny steps, and so the chase in the courtyard was soon over.

Federico, who had simply participated as a witness, followed them outside. The bitch, having seized the mouse by its tail, was swinging him violently from side to side in order to stun him and also, by the very violence of that movement, to prevent him from sinking his fangs into her delicate flesh; then she would drop him to judge the effects. He, broken and battered, after a moment's immobility would try to drag himself away, and then the bitch would snatch him up again. These were the most painful moments for her quivering sensitivity, because the mouse was selling his life dearly and, throwing himself on his back (that being his fighting position), fought back as best he could with his hands (a mouse has real honest-to-goodness flabby hands) and teeth. Besides, it is quite possible that a kind of squeamishness was restraining the bitch from more direct and sweeping action, or that the tiny snout bristling with stiff whiskers, with its suggestive power, unnerved her.

At this point Federico noticed that the mouse, in his attempts at flight, was dragging behind him a longish, dully glistening string which now wrapped itself around his body, now slithered, fully extended, through the dust on the ground, so that it must have quickly lost whatever sheen it originally had. Bending down to see in the weak light of the moon, he discovered it to be a gut and was astonished by its thinness and length. Seized by something akin to horror he rushed into the house to turn on a light that shone out on the courtyard: it was in fact a strip of gut, by now grimy and unrecognizable, which refused to detach itself from the animal and issued from it like an umbilical cord. But now, during one of the many attempts at escape, the gut caught on a jutting stone and snapped in half; a long section, nevertheless, continued to trail after the small body in its writhings.

At best the mouse had been subdued and lay in a queer position, limp on his belly at the hind part, while the front part rested on one side, so that the front hands were parallel to the ground and the hind ones desperately flung apart and practically flat. His body was wracked by the convulsive shivers of the death agony and the tiny snout gasped for air. Federico found himself unable to endure the sight and prodded the bitch to finish him off; but she was satisfied by now and refused to understand; since the enemy was felled, why endanger her throat's vulnerable softness again? Federico went to fetch a small coal shovel and with it did his utmost to kill the mouse. He was loath to hit its head for fear of splattering himself with blood, yet, on the other hand, at all the other parts of his body he could feel the soft fat flesh under his blows. The mouse seemed to have no bones and continued to writhe in a spasm that looked conscious, now and then scratching the ground with one hand. His eyes, slightly protruding from their sockets, were completely blank. What struck Federico most was the aura of innocence surrounding that body.

The mouse continued to toss and Federico decided to choke him, so he held the shovel perpendicularly and pressed it for a long time against his throat. To no avail: the neck yielded and there was no way to feel the resistance of the vertebrae under the thick padding of flabby flesh. However, the skin, drawn taut, exposed the minuscule fangs among the now drooping whiskers and, pulling back the head, slightly opened the tiny V-shaped mouth in an expression of indescribable charm. Now the mouse looked like a child about to cry, and yet without sadness. You would have also said that he had assumed that pose deliberately. Federico, at his wit's end, once more called the bitch, who at last gave in to his wishes; a sinister crack marked the end of our mouse's earthly sojourn: the dog had crushed his skull.

The struggle had been completely bloodless, not a single drop of blood stained the ground or the mouse's brown fur, nor was any dripping from his mouth. Federico picked him up by the tail whose tip had been stripped of its skin during the battle, exposing its muscle free of its hairy rings, and examined him under the light: a kind of arid and granulated mushroom, and what was left of the long string of gut issued from a gash in the belly, obviously inflicted by one of the dog's fangs; and here, too, there was not a drop of blood.

Federico laid the animal in the middle of the courtyard so that the maid who came every morning might admire it and, possibly, be frightened by it. Then he whistled to the dog and went inside.

Having prepared his salad, gotten a pitcher of water, turned off the lights in all the other rooms, and continued to irritate himself in a thousand different ways, he finally sat down at the dinner table. There is one more thing we have forgotten, the book—there, now we're ready. Ordinarily the chord introducing these solitary evening meals was a chat in French, quite informal, with an imaginary interlocutor; transfixing the first slice of potato, Federico began, *"Ah, oui monsieur, je vous l'assure, c'est un spectacle dont vous derriez vous régaler . . ."* and he went on with his mouth full, staring across the table. But the sudden thought of the mouse flashed through his mind: more than a thought, an intimate and subterranean sensation, something that clanged unexpectedly inside him, gave signs of wanting to burrow deeper, and rapidly faded. Federico resumed his conversation, the inner apparition returned several times, and always with greater intensity: it seemed that a great deal of time had elapsed since the first one, yet only a few seconds had gone by and he had already acquired the physical awareness of the dead mouse that lay outside his door. Although he continued to eat quite heartily, a great sadness, a sense of compassion and above all a restless anguish that had no apparent cause began to trouble him. The bitch stationed herself close to his chair, begging for food; she expected a special treat in view of the happy outcome of her recent exploit. There was no way out, he had to reward her; Federico prepared her a few morsels and fussed over her to tell her what a good dog she was.

After finishing his supper, he began as usual to read. He was reading about the adventures of a namesake of his, a novel called *Sentimental Education*, which had interested him very much up until the preceding session. But now the whole thing seemed insipid and, anyway, he was quite unable to follow what he was reading because his feeling of nausea and anxiety was increasing immeasurably. He kept trying to find something in the book which would be comparable to his scathing experience, and could only find, it seemed to him, things which were much less poignant. He expected the writer to help him through his ordeal, but the man was barely sufficient unto himself and continued quietly to be distressed wholly on his own account.

There is nothing that gives one the perception of flesh and blood as intestines do, with their warm stench. Federico felt suffocated, throttled by mouse flesh; the taste and putrid smell of that fat and tallowy flesh had become a condition of his being, and he savored it directly through his blood, irremediably. He considered going to bed; but how to sleep, he said to himself, with the murdered victim's body at his doorstep? It even seemed to him that the spirit of the dead mouse hovered over him like an almost tangible presence, both menacing and indulgent, and that it was linked to his own spirit by deep, everlasting ties.

That murder could not be atoned for; it would remain forever unavenged, beyond ransom.

He slept very badly and dreamt gloomily about a long procession of mice wearing plumed helmets who held on to a dark rope with one hand and filed past him one by one, bowing gracefully. A medium-sized mouse arrived, and stopped the column, gazed at him for a long time with great sadness and said to him in a grave human voice: "I have decided, I forgive you"; then everything ended in a storm of squeals and chitters and a kind of saraband that dispersed in the dark air of the night. "I will find him again, I will definitely find him again!" Federico promised himself and thankful for having a lead, he flew off along a slender gut (for that is what the dark rope which the mice had been holding turned out to be), and strained toward the leaden horizon; but there seemed to be no end to the gut and Federico, who had been flying over dark valleys for many hours, felt his breath and strength fail him, and so he woke up.

Dawn was rising over the mouse's small corpse; his protruding eyes, by now curdled, vaguely reflected its light; a great many industrious ants bustled all around him like diligent clerks, still sleepy and puffy-eyed, whom one might meet along the city's streets on winter mornings. The acacia trees in the courtyard were trying to clear their throats for the start of the day. The piece of gut that had broken off lay a little to one side and already half withered. The dog huddled in a ditch, shivering in the first gust of wind.

Federico went outside in his night-shirt, lifted the mouse from the ground, shook the ants off him and examined him again: the torn intestines were covered with dust, poor living flesh. Federico smoothed his whiskers, and clutched him to his breast, rocking him to and fro, belly up like a child. Holding him against his cheek, he stroked his fur smoothly with the grain; he noticed a tooth mark, a bald spot on the tiny shoulder, and delicately caressed it with his index fingers, as though to assuage the pain. "My little mouse, my poor little mouse!" he moaned, and still moaning, he descended the steps to the orchard with the mouse in his arms. There he intoned a strange dirge and walked like a little girl who, singing a lullaby, gives a funeral to her doll; he knelt, dug a small grave, placed the mouse in it with the utmost delicacy and covered him up. "Rest in peace, my poor little mouse!" he repeated and lingered for a long time, contemplating the tiny patch of freshly turned earth; from behind the panes of a window a peasant woman watched him with curiosity. He rose and, full of dignity in his long night-shirt, went back up the garden, loudly singing a church psalm, which had suddenly surfaced from his days as a choirboy.

This is not at all to mean that Federico had gone crazy. On the contrary, I believe that he became one of the best lawyers in his region, and there is no doubt that he got along very well with his little bitch until the end, but he retained one weakness: sometimes, even after his hair had turned gray, he roamed at night through the uninhabited rooms of his house, the storage rooms and odd corners, calling: "Come to me, little mice! Oh, come little mice, and rest in my arms!" The little mice, whenever he chanced to run into them, were amused and frightened, and gazing at him with their tiny round glistening eyes, trotted daintily ahead of him with a faint roll of thunder.

Stefano's Two Sons

◇◇◇

◇◇◇

To seal his failure in literature and life, Stefano got married. Which in any event means that between the two, whichever might in reality be the more important, the latter had won. But precisely now, when all had already been given up as lost, the former seemed to want to resume its exclusive rights. Like all weak spirits not sustained by a powerful vocation, Stefano used to carry around in him and turn over within him for long periods his "things," that is, his ideas and characters, which, there is no need to say, most often remained in the larval state: dreams of ideas, embryos of characters, blind, vain yearnings. Yet now, contrary to all expectations, one of these larvae seemed to assume a particular substantiality, almost a human face.

It was his remote and well-nigh mythical ancestor, a certain Patrizio, who had been a man of war and the great world. Stefano, though, for some time called him his son, meaning that if he managed to resuscitate him, or, rather, procreate him, he would not only have made blindingly clear to himself the profound motives of his own person-

36

ality but would have at last delivered the exact measure of his possibilities as a writer; since in his being and his obliterated deeds Patrizio
really seemed to sum up the vision of his descendant, or at least seemed
inclined to receive all the emotions that his descendant wanted to attribute to him.

So this son or favorite ghost, this Patrizio, began with a certain
urgency to demand the honors of the world: Stefano sometimes imagined himself just on the point of seeing Patrizio before him alive
and speaking, dressed in state robes, and it seemed to him that this was
his last, his sole chance as a poet—in other words, a matter of life or
death. Something, however, prevented him from giving a full audience
and full satisfaction to his projected creature.

In fact, fate had played an atrocious trick on Stefano who, mature
and weary, had married (as we said) out of desperation and as a kind
of challenge. His wife's womb announced a new and undesirable being right at the start, whom the woman (who on the contrary awaited
it in a mood of exaltation) had already baptized Andrea. He too demanded Stefano's attention. In truth his marriage had been the best
possible, yet for this very reason seemed inconvenient. His wife was
little more than a child, alone in the world, poor, loving, and, what's
more, physically small, and she leaned on him with all the faith of
which precisely an eighteen-year-old is capable: how could one abandon
her in that moment of grave travail? A travail which moreover also
concerned him, since if all the physical and (as people say) moral faculties of the young girl seemed involved in the transformation which was
being wrought in her, Stefano also had to, with fierce imaginary birth-
pangs, accustom himself to his new condition as a father and, to begin with, accept it. And yet it is not so much that his work was materially disturbed by the continual assistance which the pregnant woman
required (a circumstance not without value), but rather that part of
his more exquisite self was distracted from the effort he had under-
taken.

In sum, it was clear from the start that an incompatibility existed between Patrizio and Andrea, which quickly turned into open, mortal enmity, and then crumbled into many rancorous conflicts. If anything, Andrea manifested a special malice: for Stefano's happiest and most inspired moments were usually matched by his wife's pains, faintings and varied disturbances which aroused the anxious solicitude of the future daddy for mother and child, produced disturbances in him, too, and of course shot to pieces his real or imagined state of grace. Whereas Patrizio seemed even disposed to tolerate the intruder, almost as though he did not for a moment doubt his own preponderance and was unable even to imagine being surpassed by anyone. The upshot was that Andrea proved more fragile than his brother (if we may call him that).

As for Stefano, he saw quite well that to bring one of the two children to fruition with honor—or even without honor—it would be necessary to abandon the other to his fate; but he was, let us repeat, a weak spirit, and furthermore (or therefore) he had never been sure where the truth lay, whether on the side of so-called poetic reality or reality *tout court*. At times it seemed to him that the most important thing would be to give birth to a creature not subject to death (his Patrizio), then a moment later that his glory would lie precisely in giving life to a mortal creature, because of that creature's mysterious and glorious unhappiness. So how could he come to a decision? Therefore he continued to carry both children. With the saddest of consequences.

Even amid the above-mentioned difficulties and with great effort, Stefano (who had by now assumed the role of a dramatic poet) proceeded with his labors: slowly, like someone sifting gold from dross, he was isolating from the obscure life of the historical Patrizio those events, sayings and impulses destined to become almost the blood of the work in gestation. And running parallel to this, the minuscule Andrea was offering ever more clear and arrogant signs from the womb of his mother, while the father's bowels were softened by a still alarmed yet already somewhat satisfied paternal feeling. But one morning the conflict between the two assumed an exemplary aspect.

Either because of a simple desire to get his own back, or because he really felt his future life slipping away, one morning Patrizio appeared before his father. It was the fertile hour when ideas, not yet withered by the fetid breath of daily reality, appear young and exuberant before the freshly awakened and still dreaming creator; Stefano's wife was snoring at his side. And Patrizio spoke out: "Don't you realize that the ultimate significance of myself, your work and you yourself is concealed in the dialogue that you were confusedly trying to fashion . . . yes, in the second act, right? You just didn't know, and don't know, exactly what I was supposed to say and how. Very well, I want to help you: I will say . . ."

But at that the sleeping woman woke up with a start: "Oh, what a bad dream I've just had," she moaned. "What a terrible dream. Listen, it seemed to me . . ."

Stefano was still straining his ears to catch Patrizio's words. A moment ago he had at last been about to cast light on his father's obscure emotions, establish a superior order among his thoughts, introduce in them distant connections, and infuse the work with the quick tremor of genius: no, Patrizio *must* continue to speak.

"You're not listening to me," the woman went on. "I feel terrible, awful; I feel as if I'm going, you understand? Yes, already last night . . . last night, just as I was falling asleep, some terrible voices were persecuting me. Run, please, call the doctor! This time I really . . ." And she began to vomit with choked gasps and cries into a small basin she always kept next to the bed. Then she clutched his neck and began weeping with big, silent tears.

Patrizio's figure, the echo of his voice, wavered and drew farther away. "Oh God," the woman finally sighed, and she fell back, mortally pale, on her pillow.

While giving his wife the help needed, telephoning the doctor, waiting for him and then talking to him, Stefano vaguely tried to detain that son of his and solicit the rest of the communication from him; but his image retreated farther and farther, grew smaller and smaller, at last setting behind the squalid horizon of family concerns—in short, chased away by Andrea.

In this way, as God wished, Stefano went ahead, deluding himself that he could save, within and outside of himself, both of his progeny. By now, imprudently, he gave them both equal affection, though he still told himself that if he were forced to sacrifice one of them he would not have hesitated. But meanwhile, beyond the father's apparently peaceful sentiments, the struggle between the two continued without quarter. Until the final crisis was reached.

Stefano had shut himself up in his study since the morning. Patrizio had not shown up again in the ambiguous and, after all, untrustworthy garb of a twilight apparition, yet something better and more serious had taken place: on that very day Stefano had had an illumination, actually a lightning flash. All of his work suddenly appeared clear to him and the very words began to bubble up in him like a fresh and limpid spring, not at all tainted; each thing gradually arranged itself in its correct order and attained its proper proportion.

It was in short the true state of grace, and the great moment that was to decide his entire life. Moving restlessly about his study, without being aware of it, Stefano reproduced or, as is said, performed the physical attitudes of his character, now meditatively dropping into the antique chair (fake) with his elbow on his knee and his forehead on his fist, as though listening to somber messages, now proudly erect and with his hand at his side, as if resting on the hilt of a sword; and distinctly, inexorably, laden with (to him) inscrutable justifications, gestures, speeches and replies surged out of him. The barrier of perplexities and contradictions, the blind resistance of the material, had been overcome, as when the voice of a singer with a cold breaks through the mud of catarrh and rises purely above it. The least of phrases became necessary and definitive. Of course, the noises of the street and the smells from the kitchen were also abolished—in a word, the world. And finally Stefano flew to his desk and started to dash down the main scene of his drama. The pen scraped away almost by itself, as if not guided by his hand.

And at this point a sort of hubbub of voices, and then of steps and other noises arose from the bowels of the house. At first Stefano did not even notice it; then, however, it gradually rose to the surface as from a remote depth and finally reached his consciousness, from whereever it had been. Yet he stayed where he was: whatever might be happening over there, he could not, he must not move at that supreme moment, and he continued to write feverishly. A bit more and Patrizio would rise up before him, before all of humanity, rise up in his full physical and moral stature, with all his smallest characteristics; the hero had already begun to speak his fateful words. (But a subtle anxiety, a stirring of human affections had, nevertheless, surreptitiously wormed their way into the writer's mind.)

From the other rooms, from that distant planet, came a woman's atrocious screams, and Stefano thought he recognized his wife's voice; and Stefano, a hero himself, still was not shaken and still went on writing. And now at last—Patrizio spoke and said what he had to say to men, to the future, to destiny. Patrizio was born. Both of them were free, the creature and the creator: the former could now run about the world and the universe on his own legs; and the latter could saunter on Olympus. He was consecrated as a great poet.

His feverish hand rested for a moment on the sheet of paper. As compared with what had already been accomplished, what remained to be done was a mere nothing, a bit of child's play: negligible details, sutures, statements, slight modifications of perspective, all things which one could attend to at one's leisure. His hand, therefore, rested; and then another shriek rose from the other part of the house, but different from the preceding ones.

A strange cry, not acute, in fact gurgling and yet penetrating; a

cry (how can one put it?) not human, but in some sense similar to the
baying of a fox; a cry that shook the most intimate fibers of one's being
and made the hair stand up on one's head. It died out immediately, but
this time Stefano could run to it, and he did.

In his wife's room there was blood scattered almost everywhere,
on the bed and the floor. Stefano's elderly relation who was watching
over the pregnant woman day and night, had collapsed in a faint across
the sofa, her shoulders and head on the floor. His wife was lying with
her eyes closed and her legs apart on the bloodied bed, gasping pain-
fully, almost giving the death rattle. Tumbled on the rug at the foot of
the bed, also covered with blood, still tied by the umbilical cord to his
mother, lay a monstrous creature, fragile, swollen, wrinkled. From his
body hung shreds of a whitish membrane; his small, thin, knotty legs
trembled, a bloody froth dripped from the corners of his distorted little
mouth. But as Stefano looked, even that feeble movement ceased completely.

The tiny creature had the fingers of the hands and the toes of the
feet joined and furnished with one continuous nail, the skin divided
into zones or stripes, some yellowish and tallowy, others brown as
leather. On his forehead were two bony, pointed protuberances, horns
in fact; the huge round eyes, bulging, shiny (not yet coagulated) appeared so far apart that each one was differently oriented, as in insects;
in place of the sex organs was a kind of immense navel or rather an ear,
with lashes, a small gorge or volcano out of which a greenish pus had
been discharged.

This creature (leaving aside its sex, in any case indecipherable) was
Andrea.

That night Stefano said to himself: "I have lost a son, it is true,
perhaps I shall also lose a wife. But another son is left to me, the one
whom, although I never admitted it to myself, I loved most." So, in

order to console himself for all the horrors he had been through, he shut himself up in his study as soon as he could, set the lamp in a convenient position, and with proud trepidation took in hand (or in his arms) the pages he had written that morning. And suddenly he was like a man who imagines himself to be brandishing a sharply honed, glittering sword, but finds that he has a willow wand in his fist.

My God, where was the vigor with which he had thought he had infused his work, what had become of Patrizio's fateful words? Chitchat devoid of new and profound meaning, to which only a certain professional skill lent an external cohesion. What had become of the dazzling adjectives, the definitive epithets, the unexpected verbal relationships? In the lifeless text Stefano was examining, Patrizio, reconverted into an ephemeral larva, spoke now a trite and trivial language or, worse yet, the cold idiom of reason, not inflamed and illuminated by madness, which regenerates the world.

How could this have happened? Had the delirium, the fever, the ecstasy of that morning been nothing but deception? In anguish, Stefano contemplated the remains of his shipwreck, the poor sheets of paper in which, whatever the circumstances which had deceived him in the morning, he must now recognize nothing more than one of his usual compositions.

Patrizio was also an abortion: like the other, he had not given anything but a hoarse, low, bestial cry as the sign of his existence; and now he too lay there without even a moan, shapeless, resigned not to live. And with him collapsed forever Stefano's life—his real life, his faith, his dignity, his hope of salvation. Or should he perhaps think of Andrea as a frightening incarnation and imagine that he had returned sound, safe and triumphant to his inferno? There's no point, Stefano concluded, in yielding to literary temptation. The fact remained that, at least in appearance, his two sons had, like good brothers, shared the same fate—their own or their father's.

What this fate might be or what name it should have, we shall let the reader decide. And with that this gloomy story ends. If afterward Stefano did generously put an end to his days, or if he preferred to drag himself through life without living (as most people do), it is not such a great matter that it must be related.

Autumn

The couple are lying on the bed, dressed. Almost twilight. Toward the end they move, in accordance with their remarks.)

—It's been raining for three days now.

—Four.

(pause)

—Just think of your name for a moment! Maria—a large diamond clasp, all loops, but of course with something square at the center, maybe two or three squares.

—Oh no, it's a veil . . . a blue veil . . . sort of green. Anyway, it's the color of the moon during certain winter twilights, when it's shrouded by light mists and there's a wind.

—No, no. That's not the way it is—you're wrong.

—And think of yours. Alberto is like a small—not that small actually—rod of glass, no, rock crystal, let's say.

—And what about someone called Pasquale? A rubbery surface, but elastic, as though stretched on a small embroidery frame. But most

45

likely that's because when you say Pasquale you can feel your cheeks vibrate, or rather, swell up and then sink back like the bubbles when you cook oatmeal.

—Tommaso is like a ball of tar.

—Ada's made of wood.

—Iole is a liquid, pinkish, almost like blood.

—That's because it reminds you of "iodine," I assure you.

—Eugenio is like ragged shreds of grass. You know, those green shreds in mountain puddles which dogs drink from, and hunters, too. They're all soft and almost rotten, they look like mucus.

(brief pause)

—This is the moment of death. In torpid-growing waters somewhere, the sweet herbal flesh is now decaying.

(brief pause)

—I'm not so sure I really like that.

—But it's beautiful . . .

—No, I mean, torpid-growing waters.

(pause)

—Viareggio.

—No, it's a large seaport, don't you see? There's also a tall bridge with one . . . two . . . six . . . with seven arches.

—Oh, but which one do you mean? The one to the right of the center beam? That's not the one I'm talking about. I mean the one to the left, between those two small beams; there's also a crack along the middle and that's the beach with the bath huts, but seen from the sea.

—Oh yes, yes, now I see it, also the trees are there, on the promenade.

—And the clouds, the blue sky.

—Yes, yes.

(pause)

—Have you ever noticed how much Vittorio resembles the button on a shoe?

—And Eva was crushed between the pages of a book when she

was a little girl; if she had both eyes on one side she'd be exactly like a fluke.

(pause)

—That portrait by Domenico Veneziano is beautiful.

—If it were by Domenico Veneziano, but in fact it's by Paolo Uccello.

—See, that's how you act all the time.

(pause)

—Just look, look, it's still burning.

—What?

—Over there on the table, your cigarette.

—You're right, that smoke is beautiful.

—Beautiful. But slightly perverse.

—Why perverse? I don't get that.

—Sure, don't you see how it twists in a thousand different shapes, all those waves and curlicues? It's no good.

—But just look, now, how calm and evenly it is flowing. "Smooth as oil."

—That's just meant really to deceive you. . . . See, see? Now it's flattening into a ribbon, making all those small stiff pleats. Actually, it's some woman who's dancing and keeps throwing back her head with her hair and her arms and thrusting out her breasts. Lewd.

—Finished?

—No, not yet.

—Yes, no.

—Finished.

(pause)

—When I was a boy I once wrote a poem called "Ballad for a Veil of Rain."

—Let's hear it.

—I don't remember it.

—A few lines.

—No, I don't remember . . . I'm embarrassed.

—You're mean.

(long pause)

—It would be nice to go on like this . . . but . . .

—You know, I don't think we'll ever meet.

—What? . . . I don't know.

—It's three and a half years now. I was thirty-eight, my husband was still alive, when we first met. You're young.

(short pause)

—We both want the same things, only we never want them at the same time. . . . How shall I put it? We're like two watches that can't be synchronized. But perhaps we don't even want the same things.

—I love you.

—So do I, but . . .

(pause)

—Then I'll leave.

—Leave? Don't.

—Yes, hand me my bag.

—You're losing a hairpin.

(pause)

—The piazza is empty, there are no cabs.

—Never mind.

—Dante! He's got a pigeon on his head even now, ruffling its feathers. . . . Well, I don't know. . . . It's almost dark.

—So, farewell, Alberto.

—So long.

—Farewell.

—One more kiss?

—Yes. But what's the matter with you now?

—Nothing. Farewell, Maria.

—Farewell.

Cancerqueen

◇◇◇
◇◇◇

I

March 23, 19. . . .

These smooth or contorted instruments, these push-buttons, these keys, these levers, these complicated systems, clusters, clumps, tangles of parts made of steel, glass and God knows what else; these instrument panels, these switches, these gears, these monitoring lights, these indicators, these dials; these articulations, joints and couplings; in a word, this whole infernal machinery glitters cruelly before me, picked out in its most minute parts by the spectral white light, which in fact draws from it small, vague, bluish shadows, like those fleeting shadows of a summer afternoon which, with a similar deceit, speak of rest, of hope in that other, so much vaster yet equally constricting world. I hear the usual, uninterrupted, sharp, sibilant hum, though it rises at times in tone, going beyond my ear's power of perception to lose itself in an unseizable, mute sonorous vibration.

49

The earth lies below me, always more or less in the same attitude, I mean to say with the same grimace inscribed on its face by my native continent, Europe; a grimace incessantly covered and revealed by the passing clouds, at times altered, contracted, but substantially always the same, just as the general expression of a human face is basically constant, even when gripped by emotions. Oh, why couldn't I at least have been condemned to contemplate a part of that earth which I don't know and which I hate less?

Above me the moon, the romantic moon . . . which has never breathed so much horror from its white and black, engulfing, suction-like face, its gaping chasms of calcified stone.

The murdered man's corpse follows me implacably.

Well, now that it's quite some time ago that everything that could have happened has happened, I feel the need to tell this story, to tell it from the very beginning. To whom, and why? To justify myself, perhaps? And for what? To whom, I say, should I send this message? And let us even suppose that it reaches men, what benefit could they obtain from it?

I do not know. I do not care to know. Perhaps, since I shall have to pretend that I have a reader, I shall be less alone, and that is enough. Perhaps I shall be more alone, and that is even better: it will hasten the inevitable end, give me the courage to . . .

I was alone and disconsolate. My huge gambling losses and grave amorous disappointments, not to speak of other matters, had confined me to my ancestors' village and house. I had no hope. These were not exceptional episodes in my life, but rather its natural configuration. I nursed a mad plan, I dallied over it, considering its possible, imminent, every day more inevitable actuation. The world seemed to me without sense and, at least for me, without a future: I prepared myself, or at least I would have liked to prepare myself, to leave it . . .

One night (but how long ago, in what remote past did it take place?) while I was, as in Poe's "The Raven," *weak and weary,* immersed in the reading of an antique book or, to tell the truth, holding this book stupidly in front of me and not reading it at all—one night I heard someone banging on the door of my house.

I lived alone and was not in the habit of opening my door to anyone. But the unusual hour and some mysterious instinct led me this time to break with my custom. A man unknown to me entered; after a brief greeting and without further explanation, he preceded me up the stairs. I suffer from sudden spells and I did not dare detain him physically; indeed he did not seem to give much weight to my feeble remonstrances. "Quick, shut the door, I beg you," he said, "and go on up ahead of me." I obeyed, as though in his thrall.

In the light the stranger revealed a sturdy physique and deeply accentuated features; a black moustache shadowed his upper lip, and his voice had a richly resonant timbre; he could not have been more than forty. He dropped on a chair beside the table and seemed to have wholly forgotten the reason for his visit, nor did he even think of offering me an explanation. My dominant emotion was fear, in fact the wildest kind of terror, though nothing in his behavior justified it. Yet a vestigial habit of keen observation soon made me notice that, despite an external air of self-assurance, he had a kind of deep gentleness or even outright weakness which, however it might match his outward appearance, revived my courage. If I had known the real reason for this quality, I would have lost the little courage I had left. His eyes glistened with a truly extraordinary light.

With a nervous hand he riffled through the pages of the book which had remained open on the table, making some erudite comments on the subject it treated. He had the air of someone resuming a conversation with an old friend, talking in a somewhat lackadaisical tone, when there's time aplenty and nothing better to do. "Sir . . ." I ventured, taking advantage of a long pause. He broke in to continue the course of his argument, which, however, he also did not conclude. At the most interesting point he halted in mid-sentence, and, without looking at me, said softly:

"Sir, I am crazy.

"That is, the others think I am crazy," he hastened to add after my involuntary startled gesture. "I hope that I do not seem so to you." (And he looked at me for a moment with a sort of timid smile.) "I . . . I have heard talk of you. I have read your book. To whom else could I turn, in this part of the world? You will listen to me, I am sure. . . . Either I am really crazy or I am not, depending, of course, on what one means by this word. But you certainly aren't the person to be frightened by words, attributing more importance to them than they deserve. Nor even to the ideas they express. You are not afraid of anything, I can see that. You are a wise man . . ." Was I mistaken, or was there a touch of irony in the truly unnatural glitter of his eyes?

"Now hear me out and listen attentively," he went on. "This very night I have escaped from the asylum of . . . (and he named a well-known lunatic asylum of the region). For two years I have waited for this opportunity, and you will readily understand me when I say that I must lose no time in making use of my reconquered freedom. Throughout all this time they have never wanted to put any faith in —or even listen to—all the explanations and revelations which I tried to furnish them with the greatest calm (since I am not crazy, I have already said so). They even refused to believe in the existence of my creature. I pointed out the exact spot where she was hidden and they simply laughed and shrugged their shoulders, when indeed the basest and most vulgar of them did not resort to certain special methods to keep me quiet. I begged them to look for her, to give her publicity for the benefit of the rest of humanity, if not for mine. I would have been content to remain for all my life in that horrid prison, among those unhappy beings bereft of all light of reason, provided only that she, my creature, could show new paths to all men of goodwill, paths for their bodies, mind you, as well as their souls—provided only that she might light up the whole world, and *especially* that small world composed of thoughtful seekers after the truth, light it up with the principles which had generated and informed her; principles which could and inevit-

ably must be put to a much vaster application in the very near future.
Alas, all was in vain. I do not know, I can never know what act of mine
(since in this world of ours only acts are punished and feared) brought
me to the place where I awoke after a long period of unconsciousness.
Yet it must have been violent, ill-advised, or at the very least contrary
to the rules of this genteel society of ours, even if justified, indeed it
must have been some act of great violence (since I am crazy, I have already said so), the sort that absolutely cannot be forgiven since it en-
dangers the very structure of the precious human race, and which certainly struck and frightened them to the point of inevitably judging all
my subsequent acts or arguments as of the same nature. Finally, you
know quite well that they do not recognize an insane man's right to
reveal the truth, much less demonstrate it, since their entire edifice
would collapse if they did so; and so, just like Galileo, for two years I
vainly offered them a telescope which they refused to look through."

I felt drowned beneath that torrent of words, and yet a strange feeling was already creeping through me. I had neither the strength nor
the courage to interrupt him, nor even the desire.

"Now, the idea which I tried to make plain to them is very simple,
and it is quickly presented. If time, as was already made clear by the
poets, long before the men of science (and particularly by one of them,
who was both more than a poet and more than a man); if time is a
method, a concept to which no physical reality corresponds, an interpretation; if time and space are—and keep in mind here the preceding
qualification—one and the same thing; why then cannot space be a
method, a concept, an interpretation? Obviously this is simply a rhetorical question. Very well, I shall not trouble you with the specific de-
velopments and considerations which are mostly of a strictly physical
and mathematical order: besides, since you are not in the field you
could not possibly follow me. It will suffice for you to know that in the
light of this principle, or rather of its physical configuration, all the be-
liefs concerning the density of the planetary atmosphere, the nature of
cosmic ether, and many, many other matters, which have been generally

accepted till now, are completely overturned, in fact have lost all their meaning. And the practical and tangible result of all this, which represents barely a beginning, is precisely my creation, my creature: that is, a machine, vehicle or whatever you wish to call her, capable in theory of traversing any sort of interplanetary—and why not?—intersidereal space, and capable in actual fact and positively speaking, of covering the distance that separates us from our satellite."

Here the stranger paused. Not in order to ascertain the effect of his declaration, his eyes in any case being turned elsewhere, as if gazing into the distance, but instead like a man who has reached the most crucial or difficult point in his discourse. He paused, while I would have liked him to continue without delay: the strange emotion I mentioned before had by now overwhelmed me and dominated me despotically. Besides, I understood what this preamble was leading up to. Nonetheless, without being able to stop myself from stammering, I blurted out:

"I am happy for you and your success and, since that is what you wish, happy for all of mankind. But how do I come into this affair?"

"You mean, what do I expect from you?" he retorted, this time staring straight at me. "This too can be quickly said. I am preparing to go to the moon. For numerous reasons I cannot go alone. Would you like to accompany me?"

Well, now it was obvious that I was confronted by a madman, and what's more, a madman of the most dangerous species: a logical madman. I too did not believe in his discoveries, whether physical or metaphysical, much less in the existence of his creature, as he called her. And yet, apart from the fright natural in such a situation, what had I to lose? Wasn't I preparing, wasn't I trying to prepare myself, to leave the world? And here he seemed to have penetrated my intention and wanted to further it, though in an unexpectedly literal fashion. Moreover, wasn't anything better than this life of mine, perhaps even than that death for which I so longed? I certainly could not be going to something worse. Whatever this machinery of his might amount to,

I was desperate, and he was speaking to me of hope and, at least, of something new. I abhorred all of existence and he was offering me a chance to possibly reconcile myself to it, if only by making me believe in something, helping me to break out of, perhaps not materially as he claimed, the narrow confines within which I struggled as in a dark prison. Anyhow, was it so obvious that he was mad? In truth, he had not yet irrefutably proved that he was. Must not all men of genius, all bold initiators, have at first appeared as crazy as he, if not more so? At any rate it was quite clear that I could not hope for anything good from the sane or those so-called: then why not try my luck with the insane?

Besides, a strange force of persuasion seemed to emanate more from his entire being, rather than from his mere words. Nor could I exclude the possibility that his power over me was aided by some secret affinity that linked us together, or, in simpler terms, by some latent madness in myself. And, finally, I must add that going to the moon had been the great ambition of my adolescence, as it is, I believe, of every man at all equipped with intelligence and lively senses. Everything considered, the stranger had managed to hit upon a particularly favorable terrain.

It would otherwise be impossible to explain why I did not pretend surprise at that singular proposal; on the contrary, it infused me with a peculiar sense of security.

Nevertheless I did not reply and he too remained silent, continuing to stare at me with his fiery eyes.

"Tell me at least," he finally asked, a trifle abruptly, "whether the idea in itself of going to the moon perplexes you, or if you too doubt my means and, in general, all that I have laid before you."

He was in any case a madman, and I had to handle him with the required tact, but at the same time, since he was an intelligent madman, not make it too obvious. In other words, I had to treat him more or less as if he were a reasonable man.

"I don't doubt a thing," I consequently replied. "But you must certainly realize that your proposal is not the most common, and the de-

cision you ask of me is one of those which . . . well . . . which have
real importance in a man's life. . . . So that . . ."

"Of course, I understand," he said, mollified. "In other words you
require ample guarantees before making such a momentous decision.
That's more than just. Well then, just tell me if you would be disposed to come to the moon if I were to assure you, and prove it also,
not only of a happy voyage and sojourn there but a prompt return, if
you so chose. The rest is my affair. You will see that I can convince
you as to these two possibilities—what am I saying!—these certainties!"

Things being put in those terms, there was nothing one could
say, or, at least, I could only say:

"When it comes to going to the moon *per se,* I am not averse to
it; just the opposite, I must admit that I desire it greatly. But . . . but
to begin with, where is this creature or machine of yours?"

"If that's all . . ." he replied quietly. "She is well hidden in a place
in this region where the people whom I begged for two years refused
to go. Where by now nobody else will go but myself, or us two, if I
dare say that already. . . . What time is it?" he exclaimed, jumping
to his feet with unexpected enthusiasm. "Not yet midnight. Let's go!
We will be there before dawn. You must understand that it is in our interest not to call attention to ourselves in any way, because we cannot
leave immediately, we will have to prepare some things, gather provisions, check some of the instruments; leave on this great, this extraordinary expedition. . . . Sir, don't you feel your heart beating impetuously, your chest expanding with the afflatus of another world?"

Now he seemed gripped by a fever and paced restlessly about the
room. Suddenly he halted, looking at me almost menacingly.

"But you haven't told me whether . . . In short, are you going
along, or aren't you?"

With my usual cowardice, I tried again to stall for time.

"How far away is it supposed to be—this place?"

"Four hours walk, perhaps less, if we keep up a good pace."

"And . . . in what direction?"

"On the mountain, of course! It is there day by day, before that unfortunate incident, either living there or hiding on the spot, or going there every night for many, many years, that piece by piece I constructed, generated my creature. . . . Well?"

I have already said that I did not believe in the existence of this creature of his. So, even if that nocturnal foray hardly suited my cowardice and laziness, it did not appear to me an exceedingly compromising step but rather another way of gaining time (but in relation to what?).

"Very well. Let's go."

With a roar of joy he rushed to the door. And off we went on that singular excursion.

We crossed many valleys and hillsides; only the light of the stars somehow lit our path. We proceeded in almost complete silence. Two hours away from the village, however, the mountain became more rugged and wilder; and its woods almost impenetrable. Yet he seemed to know the tiniest trails amid the tangled underbrush and the boulders, so that our ascent continued swiftly. At one point, from the top of a hill, we saw the waning moon which, just risen, frayed and rusty, seemed to founder at the bottom of a distant valley. Yet this far from comforting sight excited my companion like some radiant vision, and he began to speak:

"Gaze at our goal: we shall reach it before much longer. The moon will be ours. And we—have you thought of that?—we shall be the first men to set foot on those distant shores. Not the only ones, no, because I want all of humanity, though it certainly does not deserve it, to benefit from my marvelous invention, and every other discovery of mine. But at last, the only human inhabitants of the silver star (which, as if on purpose, just then was made of the cheapest and sootiest copper), we shall be able to stay there as long as we wish, waiting for the world to pay us the proper homage, meanwhile being lords of the vastest domains. From up there we shall send the world a message, and . . . oh, by the way, where would you like to establish your first residence, in the Pond of Dreams or the Sea of Nectar? I'm joking, of course, particularly since these lunar seas and ponds are definitely not, as everyone thinks, dried-out basins, but real and proper expanses of water. Forgive me, in fact, if I give way like this to my emotion and enthusiasm: after all, these feelings must only seem natural to you in someone like myself who . . ."

And so on and so forth. But he soon calmed down and, after a few bizarre variations on lunar place-names, his conversation took a patient, nearly scientific turn, like that of a professor who has to deal with a slow or crassly ignorant pupil, as I surely was. Among other matters, he also furnished some details on the moon's physical composition, laughing in fact at the astronomers' universal opinion that this celestial body lacked an atmosphere. He, on the contrary, did not entertain the slightest doubt of its existence, though he admitted that the air might be, indeed must be, extremely rarified. He also said that he had taken every precaution in case his surveys and calculations should prove to be mistaken, precautions which he promised to explain to me point by point at the proper time. He also mentioned his hope, supported, he claimed, by solid data, of finding up there not a desert but a flourishing civilization.

The most troubling point for me in all this talk was that by now he regarded me as totally committed to the undertaking and his sworn companion. But time and circumstance would decide and, I hoped, would help me.

Thus we reached the foot of the loftiest crown in our massif. It rises like a tumultuous confusion of peaks, cliffs and inaccessible or almost inaccessible crests which often fold back and curve into rings or craters so as to form gigantic stone nests, many of them containing a small glacier. The tallest peak, called the Devil's Horn, which rises well above the others in the shape of a ruined tower, in fact like a decayed tooth, is—or until recently was—considered inviolable because of a certain very dangerous crossing; inviolable at least to the common run of men. In any event, I had a very vague notion of all this, nor had I ever ventured all the way up there. The fact remains that this rugged mountain area, just to judge it from what I was now rather dimly seeing, was a place more suited to eagles than to men.

And it was precisely at the Devil's Horn, feebly reddened by that crumb of a moon, that my companion pointed and said:

"Within an hour at the most we will be there. Stay very close to me, follow me step by step. The trail becomes quite difficult but not dangerous as yet."

(This to me, who was already utterly exhausted! As if it were simply a matter of following his footsteps!)

So he resumed the rocky climb with me close at his heels and, after a short stretch, attacked one of those cliffs obliquely, choosing his path in order also to reduce the exertion of the ascent. Soon afterwards, however, he disappeared, or rather we disappeared into a tunnel, in which we had to use our hands, and whence we reached the top of what, if I'm not mistaken, mountain climbers call a narrow ledge or foothold. And in this fashion, sometimes using our hands, sometimes our feet, partly crawling straight up and partly traversing the sides of the peak, we turned almost completely around it in a spiral. But another peak awaited us, joined to the first peak by a jagged saddle; and then more peaks, each one more impervious and difficult. On this aerial route and these vertiginous crossings I was partly helped by the dimness of the light, which veiled the full extent of the danger and the depth of the chasms on whose brinks we prowled; although on the other hand this lack of light rendered both the distant and nearby details of that already sinister landscape all the more horrible. Often I found myself as though suspended over an abyss, whose walls were illuminated by the pale reddish rays of the moon to a certain depth only, leaving the bottom sunk in a slightly tawny obscurity; but before the eye, invincibly avid of horror, could pierce this darkness, I had passed beyond; and so I went forward in a sort of daze. Of course I was gasping like a pair of bellows and was often forced to beg my companion, who on his part did not show the least weariness, to slow down.

By now almost every step revealed new, confused prospects. The largest peak, which seemed within easy reach, though isolated by an incalculable void, had lost a good deal of its hauteur and height. Then we reached the edge of a wide cleft or crevasse which, extending on either side so far that one could not see its end, barred our path. But soon a far-off splashing sound rising from an unfathomable profundity struck my ear and, peering down into the darkness below, I felt that I could see the very distant glimmer of water. In short, without going into further details, the mountain, owing to some formidable telluric shift, was at that point split all the way down to its base, and the proud Devil's Horn was completely separated from the rest of the mountain chain. So this was an obligatory path! I estimated the crevasse to be not less than five meters wide on an average.

"One last effort," that demon of energy said quite simply, "one last effort and we shall be there. On the other side the slope becomes child's play."

But I had been seized by uncontrollable terror and at the same time a great feeling of lassitude. What was I doing, I asked myself belatedly, on top of those savage mountains, at night, alone with that madman, searching for a chimerical flying machine; and just as uselessly I cursed the frivolity or desperation which had brought me there. In the meantime I was invincibly retreating from the abyss, all the more frightening since it was so narrow, and I was quite determined to go back the way I had come rather than attempt that crossing. Also I hadn't the faintest idea of how it could be attempted anyhow. My companion kept on comforting me, claiming that there was a way to negotiate the crevasse; and I, digging in my heels like a mule, at a respectful distance from it, refused to listen. Finally, seeing that every attempt at persuasion was futile, he said roughly, staring at me with his scintillating eyes:

"Sir, we do not have time to waste. Dawn will soon be here, and from this point we shall be visible to the entire region below. Now then, would you rather follow me safely or end up at the bottom of this abyss?"

"You . . . you might end up there yourself," I replied in horror, my teeth chattering.

"Yes, yes, sure," he snorted, coming resolutely toward me, as though to begin the struggle right away.

"Calm down, will you? Try to be reasonable. How do you propose getting over there?"

"I have been telling you for quite some time now, but you refuse to listen! The way I have done it all the innumerable times I have come up here."

After saying that and seeing that I was subdued, if not willing, he walked a few paces away and began searching among the rocks behind a boulder, and pulled out a coil of rope.

"To start with, this is a rope. Now give me a hand."

From a deep crack under another rock covered up with stones, we took out two long tree-trunks, which were in fact young pine trees stripped of their branches. Handling them as though they were straws, he pushed one across until it rested on the opposite side of the crevasse, that is, traversed it, then placed the butt end in a slight indentation on our side and wedged it in with stone slivers to prevent it from rolling; he propped the other trunk against an outcropping on the rock wall opposite, and lowered it on our side so that it remained, just below the edge of the cliff, obliquely but firmly wedged between the two rock faces. Now he slipped the rope around the first trunk, knotting one end of it in a broad loop; and finally, turning to me with the rest of the rope in his hand, he said:

"I will go over first. Watch carefully how I tie myself on; a moment from now you'll have to do the same by yourself. Above all," he added threateningly, "don't try to run away. It would be useless: I would overtake you in a flash and . . ."

He tied the rope under his armpits and then in the middle of his body to form a kind of harness. He got down on the lower trunk and, thus anchored to the upper one, making the loop slide rapidly along it, in less time than it takes to tell he had passed with monkey-like agility to the other side.

He untied the rope, coiled it up and threw it across the abyss, urging me to repeat the entire operation without delay.

This was obviously the most favorable moment to make my escape, and for an instant I had the idea of doing so. But that demon was quite capable of coming back over even without the rope. Besides, the method he had used convinced me and, as he had said, it was really without danger; the worst that could happen to me was to remain dangling in mid-air at the end of the rope, like a spider, but in that case he would come to my rescue. In short, I was beginning to have an enormous trust in him; and, in no time, having tied the rope as best I could to the trunk and around myself, I warily stepped down in my turn on the improvised gangplank.

I kept my eyes closed. The crossing went well until I had to pull myself up on the opposite side, for here, it goes without saying, I lost my footing and my hand slipped and I would have undoubtedly suffered the fate mentioned just above if he had not grabbed me by the collar, and for a moment supported my entire weight with only one arm.

He retrieved the pine trunks and, with a changed and happy face, said:

"You will forgive me if I was forced to frighten you, over there; but I have heard it said that this is how one must act with beginners."

We resumed climbing up the trail to the now-tamed Devil's Horn: a trail which in fact did not prove to be particularly difficult.

We were about to reach, so he claimed, his creature's shelter. Did I, having gotten to this point, believe in the existence of that creature (if I must call it that) or of something, at least? I was truly unable to give myself an answer, which nonetheless was in itself already half an answer. During all that time I had not succeeded in making up my mind as to my companion's mental condition, or, more precisely, as to what type of madman he might be. And, on one hand, would he have led me all the way up there just to pursue a fantasy of his? While, on the other hand . . . basically, for the moment, there was no "other hand," except for reason's invincible repugnance to crediting the marvelous. Finally, my attitude toward him was (save for my curiosity) aloof, judicial and observant; I had been waiting for him to reach precisely this test to decide whether he was, as I said before, one of those madmen who are a beacon-light for humanity (and I don't care who calls them mad), or a plain, and hence extremely dangerous, visionary. In the first case, one way or another, everything would fall into place. In the second . . . Well, it was too late now to think about what would happen in the second case. And even if there had been time, what was the point of such a thought, since both his purpose in leading me here as well as his future actions were by definition unpredictable?

Because of my slowness, we were somewhat behind in our schedule. A livid purplish light, presage of the dawn, began spreading through the air, and the stars began to grow pale. When we reached the highest point of the Horn, we circled it horizontally or, as they say, on a level curve. In this way we came to a wide breach in the rocky wall of the ridge, which was twisted like a spill of paper and turned out to be the entrance to the glacier. The sky was becoming brighter: it was day. Beneath us milky cloud-banks shut off the whole view and truly segregated us from the world. But here no festive voice greeted the day: a grave, unperturbed silence reigned among these calcareous peaks. Halting at the threshold of that immense doorway and spreading his arms out to the East, my companion burst into an exultant exclamation:

"Far," he said, "far at our feet lies the world. Soon it will be even farther away. Where are they, those blind men who must be frantically searching for me by now? Where are your creditors? (But how in the world did he know that I had creditors—and many of them?) How remote all their anxieties and agitations appear to us from here. Doesn't your blood throb joyfully? Brace yourself anew, my friend, in this pure air, while you wait to breathe air that is even purer. And that's not all: the infinite spaces are open to us. For one thing, from up there," and he nodded at the puny, dim moon which hovered as though forgotten in a corner of the sky, "we shall impose our will on this world below, and it is our will that it be prosperous and happy."

Just then, and somewhat to my relief, we heard the distant screech of an eagle.

"Listen, listen, to the happy omen," he cried. And without further ado, with me at his heels, he entered between the high, sheer walls of a sort of amphitheatre or pit. These walls were streaked with the most beautiful colors and glistened here and there, dampened by seeping water.

Taking great care, we crossed the small, sloping glacier, which fortunately was strewn with boulders that had fallen from the crest and was also almost completely covered by a layer of some sort of brown loam. There is no need to say that the extreme cold had been tormenting me for some hours, since, on top of everything else, we were both without overcoats; but he did not even seem to notice the cold.

We reached a low cave at the foot of the rock wall; indeed it was barely a fissure, so small that one could not get through except by crawling on one's belly. Here he stopped, looking at me with a triumphant expression. So now, how could that miraculous machine of his fit in there?

"Wait for me here," he said. And he slid into the hole, only to leap out an instant later in a fury. He pounced on me and gripped my shoulders as in a vise, his deep, soulful and, as it seemed, tear-blurred eyes staring into mine. He declared:

"I am about to show you my creature, the fruit of long years of study and work, the thing, and I can well say the being, that is dearer to me than anything else in the world, the daughter of my blood

and bowels. I am about to reveal her hidingplace to you and put her
at your mercy. Will you be worthy of this? Will you betray me? Since
the moment has really come for you to decide, since, as I have well
understood, you are waiting for this test to judge whether I am crazy
or not—will you also tell me that you will accompany me to the moon
if she does exist? Will you solemnly promise me to do so when you
have, I repeat, ascertained her existence? Or could there be something
else to hold you back?"

He stared at me with incomparable intensity. I babbled I don't
know what, such as what else could there be, and what great faith I
had in him; finally, I gave him my formal promise, because of an inner conviction that I had to do it, and in all good conscience, though
not without some mental reservations. He loosened his grip and
squeezed back into the hole. I heard him moving stones and variously
pottering around inside there. Then he pushed some of the stones and
they came rolling out; at last he himself stuck out his disheveled head
for an instant and invited me to follow him.

It was easy to say. Anyway I crawled through the fissure, which
widened inside and became a fraction higher, permitting a relatively
free movement, though you still had to wriggle along on your belly.
In that sort of dark culvert or tunnel his feet were my guide.

We crawled along in this fashion for a brief stretch like two
earthworms, our chests furrowing a sticky slime. I was not thinking of
anything, I could not see the faintest sign of light, and was almost suffocating. Suddenly I felt the shoe I was clutching with all my strength
slip out of my hand, I had the sensation of breathing more freely,
and an instant later I heard, below me and to one side, his voice singularly magnified as if he had reached a place of spacious proportions.

"Don't move," he was saying, "wait till I turn on the light."

I heard his muffled fumbling some distance away, and a moment
later a vivid beam of light cut through the darkness. I saw then that
I was, as I must point out, wedged just a bit this side of a sharp turn
in the tunnel; the light which struck me, and which at each instant

grew brighter and more violent as if powerful lamps were being switched on one after the other) was therefore indirect, reflected by the tunnel's curved wall, and I could not guess its source. In a word, my position, from a physical point of view as well, was insane, idiotic and ludicrous.

"Stay where you are, please!" his voice begged and thundered at the same time.

Well, of course. The good man set great store by his theatrical effects. I was about to continue on just the same when, the light having become dazzling, almost blinding, he at last gave me permission to do so.

After a small hump, the tunnel opened into an immense cavern which, in that bright light, was revealed to me in all its fabulous magnificence, with its enormous vaulted ceiling, its columns and stalactites. All around the walls were fixed rudimentary sconces, which instead of torches held certain beaked cylinders. From these with a low roar and hiss rose small, lively flames, undoubtedly produced by the combustion of some gas, as bright as the flame of an acetylene torch, but slightly bluish; and all together they lit up the place better than the most brilliant sun could have done. In the rear a large workshop with an adjoining laboratory was set up, with a rich variety of equipment.

In the center of the cavern I had immediately seen and now contemplated with more horror than amazement a large object of bizarre form that emitted a different quality of light; and, if I must report my first impression without any comment, it squatted there, quietly looking at us with a thousand eyes.

My companion approached me and, having triumphantly studied the expression on my face for a moment, pointed at the object with both hands in a rather melodramatic gesture:

"There she is. Her name is Cancerqueen."

From that moment on I was pledged to him and his machine (which henceforth I shall refer to by the name he gave her), or rather, one might say that I was in their power. To begin with, I had made up my mind: he was not a madman, or he was only one in the vulgar acceptance of that term, which did not concern me. From the standpoint of reason, one could have suspected that he was an inventor, a genius, unsuccessful, perhaps a trifle impractical; but such a suspicion did not even pass through my head. As for the act or acts which had put him into the insane asylum, and of which I should have also feared a repetition, I attributed them with touching goodwill to a temporary obfuscation and to some serious provocation: certainly the kind of provocation whose gravity the person causing it did not realize, but which can prove unbearable to a lofty intellect. In conclusion, I was trusting and blind, nor did I have any further doubts on his account.

He remained up there and I, accompanied by him all the way to the dreadful crevasse, returned to the village with the task of procuring many indispensable things, but chiefly provisions for himself and for the journey. These I had to leave every night at a certain place on the mountain, and he would then compress and synthesize the greater part of them in his incomparable laboratory according to certain processes of his, in order to assure us nourishment, as he said, for years. On and off we would meet, always on the mountain, to make further decisions.

These preparations promised to take much longer than we, in our impatience, would have liked. To start with, many items, indeed almost everything, were the strangest of substances and the most unusual objects and had to come from the city. And in fact many days went by before we could even think of setting the date for our departure, days which for me were filled with intense anxiety. These delays seemed to rekindle my enthusiasm rather than douse it: oblivious to the world, I lived only for our undertaking, and would have liked to hasten its inception. But he, inwardly just as impatient as I, kept saying that he did not want any surprises, and that everything must be meticulously prepared in advance in order to cut down unexpected occurrences to a minimum; and so, with the cautious and methodical procedure of men of science, he unhurriedly went forward with his extremely detailed and scrupulous preparations.

In the meantime I had received, the very next day after that first night together, and while I was still recuperating from my fatiguing mountain climb, a visit from the director of . . . , the province's insane asylum. With great circumspection, as though he didn't want to frighten me unduly, he informed me that the previous night a certain very dangerous lunatic, who had inexplicably escaped the surveillance of his guards, had been seen roaming about near my house. It was feared that he might have hidden in one of my house's many uninhabited outbuildings, or in my park which had grown wild and was bordered on one side by a small wood. So the director asked my permission to make a search, accompanied by two gigantic male nurses who were waiting for him at the door; he would be doing this for my own safety. But they could talk all they wished, they did not shake my faith, nor did I think for an instant of betraying . . . but how could I tell them his name, since I myself had never learned it? Well, for convenience's sake, I shall call him Filano.

After having searched my house to his heart's content, the director left, still perplexed. At any rate the man was being actively hunted; of course, his hiding place was such as to challenge any and every search for a long time. During the director's visit, I should add, though in what connection I am not sure, that I had the disagreeable impression that he spoke to me as if I were one of his patients; he often repeated his remarks, as though to make their meaning quite evident and drum them into my head, and all the while he examined me with the eye of an expert. No doubt the result of habit, and yet his behavior made me so angry that at the end I became almost rude.

I returned a few more times to the Devil's Horn and began to get on more intimate terms with Cancerqueen. She was a machine of bizarre moods, at least that is how she seemed to me from the sounds she emitted while Filano was working on her, from her snorts and various reactions; at least to me, I say, who knew little or nothing about her multiform and complicated entrails. But all in all at that time she appeared to me as a beneficent force, and her glitter propitious, even though metallic; I even became accustomed to her "dreaming devil's" stare, a stare at once obtuse and metaphysical, most often hard and opaque, like the stare of a grasshopper. Moreover, she was my liberator, whose wings (wholly metaphorical) would transport me (not metaphorically) beyond my disagreeable, unrewarding world and—but enough, for I, unlike my companion in the expedition, did not, after all, concern myself with the world's future, and only wanted to leave it.

Inside she was comfortably, even elegantly, arranged for two persons, with everything that was needed for rest and the other necessities of daily life; in fact according to what I gathered, she would not, as one might have supposed, travel the huge distance that separated us from our goal at high speed but relatively slowly. In her pantry there would be—or already had been—placed foodstuffs, as I have said, for two or three years: in her tanks oxygen for an equal period of time, reduced by some magical procedure to minute whitish pellets. Of this, according to Filano, we would consume only a minimal part, but in any case it was better to have too much than risk suddenly running out of it. Exactly how the numerous and very serious problems of aerodynamics and God knows what else, inherent in an interplanetary flight, were solved, I cannot in all conscience say. Not that in general I wasn't given explanations, practical demonstrations, and so on, by Filano himself, who at all costs wanted me to become familiar with his creature's organs and functions, since after all I was to be not only his companion but also his assistant. But the infernal impatience which devoured me, a source of distraction and absent-mindedness, the blind faith I had in him and the success of the enterprise, and finally (or rather in the first place) my constitutional inability to understand anything about scientific matters, had the precise result that I did not understand a single solitary thing. And the little I did understand I forgot,

to my great misfortune—oh, why didn't I realize then that because of
my distraction I was endangering my very life? And if it were only a
matter of my life; oh, if I had only paid all the attention of which I
was capable! . . . So in truth, as regards Cancerqueen, I must repeat
that I know and can say nothing precise, in fact nothing at all. What I
remember of her informing principle is not very certain, and what I jot
down here is done at the risk of giving currency to a bit of solemn nonsense. It seems that in those regions of space where the medium she
traverses is too rarefied to support her, she moves by emitting ahead
of herself an atmosphere, on the general order, let's say, of the terrestrial atmosphere, and to which she, so to speak, holds onto from moment to moment. I am much less clear as to where she draws her motive or propulsive power or what damned sort of power it might be,
and all that I do know is that she must periodically be fed through her
internal and voracious mouth with other pellets, which are brown in
color. I do not know how she is driven, nor how she is made to stop.
She does not have external equipment like propellers or things of that
kind.

As for how to get her out of that cavern, a problem I had been
pondering from the very beginning:

"Look," Filano said to me, "as you see, on that side, that is, toward the outside, the cave's wall curves like a sail swollen by the wind;
careful measurements have shown that this wall has a minimum
thickness of seven meters; which is not too much for a charge of good
dynamite. So now you've already understood. When the time comes we
will simply blow up the curtain of rock, as much as is required. And
that won't be much, an opening large enough for her to pass through
will be sufficient; for I," he proclaimed proudly, "can pilot Cancerqueen with millimetric precision. Or, to put it more accurately, she
docilely allows herself to be piloted by me."

And in proof of this, he invited me on a brief experimental flight.

Cancerqueen grumbled a bit, sneezed, yawned lazily, as if she
did not fancy flying about just to be exhibited, and then she rose up,

still unwillingly; but soon she emitted her hiss and began looping about the cave. She rose to within a few inches of the ceiling, turned adroitly about a column, slipped with élan through a very narrow passage between two other columns, performed various other gyrations, and finally settled daintily on the ground again. My enthusiasm was boundless.

And at last the great day arrived. The sun had just risen; but only for us, not for the rest of the world, which was still wrapped in nocturnal mist; the air, freezing at that altitude, was of an incomparable limpidity. In short, it was a radiant October morning, a morning of hope, when we set about putting a match to the powerful charges of dynamite already expertly disposed by Filano deep in the rock.

We lit the fuses, left the cave and hurried away from it, crossing the glacier and taking shelter past its entrance, behind the ridge of the crest. After a few minutes, the mines exploded almost simultaneously with a hellish roar, dully reverberating off the curved wall and followed by the whistling and drumming of boulders and stone splinters. When we returned to the spot, we could immediately see the excellent results: a long smoking gash had been opened in the aforesaid rock wall and about the middle looked wide enough to provide a passage for Cancerqueen.

"Let's not waste time," Filano cried. "The explosion must have been heard throughout the region."

Although the dynamite charges had been placed so as to explode toward the outside of the cavern, and Cancerqueen had been pushed behind massive pillars and protected by a metal net with the idea of reducing the effects of the formidable displacement of air, we still were worried about her, since her delicate organs could well have suffered from this displacement or the fall of rock fragments. But it was not the case and wholly intact, she greeted us with a gay, even mocking air.

After looking things over for the last time to make sure that everything was in order, we took our places inside her, Filano pushed down some lever or other, and Cancerqueen moaned. It always seemed to cost her an effort to tear herself out of a state of repose; but also, as I thought I had noticed, to return to this state from a condition of motion; in fine, she seemed endowed (if such an expression has any meaning) with a great force of inertia.

She moaned, trembled, detached herself from the ground with a feeble squeak; made a short turn about the cavern, as though caracoling, began to hiss; slipped through the gash in the wall and was over the glacier, skimming it at not too great a height, still with a slightly oscillating motion; steadied herself in the air and came out into the open sky; and once there, she began to climb.

Cancerqueen could not, so it seemed, rise except at a very slight incline, that is, by means of extremely wide circles. Considering this fact now, in other words that she was circling her way to the moon along a spiral of short, though variable, measurement; that the distance to be covered was therefore ten times more than the actual distance between the earth and its satellite; and finally, taking into account the fact that Cancerqueen proceeded at a speed of about a thousand kilometers an hour, it was easy to conclude that our voyage would have to last several months. That, of course, without reckoning with all that might happen once we entered the moon's sphere of attraction, where the conditions of flight could be changed. This, however, was my thought only: Filano had no doubts and behaved as though he knew in detail exactly how things would go.

The first circle brought us, after about twelve hours, over the Sunda Islands, at an altitude, I believe, of twelve kilometers (since we had taken off from a very high place); then, the next day, back to Hawaii, at a not much greater altitude; in any case, these facts could have been ascertained from the dials on our instrument panel. The next day we were again passing somewhere in the vicinity of the Malesian Archipelago; and so on, very slowly, yet constantly climbing higher and higher. During this traveling to and fro in the lower layers of the atmosphere, our passage was noticed. Cancerqueen's bizarre shape obviously had aroused curiosity and fears, since our radio aboard started to splutter excitedly: many places were asking for all sorts of explanations. We did not answer any of them.

The days went by. Each day disclosed a vaster horizon, although the terrestrial surface still did not reveal its curvature, in fact it looked somewhat concave, nor had the apparent size of the moon increased. But already the water masses were growing darker and, conversely, the land was growing brighter, while later on the oceans were completely opaque and dull and the land was extraordinarily brilliant. (We got our first sense of the earth's rotundity at a height of about one hundred kilometers.) Naturally, the apparatus which produced our oxygen had been set in operation on the day of our departure. The outside thermometer already registered extremely low temperatures.

Life on board went forward quietly, without external incidents of note, rigidly regulated in its essential phases by Filano, who wanted our strength to be kept fresh, although, having by now recognized my ineptitude, he alone performed the necessary tasks. In any case, Cancerqueen required surveillance more than actual physical care, and she did not even have to be piloted: once certain instruments were set in a specific direction, she went ahead, rose, turned, and did everything all by herself. As a result, we spent most of our time in elevated discussions of science and philosophy, in plans, conjectures as to what awaited us on the moon, in obstinate and vain attempts on his part to make me understand the principles of higher physics that were involved in our flight.

Among the daily, or almost daily, operations was the production of water, an operation which, given its extreme simplicity, I myself, for a change, was soon in a position to perform. In fact we had not carried along water, which in the quantity needed would have burdened us with an excessive weight and volume, for the good reason that Filano manufactured it as we needed it. He put his white oxygen pellets and others, obviously of hydrogen, in a large retort, connected with Cancerqueen's internal organs, where no doubt the principal reaction took place: one saw a great frothing tumult and upheaval, and soon after water dripped out, as clear as from a spring.

My companion had other machinery with which he turned our excrement, reduced to a minimal quantity as a result of our synthetic nourishment, into gases and other useful substances without residue, which were then duly bottled. Of course it is obvious that one couldn't think of throwing the excretia outside, since the slightest intrusion of outside air could have been fatal to us. Here I will say that our cell communicated with the outside only by two apertures, both of course hermetically sealed, and both conceived according to the same principle: that of the valve. The first aperture was the vent for the carbon dioxide produced by our respiration, which, as Filano explained to me, accumulated in a certain conduit and pressed against a massive operculum until there was enough pressure to force it open; the operculum was equipped with a powerful automatic closing, or reclosing, device. The second aperture was the large door by which we had entered: it too only opened outward, and a similar device, together with sturdy internal bolts, kept it closed. It would thus be impossible for something from the outside to penetrate through it into our aerial abode, but in some extreme case of emergency we would be able to force it open.

At an altitude of about two thousand kilometers we left the terrestrial atmosphere, or at least the earth ceased dragging us along in its orbit. For some time now we had had the impression that that last, very tenuous fringe of our planet only had a feeble hold on Cancerqueen, and we had even noticed some slight deviation of the earth from that which, taking into account our movement, should have been its position relative to us. Meanwhile the sky had gradually darkened, the sun had taken on the color of red-hot metal, and the moon and earth a violent, aggressive, yet chalky luminosity; this finally resulted in complete darkness, in the midst of which these three celestial bodies and the stars all shone steadily, without, however, impregnating or tempering it and without the least scintillation. That is how I see the sky even now, except that from here the moon looks much larger and the earth, a trifle flattened, does not occupy more than an eighth of the celestial vault (the earth is larger, if I am not mistaken, one hundred times larger than the moon itself). To anyone who might have seen her from the outside, Cancerqueen must have looked like a small body radiating indirect light and, owing to the atmosphere she emits, encircled by a small halo (about which I later received actual confirmation). After having for some time followed, so I felt, a most capricious schedule, the darkness of the night had on the contrary abandoned Cancerqueen's interior, which was supplied with air, and henceforth only an eclipse could have simulated its return.

The days continued to pass, but now not without changes. I have mentioned above that life on board was tranquil; actually this was so only during the first days, at least for me, because soon after our departure I began to notice something abnormal about Filano's behavior. At first I did not attach overwhelming importance to these symptoms, which I judged to be the effect of the fatigue due to the great labor and tension of the spirit in recent days, excitement at the felicitous inception of our undertaking, and many other more or less plausible causes, and so trustingly waited for them to disappear. But on the contrary they grew worse with the passing of the days and weeks, and I was compelled to worry about them. And now they were becoming positively preoccupying and I was alarmed; the scales began to fall from my eyes.

What they actually consisted of is not easy to say. Sometimes it was no more than an attitude, a word, a glance, at other times they expressed themselves with greater force; what is certain is that all together they composed, to speak bluntly, a far from reassuring picture of the man's mental state. His faculties seemed manifestly altered—I mean in respect to when I had first met him; and, remember, even then he was hardly a model of normal behavior!

But how was this? How could I, I who had had blind faith in him and even downright blind admiration, who shortly before had loudly told myself that he was anything but crazy, indeed that he was the only sane man in the world, inclining rather to assign the former epithet to all the rest of humanity, I who to the remonstrances of science, personified by the director of the insane asylum, had replied with an inner smile of scorn, how could I have come to this conclusion? Ah well, it would take too long to get to that how, but my faith was forced to give way; minute by minute my admiration changed into terror, while one by one my illusions collapsed.

Had he always been like this, or had he changed? Under the present circumstances the question could not have been more academic. Anyway, it would have been more correct for me to say that day by day he now revealed his true nature, which at the cost of unimaginable efforts had been stifled and momentarily dominated, that is, during the time needed to reassure me and involve me in the undertaking; and this too also began, with the progress of the disease, to seem to me difficult and desperate, not to say chimerical, to the same degree that it had seemed before to be safe and replete with great rewards. But I was taking stock too late of my frivolous judgment and imprudence—when they could no longer be remedied.

Not that I had yet been physically threatened, or that he had given way to open frenzies; but the disease might declare itself and an explosion follow at any moment. It's hard to describe, I'm not quite sure about it all, but the whole business had begun with glum and unexpected stares, uncalled-for giggles, with sudden silences or wanderings in the very middle of a speech, with excessive irritability, intemperate reactions, and such-like slight aberrations; and it had, as it grew and grew, reached paroxsym-like or seriously pathological forms, such as rash gestures, temporary aphasia, stammering, arbitrary deductions, merely verbal associations, compulsive actions, automatisms and so on. On the whole his speeches now evoked the image of those cans of shoe-polish which street kids pierce and twirl vertiginously on a piece of string; or to use a modern image, they were geared in neutral; once having proposed any sort of fact, most often secondary, he pounded away at it indefatigably and unrestrainedly for hours on end without managing "to gear it in" with the other facts of his discourse or extract any sort of meaning from it. Nonetheless, he seemed to be, though very hazily, aware of all this. Furthermore, he talked to himself ceaselessly, and often in the middle of the night (that is, during the hours devoted to rest, since night, as I said before, had abandoned us for quite some time now), whenever I had managed to fall asleep in spite of my terror, I was awakened by certain bursts of laughter that made my flesh creep. But the laugh which he personally developed in the very last period, and which could more accurately be called a violent attack of nerves, was by far the most horrible: point-blank, perhaps even interrupting one of his fruitless, rambling lectures, and when, it is superfluous to add, there was nothing to laugh about, he threw back his head, brought his fists to his temples and, as a frightful grimace distorted his face and bared his teeth, he shook all over or, more exactly, vibrated in the grip of an uncontrollable convulsion, though not a sound issued from his lips. These seizures sometimes lasted for several minutes, after which, as though nothing had happened, he resumed whatever he had been doing or his incoherent babblings.

But why beat around the bush? He was, I had to confess to myself, *a madman*. And in case I still had any doubts, I noticed that his right pupil, and only his right, had dilated enormously; and at last he began to complain about visual, auditory and even tactile hallucinations.

In spite of his condition, Filano continued to take care of Cancerqueen, indeed he did so with a savage and jealous concern that made him keep me away from the instruments. His already passionate love for his creature had also assumed morbid, affected or ritualistic aspects. It was clear, however (or better: therefore) that beyond this routine daily commerce with her, that is, if he were confronted by a new situation, his mind would go to pieces. In short, we were truly in the hands of God. For a long time, despite the disorder of his faculties, he had continued to show a certain benevolence toward me, although he often abused me; but now this feeling, too, gave way under the inner raging flame, changing into its opposite, a more or less openly declared aversion. Among other things, the number of surly glances he flung at me could no longer be counted; he stared at me, I was perfectly aware of it, when I turned my back to him, and scrutinized me grimly during my sleep, or when he thought I was sleeping.

I don't have to describe the sort of life I now led, irremediably locked up with that madman in that cell literally outside the world. I hardly slept any more, I lived in a state of nameless oppression and terror, day by day, minute by minute, waiting for the inevitable explosion; my nerves, my strength were on the verge of collapse, I began to fear for my own mental health; nor could I imagine what would happen after that explosion, even if I came out of it alive.

And so the fatal day arrived. Events which have a profound and lasting significance for a man's life or psyche, even events that for all of humanity prolong their good or bad consequences into an age-old, perhaps eternal future and derive their premises from a past of indeterminable duration, even these events take place in time, a brief, terrestrial period of time, and though long foreseen are always to some extent sudden. It seems to us that so portentous an event cannot possibly have taken place so quickly, and we do not know that actually that time is often concentrated in no more than an instant. Moreover, whenever anything irreparable, and even more when something sadly irreparable has to come to pass, it seems impossible that an instant later we cannot, by means of something akin to what in space is a step backward, call everything back to its previous condition, so as to start all over, think again . . . and, if we wish, perform the same act. But true it is. I mean, everything is like a dream; and what has happened cannot be part of reality; and everything is so real that it is already part of the past. (A pompous exordium, my non-existent reader will think, for this insignificant event of mine. Let him think what he wishes, since he does not exist, and let him get accustomed, if he can, to my tirades.)

And what I had been expecting for so many days seemed just as sudden.

Filano's condition had especially deteriorated after we had passed one hundred thousand kilometers of altitude, or elongation. The event took place at about two hundred thousand kilometers, that is about halfway between the earth and the moon. A little more than two months had passed since our departure.

One morning Filano got up from his berth, where by now he did everything but sleep, and seemed particularly overwrought, giving way to speeches and acts that no longer had the slightest trace of coherence, and displaying toward me an open hostility. He milled about the cell frenetically, like a wild beast, planted himself suddenly in front of me, resumed his agitated gyrations and always seemed about to pounce on me. His inhibitory centers seemed completely destroyed. His daily occupations had also lost all semblance of coordination: in his daze he moved to and fro, jerkily touching the instruments, and without any necessity whatsoever, teasing Cancerqueen's various internal organs, which in the long run could constitute a danger. He laughed, cried, howled, cackled, shivered, gave sudden starts, shook, a prey to uncontrollable fits. He seemed to want to incinerate me with a glance; once, however, halting suddenly in front of me, he commended his creature to my care with heartbreaking emotion, because, so he said, he would soon die and she would be left alone in the world. There is no need for me to describe the state I was in. Just slightly less out of my mind than he, I could only bow my head and stop my ears while waiting for the "final seizure," which was bound to be frightful: to try to undertake any action against him was out of the question, in view of his extraordinary physical strength, no doubt under the circumstances increased a hundredfold. All I could do as soon as he attacked me was to try in some way to kill him—yes, kill him.

Round about the middle of the day his agitation reached its peak, but the event that by now I was almost hoping for, to resolve my unbearable tension, was still not forthcoming. Storming ever more violently about the cell, he suddenly flung himself, before I could even think of restraining him, against the main door and unscrewed the bolts, slinging the large nuts in all directions; he kept shrieking frantically that he needed air. So the door remained locked thanks only to the spring that closed it. But perhaps a last shred of consciousness warned him of the grave danger to which he was exposing himself, or his mind had already leaped elsewhere. He desisted. He rushed instead to the main instrument panel and turned a switch, pushed a lever. For the moment Cancerqueen did not seem to react and continued her proud and steady flight.

At this point, while his back was turned to me (a position in which he remained frozen for a time), at this point I heard that voice, which still rings in my ears; that voice which, being so much more dreadful, had nothing in common with his own: calm, frosty, blood-curdling. The voice said:

"I have been thinking about it for a long time. It can't go on like this: things aren't working out because you are here, your weight. You must die."

Not another word did he say, right to the end. Almost at the same moment he swung around and, silently grinding his teeth, his whole body shaking with excitement, hatred, epilepsy, his face purplish, splotched with red, he threw himself on me and tried to seize me by the throat.

I don't know how but I managed to escape from that formidable grip, actually pushing him against the opposite wall where the door was. From there, crouching to gather impetus, he jumped on me again. But at this supreme instant, as if by superior illumination, I made up my mind. The main door, as I have said, was now closed only by the pressure of the spring, whose force must be great, as I remembered having thought at the moment of our departure. Yet if I catapulted my adversary against the door, I could hope to make it yield at least the little that was needed to let his body through. In this way I risked my own life, because a single puff of air (or of whatever it might be) and of the outside cold would be enough to kill me, but I had no choice and risking one's life is always preferable to certain death: under the attacks of that wild man I would inevitably have succumbed sooner or later. Therefore, staking everything on a supreme effort, with all the energy of desperation, my shoulders against the wall behind me and my right foot planted in the center of his chest as soon as he got within reach; helping myself with my elbows, my occiput, my soul, my terror, I thrust at him with all the strength I could muster.

The door yielded, but not enough; for a fraction of an instant it hung hesitant, just about to slam back violently; but as the entire weight of Filano's body had for a moment been brought to bear on the crack, suddenly it grew larger. Filano plunged into the void (an expression which has here, I suppose, its literal value).

As the door shut again with a sharp crash, a gelid wind, burning my mucous membrane and entrails, whizzed through the cell; stifled, parched, as if my insides had been shredded and shriveled, I fainted dead away.

When I came to, my heart was beating furiously and my eyes were bleared with a thick mist; all the same, I was rapidly regaining my breath. My skin had become like parchment; and so it remained for weeks.

The first thing I saw was . . . Filano.

I don't know the reason for this diabolical effect, which may be familiar to physicists; perhaps because up here the earth's gravity has lost a good deal of its power, at least over such a small body, and at any rate is not strong enough to overcome the attraction of Cancerqueen's proximity; or, more likely, because he had been caught "like a fly in golden amber" in the atmosphere which she emitted, so that they now formed a single unit; whatever the reason, Filano hadn't plunged down at all but was continuing to follow his creature faithfully in space—oh, very faithfully. Filano, that is, his dried-up corpse, no doubt hollowed out, as if preserved in alcohol or, rather, in liquid air, most likely as fragile as a piece of Bologna glass, but anyway externally intact and coagulated in his last attitude, all quite visible through the rear window, set against the black sky in the tenuous gleam to which I had previously alluded, his eyes wide open, his face, I assure you, wearing the horrible, ferocious grimace which was his last expression while still alive, Filano follows Cancerqueen in space; in infinite space and eternity he follows me, his murderer.

Since he had fallen with his head flung back, the attitude of his entire body made, makes one think of those wooden figures which float on the merry-go-rounds of Piedmont, stock characters such as Gianduia, the Soldier, the Lovely Damsel and the Drunkard, bereft of limbs and their bodies, almost like sirens, elongated in the shape of fish to accommodate the children who ride them; and which as the merry-go-round turns, pop up before our eyes in the air one after the other in ever new perspectives.

The second thing that attracted my attention was a noise: a clicking sound that came from the main instrument panel. The small lever which Filano had moved just before, perhaps barely a minute ago, had suddenly dropped, and right away Cancerqueen began to shake through and through, to shiver, to pitch and roll frighteningly, while her hiss turned into a menacing growl or hoarse low, similar to the noise made by a gas jet in a kitchen or fireplace. Gathering my still prostrate forces, I rushed to the panel and tried to push the lever back to its original position. I did not completely succeed and, in the very act, I actually felt in my wrist what I would call a side-slip—if Cancerqueen had wings. For many days I did not realize, nor could I possibly realize, what had happened at that point; having finally managed to adjust the lever, the flight continued steadily as before. But at last I realized what had happened—and I might as well say it right off: what the reason was I do not know and shall never know, but Cancerqueen had deviated from her course and begun turning, like a minuscule satellite, round the earth.

At the same time her velocity nearly doubled, and matched that of our planet's rotation, and perhaps this is why the same continent is always under my eyes: the most beloved . . .

II

March 30

Well, that's it, now the story has been told. But why, I ask myself again, and to whom? Even if one day we fell to earth, she and I, who could possibly find a trace of us or of this manuscript? Won't we disintegrate and won't we vanish in infinitesimal particles even before we get there? And have I perhaps overcome anguish, terror, remorse, boredom, the cold, the emptiness within and without, and finally despair? Not by any means. And yet I have gotten through almost a week of this eternity which is my life. Not very much, for an eternity. Anyway I have acquired a taste for it and want to go on: who knows whether by going on eternally, eternity too might not come to an end? So then, what is there left for me to say?

Let us begin by summing up the situation:

"I write to you from a cell in the honeycomb, from a sphere launched into space . . ." Exactly. The trouble is that I do not know what the poet meant by that cell of the honeycomb, but it is clear that I ought to change that honey into something a trifle more bitter. Months have now passed (millennia) since the death . . . since the murder of Filano. I am alone inside here, alone and without hope, somewhat as I was before I undertook this insane flight; yet worse than before, as my words will perhaps prove. Alone, not only with myself but also in the bowels of this by now hated, mocking enemy, whose course I can in no way hope to change.

How many attempts I have made since then to tear her away from her obstinate resolve, to gradually lead her back to earth, to induce her perhaps to land on the moon, so that at last this immutable progress, this inescapable turning round and round, might cease! All in vain. I have already said that I knew nothing about her or her organs; and left alone, I have fruitlessly tried to understand something about them. Methodically, systematically, with lacerating patience which I summon up each day, I have touched, caressed, tested and moved every switch, every lever, every button, for long periods at a time, experimenting with the most varied combinations, coordinating and subordinating the movements in the most diverse ways. Nothing; she has in every way definitely refused to return to her original course. The sole rewards for my efforts have been proud and menacing growls, rattles, howls, crashes, lurches, pitchings and tossings; and so then I have had to desist, because insisting would have meant prying her loose from that indefinable stability of hers, any course at all, and plunging her, plunging us both immediately into the empty abyss. And all that I know how to do is feed her for this futile and endless race of hers. Yet I remember perfectly well that all that he, Filano, did that time was turn one key and push one lever; and since I turned that key back and readjusted that lever, shouldn't everything have returned to normal? It's as simple as that. For a long time now I have given up any further attempts; I have resigned myself, if such an expression has any meaning here. I won't even mention the radio: I was trying to penetrate its workings, and broke it right away. Besides, what could I have hoped to achieve by a message to my fellow beings?

And to think that all that is needed to carry me back to safety is here, in here, within reach; but it is as though it weren't here, since I do not know how to take advantage of it.

The food supply was for two or three years; that is, if there had been two of us. Instead I am alone and besides I am not eating, or hardly swallowing any pills at all. As a consequence, the supply will suffice for me perhaps eternally, for all of my endless life.

Alone and without hope. But how can one live like this, without anything, without even a distant hope? One can't, and in fact I am waiting for something: I am waiting for the courage to die.

Wasn't I the person whose most ardent wish was to leave the

world? To whom everything seemed preferable to living in the world? And yet, strange to say, since I have left it, since that other age, I actually no longer abhor it, just the opposite, I . . . But why did I write "strange to say"? What is strange in seeing what is good after losing it, or in recognizing the lesser evil in what one thought was the worst of all evils, after one in fact has gone from an abject state to one even more abject? Indeed, that should seem quite natural. Fine, but that is not my case. It is not really that I regret the world or desire it at least as a lesser evil; on the contrary, I do not regret it and do not desire it at all. Instead—and this is the point—I love life itself, which I had never even been able to consider tolerable. Yes, I love it, I began perhaps to love it (whether this is a law of the heart or an anarchic and personal impulse) when my own life began to be hopeless, and the more hopeless my life became, the more I loved it. So that now I love it above everything else. If therefore I say that I want to die, I mean that I want to be able to will.

What is contradictory in this? Isn't it possible, for instance, to be madly in love with a woman, and at the same time realize that any relationship with her is impossible, even a relationship with oneself unless it involves her? And what does one do then, hate her perhaps? No, one wishes not to love her, which is the most passionate form of love; and yet the relationship remains impossible, literally impossible; but perhaps it is precisely this that pleases us, and perhaps our very love for her is inspired by this condition. Isn't it true that also in this case one loves what one rejects, or rejects what one loves?

Why then, I ask once more, did I speak before of courage? Well, I want to say it all (prevaricating would be utterly absurd, since I am my own imaginary reader): I am also afraid. Yes, the physical fear of death, but also fear of what comes after death. And in fact, if from one extreme evil I have fallen into one which is more extreme, is it not quite probable that from this I might fall into the most extreme? Because it must be taken into account that in this whole affair my direction is clearly indicated: that is, I am not moving through time—and I refer to my entire life considered from its inception—toward the good or at least toward a mitigation of suffering, but decisively toward the bad and the worse. To be more accurate: in this intermediate state between life and death which is my present one, I have come from one impossible life to another even more impossible; and it mathematically follows that . . . Besides, it doesn't matter and it wouldn't solve anything if I were to devote a proportionately greater love to the third stage.

April 6

To die! How does one die? Today I awoke from my brief sleep with the following sentence on my lips, a sentence whose meaning escapes me:

"One is born and one dies from the same matrix."

What can it mean? Does it allude perhaps to the blind suffering of dying, or to a hidden identity between those two supreme events? I imagine, though, that it means that in order to die one must find the way, in fact the opening; as, basically, it is necessary in order to do anything. (But is death a doing or an undergoing? Well, it all depends.) Some explanation! . . . Oh, what a dreadful confusion fills my head! I no longer understand anything about myself or the . . . I certainly can't say the world . . . about myself and all the rest.

And yesterday I awoke with another sentence: "If we arise from sleep so restored, will we not rise from death with a newer and greater strength?"

Now what does this mean? What relation does it bear to the previous sentence? How should I know! Anyway, just to try to dominate my mental confusion, just as a detached exercise (but that's not true either, there's another reason; ah yes, because these words want to be hopeful), I have for long pondered and calculated either on these sentences, around them, or independently from them.

"If we arise from sleep" . . . and so on. The concept and the similitude are certainly not farfetched, but if one went beyond the similitude one would arrive at data that I would claim to be of a scientific order. When, in other words, one affirms that sleep represents death, or vice versa, as in all religious doctrines, that death is only a sleep, such an image has only a poetic, figurative value, that is, it simply refers to man's most exclusive, most questionable and least definable activity. If on the contrary it is transferred to the sphere of physiology itself, of course in accordance with the comprehensive idea that the philosopher and poet have conceived of this science; if, in short, one were to consider death, not figuratively but actually, as the evening repose after the terrestrial day, caused by weariness and the need to recover our physical and spiritual energies, the following are the sort of results that can be obtained:

If one calculates the average span of human life at seventy years, or in round figures twenty-five thousand days, one would obtain, for the life that best deserves the name, a value of one million, seven hundred and fifty thousand years. But wouldn't this millionenial life itself have to be regarded as one day in a still vaster life? And this life would have to be set at a value of forty-three thousand billion, seven hundred and fifty million years. And so on, if not to the infinite, at least to the indefinite. Reciprocally (since symmetry, in truth a wholly arbitrary dimension, seems to be the prime necessity and almost a point of honor in our hypothesis), one could, following an inverse direction, count in each of our twenty-four hours an indefinite number of deaths, preceded in turn by lives retracted in time but not therefore less complete, or by cycles of lives one inside the other; deaths or sleeps, that is, those periods of repose, those long or short losses of consciousness from which, as I have said, our spirit and our body both draw strength in order to live. It would then be beautiful to be able to think that by an upward motion these teeny days or weeny decades and eras, I mean all these personal units of man, help him each in turn to take a step forward on the road toward a higher perfection, and all of them flowing together thus compose his perfect life, which it will be possible to assess and morally evaluate only when it is completed . . .

And blah, blah, blah! Why go on? To hell with this gibberish!

What a way to kill time! In fact the above speculation has addled my brains altogether; consoling possibly for somebody else, for those people down there, but certainly not for me! In substance, it leads to the conclusion that human life is practically eternal, that in truth when one dies one does anything but die, etc., etc.; not such a bad result. All the advantage I gain from it is, if you wish, that death, that is to say the passing away itself, is not painful: and that's not much. Yes, because I have plunged into these meditations with a definite aim: to get over my terror, less of death itself, as I have previously explained, than of the thereafter. And instead! For example, it might be a good thing that all that eternal life should foster a perfection, and even a superior one, but perfection in what? This is the point. Truly I cannot help but think that, so far as I am concerned, I would and I shall reach perfection at the end of time, yes, but it will be perfection of suffering, anguish, boredom.

Down there on my native continent, night is falling. Down there there is night, which I have not seen for months. And there is also the sunset, with its gradual, so delicate and rich transitions, with all its thousand colors, shading one into the other, and not only this black and this white, the two colors of horror. And there is a tepid breeze which awakens the grass and the flowers of the fields, the tops of the trees, which ruffles the surface of the water. There are animals on their way to their warm lairs or nests, there are . . . There is also a person, a man like so many others (my fellow being!), who sets out for home after a day of work; and waiting for him at home are his wife, his children—and why not?—the well-known plate of steaming soup on the table. . . . And there is, there is . . . Oh, how many things there are! . . . Alas, didn't I just before swear that I did not regret the world at all? And if I really must regret it, should I end up regretting precisely those things I used to despise the most? Men can be friends, can unite in families, societies; men join in brotherhood, they marry, produce children—and before, what most enraged and nauseated me was to admit and to do just this.

April 7

I reread the last words I wrote yesterday. No, not at all: this life and that are in reality identical. Or at least, my life has always been this one. I was detached from the world, but not completely; I had laboriously lifted myself up, but I remained halfway between the point of departure and the goal; and there I began to spin and buzz without end and without a goal, still attracted by the world I had left, while in my sky, close but unattainable, was the other world. . . . And our deeds which follow us. . . .

It isn't like this either. The truth is that by some mysterious fate I was excluded from the world, from all of its simple and natural things; two paces away from me my brothers (only in Christ) were fighting and dying, and all that was obscurely denied me. Even if I possessed something, I did not possess what all other men did. Thus inevitably I had to assume that attitude, inevitably I had to detach myself from the world and disdain it, precisely because it gave me nothing; and I did it out of pride, like the fox with the grapes. I have always wanted to die, or wanted to want to die, out of despair, not by vocation or choice. And so it is not that I did not love my fellow beings, it is that most times they were my fellow beings only in name. . . .

Well, it is understood that if I should live on and so have readers, critics and literary concerns, I would never have written all that precedes this. I do not have to be told that certain relationships are best insinuated surreptitiously into the reader's spirit; they absolutely should not be flung at him so openly, this runs counter to all the rules of modern literature. In fact the critics, who have the lofty task, which they carry out with great distinction, of molding authors, the critics understand, to put it bluntly, nothing, but if by chance they do manage to understand a single thing, we instantly see them up in arms, shrieking that a certain passage is too obvious, a certain comparison too immediate, a certain image commonplace. And this makes it quite clear that they would rather not understand even the little they do understand, that they consider such attempts to expose their bad faith offensive and indecent, and that, finally, their true passion and the ultimate need of their spirit is not to understand anything at all.

April 9

And always the same spectacle, the same route, the same orbit, however ample, the same few celestial events; and so on, as I said, without an end and without a goal. The marvels of the sky! The marvels of the sky are this darkness, it too endless, in which the globes, so tiny when compared to so great a void, are stuck at as infrequent intervals and as far from each other (in fact much farther) as islands in the Pacific ocean. If at all, I say the marvels of the earths, that is, if one must speak of marvels: only around the earths does life clot and precipitate, and barely a palm's breadth from them everything is death and darkness.

The large yellow sun set in the darkness, yellow stars that do not throb; the phases of the moon, the phases of the earth, new moon, new earth, full moon, full earth . . . and then? Here nothing ever happens. Say you, you down there! So you think you know anguish, loneliness, BOREDOM?

In any case these are the only events that have taken place since the death of the undeparted Filano. Once I saw a tenuous, greenish veil, almost a vapor, cross the broad face of the moon. I decided that it was a diaphanous cloud; precisely that, a cloud, in contrast to what the great savants down below would think. Illusion or reality? Was the undeparted Filano right? On three other occasions I saw a small luminous dot rise from the depths of this night, come close, move away, disappear. In fact one of those small celestial bodies, which I cannot otherwise identify, came close enough for me to see something of its texture: it was a large desolate rock of irregular shape with ferruginous streaks, arid, sepulchral, it too flung out to roam without a goal in the immensity.

If only one of these ethereal boulders would hit me! But I have as much chance of seeing this wish granted as someone throwing a grain of millet at random through an open balcony window would have to hit a hungry spider's thread stretched from jamb to jamb. Oh, I forgot to say that I also sometimes see, on the earth or nearby it, small fires flare up like a match that's been struck. And that is all.

And this eternal silence! And yet, I repeat once more, basically this is the same as that. I am almost glad I didn't go to Singapore, as I wanted to do in my youth; indeed, what could I have found there that was *different?*

Filano, dear Filano who watches me, dear murdered man, find a way to call me to you; I too am beginning to have need of air. We would then proceed side by side for eternity, following this executioner of ours.

But why in the world did she decide to change her course, or to give up any course whatsoever? I can't stop thinking about it: it could not have been a vulgar accident, a matter of chance. No, there's premeditation here, as in everything that she does. And I am almost sure I understand, with horror: she too, like her putative father, has gone crazy. But hers is another form of madness: stubborn, monotonous, without fits of frenzy.

April 11

In my rare moments of sincerity, I used to say:

I love life more than each of its greatest gifts and more than all of them put together, more than honor, glory, power, creative genius, goodness, gold, freedom, light, wine and gambling! (But now I wonder why it is that love and women are not included in this list. There is a reason.) May I be deprived of it all, as I have been, and of everything else that makes it divinely beautiful: may the eyes in my brow be blinded, the limbs of my body mutilated, may I just be allowed to breathe quietly in the dark, forever hearing on the threshold of my lair the steps of a mortal enemy; but may I be given life! And without protest, indeed with gratitide, I will accept the legacy. Plague, leprosy, cholera, shame do not frighten me, provided that I live! If at the cost of the most abject humiliation I had to beg for life from the vilest and most abject enemy, smiling I would bend my knee in the mud, bowing my head before him, even if he were the last man on earth.

Is that true? Yes and no. Because in any case I was speaking of life, not of this half death, of this existence which isn't life anyway. But let us see: what, after all, is missing? Take a man condemned to spend his entire existence in a cruel prison—the Iron Mask, let's say—would he be as unhappy as I am? I cannot be sure, but I do not think so. No, for he at least would still live on earth, among his fellow beings even if segregated from them, and even in that situation he could set his heart at rest; yes, certainly, even in that most unfortunate situation. So we've come to the point: a peaceful heart. And for what accursed, diabolical reason can't I find peace? Yes, perhaps it is precisely because of a diabolical reason. For example, couldn't I resign myself to this state, whatever it might be, and endeavor to wait serenely for death, natural death? My work could be literary, and under circumstances I have always dreamed of: continuous, calm, consistent work in absolute tranquility. Where, indeed, could one find a better opportunity? I have a superabundance of memories, and inside this cell I could truly employ a Flaubertian tract of time in the composition of my works. If these were doomed to destruction and I were not to have readers, what does it matter? A great genius has already made it clear that a work of art does not need history; and didn't I use to say, more or less felicitously, that literature begins where literature ends? Where, I ask again, could I find a better opportunity? No one would even talk about this second literature in here. . . . So it's easy, get to work! And how can one work when one is so uprooted? My God, is it true that one can find peace of heart only in the world and among one's fellow creatures? Nevertheless, the same question arises: was it my fault if I was as I was? To live among one's fellow creatures is good and well: but what if one does not have fellow creatures? But everyone, you say, has fellow creatures. Yet now it is obviously useless for me to rave on about this problem. . . . Or did I do everything wrong from the start? Evidently one can live neither here nor there on what I lived and still live. Should I not have, will I not have, to give my life another turn, a different direction? Isn't there something that can illuminate that life, this one, death and all the rest? I have an inkling that there is, and it would suffice to name this thing, that is, it would suffice to find the word to indicate it; but I cannot find it. Or maybe I don't want to pronounce it, or something prevents me from pronouncing it, something close perhaps to pride, to a radical, blind, even unconscious pride? Could it not simply be that I do not want to admit that I have been defeated? . . . Come now, defeated by what, by whom? . . . So I have almost pronounced that word.

Besides, I must stop chattering so much, even to myself. Above all I must stop asking myself for explanations: the confusion in my head increases, increases, and it is impossible to make any sense of it. I said that I have memories: I had them, and now I have lost my remembrance of everything.

It increases. You see, I did not want to say it even to myself, I delayed saying it up till now, but now I am forced to. I . . . Isn't everything that I am writing today comic? It must be comic, because looking at myself in the steel mirror on the wall opposite I see that I am laughing. I am laughing convulsively, without a sound. I am laughing, tossing back my head, with my fists at my temples. . . . I laugh like the undeparted Filano did on those other occasions. Oh Lord, help me! (Now I have said it.)

April 15

Truly I seem to be following Filano's path. I talk to myself, laugh in that peculiar way, move furiously about the cell, and so on. I will soon end up like him. But I do not want to die damned! And where, out there? I do not want to be without a grave. I want a merciful hand to arrange my body in the coffin, I want my grave adorned with the flowers gathered by memory, by affection. . . . And once again I desire exactly what I despised most before.

Coffin, grave, flowers, affection: things of another world, of the world. Don't let your imagination run away with you: out there or in here is your tomb, he is your perennial companion. ("Destiny has also given me the sign/To continue alone and without heirs/When the hour must come,/To die without a hand in mine.")

Yet, thinking it over carefully, do these things that I see, that surround me, really exist? Might not Filano and this whole story, even Cancerqueen herself, only be a product of my somewhat diseased imagination? Will I not awaken in friendly arms, perhaps in bed with my wife?

Oh, how my poor head aches, here at the back!

And Cancerqueen, she does not want to release her victim. She poisons me, stifles me with gases from her intestines; or, more classically, with the vapors of her spleen.

April 17

I cannot understand how he manages to live, that little clerk whom I see down there between the forty-first and forty-second parallels; a little clerk with eyeglasses and a bowler hat (but isn't that an oddity nowadays?). He hurries to his office after having had lunch with his beloved family; he will return home in the evening, too tired to do or think anything; he will have dinner, will go to bed with his wife, with whom, however, he makes love only once a week; and the next morning he will start all over again. The money he earns is not enough even to renew his wardrobe: his elbows and behind are shiny. His breath smells and he always has a few pieces of putrified meat between his teeth. And then? What else is there in his life? Nothing. How can anyone live like that?

That is, I did not understand in the past. Now I envy him.

She did not go crazy with her father, that's quite clear to me now,

I mean it wasn't the father who made her go crazy, it is she who drove the father to insanity, who makes everyone insane. Thus a woman will sometimes suckle a siren, who stares at her with poisonous eyes, or even a serpent, or conceives a child who eats her bowels. This last has perhaps never happened to a woman but to some other animal, yet it amounts to the same thing.

April 27

God, I thank you, finally the deep silence is broken. I heard a voice, and I could not understand what it said nor where it came from; in the end I realized that it was Filano who was talking. From out there the poor man was gesticulating excitedly and seemed to be shouting to make himself heard, but, of course, with this pane of glass more than two feet thick . . . I put my ear close to the glass, and managed at last to hear his words. A few. He said only: "I am happy, I forgive you"; and went back to his usual position. Well, that's good to know.

Yet one thing is puzzling: it wasn't really only one voice speaking. And what does that mean? Obviously there was someone else. Perhaps it was Cancerqueen herself, perhaps she is a ventriloquist.

May 1

Today is the workers' festival in almost all the countries of my native continent. There they are in fact, going down the streets of Milan, a great number of them parading, with posters, standards, flags, banners, pennants, in short all the usual trappings, songs included. So what? What do I care about the workers? But easy now, I care, or at least I did care, a great deal, and I'm not saying that they shouldn't be agitating or that they aren't right; but the fact is that, as far as I'm concerned, nothing is more boring and depressing than parades, songs, posters and flags; and organized parades are the worst! I say it again, I can't think of anything more sordid and tedious. Since there's an awful lot of them, all those who are endowed with sensitivity and intellect are there. Couldn't they do without the posters and flags? And then they should at least get their name changed, the workers, if they wish to gain credit for their cause among the best people. I ask you, how can one go on using words like the working masses, labor councils, labor confederation, together with that other word that sounds like the noise of diarrhoeic belly, proletarian, and its derivative proletariat, etc.? And they should do something about changing the names of their leaders (another lovely word, honorable too, for those being led). Did even one of them ever bear a name with some inkling of intelligence or sense of destiny? When the most recent of their wars began and they put a certain Gamelin at the head of the French forces, I immediately told my friends (which friends?) that France had lost. A facile prophecy, actually, since one can see right off whether a name, if not a man, is destined to accomplish something great and noble. With all due respect for his undoubtedly high qualities, can you picture a Gamelin entering his country's Temple of Fame, bearing a great victory? Now just look at the names of these leaders: can one imagine anything more boring and dull? Is there the faintest hope that their bearers might be superior people, generous minds, liberal, and of distinguished intellect? And without any intellect at all one cannot even solve the problems of the belly, which seem to fill these personages with so much passion. And how is it that the workers believe in those names? To go back, then, to the terminology based on "labor": why refer everything to this curse, abjection, human shame? Is there a single worker, I ask, who in the depths of his heart is not convinced that labor degrades man? (It is odd that man has decided to attribute nobility only to a few natural functions. Anyway, labor rates as a natural function only in the best of hypotheses.) After all, only one great man devoted himself to the field and he made sure to be called Lenin, which is the same as saying lazy. And besides, what is the reason for all those disgusting initials which make it impossible for the less vulgar to read the newspapers, due literally to physical nausea? Whoever invented those initials? They are the graves of words, and consequently of . . . That's it—why, I'd like to know, insist on banishing from that poor life all poetry, which is still the only thing that can help the workers too? In poetry, not in organization or technique, which only serves the demagogues, lies salvation.

But above all why this philippic? Well, perhaps it could be considered a justification. The fact is that man is neither encouraged nor helped to live among his fellows and concern himself with them; on the contrary, everything is done to make them disgusting to him. One must, I repeat, speak to our, to their divine part, to the divine imagination. And that part exists in everyone, even in those characters with a top hat, a diamond on each finger, a thick gold chain across the belly, whose pictures one sees in certain periodicals.

Obviously, if I were still alive, I would never have written the preceding stuff either: for you know how they would have taken it. Some would have said: "Who does he think he is to lay down the law?" . . . et cetera. The others would grant me the right, et cetera, and would say: "So-and-so (and here my revered and unknown name) affirms that . . ." and then would twist what I say to suit their cause. Indeed, these people would have done everything to get me on their side. Not so fast, my friends. I speak about the workers because I feel affection for them, an affection so deep that I feel betrayed by them. I would find it hard to speak about the others, for the good reason that, even if they are so dangerous, they do not exist.

But to whom and to what are these explanations directed? In short, let's decide: am I alive or dead? Anyway, once again, what have I to do with those people down there? Nothing, unfortunately. Oh, I wish I were a worker; worse, a leader; worse yet, a priest or a pope, if only I . . .

May 5

Death of Napoleon Bonaparte. Is this, for instance, a true name, or isn't it? And how do I know? I had no intention whatsoever of talking about Napoleon Bonaparte. Instead I wanted to say:

God, I thank you again; now I also have company.

They have come out of my mouth, nose, ears, belly-button and anus; some even, though much more tiny, out of my eyes and pee-wee. Most of them are black and shiny; it's a shame that they stink; those I have sampled taste of ants, iron and the female breast. But now they are here and I can even talk with the larger ones. To the most intelligent, or the one who seemed to me the most intelligent, I have even read some passages from the present manuscript, which he approved. However they seem immortal, and that worries me a bit. Yesterday when, for one reason or another, I got a little furious, I slammed several against the walls and onto the floor (not, however, the most intelligent, who serve me as a kind of general audience); then, to make sure they did not taint the air, I ate them. And do you know what they did? After a few minutes, here they came again out of the usual holes, alert and shiny as buttons on a boot.

I speak, I speak; we speak, we speak.

May 7

This is dust, really dust, and can only be dust from my native planet; a minute part of the earth which I carry with me. But this other dust which I have in my head, this comes from here. Dust and cobwebs in my brain, as when one awakens from an unhealthy sleep, yet much, much stronger. And devouring flares of flame, lacerations, wrenchings.

Lord, Lord God, you who died on the cross, save me! Save me from this evil, this anguish; from this solitude. There was no place for me on earth, and there is no place for me even here. I do not know how to pray to you; now my words too are becoming useless and trite, literary. And yet what does it matter to you? I speak as I know how to speak, and you see what's inside of me. Listen: *"Nous sommes nombreux, nombreux, nombreux:/ n'en demandons pas plus pour être heureux./ Une petite maison de campagne au bord de la mer,/ ou en proximité d'un petit ruisseau clair. . . ."* There are the humble words of a song; and combine with this, friends, the companion of my life, children; at peace with you, with your law, which is the law of our heart; this is what I would have liked to feel and to have, what I would have liked to sing in thanks, this is what I would have liked to be my prayer. You are my witness that when I said that I was no one's fellow, I did not mean that I was superior to anyone. Not even to the last worm of the earth, an animal worm. In fact it at least can have children, and never mind if the little ones eat its entrails. Not I. Children. For the third time, children. How does one go about making them? . . . May you be blessed for all that you have not given me!

Oh Lord, have pity on your poor son, shed a tear, a tear of celestial dew, on his flaming head! Let peace descend into his tortured soul, his convulsed limbs!

Oh, my goodness, didn't Gogol say something like this already? And so what? Are not their words the most appropriate for speaking to you?

Either call me to you, or at least land me on the brilliant shores of the moon; perhaps among those gentle inhabitants I will find peace and happiness—if those two things are not the same.

May 12

I have exterminated all of them by an ingenious method: they were beginning to get on my nerves, and to take up too much space, because they were multiplying (lucky for them) endlessly. But it would take too long to explain the method; indeed, to be honest, I don't even remember it, though I do remember that it was very ingenious. The general principle was substantially this: since they were immortal, to kill them I had to surprise them, that is, not give them the time not to die. And I succeeded in doing it. After killing them, I did not eat them, for fear that my inner fluids might revive them, but (since I am not so crazy as to open the door again) I manipulated the largest as one does dough for lady fingers, that is, I stretched them like worms and introduced them one by one into the carbon dioxide conduit; from which they were expelled outside as the pressure gradually forced open the operculum. What vexed and, literally speaking, long faces they had, even when dead!

There's just one trouble with it—they have begun to follow us too: they have deployed almost in a semi-circle, some to Filano's right, some to his left, others behind, and they press after us, right on our heels. This black swarm bothers me a little; but I did put a halt to their intrusiveness.

But now I have these others, male or female, underfoot. I don't know: I don't see anything, but every now and then I happen to touch certain large forms in the air, sometimes very large, unbearable and impossible to swallow, I think, like the breasts or thighs of women, but hairy, although smooth and pleasing to touch. And if I try to seize the whole thing, it escapes me. Who knows who they are and what they want from me; but there is no doubt that I absolutely must invent a system to get rid of them too.

A strange accident has cast a gloom over the montblanc (that's what I call it, jokingly). A pipistrelle, and I don't mean a bat, but a large pipistrelle precisely, has entered, I can't imagine where from, and begun flitting about. Entered in here, flitting about the cell? No, sir, right inside the walls of my skull. At first it got caught among the strong cobwebs, then it tore them to shreds by dint of thrashing about, bang, bang, obstinately against my forehead like bluebottles banging against a windowpane: it had gotten inside from some place, I don't know where, and I didn't know how to get it out again. It goes without saying that by sneezing more and more forcibly I blasted it out, grabbed it and flattened it between my palms with the help of an iron bar; then I folded it eight times, stretched it a bit more, and introduced it into the carbon assoxide conduit as before, whence it has gone to join the others. Boys, the crowd out there is getting larger.

Cancerqueen is getting more and more despotic, surly and sour. Now she would like me to keep motionless and silent: she'll have to wait awhile! Her nasal, stinking and broth-colored voice excites my antipathy more than I can possibly say. By now it's all-out war between us; we'll see who wins.

Ate sesquipedalian and jackstay; purpose: combatting anguria.

May 13

The inhabitants of the moon, whom I can now see clearly, are exactly what, through superior powers of divination, I have always in all my works maintained they would be. The third foot is ivory-like in the Angevin males, mother of pearlish in the females of the sacred wood. The most striking thing about them is the extraordinary serenity of their hair. Of the kind Fallopianism of their gaze and foreheads I need not even speak. That's why I so much hope that . . .

May 17

The quantity of disparate (and desperate) objects which somehow penetrated inside here during the last few days was unheard of. What a chasing of the Duke of Athens, what a Prague deoperculation I thereupon performed! I flung myself on each and every one, and at the end of forty-eight hours I had made a clean sweep. But what a job it was, because some of these objects, never seen before and of unknown use, refused to be flattened out. In any event, a boundless and tumultuous (as regards their position) mob of dead objects and personages is now flying behind us two mortal enemies; I almost have the impression that everything that was in the world is out there, with infinite eyes, mouths, eyebrows and limbs of iron.

Ate a round dozen rubber balls (12 pieces), oh, their unceasing bouncing hammering cerebellum!

This is what I did to get rid of those round and hairy creatures. Ready with my iron bar, as soon as I happened to touch one, slam, a fantastic blow on my own hand, with which I had to hold on to it. In this way I inflicted on it a dent, a bruise, a stab, with the result that it stayed put and took the rest of the wallops, which little by little

softened and deflated it. At the end of this great labor, and after carefully dredging the air to catch all of them right down to the very last
one, I gathered together the empty husks in the same way; at first I
wanted to keep some of them for a fur coat, but then I thought it over
and eliminated all of them in the usual fashion.

Now finally I am all alone again. I have broken my hand, but there
was no other way.

May 22

Two months have passed since I began the present notes. Two
months: an eternity? An instant, rather. Or the two things in one:
here time has no time.

And still and always this bottomless, endless life, this space and
time without purpose. "And one will live, alas,/one will live in any
case . . ."

I suspect, rereading the last pages, that I have suffered a long fit of
madness. "Suspect" of course is just a way of putting it: how can one
doubt it, just running through this stuff? But now I do not know
whether to write: luckily or unluckily, it has passed. I am lucid and
calm as never before. What's the point, really?

Tomorrow I shall make another attempt, the supreme attempt to
lead Cancerqueen back to earth, or at the worst, induce her to land
on the moon. I want to, I must do it after yielding so long to events—
if that's what you can call them.

May 23

The attempt has failed!

1: Are you going to make up your mind to stop this useless race at
last and set down somewhere?

CANCERQUEEN (from the liver, with a muddy, keggy voice): No.

1: But I will make you do it.

CANCERQUEEN: Krr, frr, trr, hoo, hoo, mooo, booaaf, booaaf, kraah, crash, wham, bang, slam.

1: Calm down, I was only kidding; let's talk calmly. Why the devil do you insist on doing this?

CANCERQUEEN (from the spleen, saffronanusly): Because. (The nasty aunt's reply to all my inquiries.)

1: But let's see, is there no way of coming to an agreement? Don't you have a heart? Don't you feel any pity, if not for yourself, for me?

CANCERQUEEN: (from the ovaries, with the voice of the thorn-apple): In the order of your questions, I reply: No, no and no.

1: Damned slut, cockeyed whore, I'll show you!

CANCERQUEEN: Ffff, Ssss, Zzzzz.

1: No, no, what are you doing! No, let's talk about it reasonably. I'm sorry. And, in God's name, take pity on me.

CANCERQUEEN (from the Fallopian tubes, gingerously): Let's hear, who do you think I fornicate with that you call me a slut? You're the one who's got plenty of mistresses and not a single friend, or at least a wife. And anyway don't utter the name of Him who is alien to you.

1: He is alien to no one. But why am I wasting my time, arguing with you? So, can't we come to an agreement?

CANCERQUEEN (from the stomach): No.

1: Must it go on like this for eternity?

CANCERQUEEN: For eternity.

1: Even after death?

CANCERQUEEN: Even after death.

1: Oh Lord, help me.

CANCERQUEEN (from the heart, from all of her guts) : Ha, ha, ha!

Must I admit that I am defeated!

May 24

Verses in a Time of Insomnia
The Porrovium

The porrovium! What kind of beast is this porrovium? It pains me to say that I myself do not know, and it's the same with the Beca. He looks something like a tapir and a pig or a babiroussa, and has almost no neck. He appears when the night scurries like a hare under the sun, its ears transfused by the light; and when from the shadows madness, crouching like a cat, or rather like a cowpat, spies on me and lies in wait for me with its yellow eyes.

For a long time my life has been obsessed by the search for or ordering of words. The porrovium prowls about gray in the darkness, the porrovium comes, goes, the porrovium is a mass that I cannot swallow.

The porrovium is not a beast; it is a word.

And what does this matter to me? In fact I observe that my life is not at all obsessed by the search, etc.; and that besides here there is neither night nor darkness; so that to speak of night is, to say the least, out of place. And more—I hope that no one has tried to attribute to me this poetic fart or to deceive me. In the first place, my writing is not even halfway decently imitated; in the second place, who would recognize my style? Oh no, here I can see the hand of hoodlums, or at least hoodless, hooded, or lums without hoods, in short shameless characters; this is the work of harassers or sheassers. And what do you want from me, pray, what do you think I can do? Useless to hope for my support, useless also to try to stifle me with these idiotic jokes: I advocado and rebanana my original position.

Anyway here is how it went. I was there, near the glass, tranquilly observing the cataslows of the sky, constructed according to a very interesting musical system, when all of a sudden this sheet, placed on this sort of desk, rose by itself, flew through the air and settled itself right before my eyes, as though to give me every opportunity to read the writing on it: the stuff that I just mentioned, penned, as I have already said, by an unknown hand (I have added the date). It isn't that someone invisible had sneaked in here, because I am certainly not a fool, after all, and I immediately began to paddle my hands all over the sheet. And the sheet returned to its place, just as it had come. What does that mean, I ask? The event is truly inexplicable.

I shall soon die, I feel it.

I shall die and then, among other things, she can say anything she wants to, I'll show them, Cancerqueen, Cancerking, Cancerprincess, Cancerroyalfamily, Canceretceteraetcetera; Cancercancer. Has this Cancer gotten the idea of ruling the universe?

May 30

Didn't I say that I felt it? I have been dead for two days. But nothing has changed, she was right. Ah, if I had known that it was so easy and that nothing would change, I would have died sooner. But to do what, since nothing was going to change? Well, I don't know, but it seems to me that in all ways it is better to be dead than alive.

Now that I am dead though, I feel the need to tell this story, to tell it from the beginning. I was alone and without hope . . . oh, forget it, to hell with the story! Why should I go to the trouble? For what twisted reason should I tell it, since I am dead? Better, with the serenity that befits the wise man, better by far to contemplate these bedroom slippers. Because doing nothing is the most excellent way to elude every uncouth siege. Behold, here I am happy and content, and with complete calm within myself I can sing: Long live England and Engsea!

But now as I am contemplating the slippers, I feel the need to tell this story, tell it from the beginning. I was alone and without hope . . .

1950

Fable

A long time ago, my dear children, I was just a puppy like you and roamed the world in the retinue of a bizarre gentleman. My memories of that period are somewhat confused, I was so small and so much time has passed, nonetheless I will search through my old memory and will tell you the most beautiful story of my life! It is well that you should know this about your mother who is going to leave you, she feels, alone in the vast world, and if anything, entrusted to man's deceitful protection. Many small animals, our most terrible enemies, are nested, as you can see, in my hair, the sign that my hour has come. You are merely the last of a long generation of dogs to whom I have given life, and who were then dispersed through the world. Besides, a persistent cough shakes my head, my breathing, as you can hear, is no more than a death-rattle. So even if I were not to die, do you think that our present master could tolerate such a decrepit and repulsive companion for long in his house? Certainly not, he will soon hand me over to that servant of his who wears the corduroy jacket which you also know, the man-with-the-thick-boots, and one day he will take me with him into the countryside, together with his dry-sounding rifle, and so it will end. But do not grieve, instead prepare yourselves, like wise dogs, for a similar fate sooner or later, and listen to my tale; who knows but that one day in your wanderings through the great world you may not come upon a memory of your poor mother, which will speak to you of the time when a golden hope lived in her heart, too, freshly budding in the light of the sun, as I hope it now does forever in yours.

A strange perturbation, I confess, comes over me at telling this story, which you are the first and last to hear, but my imminent death helps me to look at everything with a more tranquil eye; everything appears to me more distant and almost not mine, and, as for you, I am sure that you will not think badly of your unhappy mother.

The gentleman in whose retinue I traveled during that very distant epoch was, I have already said, a bizarre person. In his wanderings across unknown lands and cities he did not only carry me with him, and also my parents, but many other animals too. Certainly he must have been one of the powerful of the earth, though he was almost always by himself; perhaps he was just rich and melancholy. In fact one often saw him in the company of those strange objects whose use we of the canine race have not yet succeeded in defining, though many hypotheses have been formulated by our elders. Wicked objects, certainly, which men hold in their hands and with which they are long occupied, immobile and silent, scrutinizing them attentively for hours on end; wicked, since in the long run this mute colloquy scores their brows, I have noted, with deep wrinkles.

However that might be, my master in those days, dark, handsome, with ardent and imperious eyes which I found impossible to look at (alas, I am always losing the thread of my discourse, forgive an old story-teller), my master, I say, only traveled accompanied by many animals and many servants. Arousing everyone's astonishment and reverence, he passed through unknown cities in a sumptuous coach studded with, I believe, precious stones, and behind it came other coaches, and in these were peacocks, monkeys, parrots, dogs of every breed, ourselves and other strange animals from remote regions. After that, a dense entourage of footmen mounted on shiny horses, on this side and that, in front and behind the master's coach, wearing multi-colored garments gaudy with braids and laces, and entrusted with the task of keeping order among the rowdy swarm of other coaches. How many times, when the throng of foreigners inhabiting the cities we passed through prevented the convoy from proceeding quickly, I escaped my parents' vigilance, and leaped over the door of the coach to sniff for a while at some of the wondrous things I saw! But always, in less time than it takes to tell, a footman would catch up with me, dismount, manhandle me a bit and then set me safely back among my already worried parents, and the parrots, peacocks and monkeys.

Then, on the other, less fiery horses, servants, majordomos, retainers, most of them garbed in black, with heavy chains of gold and silver hanging around their necks, followed and closed the procession. But of all this, the master, his servants and the many strange animals in his entourage, I shall tell you some other time, if I live long enough; now I want to come straight to the most important matter.

One evening, or rather one afternoon in autumn, our party entered the walls of a city, unknown like the others, but what a city! Indeed the surrounding countryside had already alerted me: although it was unfamiliar to me, and although it appeared splendid to my eyes, I felt that I had always lived in that city, as if after long wanderings I were finding again my true and portentous homeland. My master decided to spend the night there and so we took rooms in an old tavern.

What can I say? I'm sure that I won't find the right words. The air was more limpid and at the same time gentler and warmer in that city and its outskirts; a soft wind stirred in it with great love, barely moving the branches of the trees growing among the houses; the people spoke a sweet tongue, that is, which tasted sweet to the palate of the speaker, not to mention my own ears, quite different from the language spoken here in the North, a language of command whose sentences never founder, harsh as a whistle. Down there they all seemed women when they spoke; and the indolent people watched us pass by with a smile. Tall, embattled towers, palaces of gold gray, cathedrals with façades encrusted with many-hued marbles (and I recall that there stood a church, just like that, in the middle of a square) rose one after the other along our route, and to my naive and wonderstruck eyes everything seemed of the right size and height and the right color: the sky was not too blue but rather almost gray, and gilded like the palaces, and with what beautiful harmony the color of the pale blue clouds merged and shaded into them! The trees were not too green, no, but almost dusty, and even the smells, which sometimes offend us so much, were as they should be, neither too strong nor too light and delicate; what's more, I noticed that they were all female smells, down there I never encountered a male odor. I don't want to be prolix: in brief, it perhaps was Italy, which you have surely heard of. The season down there was mild, not like our autumns; a few leaves had barely begun to redden.

That night we dogs were shut up in a stable, where in truth we were very comfortable amid piles of warm straw. But for me there was no thought of sleeping that night, as you can imagine: a curious disquietude had seized me, that enchanting city drew me into its streets with too many temptations. So after a while, as soon as I was sure that my parents were fast asleep, I began sniffing around to try to find a way to get out of the stable. Wall by wall, corner by corner, in the end I discovered a cat hole at the edge of a door, one of those holes through which our century-old enemies instantly avoid our pounce. The other dogs, of course, would not have been able to squeeze through it, but my youth was a great help on that occasion and, soon after, having cautiously crossed the courtyard where the grooms were sleeping, I was free to wander in the streets of my city.

I cannot tell you how happy I was; for a long time I roamed about, voluptuously inhaling those smells which were new to me, and yet, as I told you, so portentously familiar. The city was immersed in sleep; enormous nocturnal butterflies, large as birds, brushed softly past my lifted muzzle. I reached a square completely encircled by splendid, slim and airy arcades, where two fountains shaped like small boats, or something of the sort, gave forth a subdued gurgle. It was round about then that the moon rose. I continued down this street set between rows of majestic buildings, nobody disturbed my stroll, I reached another square, smaller but even more beautiful than the first! I won't even try to describe it and, anyway, strange to tell, I remember it only vaguely; I seem to recall that on one side there was a long vista of houses all the same, extending to a river or a hill; a street, I mean to say, or an arcade that ran into that square. On the other side, perhaps a short portico . . . anyhow, I'm not quite sure.

There must have been tall houses all around it, because the bright moonlight did not fall on the square, save on one side, fully illuminating only one corner of it. You know better than I how distressing the moon can be for us at times; we bark and bark at it for whole nights. But there it too was my friend. In that corner stood a man's statue, the most beautiful statue I had ever seen, or have ever seen since.

Young as you are, you probably do not know as yet what a statue is. It is one of those cold, white creatures which you might also see here if you were permitted to go out. They are men, men in every way, but always silent and motionless, and most of the time naked. Moreover, their eyes do not look and so one can gaze at them as much as one wishes. That statue, however, was not completely naked, strange drapes covered it, and its hair was weirdly arranged. I do not know for certain whether it was a man or a man's woman.

And now I have finally come to my story, so listen more attentively. You already know, every dog knows it from his birth, what it means for us to inundate a familiar and beloved thing or person with warm homage. Do we not entrust to it perhaps the best part of our soul? And, puppies lost in the vast world, do we not thereby intend to prove our gratitude to the man or thing that surrounds us with its protection? And, at once dismayed and reassured, is that not perhaps the way we loosen all the cords of our heart, and offer fidelity and affection? The dog who lovingly sniffs the corner of a street, and gracefully lifts his leg against it, does he not show that he has recognized in it a good, familiar and ancient presence, and does he not vow himself to eternal friendship? Man, it is true, does not appreciate our homage, I do not know why.

I could not reach the feet of the statue, it was placed too high, but the white pedestal seemed to me almost a part of its body. I did not grow tired of contemplating it; it looked into the distance, or rather did not look at all, being deprived of sight, but nevertheless looked with its white limbs, especially with the fold of its cloak, its shoulders and thighs; perhaps one can find no explanation for such strange things, I cannot explain them to myself. I must certainly have always known it, I cannot say what feeling held sway over me—it was unendurably sweet, but racking, shaking me utterly, and yet bitter. I would have liked to cry, complain, whine and gambol with uncontrollable joy at its feet for eternity. I loved it with an immense love, and yet, perhaps it was the moonlight pouring down on it, I felt at moments that I hated it with all my strength, a desperate and remote aversion that made it glare almost greenish in my eyes; but no, I loved it. It smelled of carnations, perhaps, of lilies, damp stone, a smell so strong for me! I have never found it again.

At last, in a sudden fit of madness, I crouched at the base of its throne and deposited there an abundance of my golden liquid. . . . And immediately so natural an act seemed to me monstrous, an immense shame seized me, and I fled away from there almost as though crazed, far away, and returned to the tavern and my parents. I did not dare tell them of my night's adventure. . . . The next morning we left with our master's retinue.

The years went by, but I did not forget my statue. Sometimes, when I was already an adult and a mother, I would whimper in my sleep; my husbands thought I was dreaming about furious chases of cats or chickens, but it was still the memory of my statue which filled my nightly dreams, and the sad hours of my day. Life brought me all sorts of preoccupations, dragged me far, very far from that place, where you now see me; the lively throngs of children came, every year travail and new sorrows for a mother's heart; I changed masters, my husbands did not turn out right, they were almost always dissolute and bad family men, except for your papa who, just because of his goodness, died so prematurely. There was nothing left to comfort me in my sad life, amid my tasks and duties. So it was that one fine day I could not bear it any more; forgive your poor mother for having neglected her duties, for having been a bad mother only once. Oh, that did not help her, except to make the old wound in her heart even more painful!

My husband betrayed me, my children—your brothers—paid back my most tender care with indifference or hostility, the times became even harsher; whole generations of puppies, the fruit of my womb, my then master killed almost before my eyes; no, not a single ray of sunlight dispelled the grayness of my existence, I had lost all hope; would you dare condemn me? Abandoning husband and children, and the house that had seen me as a flourishing mother, I ran across our land, and then beyond the mountains, beyond the rivers, valleys and forests. I was guided by an infallible instinct; I already knew where I was headed: I was running to the statue of my girlhood, to my statue!

I went through unknown lands, I lost my way a thousand times in deserted regions and was somehow able to find it again; I recognized the lands my master had passed through so long ago; I recognized the populous cities with their superb edifices; from men and my brothers I would beg a piece of bread for my sustenance, I attacked the mice of the fields, nourished myself on putrid carcases, lived for whole days on a single grasshopper . . . and, finally, I reached the city of my heart. Anxiously I roamed its length and breadth, rediscovered the street I had gone down that night, found again the large square, the smaller square, the fountains, the garden. . . . Do I have to tell you? I did not find the slightest vestige of my statue. The same benign sky, the same soft breeze and the veiled green of the trees greeted me, but the statue was no longer there! Where had it gone, where had it vanished to? Or was it that I did not know how to look for it?

I shall cut it short, my dear children. Sadly I set out again on the way back, all the more disconsolate now; I confess to you that I thought of death. But it was heaven's will that I should continue my useless life, continue it to such an old age. Life itself, which inflicted such a cruel blow, partly mitigated my torment, I was caught up by other concerns; I lived and acquired a melancholy wisdom. I prepare at last to leave the world, and this too is now sweet to me, although with the world I leave you, my loving children.

Now listen. Certainly, when you are older, you too will get the chance to travel through this world, which is not worth our tears; may the sky everywhere be benign and the wind caressing, as it was for me in that far-off country, that far-off time. Be happy, my dear children. But, unfortunately, hard tests await you, and for them you must be prepared.

And if the circumstances of your life lead you to that distant country, that distant city, which you will recognize by certain signs, look again, I beg you, for my statue. You could not mistake it, there is only one like it in the world. Beneath a benign sky, which later became so dark and sinister over my head, amid the zephyrs of that eternal spring, you yourselves in the springtime of your lives and the boldness of your youth will perhaps nevertheless have a thoughtful moment and say to yourselves—here our poor mother loved and suffered.

Farewell, children, I feel my strength ebbing. Perhaps in another place on earth, who knows where, you may meet the statue of my youth. If so, bring it my last salute, deposit at its feet floods of golden liquid. But perhaps it too grew older as I grew older, perhaps one day it too was covered with disgusting insects, and thus perhaps it ended miserably, as I now end.

Misdeal

◇◇◇
◇◇◇

I

She was a very beautiful woman, and haughty. So haughty that it seemed hard to resist the desire to subjugate her or—how should I say?—humiliate her in that which she cared for most ardently: her sex, considered not as an abstraction or category, but as a set and system of physical attributes. There are such beautiful women; in whom the natural instinct of display is turned about and converted into a modesty which is as fierce and sensitive as it is unjustified, and in direct proportion to the degree of their beauty.

She was tall, blond, of foreign birth; her name was Gisa. Nobody knew of or even imagined her having affairs; her suitors' cravings were therefore devoid of all salaciousness, they were elementary, even pure. Not only that, but singularly limited: by virtue of something in her, each man dreamed of undressing her, true enough, but the lewd fantasies never went any further. In a word, by general consensus, what mattered was to see her naked; all the rest mattered much less; or, on the contrary, all the rest figured as a means and token of revenge (to have her standing before him naked, and then to disdain her, was probably what each man, step by step, imagined). Yet it was a labile desire or emotion by its very nature; in any case, not surpassing the limits of a mannerly ardor.

For the others; for Marcello, on the other hand, whether it was his temperament that led him that way or other factors which came into play, it had become an obsession. Perhaps, the young man said to himself that Gisa's modesty was, like all modesty, destined to be regenerated, liberated, and he expected especial delights from this liberation; or he was actually in love with the girl—though difficult to believe (since those in love regard the beloved's body with a certain horror). But let us affirm that Marcello was in love with Gisa: provided we put the emphasis on the particular sense involved in his affection. Sense, or better, organ. In conclusion, he wanted to see her naked like everybody else: save that he could not do without it, he had to.

Yet the girl seemed unapproachable, beyond the occasional social relations, and besides, Marcello was terribly shy; so that if he loved her, he loved her with little hope. He followed her here and there, knew her habits, but had not the remotest idea of how to take advantage of all this. What he needed was an opportunity, an opportunity. . . . But of what kind, exactly? He knew very well that there was none that could help him, with his character; he would have needed a miracle, in fact. While he was eating away at himself in this fashion, one evening he found Gisa (who lived a free life and frequented the company of artists) in the studio of a fashionable woman painter, who was entertaining some friends.

It was one of those places where everything is permitted, so long as it stimulates the intelligence, no matter how much or how feebly; where the rule is a perennial and somewhat rhetorical state of war against bourgeois sentiments, with their accompanying, at times merely presumed customs; where everyone, without too much hope of being amused, out of boredom, to prove his unconventionality, or because of inner desolation, is ready for everything that might appear slightly outrageous. The party was not large: the usual Prince of royal descent, emaciated, foolish, convinced he was traveling in the realms of the spirit, a couple of celebrated painters or sculptors, a couple of literary men, a notorious pederastic art dealer, and also of course, a grocer's delivery boy or whatever he was (to satisfy the voracious snobbery of some or the base lust of others), and a corresponding number of women of diverse provenance and equal intellectual avidity. The hostess had served a dinner consisting of an enormous krater filled with blond honey, into which the guests had freely and promiscuously dipped. Then there had been parlor games, infantile or folkish jokes and pranks, since the guests made it their chief point of honor to repudiate their own high qualities, or meant to cast a brighter light upon them through the very pettiness of those entertainments (even playing "knock, knock" can display one's genius); but by now the party, with its largely fictitious excitement, more exhausted than revived by the drinks, was definitely languishing. And at this point Marcello had a brilliant idea, or so it seemed to him at that moment.

"I think," he said, "that the time to play poker has come."

"What kind of poker?" someone asked wearily.

"I propose," he went on, "that we play in heats, so to speak, hand by hand, so at the end only the winner is left."

"Then what?"

"The winner will remain dressed, or at least will have the right to do so, and all the others will have to undress, strip completely— what do you say?"

"Hm, as proposals go it's pretty old hat, don't you think?" replied the sculptor Marquis, son of an ex-minister; while the women emitted shrill noises simply for the sake of the sisterhood's honor.

"I know, but still it could be fun."

"Really?"

"Why don't we at least try?"

"So, let's try," the other man concluded indifferently. But nobody moved or showed any particular eagerness to move on into action, which served only to intensify Marcello's desire.

"Well, come on," he insisted, "you really don't want to." Then, walking over to Gisa and staring straight into her eyes, he added: "What do you say?"

The girl, of course, had understood from the first that Marcello's proposal touched her personally, although she could not guess the furious exclusiveness of his desire; but up until then she hadn't batted an eyelash. Now, questioned directly, she was somewhat upset perhaps, although her habitual pallor protected her; in any event she returned the young man's long stare and did not reply immediately. Marcello, however (who was standing before her as if naked), during this short pause, suddenly saw the adventure into which he had so thoughtlessly plunged in its true light. In fact the proposed game carried with it the possibility that he might have to strip before her while she remained dressed: a prospect that made him shiver and horrified him.

"I don't see why you ask me in particular," she finally replied, continuing to stare at him.

"You? I could have asked someone else just as well."

"Very well, I shan't be the one to spoil the fun," she retorted with a certain tone of defiance.

"Hear that? She accepts. Give me a pack of cards: who starts?" Marcello began shouting in an unnatural voice. Actually by now he hoped that some obstacle would supervene and that the whole thing would fall through.

Instead the hostess, though listlessly, supplied the pack of cards; and they went on to establish the rules of the game, to discuss the system of heats, etc. And meanwhile Marcello's embarrassment or even anguish increased: on one hand, it is true, glittered the girl's coveted nudity as the prize for the winner of the coming contest, but on the other he so vividly pictured himself defeated and naked, trembling with shame before her and all the others, that there was no doubt on which side the scales tipped. Yet what could he do? Pull back, after having been so zealous, and thereby publicly admit to his shyness, his cowardice, admit it, oh God, to the girl who, besides every thing else, had been firmly on his side? The one thing he mustn't do: but what else then? His imagination, his will, were as though seized by a stutter, but still went on groping, and groping guided him to a way out (though it too was fraught with danger): it was necessary to give the losers an alternative. The losers must be able to choose between undressing and something else; thus, if he should wind up among them . . . He was just going to propose this felicitous variant, when as could be expected the Marquis said, lisping:

"But look, this little game, at least the way we're going about it, doesn't seem, you know, awfully promising. The whole business is somehow too literal: one guy wins and the others get undressed, and then they'll all have to get dressed again, and that's all there is to it. I mean, is it worth so much effort to achieve such a banal result? No, personally, I instead would, what should I say?—give the losers an alternative. Which would have to be gauged very carefully, and all that, and would at least give us some hint as to each person's degree of pride."

"What do you mean?" asked a female voice.

"Never mind, dear," one of the painters replied, "it's a little too complicated for you. But actually I think the idea of our noble colleague here isn't bad. So let's agree on this alternative."

"Why do that?" said another. "Let's leave it to the winner's imagination."

"No, no!" Marcello broke in heatedly. "What are you talking about! It must be decided on beforehand, so that each one will know what he's letting himself in for."

In truth the young man, who at first had been happy at that unhoped-for, almost clairvoyant assistance, saw now, belatedly as usual, how treacherous in fact the situation was. That is, the alternative could not be unacceptable (because then it would harm him too), but it could not be acceptable either (because, if she lost, Gisa certainly would seize on it). And in sum, he was again caught in between and did not know what to think.

"Oh, all right," one of the people was saying, "so let's specify this alternative. Come on, what should it be?"

They discussed various bland proposals, without coming to an agreement. Finally another man said:

"Oh, the hell with it! Listen, you tell us, Marcello, since you invented the whole thing; say anything you wish and we'll accept your proposal without any more discussion."

"You want me to establish the alternative?"

"Yes," several people cried.

It was the moment to decide; to decide in one fell swoop between cowardice and boldness, renunciation and will, certainty of conquest, wretched timidity and raging passion. This time passion won. Yet there was a further difficulty, and Marcello realized it: to propose something truly unacceptable, extreme or injurious, wouldn't that be tantamount to dooming it in advance? Nobody would even take it seriously. But the young man was now fully launched and (as often happens to the timid) inevitably went beyond all bounds.

Silence had fallen. In this silence Marcello said:

"Well, the alternative should be . . . death."

"What?"

"What's that?"

"Death!"

"No less."

"Yes," he continued, "death, or let's say suicide: whoever refuses to undress will instead be allowed to kill himself, immediately, and in our presence."

"How very interesting!" said the Prince, mewling like a bogus connoisseur examining a painting.

"Not at all," snapped the sculptor Marquis. "The alternative does not seem to me well chosen or fecund in any way. On the contrary, I would say, you know, downright useless, in fact it's not even an alternative: who could even take it into consideration, choose to kill oneself rather than get undressed!"

"One never knows!" Marcello replied, exasperated and vaguely upset.

"But it's a joke."

"So be it. After all, you left it up to me and promised not to argue about it, if I'm not mistaken. So do you accept or don't you? That's all you have to tell me."

"Of course we accept," the hostess said after a moment.

"Yes, yes, we accept, if it comes to that," some agreed.

"And what do you say? Do you like the decision?" Marcello asked Gisa.

"Look at that," she laughed, without any apparent emotion, "he's gotten into the habit of always questioning me in particular. I didn't know that my opinion was all that important. Sure, everything is all right with me: why not?"

"Then we are agreed on everything, and we'll start," Marcello added gravely.

That prompt and general acceptance was easily explained: each on his own had decided that in the last analysis the alternative could be set aside. If Marcello felt like kidding, he could please himself; if the joke wasn't awfully amusing, well, too bad; and finally it simply came down to undressing, if one lost, and that wouldn't cost anything.

And yet among them, unknown to them, were two people to whom showing themselves naked would cost a great deal, no matter what the nature or urgency of the reasons for it might be. The struggle would flare up, invisible and desperate, between these two.

I I

The heats proved to be quite wearing; the games followed one another slowly, each time leaving the major part of the company inactive. It was getting late; the booze occasionally gave some of them a boost but somewhat befogged most of them. Marcello, not by chance, found himself next to Gisa and, himself astonished at the sound of his voice, suddenly said to her:

"The two of us will overturn the world."

"I know," came her surprising and simple reply.

But all of them were more or less bored. At last it was Marcello's turn to play; to tell the truth, he and the girl had each previously lost a hand, but on the basis of the abstruse rules drawn up by a literary man specializing in these little games, they had the option to appeal or play again. There was a painter who had been in the lead for three or four hands: Marcello and two others were called to pit themselves against him for a final ruling.

He had to win all the way; and it was necessary in the meantime, quite obviously, to win this hand. The young man's anguish, lulled for an instant, rose up in him convulsively.

The cards were dealt face down, and each player turned them over; then came the discarding; finally the results obtained were read and the winner of the hand proclaimed. During the dealing, he concentrated his will, trying to coerce fate; then, instead of following the example of the others, who were hesitantly lifting the corners of their cards and squinting at them with their heads almost resting on the table, he uncovered all his at once. And he was dazzled: five hearts, though not all in order, were lined up before him. A flush. Nevertheless his joy was quickly soured by the sight of the other hands, among which two players had three of a kind, which could have become four of a kind (the fourth hand could at the most turn into a full house). Marcello was in a cold sweat; but the people with three of a kind changed cards and remained with their three of a kind.

He had won. But what about the coming hands? There still remained quite a few tests to surmount. . . . In any case to be dealt a flush already signified something, a sign; perhaps fate had meant to declare itself. But keep calm! It was too soon to cry victory; giving into a sense of security, euphoria, could be dangerous. (And why dangerous? do the cards perhaps change according to our feelings or can they change their faces out of spite? They certainly can, according to feelings and also persons.) The new players came in. And Marcello won again: easily, "peg-wild," as the people of the "trade," the noble art, put it. He won again; then he won again with the next team; and again and again. And he could no longer defend himself against the sense of security, euphoria, etc.: he held luck in his fist!

And so came the last hand, the most decisive of all; it would suffice to lose it for all the preceding efforts (which is what he considered them, rather than the benignity of fate) to turn to nothing. In this last hand he had to play against, among others, his direct antagonist; he had almost forgotten about that; he realized it suddenly, saw her before him, and all his bumptiousness melted away like mist. Here, here was the real test, here the solidity of his good luck had to be proven.

The cards were dealt again. Again, too agitated to delay, he turned them over all at once: two tens, the skinny hooks of two sevens, a fifth, manifestly useless card (a queen of hearts, however!). What, could it be? Could it be that fate would betray him at this supreme moment? He looked at the others' cards: two of his opponents had better hands than he from the start, although none of the hands were final yet, but that hardly counted. By all means, let's not get frantic. Now then: two double pairs better than mine; but the danger probably isn't from that quarter, to fill out a full house is much harder than people think; the danger is rather, and precisely, in that straight open at both ends; it is so easy for a straight open at both ends to be filled. Look at it, it's a bare, miserable, shivering straight, or, better, it's only a project; but these wretched little straights, if filled, end up by beating even a radiant three aces (and that, frankly, is unfair). . . . He had the impulse to discard the three cards, keeping the pair of tens; that way, if he only made three of a kind, and if none of the others managed a full house . . . If, if; what madness. Nevertheless, any full house which might be made by the others would be superior to the one he might make. . . . Oh, indeed it was madness to reason in these terms, to give way to dismay. . . .

The discarding began. The two pairs did not change; *her* straight, on the contrary, was closed. Closed from below, with a miserable seven; but that seven gone over there made his full house even more improbable. . . . At this point the game became a hand-to-hand combat: now it was a question of beating her straight or not beating it; it had really come down to his stripping in front of her dressed or of remaining dressed in front of her naked.

Marcello, who eventually decided to discard sensibly, also got his card; and he didn't have the courage to turn it over, his cowardice was stronger than his anxiety; he asked permission to peek. He gathered the four already uncovered cards, the pair of tens and the pair of sevens, into a tight pile and turned them over; on top of them he placed, still face down, the unknown card, the card of fate; then he turned over the entire hand and grasped it firmly. For the last and definitive hand everyone had drawn close around the table. She had not even raised her eyes; impassive, she seemed only to be watching the young man's blind flounderings.

"Take your time, there's no rush," someone said with a hint of irony.

Marcello spread out quickly, fan-wise, the first four cards; and, with an almost imperceptible quiver of his wrist, making it slide with his index finger, he began to uncover the pip of the fifth, in the upper corner. But the action proceeded with a slowness that was exasperating for him too; instead of executing the necessary movements, one might say that he avoided them with great care, like someone miming the act of marching without moving forward. Or perhaps the card was a "deep" one; the fact is that the tiny corner he was watching remained white, nor did the pip announce itself in any fashion, with one of those dots or hints at lines or corners or curves that a gambler knows how to recognize.

"Come on, show some nerve; it's four o'clock," someone else said.

Nerve! But that's just what he lacked! The gravity of an event is not in the event itself, or, so to say, outside of us, but within us, in our emotions. What did they know, those who told him to hurry? For him that card might be a matter of life or death; he was most likely exaggerating, but that didn't change a thing. And besides, was he exaggerating? On that card depended the fulfillment of his most ardent desire, and at the same time his salvation. Salvation, no less? Without a doubt: now let's hear, what would he do if he lost? Lost, one mustn't forget, against her, and she would be steadfastly, proudly dressed. If both of them had lost, it wouldn't have been so bad: but now? Naked! "Naked as a worm." And he wasn't good to look at; one of his mistresses had assured him that he was very handsome, but how could he believe her? She was a middle-aged woman, and in love. . . . What do you mean, handsome! His shoulders were too pointed: and that's a fact. Pointed shoulders! He was playing at hiding from himself. The trouble was his sexual organs, forget about the shoulders! To begin with, they were attached "fig-wise," too far back; and, moreover, that general puckered look of . . . and, to top it all, the element, the principal member of the system was exceedingly tiny. Yes, that was the crux, it was tiny, this was the only, but perfectly sufficient, curse. No, not the only . . . How did other men carry it? Exposed, covered, semisheathed? And he so brazen about the whole thing, despite his puniness (which, as a result, would appear even more glaringly exhibited), what sort of figure would he cut? What a disgrace, what a disgrace! They would, she would, consider him an aggressive type, with an inferiority complex, like those short people who stalk around with their heads high. . . . Or were these just fantasies of his, and anyway, women didn't notice such things? Maybe women in love didn't—but she! . . . So then, what was he going to do if he lost? He certainly wouldn't have the nerve to avail himself of the alternative he himself had established, and he would make an about-face, he would, so to speak, slobber in their presence, in her presence, irremediably, neither man nor worm, that is, a real worm. . . . But leaving all this aside; his most ardent desire—what was it in substance, this ardent desire of his? He wanted to see the girl naked, but why? To ask why was senseless, agreed, since he did want it. But didn't that ardent desire of his contain a wish, a necessity almost, to tear her down, actually to spill the girl from her high horse, to undermine her strength itself? Perhaps; but if so, what did his more or less inevitable accompanying eagerness (since we all tend to humiliate the thing we love) mean at the present juncture, or in which way could it help him to take his stand with real manliness? . . . And she, what did she think, what was she thinking? . . . He stared at her and this time, cold in appearance and calm, paler than usual, she stared back at the young man, intently. . . . Whatever else it might be, it certainly was a terrible duel, a mortal duel between the two of them.

"Well, make up your mind!"

Yes, he had to make up his mind, this tension must end, everything has to end, desolately, if it must; Marcello moved the index finger of one hand, giving added force to the vibration of his wrist, and with two fingers of his other hand resolutely pushed at the fifth card. His hope was for a ten: there still were two that hadn't been played, whereas there was only one seven.

Well, what did that tiny shadow that began to appear on the corner of the fifth card, just at the edge of the card covering it, announce? My God, was it true? The shadow did not look round (like that of a queen, nine or eight) nor did it look pointy (like a king), nor did it jut out a little at the bottom (like the hook of a jack would have), but it slowly unveiled itself, even, straight. My God, could it be true? It could only be the foreshadowing of a ten or a seven, with its peculiar, straight-angled hook! Another vibration of his wrist, a push of the index finger, and the shadow took on substance, became definite, emerged, becoming a clear pip or part of a pip: a seven! The fourth seven.

Marcello had won his hazardous, dreadful gamble. His first reaction was one of uncontrolled elation, his eyes blurred with pleasure, relief (and sweat); the second took the form of a glance at the girl. She stared at him, still unperturbed, but observing her more carefully, there was something grim and withdrawn or involuted in her expression, as if she were pursuing a secret thought, and in any case had some objection; there was an indefinable, incomprehensible reproach and, for the first time, a touch of dismay. The young man understood that in her spirit had unfolded, unrolled, a sequence of corresponding emotions, which had come to a very different conclusion, and for a moment he pitied her.

An utterly misplaced pity, by God: he had risked as much as she, he had won, she was his prey by right of war. She lay at his feet, at his mercy; and his vehement desire was about to be fulfilled; and he himself was safe. Why shouldn't he abandon himself to his intoxicating triumph, or (in the name of what?) should he be asked to contaminate it with embarrassing emotions, extraneous weakness and trite afterthoughts?

III

They all lackadaisically began to undress and soon were naked; or almost, since two or three women, not very sure of one aspect of their charms, had kept on their brassieres. Marcello in fact did not know how to consummate his victory; as regards his public or apparent behavior, what should he do exactly? And, on the other hand, in what way could he introduce or justify that prolonged contemplation which was his sole and true purpose? He decided to take a stroll among the naked and linger before each one, which would furnish him with the excuse of lingering as long as he pleased before that one naked woman. Of course, he had avoided looking at her again; and now, starting out on his stroll while the slowest were still fiddling with hooks and buttons, he turned his back on her.

"My dear girl, you really have to be more daring, take off that brassiere." (Which the woman addressed did, lifting her arms high, to save the savable or support the supportable.) "Bravo, who would have thought it! Congratulations"—and so on. And meanwhile, concentrating on not turning around, he tried to look at her with the nape of his neck and it seemed to him that he was struck by the breath of *her* nudity.

But when he had finished his tour and the clownish comments had come to an end, he actually turned to face her with a shiver (the kind which in private precedes the pleasure), he saw that the girl, as though undaunted by that naked crowd and seeming in fact completely at her ease in the midst of it, was still dressed from top to toe. Her stance was proud and at the same time supremely graceful, in short, feminine in the true sense; she rested more on one foot than the other, so that one hip took on prominence and a flowing roundness, and her knees were partly crossed, showing the silhouette of the calf of her less burdened leg; higher up, her small head with its casque of blond hair, flung back and slightly inclined over one shoulder, seemed to defy bleak fate and the whole world. Faced with so discordant a sight, Marcello felt inexplicably shamed, rather than surprised.

"But what about you? . . ." he finally stammered.

"None of these ladies and gentlemen," the girl replied quietly, "has seen fit to invoke the established alternative, and that's their business. But that alternative does exist, and specified by none other than yourself. Very well, I choose it: that's all."

A general silence fell, followed by an indistinct murmur; one would have thought that these intellectuals, inured to all sorts of adventures (of the intellect), had been caught by surprise.

"But how," Marcello stammered again, "how can you . . . ?"

"Do we or don't we have this blessed alternative?" she cut in coldly, and even with a hint of gaiety in her voice. "But we do; and so it does not seem to me that there can be any objection. I'm not getting undressed; so tell me with what means I must commit suicide, immediately and in your presence, according to the rules. I will do it, don't you worry."

Incredible! She was eluding him with a joke. What else could it be? Who would have had the courage to seriously impose on her the observance of the agreement? . . . And yet, was she really joking? Her eyes were dark. Marcello couldn't recall ever having met so dark a gaze; her breasts quivered; and that hint of gaiety resembled, if anything, the twisted smile of the condemned. . . . But even if she were ready to go through with it, it still was not nor ever could be a serious matter. And that in the end meant a new defeat for him, a defeat in victory, hence more crushing, irremediable, something atrocious, unbearable! And the young man did not know what to latch onto in himself, or in what damned way to handle his absurd position, or what words he could add.

But, whatever it might be, the situation was for many of them a very tasty tidbit: a fecund situation, the Marquis would have called it. Fecund of what? Of talk naturally, but in the end also of audacities (another's skin being at stake); many perhaps were not averse to accepting at least as a matter of principle a literal solution, as one of those critics or writers would have put it—that is, the girl's suicide. Finally, they had come awake; and each one feeling his little gray cells tingling pleasurably, each covering himself summarily, an argument soon broke out.

"Well, obviously she has something to hide," the silliest of the women whispered. But this nasty crack went almost unnoticed.

"Now, let's see, isn't it true that it was a joke, it's been that from the start," the Marquis said, making an effort at good sense, but leaving his thought rather vague.

"Not so fast," a literary man butted in, fluttering his bloodless hand. "Everything is a joke and nothing is, you understand what I mean, or we should say that the very concept of a joke is merely subjective. To put it even more clearly, it would indisputably be a joke if she, the concerned party, had understood and had always understood it as such. Otherwise, how would we dare . . . ?"

"The only thing clear is your damned literary man's petulance, with all your paradoxes and distinctions and eviscerations, of which you have given us so many examples, and even now you would like to push a thousand more of them down our throats, if we didn't stop you," a fat painter broke in good-humoredly. "Never mind; side by side with what you claim for them, things must surely have an objective value of their own, and it's not for nothing that common sense does exist. Now, come, are you telling me that you would like to kill Gisa, or allow her to kill herself, which comes to the same thing, just because she doesn't feel like getting undressed? What's going on in your head?"

"You haven't understood a thing, as usually happens with you," the other man retorted, with not too sour a smile, "and as for your famous common sense, that's what you use to paint your paintings. No, I'm saying, and try to follow me, that one never knows what place a specific thing will take or what its purpose may be in an inner context; that is, someone else's inner context, by definition unknown. Let's assume, for instance, that consciously or unconsciously she wanted to kill herself and needed this tortuous preparation to attain her goal; or that at a certain point, for whatever motive, suicide took shape as the inevitable effect of some unknown combination, or God knows what. From this point of view, we certainly would not have the right to stop her from doing it or even to put obstacles in her way, you'll admit that. And there's more: you must also think what tremendous guilt would be unleashed in her if she defaulted; and I don't refer to the default directly connected with the rules of this nonsensical game; no, any default that might appear to her spirit, even if it was expressed by a twist of the intellect or heart. Besides, you should realize that a feigned or merely formal default still can unexpectedly be transformed into a deeper one owing to manifest or mysterious causes. It might impersonate, if I may put it that way, or represent or symbolize an inner state, an inner relationship which demands a solution; or, again, bring out a latent conflict. My dear fellow, we are not in other people's souls and never will be. Now this being so, it would evidently not be enough to say: 'Don't do it,' but it would be more appropriate to examine carefully the case itself. . . . Do I make myself clear?"

"If you ask me, he puts it very well," the Prince said, raising his eyebrows; unheeded, but thanked by a new and modest smile from the speaker.

"Oh you, with your guilt feelings and your latent conflicts!" contradicted a second literary man, envious of the first man's notoriety. "Guilt feelings must be a mania of yours, and your books would seem to confirm it. For heaven's sake, don't you think that you sound like a textbook? You're like some professor standing over an anatomical specimen; don't forget, my friend, that the object of your disquisition stands right in front of us, alive and kicking, and all we have to do is question it."

"As if by questioning anyone you could find out something about him!" the first retorted demurely.

"Come, you've just asserted that we cannot know anything about anyone, and now you're trying to say that no one can know anything about himself—where is it going to end?"

"Yes, everything is unknowable," the Prince inserted thoughtfully.

"Calm down," the first literary man replied to the second. "All right, then: though it is not wholly conclusive, the experiment can always be made. Why don't you question her?"

"Gisa," the second man continued, "come, tell us, it's a joke, isn't it?"

The girl, who during all that pompous nonsense had remained motionless and indifferent, turning her eyes from one to the other as if they were not talking about her, stared at the questioner before replying. Marcello, who had drawn aside and had perched on the edge of an armchair, thought her face suddenly seemed to cave in; certainly her eyes glistened with incipient tears.

"What joke?" she then answered, passing a hand over her forehead. "I don't even understand your question. I played, I lost; and I only want to fulfill my obligations. I must fulfill them."

"You see: 'I must,' " said the first literary man.

"What are you talking about 'you see' and 'I must,' " the fat painter barked back, "if she's a moron, is that perhaps a good reason for us to be morons, too? She may have some stupid reason for talking like this, because she surely doesn't mean it; we would be potential murderers if we added another word. But why waste my breath? You're all morons, the lot of you."

They continued in fact to argue and exchange insults; very deeply felt, but passed off as friendly.

IV

Someone said:

"My dear friends, the company is fine, but it's now five o'clock in the morning: soon we will be surprised by the misty, slothful and torpid dawn. Ghastly!"

" 'Turbid,' says the poet."

"It's all the same. Anyway, it's time to end this lovely party. Or what else should we do? Despite all the chatter we haven't found out yet; so let's pretend that everything went as it should, let's leave Gisa all buttoned-up, let's get dressed again and go to bed as we should like good little boys and girls."

"No, no!" the girl exclaimed.

"Too easy," the first, impenitent literary man echoed; but nobody paid any attention to him.

"Why not? Isn't that what you want?" the painter said to the girl.

"I, I . . ." she began.

"Don't you see, Gisa," the hostess intervened, "all the unpleasantness and arguments you've caused? Wouldn't it be simpler to undress and get it over with? You would leave us all happy and satisfied, we wouldn't have to be embarrassed at infringing propriety and convention, and so forth. Is it that hard?"

"You can see that it's hard for her," murmured the usual good girl friend.

"I'm not getting undressed," Gisa replied with a movement of childish irritation, "and I have nothing more to say; so let's proceed according to the agreement."

"But what agreement, what's going on in your head? If you don't undress, it'll just mean that you won't undress and that we shall have to forego seeing you naked—that's all. There is no other possible solution: it's almost dawn, by God, and at dawn vapors clear away; squalid reason, if only for the space of a morning, regains the upper hand."

"No, that isn't right, either," Gisa insisted, almost with a snarl; her lower lip was thrust out, its corners ready to droop again, like the mouth of a fretful child.

"Oh dear, it's either one or the other."

"What do you mean, either one or the other? An alternative was, has been, set down; and I have invoked it, and it's my . . . my . . ."

"Of course, her right," completed the literary man, raising his voice to dominate the hubbub, "it's her right that the alternative should be somehow, and mind you I'm saying somehow, implemented."

"What is 'somehow' supposed to mean?" said the fat painter.

"Somehow means somehow," squeaked the other man. "I am not

bloodthirsty, as you perhaps do me the honor of thinking, but neither am I the farmer's almanac: how do I know what way? But why don't you think about it for a moment, my precious and unrelenting heckler, let's suppose that she . . ."

"Back again at the suppositions," said the second literary man.

"Well, yes, let's suppose that on some part of her enchanting body she has a repulsive wart, a monstrous birthmark, or something."

"Isn't that what I said?" the good girl friend whispered again.

"And so?" asked the second man. "That would explain why she does not want to get undressed, but it would not at all explain why she does not want to not get undressed, that is, why she does not accept the solution of staying dressed without a fuss, so that we can all go to bed."

"Quiet, just a moment," the first man replied, closing his eyes and wincing with obvious vexation. "So she has a wart . . ."

"Remember, hypothetically . . ."

"All right, hypothetically; and so she does not want to undress. But who's going to pay for this wart, who . . . who will redeem it?"

"But what the devil are you saying?" his interlocutor exclaimed after an instant of perplexity. "What does it all mean?"

"I mean to say that if she has a desire, a craving, even though blind, for self-punishment due to such a defect, it is or would be legitimate, and we do not or would not have the right to contest this right of hers."

"Ah, now we're getting somewhere!" the other man was content to retort, conscious that when it came to the unconscious he could not compete with his colleague and rival.

"Interesting, though," said the Prince.

"Nonsense," the fat painter commented.

"In fine, I must point out to you," the literary man shouted, "that for her, if undressing right away could have been an act without consequences, now, after all our discussions, it has of necessity become something very important."

In short, the argument flared up again.

"Come, come," the hostess, who wanted to get to bed, finally said. "Gentlemen, please. . . . Now, Gisa, what have you got to say?"

"What I have said."

With a gesture of resignation, the hostess took Marcello aside.

"Listen, at this point perhaps the best thing would be to play along with her, that'll change her mind, and take care of it. Don't you agree?"

Marcello did not answer.

"All right, Gisa," the hostess continued, "do you really insist that things be done according to the agreement, to the letter?"

"Yes."

"Very well. How do you want to go about killing yourself?"

"But . . ." the girl replied, "any way you say."

"No, no, in the agreement to whose rigorous observance you hold us, it is not said that we must or can impose on you a type of suicide that might prove disagreeable to you. At least, that's how I understand it: does everyone agree?"

"Of course," confirmed the specialist in the subliminal, "let her choose." Naturally he and all the others had more or less understood what was afoot.

"So, Gisa, what do you choose?"

"Oh, for goodness sake, I don't know. . . . Give me a pistol, it's the fastest way."

"Coming up," the hostess said; and went to fetch from the desk drawer a tiny revolver with a mother-of-pearl butt, which she handed to the girl. "It's not loaded," she whispered to Marcello, resuming her seat.

Gisa took the revolver and turned it over in her hand for a moment; she glanced at Marcello with an indefinable look (yet that look made him start); then she inspected the revolver again, and especially its cylinder. She laughed in a bitter, even vicious way.

"This *is* a joke," she said. "It's not loaded! Give me the bullets."

The hostess exchanged a glance with Marcello, but his expression remained unresponsive and obtuse. Everyone was quiet. The hostess went back to the desk, took out some cartridges and gave them to Gisa, who with painstaking concentration filled the revolver's chambers. Nobody thought that this meant anything or that the girl really intended to kill herself; yet all of them, once again, fell silent and felt slightly ill at ease. More than anything else, they were waiting to see how she would get out of it.

V

Gisa backed against a table and perched on its edge, uncovering almost the entire length of a dazzling leg. She smiled in a half foolish, half absent way and shrugged her shoulders slightly, staring at the revolver in her hands, playing with it idly: she looked embarrassed or, more precisely, she looked like someone who has been forced by simple-minded people or children to play a senseless game, and sets out to please them. But it was only a passing moment of weakness; an instant later she raised her eyes and pointed the weapon decisively at her temple, her finger on the trigger.

The gesture elicited an incredulous and amused murmur from those present, and a jab with her elbow in Marcello's side from the hostess, who perhaps meant that hers had been a very good inspiration, that with this last bit of play-acting the problem could be regarded as solved, that finally the girl would never have the courage to pull the trigger. But on the contrary in that fleeting moment Marcello saw, was warned by some secret sense, that she would not hesitate to do it. And indeed, why call it a secret sense? It was enough to know her as he did from long contemplation. There was no doubt— the girl was going to kill herself, there, right then; the uncertain expression she had worn before was now replaced by an awesome gravity, an implacable resolution, an oblivious detachment; her face was radiant, it shone like only that which is promised to death can.

For an hour the young man had been prey to conflicting and imprecise emotions, and an obscure remorse, his silence had been a kind of dark vigil in which sensations and feelings matured and disintegrated from one minute to the next, none of them consolidating or acquiring sufficient certainty, decisive weight, none triumphing: now the silence and stupor were suddenly dissolved and he felt it his duty to intervene, or rather an irresistible impulse moved him. He leaped forward, seized Gisa by the wrist, without being able to turn the weapon away from her temple, or without even intending to do so.

"Come on, what are you doing?" he cried, amazed and annoyed with himself for the inadequacy of his words. "And why?"

The girl did not reply; they stood there looking at each other intently, panting a bit. And at this point (at last, at last) the young man realized that he loved her, loved her with real love. From his whole being, from his bowels, emotions at last known, plausibly, incontrovertible and ancient, rose in hot waves: a desire of offered protection, a yearning for warm flesh, a scorn and almost annihilation of the self, and other deliciously absurd and silly desires, which abolished all the presumptuous constructions of his intellect, of his spoiled, fallacious, deficient senses, which abolished . . . his pride, pride as a male, a man, a scribbler, everything. At the cost of shame before himself, shame before the others, before the whole shabby and spiteful, conceited and unsuspecting world, he must save her; or save himself, which was the same, to save her in himself and himself in her. To save her from what, from death? Yes, certainly, and yet not exactly: from a death that was harsher than death; from pride, which mockingly opposes all that matters; from her pride, as he had by now saved and freed himself from his own. For at that very moment he understood that she never could or would agree to undress and therefore to not kill herself; or perhaps the connection was not so direct, but to establish it now would not help; that she would not be able to undress nor not to kill herself, nor, in the end, would she be able to kill herself; that her spirit thrashed about desperately, caught in a net of appearances, of false thoughts, of false consistencies . . . of pride, once again.

"What are you doing?" he repeated.

"What I must do," she answered coldly.

"But why?"

"You say why?" she flung back. "You, you ask me why?"

What did these words mean? Marcello did not stop to inquire but racked his brain with more urgent questions. Yes, precisely, in what way could he save her, free her? And suddenly the answer flared up within him, and then became fixed in a blinding light. It was simple, it was obvious, in what way.

"Listen, Gisa," he said. "I'm the one who invented the game, set up the rules, won, and as a result gives the orders. Now try to understand me and grasp the connection, which even for me is still mysterious, which . . . which, oh nothing—the connection. You don't want to undress, I don't know why, or perhaps I do confusedly understand and there's no point in talking about it; in any case, I grant the correctness of your decision. Hence you invoke the famous alternative: this too is correct, it is your incontestable right. But look at it this way: if I, in my position, that is, being the only person who could legitimately not do so, also undress, would you accept this solution as invalidating and consent to undress, without invoking this or that right? Would you give up all reckless intentions and not feel in any way diminished? Do you understand what I'm saying? I undress, you undress too, quite simply, and then everything will be restored to its proper proportions, which after all are those of a more or less tasteful parlor game. And then we'll be done with it. How about it?"

The others, either because they were bored or despite themselves were made wary by something true which they felt to be happening between those two, had kept silent; but now the fat painter exclaimed:

"I call this a brilliant solution."

"I would say so myself," approved the literary man. "However . . ." he added, quickly repenting.

"But what about the wart?" the good girl friend grumbled. The two of them heard nothing.

"I would first have to understand the connection . . ." the girl at last said hesitantly. "I can't figure it out by myself." But still she lowered the revolver.

"What connection? Oh, the connection. That's not necessary. Gisa, my dear, it's simple and solves everything, trust me; look . . ." and he threw off his jacket.

The girl stared at him, confused.

"It's just a moment, it's nothing, look . . ." the young man continued; and he ripped off his tie, dropped his pants (the vulgar act gave him the shivers, but the thought of his amorous sacrifice got the upper hand and sustained him). "Well, come, do you accept? Do you accept this solution? Come, come, it's easy, look . . ." and he began to unbutton his shirt. "Come, do it with me! But no, wait; wait till I'm naked, it will be even easier . . ."

Delicious, inebriating liberation! Like divesting oneself of a scaly carapace. What did his tiny or badly attached genitals matter now? Where had his shyness gone, the daughter of his pride, the daughter of hell? When he was naked, naked as a worm, as he had always and especially this evening had a horror of being, he looked trustingly at the girl. And she, abstracted, pensive, almost out of the world or rather inside a lost, young and marvelous world, she too began to undress. . . . Won. And what did this surfacing verb without a subject and without an auxiliary mean? Who had won and what? She, of course, had won back her own self, but there was something else. *That* world was lost, lost but retrievable each day, as our faith allows.

She began to undress, at first doubtfully, then more quickly. And it was truly easy, not just a matter of being physically able to do it. She appeared as she was and had to be, firm, white, pure; she had neither warts nor birthmarks, nor even a beauty spot; she was a diamond without a flaw, a transparent alabaster, or an amber. And in Marcello there was no longer a shadow of curiosity but rather a boundless admiration, a sense of plenitude and calm, almost of order, a pleasure in accord with nature, a soothing vision.

Everybody, including the two literary men, applauded; the good friend went pale and lowered her eyes. Gisa smiled timidly, covered her sex with her hand, and said:

"Well, now you can go to bed without a worry, right? And you'll allow me to go too, I hope," she added, putting on the first, impalpable garment.

"Yes, yes, we are fully satisfied, so are the rules of the game, and all our possible exigencies as regards justice, kindness, and, in particular, beauty," the fat painter said with gallantry, gaily, though a bit too loudly.

"But still," muttered the literary eviscerator, "there's something in this business, this solution, that does not completely convince me."

"Ah yes, and what would that be?" the second literary man immediately pounced.

"Well, I don't know . . . something missing."

"How's that?"

"Yes, just as one says 'missed beat' or 'misdeal'. . . . Do you get me?"

"I shall be careful not to. On the contrary, it seems to me that here, as you critics often say, the harmonious and generic convention which presides over the relations between men has been fully restored; or at least this solution has as much as possible approximated the very concept of convention. . . ." Of course, he just wanted to contradict, and let everyone know that he too, when called upon, could hold his own.

"Something's missing, but in your head and your whole body," concluded the painter in a philosophical tone, addressing the first man: "You missed your trade as a nag and bore."

Now they had to get dressed, which is more difficult. But everybody was in such a hurry that they set aside or forgot their painful, exquisite sensations, and just did it.

Marcello in the meantime was thinking: "There's no doubt that the Marquis will offer her a lift in his car, since they live near each other. And what will she do? She should, she must, reply: 'No, thanks, I'll walk.' Then I, the lowest among my peers, not having a car, can accompany her."

The Marquis said:

"Come, Gisa, hurry; I'll give you a lift."

And she, that angel, replied word for word as he had hoped:

"No, thanks, I'll walk."

Goodbye, goodbye, thanks for a lovely evening, your whiskey was excellent, we'll see you at the show, poor Bacon in such bad hands, actually it's nothing more than a vulgar case of alienation, no wonder he's impotent, since he copies Daumier, he does it pretty badly, goodbye, goodbye. And the party ended amid the roars and screeches of the departing cars. Gisa and Marcello set out on foot.

VI

They walked for quite a distance at random, without talking; without talking and even avoiding the slightest contact. It was cold, there was a sliver of a moon; the streets were gradually becoming more vacuous, more anonymous and desolate. But like an incumbent, indeed an inner queasiness, the dawn lay in wait for them. And with dawn, with their spectral faces mirrored in each other's, what would be left? . . . But left of what or from what? There had been nothing; it was necessary to hasten to give that nothing a form, a voice, a warmth.

"Where does this street go to?" the girl suddenly said.

"To the Colosseum," Marcello replied, automatically.

"No," she smiled, "I mean this one."

"Oh! . . . Well, I don't know. But I do know; I desire it, I hope for it; I want it."

"What exactly do you want?"

"That you love me forever."

"There's no need to desire, hope and want it; it's enough to know I already love you. And you have no need to know either, since you already knew it."

"I don't know if I knew."

"And it doesn't matter. But tell me, don't you think we've started out badly?"

"Why?"

"But dearest, splendor cannot be sustained: a dazzling light soon forces us to shut our eyes and fall back into the darkness. I did not want a certain thing, and yet I wanted . . . and you wanted . . . Yes, but now?"

The young man kept silent.

"Dawn threatens us," Gisa continued after a while.

"So let's run away from this dawn and all the other dawns."

"How, where?"

"At your place, at mine."

"In my house or yours? No, Marcello, that's not the point."

"What is it, then?"

"The path of pride is wrong, we've seen that. But so is that of humility, don't you see, Marcello?"

"I can't see that: we haven't taken it. And you aren't taking it, this way."

"Or it's simply wrong, sinful, and in any case uncomfortable to acknowledge the way things are."

"And can one avoid it?"

"How do I know? We would have to try."

"So then how should one live?"

"At random."

"But it's impossible! I wish it were."

Here the girl fell silent. They went on walking; from behind the Celio a vague malign pallor was spreading.

" 'Dawn, furious beast,' " Marcello declaimed, " 'you empty us of blood, you hollow out our cheeks, I shall see by a face, by the face, my very aspect,' and so forth," he broke off sharply, annoyed by his clowning.

They were still walking.

"Would you have really killed yourself?"

"Yes, certainly," she replied, surprised.

"But why?"

"Because I had to: I loved you and nevertheless I was empty: I didn't know where, where inside of me, or how, to put this love."

Silence, and a pause. Dawn spread like an indelible stain.

"How silly you are; infinitely, intolerably silly: this was for you, not for everybody."

"What's this?"

"This," she made a scythe-like gesture, pointing to her own body. "Since I have neither warts nor birthmarks, you've seen that by now."

"How silly I am, it's true."

"But after all you too undressed, and you feared it more than anything else. Well, suppose we try to proceed from this fear, this outrage to love, this ignominious exposure, suppose we were to start from here? From an infirmity of the intellect, a blind event rather than the perfect thing which is therefore treacherous and ephemeral and which seemed to take shape at the end?"

"What madness! Our very determination would be our ruin."

Another pause.

"A missed beat, a misdeal: that fool was right," the girl murmured. "And yet it is terrible that one cannot really understand all this: why missed, from whom, from what, from what rhythm or game? Or perhaps everything is a missed beat or a misdeal, everything that is not . . . ?"

"You mean that happiness is a misdeal? Not at all, it's our natural state, haven't you read that?"

Silence. The dawn had thrown away its mask; the old stones of the imperial and fatal ruins were whitening at the summit.

"Gisa, it's day."

"Yes, I can already see you, almost: a little bluish; I see the black under your eyes, the veins of your hands."

"Gisa, come, before it's too late; we'll close the shutters, pull the curtains—against the day. We'll light the lights; red, at this hour, like eyes that have wept."

She kept silent; nervously smoothed her wrinkled dress over her belly; turned her head to one side and found nothing to look at. A complicated and noisy vehicle advanced alongside the sidewalk, sprinkling water on the street; from the wetted dust rose a disheartening smell.

"Gisa, come, Gisa, come! Come to my house, let's hide there. Let's hide there forever, for all our lives."

"All our lives?"

"Yes, yes, what do we know! Perhaps . . ."

A taxi drove by, unreal, almost metaphysical in that desolation. The driver seemed . . . seemed to breathe, to live, to have something to live for; he stared at them with curiosity; slowed up, nearly stopped, ready for a sign.

"Gisa, come!"

"I'm coming," she said finally, dismayed. "But Marcello . . . Marcello, what about afterwards?"

Without replying he dragged her along quickly, happy and desperate.

[Untitled]

⬦⬦⬦
———————
⬦⬦⬦

Dear, oh dear. These breasts of mine aren't a woman's breasts, they're too tiny, too tender, I don't know. . . . And the tips, they're just like a little girl's. . . .

—Oh, come now, they're beautiful!

—And what about my hips? I don't have any, almost; you might say I'm nearly square from here down. Oh dear, oh dear, it's hopeless.

—What are you talking about? You look fine. Don't get such ideas into your head. Stop fussing.

—Why, just look at this face; I've even got a kind of moustache. And my hair, it's so bushy. . . .

—Now, listen, why don't you cut it out? Just relax, for God's sake. You're making me nervous, too.

—Sure, it's easy for you to talk, you're as hard as a pearl. . . . And my thighs are a little hairy, too. Oh dear, dear, there's no hope, none.

—Say, you down there! Why don't you start getting undressed?

—Sir, please . . . how far ahead are they?

145

—Well, they're going pretty fast. It'll soon be your turn.

—Are we supposed to line up here?

—Yes, stand on this side—and as soon as you're called . . . In fact, there's one coming out right now.

—Miss, miss, how did it go? Are they very strict?

—No, not really. I mean, they are strict, but anyway I got through. Don't be so scared and above all try to act natural. Lots of luck.

—Well, get moving. Actually, it isn't your turn yet, but since these women over there keep dawdling . . . Go ahead. Hey, not both though, just one.

—So, kiss me goodbye.

—Yes, yes, I'll kiss you goodbye, but what about me? . . . Don't leave me here all by myself.

—Don't act like a child: a nice way to encourage me.

—Yes, you're right, I'm sorry. Lots of luck, but you've got nothing to worry about. . . . Oh dear, dear. Sir, am I next?

—Yes.

—Oh dear, dear. Sir, sir . . . tell me, what do they do if . . . if you don't get through?

—Why think about that now? Forget it.

—No, no, tell me. Please. I think I won't be as scared if you tell me. First of all, where?

—Why . . . here in this courtyard. No, don't try, you can't see anything from these windows.

—And . . . how?

—Well . . . it doesn't hurt. You'd think God knows what, but it doesn't hurt at all.

—Oh, now you might as well tell me everything; afterwards I'll be less upset.

—Well, it's like a big wheel, that is, half of a wheel, made of steel, it's very sharp and it turns: the girl lies on a board, naked, and . . . I'm

telling you, it doesn't hurt at all. . . . Oh, there's your girl friend coming out.

—Oh, you're back, my dear. Well?

—Let's not waste any time: they're waiting.

—But let her at least tell me . . .

—Come, come, that's enough now, go on in. IT'S YOUR TURN.

Looking

I am a young girl . . . just an ordinary young girl. I'm certainly not beautiful; I am the kind of woman who was shut in a book when a child, as the saying goes. Yes, sometimes I have the feeling of not having one face but two, in fact two sides like a sheet of paper; I am formed edgewise, that's it, and I am awfully thin. But, after all, I am not really ugly; I know, for instance, that I have beautiful hands, which stay beautiful no matter what I do to them. During this winter season I see other girls with reddened, cracked hands: not me, I can put them in cold water directly after hot, even go about without gloves, and they will still remain the same. They are rather small, tapered, with velvety skin. My eyes must also be beautiful, but, of course, all young girls have lovely eyes; when there's nothing to be said about a girl, people always talk about the eyes or the hair.

My social position is humble: I am the second daughter of a café owner. But my father made the mistake of sending me to school, and as a result all sorts of ideas have popped into my head . . . including that of writing this diary. He, and I myself perhaps, wanted to make something different out of me; but then time passes and laziness remains. In short, I am here and when I feel like it I help at the bar; and that's all. Well, I ought now to say why I began writing this diary. In fact, it would have never occurred to me if . . .

For several days now, almost always at the same time (around eleven in the evening) a certain man shows up at the bar; a man who comes to drink a coffee, sometimes with a drop of liqueur, and then leaves without saying a word. And what about it? What do I think is so special about him? Nothing, of course; and yet . . . What does it mean? Why do I say: and yet? Well, let's try to find out.

He's a man who is no longer young, almost old. Stop here: did I ever have an inclination for sedate people? No; and besides this man, though old, does not seem at all sedate. So then? Then let's go on. He's handsome. That is, he's a man who must have been handsome; and who therefore in the last analysis still is (you don't lose your good looks along the way). . . . But I am expressing myself badly: he is handsome, of course, but the way I mean. And how do I mean it? I'm not quite sure: he has a mark on his forehead. From what? From . . . from thought, to begin with; and then also a mark of passion, spent, withered, disappointed, but still passion. I get the feeling that I could tell him all about myself and that he would understand everything. And he's melancholy.

Um. And what am I supposed to tell him about myself? God knows what; nothing. My long nights of sleep, the café, the sea that gradually changes color, in the evening the usual people from this little outlying quarter, and you can imagine who they are; and so on from day to day. Ah well, I could perhaps tell him just about this nothingness, and I am sure that he would understand me. . . . Forget it; as if there were anything to understand. Or ought he to understand that it is infinitely difficult for me to go on like this? No: who am I? A nobody, a nobody, and nothingness suits me perfectly. How could I dare ask for what I don't have?

Ah, it is lucky that I speak so obscurely. I guess that it comes down to his being a new face among the same coarse faces. We'll see.

December 16

Today, at my wife's house (and the house of my children: I live elsewhere) the old problem came up again. Came up, as usual, through indirect allusions, through digs, immediately checked and deviated; and a so-called problem, too. In short, paring away the myths, several years ago my wife was in a serious auto accident, which has left her in permanently bad shape: not without but within, I mean to say not in the face but the body, which in any event does not reveal to the external observer any sign of injury. Her face is still beautiful and fresh as a rose while her body is horribly disfigured.

Now it is obvious that such a brute, blind event, which is not, at any rate, imputable to her, must however have radically changed our relations: in truth, how can I, already burdened by age and moreover never too lively sexually, desire a woman so badly disfigured? I adore her, no doubt, I feel that she is necessary to me, indispensable, but this cannot be the case for her. And this is precisely where the problem is supposed to arise (which one might as well declare right off to be insoluble). She is not one of those women who can accept a fact just because it is accomplished; her love is pure, her soul generous. As a result, she cannot admit, except by cold reason, that her accident constitutes a sufficient cause for my spent desire, nor can she escape a certain rancor toward me, a certain need, I should say, of revenge or recrimination: obviously, if her love and her esteem for me are so great as not to allow her to discern a motive in her own disfigured flesh, she must inevitably consider or rather perceive fate's betrayal as mine. Could the man who loves me, she seems to argue, ever stop loving me just because my body is no longer as beautiful as it was? In fact, it is even impossible to attribute this argument to her: she doesn't argue at all; doubt does not even graze her stainless conscience (hence her reactions, her sense of an undeserved outrage, an unmerited desertion, etc.).

Well, what should I answer to these true or imagined accusations? I might say (hoping not to upset some eventual righteous reader) only one thing perhaps, and that's fundamental: that any attempt to overcome the stumbling-block would take the path of sublimation; but, unfortunately, conscious sublimation and so useless from every point of view; it would in short be an abject expedient, unworthy of both myself and her. The expedient already being resorted to, it is true: that is, to love her, I do love her, I repeat, and even more than before; so what?

And that's not all. All this has made me even more uncertain—and she has certainly noticed it—of my sexuality in general, so to speak. Hence her bitter advice to find another woman who will be more able to please me; and all the rest. And, to wind up, the admittedly ignoble way out by which such or similar tangles are often resolved is closed for me: that is, she could not even let herself be loved by someone else (supposing that we both agreed to it) for what would happen the moment this other person undressed her? And she somehow knows it, in some obscure way.

Enough. In any event this appearance of the age-old problem was only momentary today. In reality I desired her dressed, and she more or less consciously wanted to be desired naked; a rather simple equation, after all. Which has remained of course without a solution; and, I don't know how, quite soon took another path, that of our always precarious family budget, of my vices which make it even more shaky, and so on. Just as well: the second insoluble problem in so far as or because it is rather commonplace, lulled for a moment the anxiety aroused by the first.

Lulled? Let's admit it for convenience's sake (mine); because anxiety is always aroused, always uselessly aroused.

December 17

Who could he be? Not that I am especially curious or that it matters very much to me, but after all it is natural that I wonder; in any case, I do not see why I shouldn't wonder if I want to. So, who could he be? There's no doubt that he isn't the same kind of person as the people hereabouts, who are artisans, small pensioners. But he doesn't seem to be a clerk either, or a schoolteacher, or a professor; he often carries books under his arm (whose titles I've never managed to read) —but this doesn't mean anything. He's elegant, too. That is, not elegant, he seems the kind of person for whom a certain external dignity is habitual and so he scorns it. For instance, his overcoat must be extremely expensive but it is far from new and he wears it negligently, just thrown on, with its collar turned up; and the same goes for his hat, his gloves. Yet, for the third time, who is he? Why does he turn up here at that time? And where does he come from when he comes? What is he doing in this place? But is he really from around here, does he really live here, or is he just passing through? Here are so many (idle) questions fated to remain without replies, unless one questioned him directly, and provided he would answer them properly.

The truth is, he never speaks; I've barely heard a few brief "good evenings" from his voice, which is quite beautiful in fact, warm, virile, slightly husky due to his smoking, and—how should I put it?—lived, full of experience, of implications. The first time he came he pointed in silence at the coffee machine and I began making a coffee for him; then, still silently, he pointed at something behind me, a bottle on the shelf. Well, it wasn't hard to guess that he wanted the coffee, now ready, with a drop of cordial; and since out of the three bottles in that section only one was suited to the purpose . . . From then on he seemed to have come to enjoy the little game; he comes, points, and leaves muttering—bit of an effort—"Good evening." And he doesn't deign to look at me at all.

But that is not entirely true: yesterday evening he looked at my hands (which, as I've said, are beautiful). He pretended to be distracted, sunk in his thoughts, but in such cases we women are not easily fooled; we know how to see, you can bet, whether a man looks or doesn't look, and he was looking; so much so that I had to slip my hands in the pockets of my apron. But just imagine! He was looking at them: thanks a lot, and kind regards to the family.

More important—last night I looked at myself in the mirror, as I haven't done for such a long time, since I was a little girl of thirteen or fourteen (and now I am twenty-two!). . . . Well, yes, when I went to bed I stood in front of the mirror, like that, without anything on, and I examined myself carefully. And the result of my examination was not very encouraging. Anyway, first of all I saw much more clearly what I already knew, that is, that my tall hair-do is completely wrong: it lengthens my face, which is long to begin with, and makes me look much more gawky than I actually am. Besides, what's the point, I'm too thin; my breasts are terribly small; and all my ribs stick out; and my arms are bony; from behind I actually look like a young boy; and instead of a belly I have a basin, a kind of hole.

Still, still, despite everything, if I must be honest . . . well, as a whole, I'm not too bad. Why I'm not bad I can't say, but, for example, I have long, well-turned thighs, and since the rest is so flat, that part down there shows to even greater advantage. In general, thinness is not necessarily a defect, it can also be an accentuation, the accentuation of certain particular characteristics. In sum, I am "interesting looking," and I imagine that I might be attractive to somebody. Naturally, not to one of these men around here; it would have to be somebody intelligent . . . a connossieur!

But I do write quite well sometimes: where do I get some of these words from? I'm amazed at myself! But when it comes right down to it I did get through my studies, I am a schoolteacher, and if I wanted to I could at least teach children their ABC's.

December 17

Today, over at my wife's . . . It was dusk, and the poor inno-cents didn't seem to notice it; I don't mean actually the dusk, but rather that constant dusk which blights that miserable house and their very lives. This time the mother was whining, about money again. On one side the house looks out onto a cramped courtyard, with little dogs put up in emergency shelters and their respective tender owners, and a buxom housewife who decks it out from side to side with the banners of her wash; on the other, onto a sordid city street, so sordid that the communal ordinances do not reach it and permit the display of its limp underwear and petticoats hanging out to dry in the sun. In the kitchen there stagnated the atrocious stench of detergents, mingled with the personal odor of the dish-washer who frequents it on and off, and had just left; in the bathroom was strung a line bearing tiny infants' underwear to dry, still dripping, and in the tub stood a plastic bucket packed with clothes set to soak. And suddenly, instead of lamenting the plight of others, instead of promising myself to deliver and to save my dear ones from so much sordidness, suddenly I was seized by a kind of furious pity for myself. I felt that I was being imprisoned there without hope, I was being deprived of air. Overhead I could hear, through the very thin ceiling, dragging chairs and a broom being pushed; schoolchildren and child-maids crashing headlong down the sonorous staircase; from the apartment next door the hoarse grating of a radio; from the windows above our terrace the flapping of sheets, obscuring for instants the small, bleak sky; and finally, in a pause of silence and again from the floor above, the sound of a fat, sick man urinating. Yes, exactly, somebody urinating into a chamberpot.

And I said: "I'll be back later. I'm going out to buy cigarettes." And I left and didn't come back; and I never want to go back again. I leave them to their fate, my children, though adored, and my little wife, equally adored; I don't want to return; I can't do otherwise. I don't want to . . . Of course, my not wanting was stronger (at that moment) than it is (now); but what does it mean? Even if my will weakens, the impossible shall not become less impossible. Let's say, for instance, that I *must* not go back: since, among other things, I can only do them harm. But I'll think about it. No, I won't even think about it.

I left; and the whole world opened out before me, not in fact with alluring but with threatening appearances. The world without them! Since I was firm in my resolve, it was definitely necessary that something should accustom or reaccustom me to that world, give me a send-off, and right away; otherwise, what would this first night have meant? There was no time to be lost, already the first doubts about the material possibility of putting my decision into practice were stirring: where to go? where to start? what exactly should I do? In truth, I have always been embarrassed by these material sequences of action which a decision renders necessary; or in other words, I have never managed to establish a solid relation between the decision itself and the actions which perforce arise from it. And now, in this instance, I wish that my resolution were enough—no, it was necessary to sustain it, render it effective, and indeed real, by precise yet not very definable acts. But enough—despite all that and even at the cost of having to go forward at random, the next morning must already find me somewhat different and inured.

My first idea was to go to the Outsiders' Club, where there is gambling, and that for a double set of motives: because gambling stuns and distracts, and also because, even without having directly examined the problem, I knew by ear that money was the beginning and basis of everything. But, having stopped in a café to check my assets, I realized that I did not have more than thirty-two thousand lire; a manifestly insufficient sum for a game with high stakes (such as is played in that club). Thirty-two thousand lire, however, could be enough for something else: a woman, for example. A rather bottom-drawer woman, of course; but at a certain point high or low class amounts to the same thing . . . Why, yes, an excellent idea: this would perhaps be the famous opportunity, I could carry out the test, see if . . . if really . . . or if instead . . . Well, how should I go about getting a woman?

But was this the city renowned for its libertine delights? The hour, admittedly, was not the most propitious; at any rate, there was such a sedate and proper atmosphere on the sumptuously lit streets that even the most intrepid of men would have been disheartened. The cafés displayed through their plate glass rare, sulky and dazed couples under the cold, operating-room neon lights; and if not in the cafés, where was I supposed to look? But perhaps after dinner the situation would improve. In the meantime it had become quite late, and so I went into the first trattoria I found, where I turned out to be the only customer. After having served me a poor dinner, though with a good bottle of wine, the proprietor went back to dozing with her elbows propped wide on the table.

I left there and resumed the hunt, if my long and doubtful peerings into every hole and corner without stopping in any of them can be called that. I was looking, more than for a place, for a mood, that is, for one of those places in which from indefinable signs or a general atmosphere a woman hunter concludes he is on the right track. I also remembered certain brazen-looking women whom I had often seen strolling along the same streets I was reconnoitering or searching, and with whom I had exchanged a few suggestive glances: this time, if I met one of them, I would perhaps do something about it. But I didn't meet any. Yet at a certain point I did actually see Ginetta, standing uncertainly in front of a closed store. Ginetta is one of the women I see on the bus, and in fact the one I admire most: a very young girl, beautiful, slender, and all hard, with admirable proportions; she must be a shop girl or something of the sort down in the center of town. And since I have nothing better to do tonight, I'll say a few words to her.

All the girls on the bus are hard to approach—but this Ginetta! Her peculiarity is a certain look, I mean a certain way of looking or rather of not looking, which the most elegant of duchesses would envy. To be precise, she looks or at least she looks at me, as if I did not exist, almost as though before her were a void and I were—how should I say?—transparent. She is face to face with me, a step away from me, her eyes are level with mine which stare at her, and yet she does not see me or seems not to see me; rather than fixing on me, her look pours out and loses itself, like certain voices without any timbre, not carried and sharpened but devoured by the wind, so that one cannot even say that they miss the target, the listener, because they aren't even aimed at him. (By the way, at moments of intimacy I used to tell my wife about these girls, especially those on the bus. But she did not seem to appreciate my confidences at all. It is amazing how naive men are when it comes to certain things: women will never be able to appreciate such fanciful thoughts, nor accept as legitimate men's claim that telling them about a particular woman implicitly proves her innocuousness—and perhaps, one must add, they aren't altogether wrong.)

But let's come back to us. So Ginetta was standing there uncertainly, and I stepped forward wolfishly, repeatedly gave her the eye . . . eliciting one of her usual looks or non-looks which robbed me of all my bounce. And luckily, because a moment later a robust young man in a leather jacket stepped out of a door nearby and carried her off. So I continued to wander around like a soul in purgatory. But the hour of mystery and folly, midnight, was near: now or never. Finally I decided that the best place of observation and approach could only be a certain café (all green, the walls, the chairs, the cloths on the tables), where I had noticed women of ambiguous comportment on another occasion: and there I stationed myself.

In fact there were two or three women, but accompanied, or sleepy, or not easily identifiable as the kind of women I required. I was about to give up the whole business, when . . . Yes, this one, this woman who had just come in, she had something in her step, the click of her heel, the tilt of her loins, and something unequivocal in her eye, or rather something that declared her sufficiently equivocal. She was on display, available; and as she drank, standing up, she looked around. It didn't take much nerve on my part to invite her to sit down.

She was as black as a raven; she had long, beautiful but rather hairy legs. Sitting down, she pulled up her sleeves, and I could see that her forearms were hairy, too: what must the rest of her body, her belly, perhaps even her breasts, be like? She spoke with a brusque, slightly husky voice. And what about me, what was I to say? She solved my problem by starting to discuss a certain movie (unknown to me); but every so often she broke off, tapped her skeletal fingers on the table top, hummed. I was put off by her hairiness and kept silent; I hadn't actually forgotten why I was there and I still felt a vague and generic desire for something, yet the wine had lost its fizz and weariness and disgust were taking over. At last she looked at me quite meaningfully and said:

"Well, dearie, are you going to make up your mind?"

"What do you mean?"

"Oh, now, you don't expect me to sit here all night and waste the evening for nothing."

And so I ran away, and here I am back in my quarter; defeated, restless, whereas I should like to relax, etc. Before going home I had the usual coffee in my little bar; a consolation in a way, though not very substantial, and almost a refuge. But now? I must have spent some time writing these rambling pages and I guess it's about three o'clock in the morning; nonetheless dawn is still far off, and before dawn there is no hope of getting to sleep. Anyway the question is not of spending the time and getting to sleep but, as always in my life, of finding the way. For me it's always a question of finding the way (to do or not to do something); one might say that the search for the way is indeed my way of being. Yes, indeed—and right now?

Rossana waited on me in the bar. Rossana is a flash, a look; a black and brilliant look (terms that are not antithetical, as is shown by certain gems and, precisely, the eyes of some women), both timid and . . . I wouldn't say brazen or even bold, but certainly revelatory or, even better, affirmative of a will for life. The flash reverberates from her forehead, lighting it up and darkening it, and, like all flashes, goes out in an instant, that is, she lowers her head. Yes, but this girl is bony, irremediably bony; her breasts are barely visible, she would have to raise her arms to show them; and, besides, who could see anything beneath that wide and shapeless apron or smock? Or perhaps she is the most deceptive or misleadingly deceptive of thin girls, and when naked she has everything in its proper place? What's more, she is too tall; or is it because of the wrong hair-do? But her hands are lovely. And besides, was it Rossana who gave me the coffee? In fact I am beginning to suspect that the person I call Rossana is in reality a kind of average image, that, in other words, Rossana has a sister who resembles her a great deal and I cannot tell one from the other. Yet how could that flash belong to two persons, how could that flash be average, too?

Fine. But now . . . ? Let's see—what if I were to discard all foolish aspirations, all rights to an existence of my own, and went back to my wife or promised myself to do so? No doubt I would sleep peacefully, and sometimes it can be worth one's while to sacrifice everything to peace, even that which one believes one has to do or say in life or to the world. . . . But no! It would be cowardice, it would be unmitigated cowardice, not at all justified, not even by a melancholy sense of duty or responsibility. What responsibilities? Responsibilities are for those who accept them, who feel them as such, whereas I have never felt anything of the kind toward my family, toward other people in general and in the last analysis toward myself. The path of responsibility would gradually lead to that notorious self-respect and—who knows?—perhaps even to democracy. God forbid! No, no, if anything, self-respect is a form of charity, but similar to that of Punch when he says: *"Prima charitas incipit a me."* Nonsense; here I am and I need a tender creature to take care of me, me alone, to accompany and support me from minute to minute: a female, of course. Whereas my wife is now embittered, and also is almost unable to take care of the children, who are mine, too, but what do I care? She is embittered by many things and for many reasons: in the first place, apart from our particular problems, by this funereal, diabolical institution, marriage, and the resulting family; and then by the children themselves, who, though dear and darling, are a real scourge. Sure, the sacred family board adorned by the bright eyes of children!

Oh the hell with it! I've even begun to preach. Let's try getting into bed, with or without the Lord My Shepherd. And anyway there's plenty of time to think it over; it won't be the first time that I have been missing from the house for several days. They won't be upset by it; they'll wait, not even suspecting that I have decided to abandon them. I am free, no urgent demands harass me, and if I did go back I wouldn't even have to save face.

But I won't go back: I don't want to, on the contrary I want . . . what I want and what is necessary for me.

December 18

This morning I was going into town and there he was on the bus, sitting all bundled up in a funny way in a huge woolen scarf, his hat pulled down over his eyes: he must have felt cold, though it wasn't all that cold. I saw him immediately and didn't sit down, because the only free seat was next to him. I stayed on my feet, hanging onto the strap throughout the whole trip and (with a notable effort, I admit) I didn't turn in his direction, but stared at the street in front of me. I didn't know when he would get off, and every now and then I had the sensation he had gotten up. And if he were to say something to me when passing me? But after all what could he say? In any case I was ready to reply: just like that, with some vague remark. Was he looking at me? Who knows? At times I thought he was looking at me, at my shoulders and my legs, too (which aren't bad either, perhaps I've already mentioned it); I felt that weight or touch which informs us women of people's looks, but naturally I could not be sure of anything. Then the moment came for me to get off, and out of the corner of my eye I saw that he was still there. I got off, feeling that my legs were moving clumsily, and the bus left; and I began walking as best I could along the sidewalk. Well, at this point I couldn't hold out any longer and raised my eyes toward the bus window behind which he was seated: he was staring at me, as I had suspected. And what should I do? I know very well that I should have lowered my eyes and kept going, pretending that I hadn't noticed; but I couldn't stop myself from smiling, as a kind of hello. And he smiled back as he was carried rapidly away by the bus.

This evening, while he was drinking his coffee, he asked me abruptly: "What does that mean?" pointing to the ring which I wear on the fourth finger of my right hand, a simple gold band, "that you are engaged?" "No," I replied, and I felt myself blush (who knows why?) and I thought it indispensable to add: "It was left to me by an aunt who died." (the truth) He didn't say anything and left immediately.

But that isn't it: it's that . . . The sea, the sea which I have always before me, the bleak, monotonous and sad sea, gray most of the time, with its distinct, desolate voice: the sea tells me, suggests to me, sings so many things to me now! And what do I read in the stars, which are almost invisible from where I am, so that in order to see them I must shade my eyes from the light? And what is this restlessness, this sudden tremor which runs through my breast in the morning, as soon as I awake? (And from what young ladies' novels have I fished up these sentences? So what, even if I don't know how to write, as he most likely does. . . .)

What do I care if he's old!

Just a moment, I almost forgot the most interesting part: when he asked me about the ring he called me by name. He said: "Rossana, what does that mean?" So, despite his show of absentmindedness, he managed to find out my name.

December 18

Rossana (now I know that it's really her, I happened to see the two sisters together and face to face). Rossana. This morning I was going into town, for no reason in particular, out of desperation, terribly chilled, huddled up on my seat; and she got on the bus. But she never turned, she had the persistency to remain there on her feet without taking her eyes off the street; I even contemplated saying something to her as I got off, but she got off before me. I looked after her, of course, while the bus was leaving; and she in turn lifted her head and smiled at me in greeting. An open, simple, friendly smile. Now, I ask myself, wouldn't most women in her place, seeing themselves looked at, have quickly lowered their heads (or continued to look, only to prove that they weren't looking)? Rather pretty, in her little cape completely buttoned-up, the kind they wear nowadays with slits for the hands; and not too tall, as I had thought; and her legs are also beautiful.

An atrocious day, made up of feeble attempts at reading, soon broken off, and of letters crumpled up after the first sentence. In short, what should I do? Images of family life, from which I protect myself with a certain effort, assail me: the way my wife holds her head to one side when she's tired or has a cold, the screeching of the baby when I walk into the house, his confident syllabification of my name, the only one by which he knows me (Pa-pa-pà). . . . For him there is no doubt that I am and must be his protection, his fortress. . . . God, what should I do? But I have decided: I must resist, I must not go back. That much seems certain: otherwise, what would I have lived for and, moreover, what shall I be for having lived?

But why do I say Rossana? I don't know, no doubt there is no special reason; and I say it because I am a man, and a troubled man—

that's all. Nevertheless, she is a tender creature. . . . Could it perhaps be she who will support me, revive my faith in myself, in an existence perhaps as monstrous as the one I have rejected, but at least different? An existence for which at least I would not blame anyone but myself? . . . Oh, what foolishness, she is just a child and I am an old man; anyway, what right do I have to attribute to her feelings which certainly are simple manifestations of her natural kindness, her benign nature? Now just look where I have got to, out of fear, out of madness: I've almost frozen her image, isolated her from all other possibilities. One must beware of that which does not have and cannot have meaning.

This evening after having my coffee, instead of slipping right off I crossed the small sidewalk enclosure outside the café to observe her from behind the plate glass: her look followed me, in spite of all the customers crowded around the counter.

Passed later, no obligation intended, under *their* window.

December 19

Today I was in a café downtown when he came in. I was with some girl friends, but by myself for the moment (they had gone off on an errand), and I stood leaning against one of those glass cases where they keep the pastries. He walked in, saw me, tipped his hat, clutched the counter and asked for a strong drink without looking at me again. And here I could tell a lie: but to whom would I be telling it? It would be hard to tell it to myself. I mean to say, I looked at him; looked at his deeply lined face, his slightly bent shoulders, and his nearly white temples. What misfortunes, or even what boredom, must he have experienced? I had an emotion like pity, like . . . ah well, I don't know exactly what I felt; I would have liked to do something for him, offer myself to him with what little strength I had, if I could at all alleviate . . . But what? And say his troubles were all a product of my imagination?

Suddenly I don't know what madness possessed me. I started to cough, to shuffle my feet, twist; I wanted him to turn around and talk to me. In fact he turned around and who knows what he saw in my eyes (something, no doubt, which I myself was unaware of), because he came closer, not much, looking uncertain, moving sideways like a crab or hunting dog. And at last he really spoke to me: "How are you, what are you doing with yourself?" or some other sentence without any particular meaning. I replied, not much more intelligently, and we began talking; I kept worrying that my friends would come back, but luckily they were late.

Luckily? Unluckily, I should say: in fact he gained confidence and our conversation took a completely wrong turn. He spoke in a rather false tone, he was like a man who flings himself into a difficult ordeal or does violence to himself—and nothing wrong with that, quite the contrary! But then all of a sudden he came out with some insulting remarks, really insulting. I don't remember them all very well, but anyway one of the things he said was: "Ah, yes, I thought you were a romantic girl, filled with a certain anxiety to rise above your station . . ." etc.; and in conclusion he asked me to go for a walk with him. Well, the walk, let's not fuss about that (anyhow it wasn't possible because I was waiting for my friends) but "rise above your station"—what right had he to treat me like that, humiliate me like that, what had I done to him? And what does he know about my station? I replied angrily that even if I were a romantic girl it did not at all follow that I would take a walk with the first-comer; and so on, using tiresome and stupid words (but why had he provoked me?). Finally he said, blushing: "You're right, forgive me," and quickly left, as usual.

And I never want to see him again.

Yet may he not have overstepped the bounds out of timidity or desperation? In that case he would be even more worthy of my compassion, of my . . .

December 19

Met Rossana downtown; spoke to her in an absurd, awkward, vulgar way. Forgive me, Rossana: I did not want to offend you, it is because I am desperate. Did you understand that? Not very likely: did you understand that? Now look, if you fail me too, what shall I do?

Three days have passed since my flight, and I still haven't settled anything. I am torn by uncertainty, nameless anguish. I say nameless advisedly; and without omen (of redemption or hope, of definitive defeat).

Rossana.

December 20

I've forgiven him, of course: how could I not forgive him? And how could I help but forgive him after a day of sea and gray skies, or petty chores or, better, of idleness and boredom? And to be completely honest, how could I not forgive him when he looked at me like that? (Now he looks at me for a long time fixedly, pensively, sometimes he smiles at me with just the hint of a smile.)

At a moment when nobody was at the counter, he suddenly said to me: "I have two children, one two years old and the other five." I felt myself blush deep red: who had asked him? And what should I say in reply? But above all, what kind of blush was it, what did it signify? I didn't say anything. Staring at me, he added, still reflectively yet in a challenging voice: "And I love my wife very much; and she's still a child," and then, in a sort of murmur and finally lowering his dreadful eyes, ". . . almost like you."

"Excuse me," I said, as though I hadn't heard; and I ran inside.

Why, why this information? Or does he think that I . . . I . . . ? If he does think that, he is wrong: this would be the logical sequel, and so probably this is what I should write and believe. But no, if that's what he thinks he is right. He is right, right: I felt an indescribable pain at his words. Even if now, as I write, they do not seem as significant and irrevocable as at that first moment. But intelligence, and a petty calculation of the circumstances, now encourage me; my heart is still bewildered.

I stayed inside until he left.

December 20

This morning, as happens sometimes, I awoke to a renewed burst of energy. Once again I reconsidered my situation, and I have become reconfirmed in my all too languid decision (to abandon everything and everybody); but then I began discussing with myself the problem of problems, money, and that's where I came to grief. The truth is, to do something of this kind one must go far away, but really far away, move to another continent; and this requires money, and a lot of it. Well, where can I get it? I wasn't able to think of any serious solution; and meanwhile my few resources are melting away. My wife has money, a certain amount of it: under normal circumstances I could draw on that. . . . But such a base motive cannot and must not be determining, nor must it even slightly influence my decision. And so now I'm back where I began, dragging my feet, waiting for God knows what. Besides, there's not much sense in denying it: it is not only a question of money.

Either I'm deceiving myself or R. is in a particular state of mind: obviously, that young heart throbs in her face, in the flash of her eyes. And I do not want her, or rather it, to believe or imagine . . . It was my duty to disillusion her, if indeed she had any illusions. And I did so; clumsily, as always. I must have upset her; but it's better that way.

December 21

I don't want to, I can't see him. This afternoon I sent my sister to make his coffee; but suddenly I couldn't resist any longer and came out impetuously. We looked at each other, I didn't know where to put my hands (which he likes so much); I began to rinse a perfectly clean cup. He stared openly at me, with a grave smile on his face. Oh my God, what should I do?

Seriously, can I think of robbing from another woman the affection that is owed her? But then why does he look at me? Besides, this isn't it, so help me, this isn't it.

December 21

R. doesn't speak; she seems to have forgotten me, not to see me any more. In a certain sense I should be happy and instead I am agitated. Didn't I want to disillusion her, etc.? Certainly, but I cannot bear to think that she is not, is not about to become a part of my life in any way at all. To renounce her help, even if indirect, unconscious: can I find the strength for that?

As a matter of fact she does talk to everybody else, simple, nondescript people, even old women, and to her friends or dazed looking classmates with their huge and calloused hands (so different from hers); and she does not look at me. This evening she was saying that she wanted to go with them to some party or New Year's Eve dance they made detailed arrangements, taking a long time to set the hour they would meet; and she didn't look at me. . . . Or did she want perhaps in this way to invite me to the dance?

Then a man, a factory worker, and certainly already half drunk, proposed the following riddle to all present: "The greatest painter and the life of the poor." What's more, I don't know whether it can be called a riddle; perhaps it is a sentence that has to be resolved in another sentence, with the further difficulty that the fellow pronounced the word "life" uncertainly. And in fact R: said: "Well, tell us at least is it *life* or *wife?*" But all he did was repeat the saying in the same way, patted the back pocket of his trousers, and promised he would give ten thousand lire to anyone who came up with the right answer; while the people there tried to figure it out in different ways ("The greatest painter is Giotto—" "Sure, and what about Raphael and

Michelangelo?"), and R. stared furiously at the puzzle-posing, swaying customer.

Perhaps R. was stubbornly trying to find a solution, hoping to
show off. In truth, what does this obsessive sentence mean? I realized
that I was repeating it to myself on the way home; and I thought of it
again when, as often happens to me, I woke up in the middle of the
night. Now let's see: "The greatest painter and the life (or wife) of the
poor": is it possible that everything and everybody, even the simplest
factory worker, must pose us stupid and insoluble riddles!

My God, what should I do?

December 22

The sea had become alive with a thousand colors; then it turned
gray again; this morning it was radiant once again. Not he, he has
nothing to do with it: it is my sea within, which churns, which is
about to break into a tempest, which demands a victim, if necessary a
thousand victims, which shatters this mediocre boat, my life.

I don't care about all the rest.

December 22

I had a coffee; paid for it with ten thousand lire. She went into
the back room; then she came out again, took the change from the
cash register, nine wrinkled thousand lire notes plus the small change,
and handed it to me. And then, while straightening out all that dirty
paper to put it in my pocket, I noticed that among it was a white sheet
folded in quarters. There and then I was (stupidly) astonished and
raised my eyes; but she kept hers lowered. Finally I understood or, to
put it more accurately, I simply felt that I must act as if nothing had
happened.

The white sheet was a note without a signature or a salutation,
written in a still childish handwriting. Here it is:

"You offended me deeply that day we met in the city. But I have
been able to forgive you: were you suffering perhaps? Why? Why

don't you tell me? After all I might be able to do something for you, if you think me worthy of your confidence and of trying.

"But now I don't know whether I can forgive you again. You told me, without my asking, that you have two small children, that you love your wife: why? What does that mean, or what do you think of me?

"Forgive me if I contradict myself, and if I write to you, and do not think too badly of me.

"Tell me, do you really think that I want something from you?

"But you, what do you want from me?"

A singular letter, adorable. Dear R.! What do I want? Everything. Or nothing, you are right.

I must talk to her, I must talk to her immediately. But how can I make an appointment with her—provided she's willing to accept it? To hand her a note in my turn is too risky; I shan't have the courage to ask her directly. Enough: we'll see tomorrow.

December 23

He must have read my letter by now. What will he have thought? what will he say, what will he do? And tonight, what time will he come in?

December 23

I plucked up the courage, deeming it to be the best way. She wouldn't lift her eyes, it was impossible to attract her attention; but fortunately we were left alone for a moment.

"Don't you ever go out?"

"Yes," she replied in a small voice, after a long hesitation, and still keeping her eyes lowered: "Well, yes, sometimes, with my girl friends."

"And by yourself?"

"By myself," she said with a visible effort.

"And when?" Silence. "I mean, about what time?"

"Around five."

"From here?"

"Yes yes, of course, from here."

So tomorrow (if she comes) . . .

I thought that I might also go to my wife's, to pay her a visit, see the children—just like that, as if nothing had occurred. In fact she knows nothing of what is going on in my head, and it would be quite easy. Just like that, simply to try it out.

December 24

Today.

December 24

I waited for a half hour but at the end she came out—alone. I let her walk for some distance from the café before overtaking her. "Well?" I said to her in a muffled voice and as though with a painful creak of all my outraged timidity, subjected to an overwhelming pressure, "Well, can I accompany you?" She halted for only an instant, and the first flash of those eyes was not for me but circular: she wanted to see if someone was watching us. She then continued walking, pointing in a certain direction with a quick gesture. Somewhat confused and stunned, and not too sure of having understood, I followed her at a distance; I felt particularly miserable, so gray, squalid and down at heel in the red light of the sunset. She was walking rapidly and not without grace: to judge from her older sister, if it is true that older sisters trace the path for the younger ones, she will be positively beautiful in a few years (not that the other one is beautiful, but she at least is a trifle more opulent; and this is the only thing that she, R., lacks).

She was going toward a very low railroad underpass; she had to stoop to get under it, and she did it without discomposing herself, that is, without losing her poise, indeed in the act exhibiting unsuspected charms. On the other side was the main avenue; she halted at the bus stop for the city. I did not know exactly what to do, but anyway I stood there too, waiting for the bus, a few steps away from her and pretending I didn't know her. The bus came, we got on; she still didn't look at me, certainly fearing the presence of people from her section. It was night now; I felt even more miserable and unworthy in the turbid electric light.

When we reached the center of town, she got off in a not too well illuminated piazza, and I got off right behind her. And only then she turned, with a strange gravity in her look.

"Here we are; what do you want?" she asked.

"Nothing," I replied too precipitously. "But anyway," I hastened to add, "anyway, yes, I must talk to you. Can you come with me?"

"Yes."

Without looking at her, holding my head low, I made for the nearest café; which was—what a coincidence!—the very same all green one in which, a few evenings before, I had thought I could consummate my freedom.

Two adolescents, a male and a female, were standing in front of the gleaming record machine they call a *juke box* and by means of fifty or one hundred lire coins, were drawing from it languid, bedeviled, always lacerating, indefinite, reticent, sometimes deafening melodies. And to that perhaps the peculiar character of our conversation is owed, which I shall try to transcribe as I recall it.

"So what do you want?"

"Nothing, I told you. Everything."

"Everything!" she repeated as though uninterested. "But tell me, don't you have two small children, aren't you in love with your wife?"

"Yes, of course."

"I wrote to you, and that's why you think . . . But it isn't true! Or, if it is true, the matter only concerns me."

"Agreed, but why not drop the preliminary fencings? You're intelligent, I know, and can understand me; in other words, suppose I were to ask you what you want from me?"

"Ah, you were to ask me: and do you think that we can come to some agreement with this little game of who wants what from whom?"

She was suffering, in some way. Not in some way: she was suffering. And she kept her eyes obstinately lowered, and no black flash illumined me, gave me courage.

"You're right, Rossana; and forgive me if I speak to you informally, I could be your father, even your grandfather."

"I know, and it doesn't matter to me."

"And I know," (I spoke with an effort, with a bloated voice, like an asthmatic and a sentimental old man) "I know that it doesn't matter to you . . . Yes, you're right. In fact, look: I know I am here for . . . Ah, I told you just now that I don't want anything, and that I want everything . . . What nonsense, what a meaningless sentence! Put this way, you might believe that I really want everything; and instead the truth is that I don't want anything, that is, I want something immense, which I care about more than anything else: I want you to be happy, or at least not to be unhappy. Do you understand?"

I was groping, groping in a horrible darkness, prey to contradictory feelings, tender, merciless, paternal and even libidinous: I couldn't recognize myself, I was beside myself. And at this point something happened, a kind of miracle. Her obstinately lowered eyes looked up, with their flash; but a flash, so to speak, that went on and on. They looked at me, those eyes, without a shadow or a cloud, terrifying for my corruption. And she said:

"Do you love me?"

And I, I who have an answer for everything, and know how to avoid embarrassment in the most dangerous logical confrontations, did not know what to answer; and I looked back at her lost, dismayed. I should have foreseen this question, even if not quite so immaculate a form: why had I not foreseen it? Or why was my soul beating its wings abjectly, fluttering and languishing? And her chaste eyes continued to transfix me; and their look dilated inside me, filled me with shame, with desperation. . . .

"Do you love me?" she continued. "That is what counts, beyond and in spite of all our words. Do you love me?"

Alas, I do not love anyone (anyone real): what should I reply? And finally I did reply:

"Yes, certainly, but . . . You see, I really wanted . . ." (an obscure, ignominious reply).

"I understand," she said quietly. "I understand!" she said again, shouting. While I . . . I what? Who am I? "I understand. You don't want my heart to, you don't want my soul to . . . What a sad role you've chosen," and she laughed frantically. "Yes, all right, you don't want me to get ideas. All right, don't worry, don't worry about me. Go. Go!"

She laughed hysterically; or was she crying?

December 25

Christmas! A colorless, whitish, stifled sea; a strange silence along the streets, till now. A Christmas of anguish, shame. And they over there, in their ugly house . . . Well, what is the matter, what do I infer from that? I don't know . . . I don't mean without me (which may be all for the good); I simply say—they over there.

What little money I had is completely gone; but this has nothing to do with it, I could always manage to get by somehow, perhaps by pawning some precious object I still possess. And Christmas doesn't have anything to do with it either; what is it to me that Christmas is the holiday of families and children? So much the worse. I myself see in it only an oppressive, intolerable and interminable series of nuisances, and of ceremonies which the soul cannot even minimally abide. No, it is not this. And yet . . .

I decided tonight what I must do; and I shall do it soon, as soon as the right time comes.

Opposite their house is a tailor shop, on the second floor, in which two men and a girl work. They know neither set hours nor holidays:

they work all the time. The girl is very beautiful, minute, with hands as delicate as they are untiring; she hardly ever lifts her head from her sewing, and when by chance she does so and gazes distractedly at the street, her dark blue eyes shine like those secret gems of the Orient, immense, astonished; and she never parts her knees, on which she lays the cloth, but through it one can imagine the marvel of her pale, slender legs. A girl who did not deserve seeing her rights sanctioned by the Constitution, did not deserve such an insult: a true worker, gentle, quiet and steadfast, a worker out of a play. We have watched her and the whole scene so many times from our balcony. Well, in a short while I shall go into that tailor shop on some pretext or other, to watch their house and my wife from there. What I think I'm doing or hope to accomplish by that, or why I have chosen such an indirect path, I cannot say. On the other hand, am I going because of my wife or for the girl? But perhaps it is the same thing.

So I must only await the right moment (three in the afternoon, I've decided, I can't remember why); I am waiting. But how shall I spend this time?

December 26

Seen from close by, the girl is much less beautiful; there's something puffy or spongy about her cheeks and her whole skin is poor, impoverished by her shut-in life; passive, let's say, even overabundant at the more vulnerable spots. I talked about a suit I wanted them to make, feigned indecision, leafed through the swatch book; and watched the balcony across the way.

Nobody was visible behind the large windows. Then the little girl appeared, just her back; and she withdrew immediately. At last, when I no longer knew how to prolong the conversation with the tailor, my wife appeared; and she sat down right there. Sat down: it was more than one could have hoped for. She was holding a sheet of paper in her hand, a letter certainly, and began reading it.

She read: and suddenly I saw that she was crying. And at that very moment I was seized, clutched in my bowels by the desire to know the contents of that letter. . . . But I must not be too unfair to myself; also I must not lie: it was not only that futile desire that shook me. She held her head to one side, in her way, in an attitude of helplessness and dejection, and I recognized in it all of her infantile need for protection, all of her unconscious anxiety, and at the same time my own instinct of tenderness, of love for her; I recognized her and recognized myself. And, cutting short my idle conversation, I hurried across the street; I opened the door quietly with my key.

"Ah, it's you," she said to me simply, without showing any surprise.

"Yes. . . . How are you? And the children?"

"They're playing in their room. Should I call them?"

"No, leave them there. . . . You've been crying, you're still crying—what's wrong?"

"Nothing."

"Come—nothing! There must be some reason."

"Nothing, I assure you. . . ." She was still holding the letter. "Look, it's from Maria."

"Maria? What about it?"

"Read it; if you want to."

Maria, one of our cousins, was answering a letter from my wife; her brother had suddenly died a few weeks ago, and Maria was thanking her for being remembered, expressing a blind, bottomless, slightly maniacal sorrow. And my wife was crying over this death and this sorrow. Though it should be said that the dead cousin was in fact my cousin, not hers, that is, that those tears were disinterested, pure, vaster than their immediate object and more precious.

Her purity: her strength, my damnation; my salvation.

"Come, don't cry, I'm here."

I'm here: with all that this implies; with all, damn it, that this implies.

"How did you spend Christmas?"

"Nothing much; but the children were happy. The little one got a top and a telephone; the girl a kitchen with all its little gadgets. Did you see the tree in the hallway? It isn't much but it's rather gay, don't you think?"

"Why, it's lovely. You are very good at these things."

And so here I am still, in my little section of town, and I haven't gone out for my coffee (to inaugurate new habits is always difficult). But now, but this time, I have a full heart, though still tormented. It may well be that if my mad and turbulent heart were placated, everything would really be over and finished.

And Rossana? . . . The first word that comes to my lips or my pen is "tangent": a line that, coming from afar, has touched this closed circle at a single point, for a single instant, and fled away forever and ever. It may be ludicrous to compare a woman to a tangent, but there it is.

A Family Chat

◇◇◇
─────────
◇◇◇

By the way, Papa, I found a thing called "an Earth" or "the Earth" mentioned in a book. What is it?

—The Earth? It's . . . It's a small celestial body.

—Yes, but where is it?

—Well . . . come here, it's quicker this way. Do you see our sun, and over there farther that large star? Well, now you must look even farther to the right, all the way to the end, so to speak. Got it? And now do you see those very small stars, which are in fact other very distant suns? . . . Sure, you can barely see them.

—Not at all. I see them very clearly.

—Well, one of those . . .

—Is the Earth?

—No, what are you saying! One of those, I don't know which, but one of the weakest is the sun of the Earth.

—How's that?

177

—What do you mean, how's that? The Earth is the planet or a planet of one of those suns.

—All the way down there?

—Yes, indeed, but I can't tell you exactly where. To put it briefly, the Earth is down there somewhere, I think.

—And why is it mentioned?

—Mentioned! What do you mean, mentioned? How am I supposed to know how it was mentioned in your book? You mean to say because we deal or have dealt with it, because we have studied and know it?

—Yes.

—Do we know it? Perhaps someone else might know it better, as for me . . .

—But then?

—My dear child, I am not an astronomer or a space explorer. What can I tell you? . . . I believe they believe that—who knows when?— some kind of civilization flourished on that planet.

—A civilization, no less?

—Well yes, a civilization, or something. But why don't you ask your teachers?

—No, tell me, you tell me what you know.

—Wait a minute—I'll try to remember. . . . Oh, that's it. They went there and found . . . actually they didn't find anything there, very few traces of this civilization; but anyway, right in the middle of a plain there was—or perhaps it's still there if they haven't brought it back here to some museum—there was a talking machine.

—A talking machine?

—Yes; what about it?

—A talking machine: but what is it?

—A talking machine is a machine for talking, there! You know what it means to talk?

—No.

—What, you don't know? . . . But nowadays they aren't teaching you anything at the university. Though I must admit, I myself . . .

—So let's hear.

—For goodness sake. To talk . . . to talk means to talk, to emit . . . something, and I wouldn't really know what for . . . to emit sounds, I imagine.

—Sounds?

—Now he doesn't even know what a sound is.

—That's just how it is—I don't.

—Ah, you're really making progress in your scientific education!

—Yes, yes, now you tell me what a sound is.

—A sound, a sound . . . listen, I myself know very vaguely, and the little I know I don't know how to explain to you. This is your professors' job, after all!

—Let's not go into that, and just go ahead.

—A sound, a sound, well, it's a way, a kind of way to signal your presence, a sign of presence, let's say . . .

—I don't understand a thing.

—Neither do I.

—All right, it's supposed to be a signal, a kind of light emitted by living creatures to inform the others of something, right?

—Not at all. What are you making up now? A sound is a sound and it's not a light, and you don't have to be a living creature to emit it, and besides I don't know if it can be used to warn of anything. . . . Let's say, more than warning or signaling, it declares, reveals something.

—And I still don't understand a thing.

—And I believe it. But now listen, they've at least taught you this— certain celestial bodies are surrounded by an atmosphere?

—At-mos-phere?

—Oh, my God! Yes, atmosphere: a medium, what do *I* know?

—A medium?

—Oh! . . . Tell me, what are we surrounded by?

—Nothing.

—That's what you think. But the fact is that all around us, right here and all around our world, we have a whole lot of waves.

—And so?

—Well, then, you just have to imagine that the atmosphere is something of the kind, but more compact, thicker, more solid, I don't know how to put it, and it surrounds everything, everything around one of those celestial bodies.

—Solid, like a stone?

—Ah, how can I make you understand it when I myself don't understand it too well? They say that . . .

—Who is they?

—They, them, the scientists, your professors or somebody . . . They say that on those distant worlds there are a lot of things softer than stones. . . .

—And sound would be one of those softer things?

—What's all this? I just said that to give you some idea of this atmosphere, which in fact is supposed . . . supposed to be some sort of soft thing which surrounds the celestial body and its inhabitants on all sides; air, I think that's what they also call it; and then they've got water, which is a little thicker. . . .

—Water?

—Oh, it's hopeless. Never mind, it would take too long to explain, and besides, the explanation would be too confused.

—Sure, what with soft and solid, there's not much to understand. At any rate, how soft is this medium, this atmosphere or air? Now let's hear, can you pass through it?

—Mmm. Yes, I think so.

—Well, even if I still don't know what this stuff is and what it's there for, I've got some notion of it. But let's go back to the sound: where does sound come in?

—It *does* come in; because where there's atmosphere there's also sound; and where there isn't, there isn't! Now we for example don't have atmosphere, and we don't have sound either.

—In that case, sound would be a property of the atmosphere?

—But no, not at all. Atmosphere is what makes sound possible, and that is that.

—But then, we're back where we started. What is sound? A signal, as you were saying at the beginning, emitted by the atmosphere itself?

—No, no, and no. What do you mean, signal? It's not a signal. I've made it quite clear to you that sound declares or reveals something, rather than signaling.

—Declares? Reveals? I'm sorry, Papa, but when you get right down to it, I understand everything you say but I haven't understood a thing.

—Sure, I can see that, but actually it's not your fault. Listen, let's try to look at it from another angle. Imagine that a sound is a wave, waves emitted or produced by objects immersed in that medium, that atmosphere; or better yet, the way I figure it, a sort of stirring of the atmosphere itself through the activity of these objects. Do you get it this way?

—Objects emit or produce these waves, or stir up the atmosphere. . . . But why, as the result of what?

—Well, that is, they don't emit them, let's say, of their own will, or maybe they do, sometimes, if they are living beings. . . . Anyway, I repeat, these waves declare or reveal a certain state of their own.

—That is, a specific condition of the object or body necessarily produces sound?

—No sir, what's this condition, what's this necessarily? Did I say "state"? Well, I shouldn't have. Now here, sound on the contrary is produced by a motion, by some action or reaction of theirs.

—Ah, at last I think I am beginning to understand. Sound is produced by the movement of objects?

—Not by the movement in itself, and also by the movement in itself, provided the object is immersed in an atmosphere, but better put, I repeat, by an action or reaction.

—On what or to what?

—An action on other objects or a reaction to the action of other objects, obviously.

—Determined by what?

—Whatever the cause might be. I don't know, let's say two objects that suddenly come into contact, an object that falls on another, and so forth.

—Then sound would be the secondary and necessary reaction to any and all interactions?

—Well, yes, I think so. It's more or less like that.

—The trouble is that that's not an adequate definition, and you know it.

—There's nothing I can do about that.

—Or could sound be the sole possible secondary reaction?

—My boy, you'd better stop all this. What's the point of squeezing me, since nothing's coming out?

—However that may be, does it mean that a body can emit this sort of wave, this sound, by its inherent quality?

—Certainly not. . . . But then, damn it, what do I know about it? You're a first-class dunce in the sciences, but when it comes to arguing and mixing people up you're a champion. How do I know whether a body can or cannot emit a sound by its inherent quality, and anyway what's so important about a thing like that?

—I was just trying to get a better understanding of what a sound is.

—But it all depends on what you mean by body and by inherent quality. For instance, can you picture a completely inert body?

—So now we're back at motion?

—What else? It can't be helped.

—But sound is not the *only* effect of motion.

—Certainly not.

—Therefore, to repeat, the fact that it is originated by motion does not define it adequately. Provided that one were to consider this point established, that is, that it is originated solely by motion. And so, after all this discussion, I must ask you once more: what is sound?

—To hell with it all! Look, I've had enough of your riddles and complications. I don't know any more and by now I can't make head or tail of it.

—Come, come, don't get angry. Let's try another angle. Sound, how does it manifest itself?

—But what have we been saying all this time? It's waves, I told you.

—Yes, but who receives them up, or maybe nobody receives them? And if someone does, how? How do we perceive these waves?

—We? We don't perceive them at all.

—They, I mean the inhabitants of those worlds.

—They . . . it says they have—or had—a special organ.

—Oh, an organ for the purpose.

—Yes, I think so. Wait, what did they call it? An ear, I think.

—And with that ear they perceive those waves?

—Right.

—And what could this perception be compared to?

—And how would I know, since I've never perceived a sound in my life? I believe that nobody can know how, exactly how, a sound is perceived. I imagine it's a clash, an irritation of the organ, or something like that.

—Hm, let's forget it. But tell me, why are these waves produced?

—They can't help being produced. If you move an object in a medium, the medium stirs in its turn and so does its atmosphere.

—That doesn't make sense. In that case, all waves would be sound.

—Please, don't start all over again.

—Nevertheless my question is legitimate—why this particular tendency of sound? Why, in short, does sound exist?

—Ask God Almighty.

—I'm trying to say something much simpler. In nature everything has a reason, isn't that true?

—Is Mr. Know-All really sure of that?

—Until proof to the contrary. Now, this blessed sound, which in any event we do not know exactly what it is, but so far as I have understood is a necessary effect, what's it for?

—What could it . . . ?

—Wait. It can't be produced just like that, for the sake of art or decorative effect; on the other hand, you tell me it's not good for warning . . .

—My dear child, how I am supposed to know? Maybe it can be used for warning too, since you feel so strongly about it.

—Whom and about what?

—Whom? Whomever can perceive it. About what? About what's happening, of course, but possibly without any specific indication—or should I say intention? It warns that a certain thing is happening, and that's all!

—But if this thing does not represent a danger for the person who can receive the warning, what need is there to warn him?

—Good heavens, what do you want from me? Maybe, I repeat, maybe it is a generic warning, which does not compel a particular resolution or reaction, and it'll be up to the warning . . . damn it, the potential warnee, or whatever the hell he ought to be called, it will be up to him to evaluate it as a danger or not, as something pertaining to him or not. . . . And to finish, you know what I am going to tell you? I don't know what sound is, God knows what it is and why it's there, wherever it is! All right?

—Great! That conclusion I'd gotten to a long time ago, and all by myself.

—Now really, that's all I needed today, sound!

—Calm down. And let's at least go back to what started this discussion. Let's go back to the so-called Earth. You were saying that they found a talking machine there and I did not know what talking meant, and from that came all the rest. So, what can you tell me at this point?

—About what, about talking? Nothing. I can only repeat what I have already said: to talk means to emit sounds, I have no idea for what purpose.

—But in the first place, emit them how?

—How, how?

—I mean, in exactly what way did they emit them?

—But who? The machine or the inhabitants?

—Forget about the machine. There must have been some kind of a system for it—I mean the inhabitants.

—Not so fast, please. Let's get this clear. I know about the talking machine, but I don't know whether the inhabitants talked too.

—They must have. If they even had a receiving organ, it's very likely that they also had a transmitting organ.

—And why should it be so very likely? They could just be picking up sounds. But in fact, don't fret, it actually seems that they did talk, and a lot at that. But I felt I should caution you that here, as in everything we've discussed, we find ourselves in the area of mere suppositions and reconstructions that have been set up by our scientists. I don't have to tell you that, on the basis of sound reason, we who are unable to perceive sounds cannot know anything with absolute certainty.

—Yes, but I'd like to know how they talked, or how one thinks they talked? With a special apparatus?

—Now don't expect me to go into any great details. I heard by chance of that . . . that ears of theirs, but I don't recall anything else. Undoubtedly they must have talked by rubbing some organ of theirs against some other organ, or in any which way, I mean producing some particular movement in themselves . . .

—Aha, I see, but for what purpose?

—I already told you that I do not know.

—But now the story is becoming more complicated. Do you realize that with this story of the voluntary emission of waves on the part of the inhabitants, what little we've clarified so far goes right out the window? If sound is emitted deliberately it can no longer be considered a warning; what would those people have warned about, something that happened in them and was provoked by themselves?

—We're back to the riddles. To hell with the whole business!

—There, he's getting sore again. . . . Couldn't we suppose that they were communicating with each other in that way?

—One supposition is as good as another. Take your pick. In fact, if certain theories, or perhaps fantasies, are correct . . .

—To communicate by means of sounds, what a funny thing!

—Well, this wave or that, in the end . . .

—But from the way you've described them to me, those waves must have been pretty heavy, pretty massive. . . . Anyhow, what I'd like to know is: why the machine, in that case? To whom was that machine supposed to communicate something?

—You see, perhaps those were communications of common interest entrusted, so to speak, to the machine, which presumably could emit stronger waves than the inhabitants, so that it could talk to many people at the same time.

—Entrusted, how?

—Yes, registered on the machine.

—Really?

—Really, nothing! It's just a way of putting it, anybody can imagine whatever he wants to.

—And the waves emitted by the machine . . . even now being emitted, I suppose . . . have not been interpreted in any way?

—No, I don't think so. Besides, by now that emission must be so unsatisfactory that it wouldn't be possible to understand anything.

—And in general, nothing else is known?

—No, at least not that I know of. Or maybe it's just a lot of jabber: they say . . .

—They say? . . .

—But I don't remember very well. . . . They say, someone said, I don't know on what basis, that the people of that world, of that Earth, were a people of great talkers.

—That is, they were continually emitting those waves of theirs?

—Yes, all they did was emit sounds, argue, communicate or something like that, just as our magpies can't stop for a moment. And they also say . . .

—What, what?

—Why are you forcing me to tell you all this nonsense? Or maybe I read it in some novel. . . . Yes, I've heard that they loved to talk, they themselves or precisely with the help of some machine, and they particularly loved to talk in public, addressing many persons gathered together who could receive their sounds all at once.

—And to what end?

—Well, hm, perhaps to convince them of something, to get them on their side, a lot *I* know; most likely it was politics or things like that. Indeed, this seemed to be the principal characteristic of their race, these eternal speeches, which obviously couldn't help but be always more or less the same. So, as a consequence, this talking machine preserved through the millennia and the millionenia could be regarded as the symbol of their civilization. . . . But maybe all this was just invented by the author of that novel.

—Ah, so that's what—how would you call them?—the terrestrials were like? Anyway I would like to know a bit more about those funny people.

—Look, son, it's gotten late: it's time to go beddy-bye.

—Yes. So long beautiful black sky, so long fiery stars, so long Earth. I'll see you again tomorrow.

At the Station

◇◇◇
◇◇◇

The wait was interminable. Every so often the number on the black-board listing the delays of the trains was changed; it got as high as ninety minutes; the snow had probably blocked the track. The man next to me in the waiting room slowly swung his leg, sometimes whistled to himself quietly and gazed outside past the befogged window, where one could see a slice of the overhead roof loaded with snow and a heavy, hanging clock which the wind also swung back and forth from time to time. We began to talk.

"This is why," he resumed at a certain point, "I declare that faith is everything: to have faith in life, in its infinite possibilities. Little does it matter whether these possibilities are realized or not; I mean to say that faith suffices for itself, that one can live on faith alone. And it isn't even true that faith, like courage, cannot be imparted. Indeed it isn't even in question, because everyone has faith, a little faith at least, since they do live; only it remains there inert, unutilized. Instead it's a matter, after all, of reinforcing it, giving it a precise direction, in

188

short, you need some diligence, get your brains working and help luck along, otherwise, you see, you behave like those people who want to win the lottery without buying a ticket. What do you think? I too was just like you before, then one fine day I began to think seriously about how things were going with me, recognized the absurdity of my position, and so, having clarified my mind, I also got clear ideas. One especially."

"What idea?"

"Well, this is a more delicate matter, for different reasons and above all because of the prejudices all around us. . . . But after all, why not? I'm not interested in monopolizing it, and as for the prejudices, I don't give a damn. The idea came to me while listening to a certain man, a rich man without close relations, who because of cancer or something of the kind was condemned to death. The doctors had given him up; he had only a few months of life left. So I went to see him. I recall that you wouldn't have said that he was in such bad shape: cancer or not, his illness was in any event sly, leaving his faculties unimpaired. Only the look in his eyes was terrible and made you think of the Devil. Yes, you know, according to some people, the Devil sometimes appears as a very handsome young man, dressed even in evening clothes, but with such sad eyes that you can't look at them without bursting into tears, being racked by despair and so lose your soul."

"All right, fine; but why did you go to see him?"

"I'm coming to it; besides, can't you guess? I simply proposed to him that he give me half of his worldly goods if I succeeded in curing him."

"I see: apart from the exorbitant demand, you obviously are a doctor and thought that there was still something to be done."

"But no, not at all; haven't you understood it yet? Me, a doctor! I am just an ordinary person, and my whole treatment consisted in a few pellets of moist bread dough in a small round box which I had brought with me."

"But this is atrocious!"

"There, I knew that this would arouse your prejudices, and that's why I hesitated. Atrocious? Yes, I do not deny that one can find a sort of subtle and perverse voluptuousness, a horrible and delicious emotion, in playing like this with desperate hope and another man's very life; but, if you look into it, these emotions or sensations have no other basis than a specific order of, as I was saying, prejudices. Consider the reality of the facts: actually I was not playing with anything. He was condemned and nobody could do anything about it; so then, why shouldn't his inevitable misfortune be useful to someone? Or rather, and this is my justification, not his misfortune but his very improbable or actually impossible good fortune; because it is clear that if he had died I wouldn't have gained a thing, indeed I would have lost something—my time, if nothing else."

"Yet you were fostering the illusions of a dying man, and by fraudulent means."

"His illusions, you've said it: and does that seem nothing to you? As for the fraudulent means, I shall just point out to you the logical error into which you have fallen, since one cannot foster illusions except by fraudulent means. But in fact my means, even though they were such, were less so than all other possible means. And here too you must consider the reality of the facts: this man had been given up by the doctors, which means that according to the common understanding and with the usual resources of science there was no longer any hope of saving him. Yet there is always a hope, even if only in principle, and in this case it could only lie in some kind of psychic therapy: which in substance was the one I proposed to adopt. In sum, not only was I holding out to him a light of hope where others had abandoned him to his fate, but I provided the only admissible basis for this albeit very weak hope."

"Never mind that; just go on."

"Certainly it wasn't easy to convince him. He was a proud man, and what's more, strangely attached to life, I mean to say to all that which by now should have seemed vain to him, such as respect for himself and things of that kind. He did not accept the 'deal,' in fact he didn't even want to discuss it because 'one does not lend oneself to such shameful games,' because he 'would have forfeited his dignity'; he asked me to leave immediately, not to bother him, and at least show respect for him in 'the grave emotion of his misfortune' of his imminent death, etc., etc. To cut it short, he too unfurled all of his prejudices, all that he had read in his schoolbooks, dragging out a complete collection of commonplaces. It almost seemed that he wasn't the person involved, or that he was a strong young man with a hundred years of life ahead of him—if we accept the idea that prejudices are necessary in order to live. For him, of course, I was only a crook; which from a general point of view might even be true. And, in particular, he said that my bright idea was even too obvious; I was like one of those people who tip you off on the numbers to play the lottery, with the understanding that they will get a percentage from any possible winnings. He was reasoning very well, I told him, but up to a point and in the usual specious fashion. It was easy in fact for me to answer that whoever gives tips on lottery numbers lets the other party pay, that is, shares in the benefits without the risk, a relationship which manifestly did not apply here, since there was neither expense nor risk, or there was only on my side; and that also the probabilities of a favorable outcome in our case were (no point in hiding it) far less. And this double justification, or rather this way of looking at things in general, seemed to impress him; so that I drew him into a discussion, and that's all I needed. Little by little he was compelled to yield to the evidence. I was a crook, he said, but since I admitted it, how could this aspect of my character harm him? What, to repeat myself (leaving aside dignity and all those other trifles), what was he losing in the deal, or what was I trying to defraud him of that he had not already lost? But, more to the point, could he say, with absolute certainty and without reservation, that I was a crook? Wasn't there at least one chance in a million —or a billion perhaps—that I wasn't and that my medicine might prove to be effective? In sum, he had no choice and had to admit it; it would be best for him to cling to that hope, no matter how remote and evanescent it might be. . . . But I am making my story too long and certainly I am boring you. In conclusion, whilst gritting his teeth, kicking up a terrible fuss, insulting me, blabbing absurdly about the ignoble blackmail and his yielding to violence, he decided nevertheless to sign the document we drew up with the assistance of a lawyer (naturally), and in exchange, to take the bread pills. . . . Well, my story is ended; there's nothing else to say, I think. Why are you looking at me like that?"

"Horrible! But what do you mean, nothing else to say? The most important part is missing. What about afterwards?"

"What afterwards? The afterwards doesn't count, neither this nor any other afterwards."

"Oh, no, you can't leave it like that, now you have to tell me . . ."

"I see. You want to know whether he died or not and whether I became rich or not. Ah, poor me, all the intelligent remarks I made to you at the beginning were wasted. In any event, if this merely administrative aspect of the affair interests you, he did die."

"Oh, he died."

"Of course. At first he seemed to recover, no doubt thanks to my bread pills, and he certainly lived longer than expected; but then suddenly and from one hour to the next . . . from one hour to the next . . . I know quite well because I visited him all the time; the fact is he did not realize he was dying, that is, he died happy, sure of life and at peace with it. You see, you cry 'Horrible!' and look at me as one looks at a monster; but he thanked me, called me his savior. Yes, he did, but you don't understand, do you? Anyway there isn't anything to understand, as I have told you myself. I sold him gratis, that is, I gave him a gift of something precious, irreplaceable: hope! Something which he would perhaps never have known, if it had not been for me."

"That's true, that's true. . . . Yet your idea proved to be ineffective."

"That's where you are mistaken: not at all, I'd sold—or presented —a gift of hope to myself too!"

"By now defunct, in any case."

"You're wrong again. The world unfortunately is full of people condemned to death, and I did not stop there; to put it more clearly, I have not stopped and have no intention of stopping."

"What, you went on proposing and continue to propose your . . . your deal to other unhappy people?"

"Yes, to all those whom I happen to know about. A deal that is a pure loss for the moment; but one never knows, one fine day one of them might survive and in that case . . . But you perhaps are thinking, as I can see from your perplexed look, that it's your duty to denounce me to the authorities. Well, you don't seem to be the type to do it, but if you are, go right ahead: when everything is said and done, at the very worst a charge of illegal exercise of medicine could come out of this. And I'm not even sure about that, either—what has medicine got to do with pellets of moistened bread dough? Come, try to think up another heading for it."

"No, I wasn't thinking of that at all. On the contrary, all that I was going to say is that, apart from anything else, your hope is one of despair, life lived in the expectation of miracles."

"If you know another way of living . . ." he said, spreading his arms wide.

Our train had finally arrived; we set out for it together.

"Come," I said to him, "let's continue our discussion on the train. You are an unusual man and I won't deny that. . . . Besides, there are some details I'd like to know about; for example, why did you ask, or do you ask, . . . the victim for only half of his wealth? No doubt to escape death one is ready to give up everything, and so you might as well . . ."

"A matter of elementary caution, my dear sir, chiefly, though not only, in view of the well-known ingratitude of anyone who has been benefited when the benefit is no longer necessary."

"And then there's the time element; I'm sure that in those legal documents of yours there must be a deadline beyond which the survival of the first party to the bargain is accepted as absolutely accomplished? That is to say that if he wants to disinherit you, he must hurry up and die."

"In the document this and other matters are all foreseen, and the question of time is explicitly dealt with."

"And what if by chance you were to die in the meantime?"

"Foreseen, foreseen!" he exclaimed, impatiently waving a hand. "But listen now, I haven't the time to explain all the ins and outs. Because I must disappoint you: you certainly travel first class, don't you? Not me, I go second. What do you expect, I am a poor traveling salesman and I certainly can't afford it. I sell medicines, to be exact; this suitcase here is full of as many small round boxes packed with pills as you want, perhaps not very different from mine but with the official blessing. Goodbye, goodbye, it will be a pleasure to see you again; because in fact, just between us, this isn't my only brilliant idea."

And he got on the train; while I, who after all could have accompanied him, stayed where I was, looking after him. But a moment later he reappeared at the window.

"It's time to leave," he said. "So . . ."

"What?"

"Tell me, you didn't really believe my story, did you? Every now and then these little ideas pop into my head. . . . You're not the only one who gets fun out of imagining . . ."

"What do you mean?"

"Come on, anybody can tell you're a writer from a thousand miles away. And there's only one way to entertain you: tell you some cock and bull story, the same that you tell us in your turn. Goodbye," he concluded with the most elegant of worldly smiles.

I didn't manage to see where he got off. I imagine around Modena, one of those cities where you'd say that everybody is concerned with business and making money, whereas in fact there are plenty of heads bubbling with all sorts of vagaries.

Venetian Dialogue

Now let's see, my friend, what do you think of the Doge of Venice?

—Hm, I think that he must certainly be rich.

—Well . . . I am the Doge of Venice.

—Oh, congratulations; and I am . . .

—Now don't be silly. I actually am the Doge of Venice.

—In disguise among his people, even here in this den among gamblers, with the purpose of inquiring into their needs, their aspirations, and so on?

—That's quite right, and not only for that purpose.

—At any rate, so far as I'm concerned it's all one; I am quite at my ease here. . . .

—At ease?

—Yes, more or less; I'm not winning or losing.

—But you will lose without fail.

—Who can know, and where does such a certainty come from?

—All gamblers lose.

—And so be it; in recompense they gamble.

—Besides, you might even be right: it is not positively ordained that you must lose.

—That's good to hear.

—But if you were to win, how much do you think you would win?

—Who knows? Maybe a thousand zecchini, maybe ten thousand, one hundred thousand.

—Now, now, not so fast, try to be logical. You know what is the highest stake permitted here and you know—or ought to know—how much time each play with its accompanying operations requires.

—And what does that tell you?

—What time is it?

—Two o'clock in the morning.

—And at what time does the gambling stop?

—About five o'clock.

—So then, quite simply, this is what it tells me: that even if you were to win uninterruptedly, without losing a single play right to the end (and that would be truly unusual), you could not win more than eighty thousand zecchini.

—You are very fast at reckoning.

—These aren't very difficult sums.

—But what are you driving at?

—First tell me if you are convinced of what I said, that is, of the exactness of my reckoning.

—Yes, most likely . . . wait a moment. Yes, it's exactly as you say.

—Well then, look at this large pouch which is lying here.

—I see it.

—It contains precisely eighty thousand gold zecchini.

—So?

—They are yours if you go home right now. Tomorrow you can come back; you are not expected to give up gambling for the rest of your life.

—My goodness, what kind of game, I mean what kind of joke is this?

—It's not a joke; take the money and go.

—But what is the meaning of this unexpected offer?

—It means what it means and nothing more or less. I am the Doge of Venice, and you yourself have said that the Doge is a wealthy man.

—But, if anything, he is rich precisely because he is not in the habit of sharing his wealth with other people.

—Ah, my dear sir, what a sharp tongue you have. But never mind, just grab the good luck you've run into.

—Huh, there must be something behind this. What are the motives for your behavior?

—You needn't know my motives, and I don't even understand why you should be concerned about them.

—Now I see! It must be because of that lady over there, who has been making eyes at me for some time now and who has taken your fancy. Ah yes, you're looking at her in that certain way. . . . In short, you want me to leave you a free field.

—She's making eyes at you, you say? Now be careful how you talk. . . . Well, that might be it; or it might be something else. What does it matter to you?

—But now it's your turn to be logical; you might be trying to circumvent me.

—Me? Circumvent you?

—Why, I don't even know whether you really are the Doge of this city.

—And say we admit for a moment that I am not?

—That money could be . . .

—Could be what? Zecchini don't have names written on them. All you have to do is take them, whoever I might be.

—In the first place it's today I want to gamble, not tomorrow.

—But today is no longer today, that is tomorrow is already tomorrow, since it's two in the morning.

—Hm.

—So what are you waiting for?

—Hm. I refuse.

—Now, now, you refuse my offer when I have proved to you, just as four and four make eight, that . . .

—You could prove anything you please, but it won't stop me from gambling.

—Now this really is ridiculous! Why do you gamble, I'd like to know?

—What a question! To win.

—To win how much?

—Again how much! The maximum possible.

—Come now, haven't I offered you the maximum and at the same time relieved you of all the anxiety?

—Sure, sure, but it's useless, I've already told you, why go on discussing it? Gambling and reason have nothing to do with each other, and this most likely is the beauty of it. If I were reasonable I wouldn't gamble, don't you agree? I'd work at something: I'd be your Doge, for instance.

—But you too make use of some sort of reason even in gambling.

—A superior reason, my dear man, that is not commonly so called, and I do not know what it is called.

—Anyway . . .

—Now tell me, what did you ask me a moment ago?

—Why do you gamble.

—And what did I reply?

—To win.

—Well, I should have replied differently.

—How?

—At least like this: to win or to lose.

—Ah, I see (just look how things work: you make me forget my motives and now you've aroused my curiosity. . . .), I understand: you mean that nothing in the world, not even the certainty of winning could take the place of the risk for you, just as the fear of losing could not induce you to avoid running it.

—No, not exactly. You must have noticed that just before I said "at least."

—So what am I to think? Perhaps you're trying to say (but wouldn't that be the same thing?) that your psyche needs violent solutions, that a peaceful solution, inherently without strife, be it winning without gambling, or breaking even by gambling, could not satisfy you.

—No, it isn't that either.

—Then I really don't know what to make of it.

—Thinking it over, the only precise answer to your question would be that: I gamble to lose.

—To lose! Could there really be a person who is consciously averse to his own interests?

—Yes, there could be; besides, it all depends on what one considers one's true interests.

—Oh, yes . . . I think I've already read something similar in the works of a philosopher of bygone times.

—So much the better.

—A certain Pico di Tomaso . . . no, Tomaso da Pico . . . I can't remember exactly.

—And it's not important.

—He certainly meant that, total loss being the only way to placate the passion for gambling with its transports and turgidities (since winning could not do anything but rekindle it), such a loss must logically represent the gambler's final goal.

—I don't know what the man meant, nor, on the other hand, do I trouble myself with logic. Nor is that what I mean.

—Oh, this is too much! I think I have made every effort to meet you halfway, to understand you, and I'm still not making any progress. So now it's your turn, be so good as to explain yourself.

—My friend (forgive me if I call you that, if by chance you are the Doge of Venice), my friend, you can take it as certain that to lose is man's true vocation. Not only at gambling, or not only at the gambling that one does here.

—What!

—Ah yes, true and in a certain sense legitimate: don't you realize how vulgar it is to win? But of course it will be hard for you, if you are the Doge, to understand.

—It is indeed. Why vulgar?

—How do I know? Perhaps because it is a way of accepting . . . or rather it presupposes an acceptance of . . . of everything. But, after all, look at the loftiest spirits, whom you seem to be familiar with. Has there ever been any among them who consented to win in life? On the contrary, they always consider winning or victory as the very plague.

—This is absurd!

—But then also look, if you please, at the run of men: they undoubtedly want to win, since winning is fundamentally their natural mode, that is, their animal aspiration, but for that very reason they do not want to admit it in public or even to themselves. You yourself, assuming that you are the Doge, wanted to be the Doge, but did you ever confess it just to yourself, that you wanted to be, or haven't you rather waited and demanded a popular delegation or whatever to plead with you to take the office? And finally even those who proudly proclaim their desire for victory, aren't they quite careful always to justify it with some idea or idle talk about the good it will do, etc.? From which I deduce, as I have said, that man's secret vocation is to lose; or that the task of the human spirit is to refuse . . . reject . . . everything and to resist at least passively the blind force that governs us. Besides, I can leave to you the definition of the more exact motives.

—Well, well, there's some truth in what you . . . But still, what has ambition, of which obviously they—or, if you prefer, we—are ashamed, to do with the just aspirations of . . . of the . . . ?

—No, no, listen; there is only one indivisible truth, at least in an argument, to which indeed everything must be led back. So it should be easy to prove that you are being sophistical; ambition and the desire for victory seem to me the same thing.

—All right, have it your way. But until now we have dealt more with symptoms than causes. Good; but why should you leave the more precise motives to me, of all people, when I'm not even able to recognize the outward appearance of this human disposition, or whatever it should be called? Instead I would like you to investigate them separately, or perhaps we should investigate them together.

—You forget that I have better things to do: I must gamble, and I must hurry if I want to get anything accomplished. I must lose, my dear sir. On the other hand I have the feeling of having said even too much already, though it might not seem so.

—All the same, I still haven't understood.

—To lose, my friend, to lose almost purposely and for good reason: that's all. Or, for the person who does not like this kind of reason, to lose in order to lose, just like that. So you see, going back to the first point, what you would be robbing me of with your zecchini on conditions—my most favorable chance, the best part. Yes. I can assure you on the basis of sad experience that there is no benefit to be gained from winning.

—Eh, I'm beginning to realize that myself (sotto voce).

—What did you say?

—Nothing, nothing.

—On the contrary, you said something that's very comforting for me, my thesis and the people of Venice.

—How is that?

—Your government, if you are indeed the Doge, is despotic and greedy, you know it yourself.

—Oh!

—But let's leave your government aside: you can reflect at your convenience on whether you should resign or hand over public affairs to someone better than yourself. What I would like to say to you, though, and what I'd like you to do right away is . . . Now do as I tell you: you see that lady, the same lady we talked about a while back?

—I certainly do. Why, you have read my heart.

—And have you thought how it will be when you'll have had her?

—What do you mean?

—All right, think about it now.

—Oh, good heavens, yes, yes, that's right . . .

—Won't you—or wouldn't you—be left with a fist full of flies? You must know that feeling when one has obtained what one passionately desired.

—Oh, yes . . . one's left with a fist full of flies, as you put it.

—So at least do this, or begin by doing this: give up that lady. In other words, lose.

—Ahem . . .

—I don't quite know what that grunt of yours signifies; in any event, if you really haven't the heart to do it, start by offering her, without beating about the bush, that pouch of zecchini. I assure you, it's the easiest way; she is a lady, you needn't doubt it, but eighty thousand zecchini are eighty thousand zecchini.

—Sir, I . . .

—Well, what's wrong?

—No, my dear man, you have convinced me. To lose. What an intoxicating pair of words: to lose.

—In that case, goodbye.

—No once again; I . . . may I?

—What are you doing?

—This pouch of zecchini . . . is yours.

—Say, what's this!

—Take it, you're fully entitled to it.

—Without the obligation of having to leave here immediately?

—Without any obligation. Lose them without a thought.

—Then that puts a different complexion on it. I thank you.

—I'm the one who should thank you. Sir! The Doge of Venice doffs his hat to you. Farewell.

—Your servant.

—He left rather abruptly, almost running. Well, there are some strange ding-a-lings loose in the world. After all, perhaps the people of Venice ought to thank me. As for losing these zecchini, I wouldn't even think of it. I can live well on them for months, for years: let us go home without further delay. Yet, if it had to end like this, why didn't I take them right away? Ah, the mysteries of the human psyche . . . Oh, there he is, coming back in a hurry.

—Of course, my dear sir, I am the Doge and I will remain the Doge. If the true though secret vocation of men is to lose, I consider it my duty to give them a hand. And if I were to renounce that woman, it would be only and precisely to spare her the affliction of winning, as she would in any case and from any point of view. Ah, women, women! But again . . . farewell.

—Hold on a moment. Don't you want me to distill the essence of my present lucubrations?

—It must be some new deviltry; but go right ahead.

—No, it's an old deviltry. It is contained in four short words: the will to lose.

—Actually, I don't . . .

—Well, if you don't have it I envy you and pity you.

—As you wish, sir . . .

—Your Serene Highness . . .

Week of Sun

◇◇◇
◇◇◇

It was a difficult time for the heart
—Akhmatova

October 15 (autumn)

These sunny days keep coming back with intolerable persistence: blue rivulets wend through the sky into the distance, from the very first appearance of dawn the air is deep and luminous, even the shriveled leaves of the orange trees, struck by the sun, bedazzle. Well, what is expected of me, if I may ask? What am I supposed to do?

I've given orders to prune both cypresses and the walnut tree; they are still small, and if their strength is allowed to flow away through the shoots and lateral branches, chances are they'll never grow tall. I've always thought that the cat is the most amusing of animals and the reason is that, although he is so minuscule, by his movements, his behavior and supreme indifference he gives himself the airs of the king of creation. Conversely, or, one might say, similarly, I should be amused by the small walnut tree because, though an infant, it is already fifteen or seventeen feet tall. Yet nothing of the kind, rather I'd say it irritates

205

me: it is serious in its giant life, cool in its stately proportions, though when you look into it, inconclusive. Oh yes, that's just what I needed on top of everything else!

Meanwhile, as I was talking about pruning with the gardener, a woman at the window of a house across the way had got it into her head to tell me some interminable story, both pathetic and obscure. She was planting basil in a pot and that by driving the wooden peg into the soil she referred to her husband's abuses, and by fluffing up the leaves she wanted to point out that, after all, she had brought into the marriage a bit of dowry—that I understood perfectly; but what on earth did she mean to say by pressing with her fingers the soil around the planted seedlings? And why so many mysteries when, if it was really true that she had to tell something to me personally, it would have been so simple to say it with words? Most of all, I was irritated by the monotony of the sordid tale, and so I went back inside.

October 16 (dawn)

Let us sum up in an orderly fashion what little is known, through family traditions and documents, about the Wastrel.

Unlike the other ancestors, all people bent on adding to the family's prestige and prosperity, a couple of centuries ago the Wastrel seems to have dilapidated a great part of his wealth and to have left his sons in straitened circumstances so that later, as a consequence, they had quite a job to get things back into shape. And actually he (the Wastrel) is less than honorably remembered by a marginal notation (a heartfelt outburst) in an old ledger, penned by one of those sons, the Stalwart, a fact which has aroused in me a friendly feeling for the father. Furthermore it appears that one time at F., in the piazza crowded with the populace, considering himself grievously offended by the capricious behavior of his very expensive horse, he drew his pistol—bejeweled, I assume—and laid it out cold by putting a bullet into its ear without even dismounting. But I don't believe that this act of bravado was sufficient to undermine a then considerable patrimony, and everything considered, the circumstances and causes of his dissipation are shrouded in absolute darkness.

By what path did so much prosperity and so much money disappear? Very simple, here is my theory: the Wastrel, judging the times to be calamitous and all possessions insecure, liquidated the major part of his estate, and *hid* the money along with the assets in a place known to him alone; having then died unexpectedly, he did not have the time to reveal the hiding place to his sons. All this, it is true, would make him unworthy of his nickname, Wastrel, but there is nothing one can do about that. In short, it is certain that there is a treasure hidden here in my house.

Of course, but that is precisely where difficulties begin: how to make head or tail of this story, where to begin the search in an old twenty-four room house with a courtyard and garden? This is what worries me. I've asked advice from the custodian and he just laughs shyly, I've questioned for details the armoire on the stairway, which must remember plenty of things, and it tells me it knows nothing: it has undoubtedly become senile by now. As soon as I went downstairs into the drawing room, the chairs rushed to meet me, overjoyed, and to lick my hands; I've petted them, poor things, what do they know about my worries? But in the end I have solved the problem: I will ask the Wastrel in person; it is easy to harp on the respect owed one's ancestors, but this is a much too important matter. At any rate they had already promised to come some evening.

October 17

I have now taken on, as the saying goes, "for worse and for better," the little ten-year-old girl, who used to help my ailing housekeeper; her mother, who is very poor, was glad to hand her over to me—one mouth less to feed—and immediately forgot about her. The little girl is at my mercy. I'm planning to make a little housemaid of her, quick and diligent.

For some time now I've been in love with her; despite her age, you wouldn't believe it, she already has a cleft between her breasts; besides, her hair is tousled and dry like hemp, somewhere close to her mouth a tuft of down grows from a beauty mark; she is tiny, very, very thin, even haggard, only her calves are a bit thick. And as far as I'm concerned, that is all I see. When she happens to stand in a doorway, the light from outside shines through her flimsy little dress and makes her look almost naked, lengthening her legs disproportionately and carving out her crotch remorselessly. Because of this, I often go to the attic, into the sun near the small round windows, to cry: "Dear little girl, with the long legs, the small protruding belly, the meager, narrow shoulders!" Of course, but this is precisely where difficulties begin: how to make her understand my love, and how to make love to a thing like that? All the more since she has such a serious and sensible expression and is terribly afraid of me; everybody here, to one degree or another, is afraid of me. I often follow her and even I don't know why or what I hope for. I don't know where to start, I don't know what to do, and this worries me. Today, just today, I followed her, without her knowing, as she started to go upstairs: it was the time after lunch when I doze, and she felt free. She went down a long hallway, swinging her small behind just a little, and made for the attic where, as I said, I go to cry about her: I couldn't say, therefore, what mad hope took hold of me. But she stopped at the top of the small steps, those that lead to the real attic and are made of polished wood, lifted her skirts and sat down on the last step, so I suppose she was sitting there completely bare; I had hidden behind a half-opened door and I was able to see through the crack along the jamb. . . . The little girl stretched out her legs and by dint of wiggling let herself fall, still sitting, onto the step below and then down onto the others all the way to the bottom, at first helping herself with her hands and then gradually picking up enough speed to continue without them or any other movement. Then she climbed up and started all over again; and every time her flesh thumped dully against the wood. I wasn't quite certain I had understood the meaning of that message (I should say that confession), I couldn't believe what I heard and leaping out, I cried: "Oh darling, repeat it once more," trying to sound blandishing, despite my agitation. The girl, seeing herself caught, got frightened and began to whimper, hiding behind her lifted elbow. "Come on, repeat it." It was useless; she suddenly burst out weeping, with loud, racking sobs, and tried to run away. I was forced to push her into a corner and got angry, lost my head. "Repeat, repea-eat, I'm not sure I understood, darling, please repea-eat!" I yelled with all my breath, while the impact of my shouts made her legs shake, her knees bend. In no way was I able to get her to repeat the message and I was left with my frightful ignorance; but it is absolutely impossible to get anything out of her.

The dog is also afraid of me: as soon as he sees me he falls silent, turns pale like a cow struck by the butcher's mallet, sits down on his hind legs and bends his body backwards, raises his head, lifting the skin over his teeth and looking at me obliquely, turns his head away to right and left, howling feebly, as if I wanted to whip him in the face or were offering him some intolerable food, his front legs rigid and planted wide apart; then he lowers his head again and points, watching me through turned-up eyes with an expression of horror such as I have never seen on any other face. And by the most insignificant thing I can actually put him beside himself in a frenzy of terror: just by whispering a word, for instance "silty." He beats it to his pad, giving me a wide berth, and tosses around in the straw until he turns his back to me, but he twists his neck and never takes his eyes off me; I follow him all the way there, raise myself on my toes and lifting my arms, hands dangling, whisper in a cavernous voice: "Silty." At that point, he no longer knows what to do or where to go, and he begins to tremble painstakingly. He is in cahoots with the mimosa trees and the front of the house . . . in cahoots! Especially with the front of the house which does everything it likes and sprawls beatifically in the sun all day long, but as soon as I look at him face to face, from the garden, he turns pale. What have I ever done to this imbecile dog to make him so afraid? I have written to Elle, and I have prayed to the sun with tears in my eyes to leave me in peace, because there is nothing I can do about it. Or at least—to speak more clearly—to tell the truth, I know what it would like, but how is it possible to do that? It is absolutely impossible.

October 18

The ancestors came; there were only four, but the Wastrel was among them. It was simpler than I had thought. At night, in this damned village, and particularly in this isolated house, the silence is such that you could hear the grass grow; a silence that rustles and rapidly slides around corners, like a gray mouse; I could swear that it too is afraid; if I catch it one of these days, I'll show it what's what. So, I was completely alone—the little girl was asleep upstairs—strolling about the kitchen with all the doors closed and looking unconcerned, hoping, if anything, to catch the silence unawares: the kitchen is its favorite lair. I even pretended I was busy with something else and just talked to myself. The dog lying on a bench did not lose sight of me for a moment, the cat on the stove, her pupils dilated, bristled her fur every time I walked past her. "I'm telling you, they aren't coming," I said. "See how they keep their word!" But just then, from the adjoining room, came a strange sound, similar to the muttering of a winded trombone or the muffled gurgle of swallowed liquid. "That must be the ancestors," I thought, but all the same the blood froze in my veins. I listened intently without moving, the gurgling became a hollow chant, subdued and intermittent, on the measure of heavy, excited breathing, like courtiers plotting in an opera. "Se-ven of spades, se-ven of spades," several male voices hissed, gradually increasing in volume. The singing came to an end with an heroic aria of the same words, followed by a rigorous choral whistling of the same motif. "Come what may, I must go and look," I said to myself as

soon as I recovered from my bewilderment, and I rushed to the communicating door, I wasn't able to open it, it was as if they were pulling
at it from the other side; I jumped back and the door began to turn
slowly on its hinges. The majestic figure of an old woman, decked out
in ancient silks and laces appeared on the threshold, her huge beaked
nose almost touched her chin.

"Once all doors used to open toward the inside," she remarked
coldly, sizing me up with obvious disgust.

"Who are you?" I shrieked, beside myself.

"Well—the Queen of Crockery," she answered with surprise; she
dabbed at her nose with a batiste handkerchief drenched in a sharp
perfume and added: "I was cook's helper in this very kitchen when
your great-great-grandfather, the Swine, married me." And then, without paying attention to my look of astonishment, she suddenly put off
her offended Grand Duchess airs, slumped her shoulders, notably reducing her stature, a slight flush rose to her cheeks, she seized my
arm, studied me with boundless benevolence and said with deeply felt
solicitude, stammering as if there were something in her mouth: "He
is in the other room with the Wastrel and the Stalwart. Come, they
are waiting for us." And she preceded me into the drawing room, moving her feet, hidden by the folds of her skirts, with such rapidity that
she seemed to glide over the floor.

In the drawing room all the lights were on, but in the dining room,
where we were headed, only the table was lit up by a quiet circle of
light. Around it three men attired, as far as one could see, in bizarre
clothes, were sitting with their heads in the shadow and their
enormous hands, magnified by the light, resting on the red cloth: in
front of each was a small pile of cards, and a fourth pile lay ready for
me before the vacant chair. As I sat down I caught sight of three disinterested faces of which only one squinted at me for a second:
their attitudes expressed a kind of irritated waitfulness, as if I had
begged to leave for a moment to see to a sudden necessity and were
now returning to resume the game.

"They've already dealt the cards, you don't mind?" said the Queen of Crockery. We picked up the cards.

"Two in the suit has been played," muttered my partner, throwing the seven of diamonds on the cloth.

"Oh, no, I won't have that!" burst out the next player, one of my opponents.

"And why not, pray?"

"Because they sparkle like lemons in the sun and besides, they remind me too much of your dissipation."

"Stingy as ever. In any case, my dear son," came the firm reply, "I will play diamonds, whatever it may cost."

"Please yourself, but you will regret it!" said the other, giving in. So then my partner was the Wastrel, the other was the Stalwart, and the third one, therefore, the Swine, who in any case was easily recognizable—my eyes were getting used to the darkness around us. Contrary to all my expectations, the Wastrel had a stern and melancholy air and his clothes looked very neglected, although what seemed to me a hunter's cloak might very well in his time have been a curial garment. But on the other hand the Stalwart's mien was positively amiable and jolly beyond words. The very color of his cheeks, his fine, thin eyebrows, contrasting with those of the Wastrel which were bushy and grew together, the satin of his eighteenth-century rococo vest and the great attention he paid to his wig, which he smoothed every other moment with his well-tended hands, confirmed my impression.

I also realized that my partner must have excellent reasons for playing diamonds: by doing so, he undoubtedly wanted to show me where the treasure was hidden. The Stalwart took the ace and changed the suit, announcing sarcastically: "Straight all the way and follow suit." The Wastrel in turn picked up with the three, to the immense annoyance of our opponents. "Hey," he said, to attract my attention, and he winked without losing his surly expression. Then he delicately placed a five of hearts on the table, grumbling: "Double straight or what is tops, alonsanfans." And so it was clear to me that he meant point H.

"You might as well give up," the Stalwart retorted with bogus politeness. "That treasure has already been found, by me, and I squandered it with the Virgin of Falasco when . . ."

"Don't listen to him," the Wastrel broke in angrily,

The hand dragged on forever, but even before it was over I knew all I needed: *the treasure is on spot H, under a hook.* At one point the Queen of Crockery, who had been knitting at the Swine's side, unexpectedly let loose a series of dreadfully off-key vocal scales, accompanying them with vivacious movements of her hands which she seemed to run over an imaginary keyboard, showing the whites of her eyes and writhing grotesquely. Then just as abruptly she stopped.

"Don't let it upset you," the Wastrel said, to justify her behavior, "she feels the approach of the sun. There's plenty of time, old girl!" I, however, thought that I had already heard the first cock crow.

At the conclusion of the hand pandemonium broke loose and I was the chief butt. The Stalwart started it, politely addressing the Swine:

"Since I said straight, and follow suit, you might have rallied around your twenty-nine, I should think."

The Swine, who had never picked up anything, jumped to his feet and climbed on a chair; there ensconced, he scratched his crotch, then, with uncanny speed opened his arms, touched his buttocks with his hands in rapid succession, traced a sinuous upward line with his open hand, croaked *ha ha ha* without laughing, turned his palms to beat his breast two or three times, dealt his head a vigorous punch and finished off with the gesture miming the dunce's ears, or the hare's, whichever you wish to call them.

"You're mistaken," the Stalwart rebuked him pleasantly. "The two of hearts was free. . . ."

The Swine's pantomime was quite ludicrous, since he wore a long robe and never lost his astonished expression: besides, his hair, which was gray at the temples, showed around the edges of his wig. But I didn't get the time to enjoy it.

"What the hell, what the devil does alonsanfans mean?" the Wastrel was thundering at me. "It means take all your winnings home, that's what it means. You're a complete beast at cards! You had capot right there!" and other things that I did not understand, especially since, to put it briefly, we were speaking and shouting all at the same time; or, to put it more correctly, they were all shouting at me, except the Swine, who addressed to me the frenzied scratching of his groin.

"Where is the ring I left to the Nag of Venice in my will?" screamed the Queen of Crockery.

"There is no treasure. There isn't, there isn't," the Stalwart kept repeating, always in the same polite tone.

"The three of spades," shouted the Wastrel like a lunatic.

"The ring, dearest heart, the ring?" and the old woman kept coming closer, smiling mellifluously.

For my part, I only said: "I do not want to marry this woman!" But the old hag came to within jumping distance of my lap, abruptly hiked up her skirts and exposing a pair of furbelowed underpants that reached down to her ankles, settled herself on top of me; with great revulsion I felt her sharp bones dig into my legs.

Luckily their frenzy was doused by a strange itch that the Swine seemed to have communicated to the rest of them. At first the Wastrel began scratching his neck, still shouting, then, as the itch increased and spread, his tone of voice grew more subdued: now he was scratching one of his shoulders. The Stalwart also was doing it, daintily, but quite soon they all gave up every pretense at good manners, following the example of the Swine, who had even pulled up one side of his robe to scratch his knees more comfortably, standing on his chair. The old woman rolled on the floor in a fit of laughter, scratching her chest with the first tool she laid hands on, a huge salad fork. The Wastrel muttered, "For the Antigods's sake," excoriating his hip; even the Stalwart finally had to rush to the door jamb and remained there glued to it, frantically rubbing his back. They all writhed and scratched themselves furiously.

But all of a sudden they stopped, approached the table again, rested their bent thumbs and index fingers on it and remained motionless for a moment, with the serious look of people witnessing the opening of a will. Only then did I see a timid ray of light filtering between the shutters and grasp the reason for their behavior. And indeed, having exchanged glances to get set, they exclaimed in unison: "Phew, the horror of the world!" and left noiselessly, one by one, with small waltzing steps.

I was dumbfounded for a moment, then I followed them into the main room, but they had already disappeared through the kitchen door. Only the Wastrel was still there and preparing to leave in turn, in a queer position, slightly bent over, one foot lifted, hands on his shoulders and a sly concentrated look on his face, like a member of the chorus who, though still hidden by the wings while the head of the procession is on stage, gets into position for his step, waiting for the person ahead to move on. Seeing me come in, he stood up straight, very annoyed at being caught unawares; when, however, I pulled him by the sleeve, my petulance induced him, wholly against his habitual manner, to smile, and just as he disappeared he pushed me back and said: "But yes, point H, protected by a hook."

Now then, there is no longer the shadow of a doubt: I heard it with these ears from his very lips. Of course, but this is exactly where my difficulties begin: which is point H and what could that hook be? This is what worries me. In any event I'm very happy with the way the night turned out, these are really people that suit me: first, I have been able to ascertain most definitely that none of them is afraid of me; second, they too cannot stand the sun.

When I went back to my room, by the way, I surprised a small, skinny ray of it which had squeezed through the slats of the shutters and was looking for something on the floor. I managed to catch it despite its attempt to escape up the wall, I shook it up, spanked it as it deserved, flung it several times on the floor, where it thrashed for a while like a snake, and then I threw it out the window. "And now, go tell your master," I cried as it went, "let him learn what it means to meddle in my business."

October 19

She has arrived without warning and her first thought was to undress completely; then she began wandering around the house naked like that, straightening out her things, making herself comfortable for a long stay. Later, she had the fire lit *despite* the sun outside, and, still naked, settled in front of it in a large armchair, with her legs spread apart and the cat between her thighs. I fully appreciated her wisdom, because gradually as I was indolently contemplating her naked body, I felt a warmth of tranquility and repose expand under my breast like an oil stain. As a result, it was possible for the little girl to come into my room, bring something, blush to the whites of her eyeballs and leave, without my being moved.

"Oh, you're in love with the little girl. Are you looking for the treasure?" Elle said to me quietly. "Never mind. There is no point in your pretending you are crazy, I will never be afraid of you, and I will always care for you as much as I do now. Go on caressing the chairs, keep on hunting down silence, beat up the rays of the sun, I will continue to rub up against your ankles just as this cat would, if she were not afraid of you; cross the courtyard on one foot, as you do every day at twilight, I will hop after you. Every time you scratch my head I will lick your wrist. You will always discover me following behind you like a shadow, I want to be your *shadow*, I want to, do you understand? For instance, Giacomo would like me to go and live with him," she added, picking up a note from the table and flinging it into the fire. I didn't understand much about what she said, only that she is not afraid of me. This makes me suspect that she might be an ancestor, or an ancestress: Elle the Nakedressed. I will soon have to play with her, and she will rebuke me severely because I will not play the three; I always forget about the three, I seem to believe at that moment that the two will take all the cards. Or perhaps she is somebody who cares for me.

October 20

The rooms with potatoes, spelt, rye, corn and barley are arranged in a quincunx; so that must be point H—it became apparent to me this morning as I woke up; and filled with hope, I went up to the attic (all the things that are important to me take place in the attic, I don't know why). Yes, of course, but this is precisely where difficulties begin: where, exactly? Going over those five rooms again and again, I discovered at last a small square hole which looked like the vent of a fireplace's flue. And in fact there was a flue, cut vertically through the thickness of the wall, but in the upper part a few centimeters above the hole, the flue ran into a stone block which was definitely not filler, and below it plunged into the wall, but stopped, also on this side, after no more than one meter; hence it could not be the flue of an old fireplace. What was it then? I measured the depth with a small vertical stick, for my arm would not have been long enough: the only way to explore the bottom of that deception was to open a breach in the wall approximately one meter below the hole, in order to get to the flue at the point where it ended. This I did with the help of an old chisel and a rock, and finally the bottom was within my grasp.

It was peculiarly soft and consisted of light filling material, dusty sand and small pebbles, which I could easily pry loose and was in fact removing with the rest. But a goodly heap of it had already accumulated beside me, and I still did not find anything, nor did anything happen. I was in a very uncomfortable position, the breach had hit a spot just above the floor and so I was forced to work with my arm bent sideways; furthermore, I was maneuvering in the dark, groping blindly, because as I kept extracting the rubble, the bottom of the flue got lower and lower, and dropped out of sight; because of this, in short, since I must tell everything, each time with each haul my hand got a less effective grip. Thus, tired out, I decided to extract one more stone, one larger than the rest, which was already beginning to give way to my tugs, and, if nothing happened, I would desist from the enterprise for that day. The stone came out at last, and amid the dust and chunks of plaster below, I immediately touched a blunt point which just barely protruded and, to my touch, did not seem to be that of a stone but seemed to belong to something stuck deep into the bottom. Clearing the space around the extremity of this extraneous object at the cost of great efforts, I realized that it was a small stick whose substance I could not determine, but although it was quite loose now, I was unable to rip it out, as if something were holding it fast at the other end. My heart pounded wildly. I imagined, I don't know why, that I would come up with a thin ivory stick, minutely decorated with carved coats-of-arms and garlands, with a spiraling inscription in Gothic letters: "I, so-and-so, called the Wastrel by posterity, on such and such a day of the year 17— have hidden in this place a treasure of Spanish doubloons totaling, ducats totaling, etc. etc.," and a quatrain: "You who shall find this treasure . . ." But what I actually pulled up was an old umbrella handle; not all that old in fact, the kind of umbrella still used by peasants. Badly broken off and chipped, with a rusty nail still stuck in it, which goes to show that it had been previously repaired. That is why it was so hard to get out: its curvature held it in place. So I had made a kind of quatrain. Never mind, this is the hook the Wastrel told me about.

Oh, with what zest did I continue to dig! Covered with plaster, sprawling full length on the floor, my arm inside the opening up to the shoulder. But I was interrupted first by the sun who came through one of the small windows and pushed me back, and then by Elle, who showed up, still naked, and, seeing me in that position yelled in a cold voice: "Get up, you little worm, enough of that!" and dragged me downstairs. There is nothing one can do with such pests. I will continue tomorrow.

At passionate moments Elle often calls me "hairy caterpillar"; but today she said "little worm" without any tenderness. This troubles me.

October 21

"Farewell Elle, farewell love!" I was able to shout quite happily today, as I accompanied her, following a few steps behind, to the bus.

She had won. During the last few days she got me to make love to her. Our raptures took place at the end of dawn or in the early afternoon, and often, afterwards, we lingered stretched out lazily in bed, the window flung wide open on the garden and the first sun, or a delicate purple reflection that fell on our bodies and the thick blankets. I stroked her hair without speaking, the light set fire to her body from her feet to her hair, then when she arose I derived pleasure from inflicting on myself, by slightly straining on the arch of one foot, a voluptuous cramp which, the moment it grew unbearable, I relaxed, straining in the opposite direction. And that's how it went this morning too, but Elle suddenly picked up a letter from the night table and said: "Giacomo has written again." That is all she said, and this time she did not destroy the letter but carefully laid it down again. Later on, without another word, she collected her things, finally got dressed, and set off for the bus station, dragging along her two large suitcases all by herself. Just as well, the way things were working out: to start with, the sun did enough reproaching anyhow, and her tyranny was becoming insufferable. Lastly, I don't want to love Elle, I want to love the little girl.

A few gray clouds have appeared on the horizon, but they are motionless; or, at any rate, they are advancing so slowly that it will take them several days before they are above us.

In the late afternoon I went down into the garden, there was a golden autumnal glow, and I had the opportunity to witness a struggle between a caterpillar and a glowworm among shrill green leaves. Not a struggle, really, the delicate and gentle glowworm was minding her own business and I saw very clearly that it was the caterpillar who attacked her; just as I realized immediately that she was doomed to succumb; the caterpillar was yellowish, as big as a thumb, soft and hairy; the glowworm shied, trembled and tried to flee, and every time the caterpillar got on top of her, staring at her with his dull lightless unseeing eyes, so that his very presence robbed the glowworm of all her strength. That is exactly how my father, in the good old days, looked at me, and moved from side to side, if I turned my head, to stare at me again, and his face and his eyes were so hateful to me that I was completely at his mercy. And in the same way the caterpillar obtained submission from the glowworn, so that before long he was able to leave behind her husk drained of blood and go on his way, heaving like an esophagus—the esophagus of someone who is vomiting. I returned upstairs disgusted, opened the windows of my room, the window over the garden, and spat out, and then I urinated, on the trees, the blushing leaves, into the sun: the sun gilded the stream of urine, fringing it with spurts (and droplets) before it struck the ground. "Sun," I cried, "forever reproaching and tormenting sun, smug-faced, cretinous sun! Please yourself, color everything a nice golden hue, like cauliflower fritters, the peaks of the mountains and the chrysanthemums of the dead; I will not go out again and I will do nothing at all. May you, oh sun, who will not ripen the little girl and dost compel caterpillars to attack glowworms, sink forever into the ocean, sizzling like a smoking chunk of firewood doused in dishwater! . . ." That is, I would have liked to cry out. But we keep our mouth shut for fear of worse. And indeed, just from thinking this tirade, I saw the sun, who was about to set, look at me for a moment as my father used to, and when I turned to the East horror-stricken, I saw him move in that direction to stare at me again. At last, God willing, he set and went away. Elle had left, the sun had set: the evening was mine.

Tonight the little girl was dressed in an unusual way: her little dress, very tight around the waist, slipped somewhat off one shoulder, and one of her stockings—long, as dictated by local custom, and crudely held up by a piece of string—sagged below her knee like the boot of a musketeer. As a result her general look was both frowsy and pirate-like. I am terribly fond of women dressed up as pirates or musketeers! No matter what you may say about it, the fact is that whereas men's clothes are held up by the shoulders or by their own rigidity, women's clothes are held up independently by the separate elements of their bodies, and this is seen quite clearly when a piece of clothing tries to slip down along one of those bodies and gets stuck on one of those elements; and this imparts to a woman's more casual attire a highly voluptuous quality. Thus the little girl's dress held up by one of her breasts emphasized it, and the stocking did the same for her calf. It must also be added that these curves were, still are, small and hard. In short, as I looked at her I decided that my only desire was to embrace her, clasp her in my arms.

But when I tried to do so we were in the dining room, night had already fallen quite a while ago, the girl got frightened, tried to fend me off, began to whimper; at the same time the dog, watching me with that usual horrified look in his eyes, loped toward the closed door before which the cat was already pacing frantically to and fro, and emitted a hoarse and sinister yelp: in all the things that looked at me, except for the chairs, poor dears, I read convulsed horror. And that made me lose my patience; "You see, you are all afraid of me, aren't you?" I cried. "Very well then, croak, drop dead from fear, all of you!" And turning round and round, facing now the dog, now the little girl, now the cat, now the silly chest of drawers, facing them all except for the chairs, poor dears—I began to move and-up and-down murmuring tomato-potato! I crouched, making myself very, very small, then I stretched out full length and became taller and taller, lifting my arms to look like a ghost, and danced around the room on all fours with measured steps, swayed my whole body, shook, blubbered, panted menacingly. Finally I grabbed the poker, twirled it above my head, and heedless at this point of all obstacles, climbed over the tables, the poor chairs, the mantel and began a wild, irresistible round dance. "Olé!" I shrieked whenever I reached a high position, the top of a closet, for instance. But I had noticed in particular that it was my stretching and shrinking that threw them into a paroxysm of terror, and so I continued to run about and never ceased to bunch myself up and stretch myself out, beyond all measure. This lasted for quite a while; the dog escaped along the walls, emitting drawn-out yelps of pain, the cat, disheveled, trembled and hissed until it almost choked; each time I passed the little girl wept.

After sobbing for a while as loud as she could, she had quieted down and was now weeping silently, in a limp, defeated and desperate manner. But how many tears streamed down her face and fell into her lap—she was sitting on one of the andirons—they made a stain on the cloth which spread larger and larger and larger, like the stain in my chest on the day of Elle's arrival; and as she went on weeping she kept growing limper and more shriveled up until at last she remained motionless, bent in two, transparent and dull like an empty husk. The spreading of that stain of tears, in fact, calmed me, and I experienced a feeling of profound well-being, solace and great joy; yes, now I could pick her up, gather her in my arms, take her to bed, give her something and see a little color return to her cheeks, caress her breasts ever so lightly. How fragile the little girl was! The small, hard things seemed not to have roots in her body.

While she slept, I continued to dig in the attic by the light of a lantern, and still I found nothing.

October 23

The clouds arrived sooner than I had thought: this morning, awakening, I saw that the entire sky was gray; of the sun, not a shadow, and all around dense, immobile air, soft and deep silence. On days like this one doesn't walk around the house, one swims; and who would venture onto the sea outside? By the way, I have managed to catch small silences, two baby silences: they are covered with soft down and are a shade darker than their mother. Everything considered, I no longer felt up to battling silence, I let them go and they rushed into a corner of the kitchen. Up in the attic I have dug and dug and still nothing. I don't know—I am quite calm now and content: autumn swim, heart at peace, says the proverb that I have invented on this occasion.

The Sword

One night Renato di Pescogianturco-Longino, browsing through the heritage of his ancestors . . . But it is necessary to explain briefly of what this heritage consisted. The Pescogianturco-Longinos—apart from one ancestor who had gone on the Crusades—had all been more or less, as one says, solid folk, had busied themselves with the administration of their properties and, in general, with the prosperity of the family. Until one arrives at Renato's father, may he rest in peace, who represented the connecting link between that edifying series of gentlemen and his own son. To put it briefly, he had never managed to accomplish anything worthwhile, was imaginative, capricious, extremely sensitive and, above all, boundlessly lazy: a melancholy spendthrift. In short, his illustrious lineage seemed fated to be utterly corrupted and finally extinguished in him; for the appearance of such a man in its midst condemns even the most ancient family to certain death. Moreover, it is amazing to consider in how short a time the aforementioned prosperity can be transformed into straitened circumstances and then into inept poverty: in the course of only two generations. And yet that's just how things went; and as for Renato, he would have been right to regard the varied and illustrious clutter strewn about the attics of his castle as the only or almost only heritage from his ancestors, outside the castle itself, where, to cut the preliminaries short, he was now forced to live bereft of all material support.

As I was saying, at a certain moment that night he extracted from a heap of weapons and dusty saddle gear, all stuff from another age, a sheathed sword which he believed he had never seen before. In the light from the chandelier he first examined the sheath and saw that it was made of noble materials, such as velvets and silks, held together by ribs of precious and vividly dyed skins, by studs and buckles which seemed to be made of gold and silver despite the tarnish with which time had dimmed them. A work of exquisite handicraft. It really looked like a precious weapon and this especially aroused Renato's attention: he wondered whether he mightn't be able to turn it into money. He decided to take the sword to his rooms and examine it at his ease.

For some time now, Renato had been suffering from strange perturbations, presentiments which proved unfounded but which nevertheless troubled him a great deal. Confusedly he told himself that it was about time to do something and to get out of the rut; yet apart from a vague sense of guilt, a bizarre excitement often pervaded him, comparable to the intuitive flash that treasure hunters experience, when they think that they are on the point of discovering their treasure. Indeed, it seemed to him that he had great wealth within reach, though he did not know exactly what it was nor how he would be able to make use of it in any case. And now, as he sat with the precious sword before the flames in the fireplace, he was seized more strongly than ever by this sensation.

After dusting it just a bit, the sheath proved to be exactly what Renato had imagined it in the attic. It was truly a noble weapon, created by the most distinguished of craftsmen! And there was now not the slightest doubt that the studs were made of pure gold or that the stones were topazes and emeralds, whose glitter was almost extinguished by their long segregation. Nonetheless, Renato did not decide to pull out the blade; an almost inexplicable fear held him back. At last he did so with a brusque motion.

The blades which the autumn sun thrusts through a closed shutter into a darkened room, the keen darts which it flings into remote corners, the vivid tongues which sometimes leap up from a fire, were nothing beside that dazzling blade! Renato closed his dazed eyes so that its burning splendor should not wound them—and there was not much light in that ancient room. The fact is that the blade seemed to shine with its own light. Furbished, untouched since ancient times, one would have said that it was made of gold leaf if there had not been a certain obscurity which glowed, so to speak, from within (not at all dimming its gleaming transparency) and which made the mysterious substance similar to topaz itself, or perhaps some rare oriental stone. For it was transparent: looking through it Renato could see the tongues of the fire in the hearth clearly, only a bit distorted. And it was so thin that it seemed to have no body at all, an edge and a flat, or two blades and a groove, like all other swords; so thin that one should have been able to bend and crush it if an arcane tempering process had not given it as much rigidity and flexibility as any other blade of good steel.

"Good Lord!" Renato cried in a loud voice, and he touched the blade with his thumb, as one does, to test its sharpness. He should never have done it! A crescent-shaped part of his nail and a tiny piece of his fingertip were cut away even before, as it seemed to him, he had exerted the slightest pressure. Or, more accurately, and this is the point, it seemed that the blade had passed through the nail and the fingertip as if without cutting, certainly without causing pain; and that only an instant after, when he made a gesture, the neat little slice of his finger detached itself and he felt a burning sensation. "Good Lord,"

Renato said again, dabbing at the blood, "this is really a sharp weapon!"

He picked up the sword again, wishing to test it on more substantial materials. He stretched it out over a round log in the fireplace, which was burning at one end while the other was supported by an andiron, and he had barely rested the blade on it, without even pressing, when the log split docilely in two along an extraordinarily precise line; just the impalpable weight of the sword was enough. As it flashed obliquely against the flames it grew red like a bright mirror of copper and flickering words seemed to appear on it, perhaps engraved or forged in the steel, faint words in the heart of the blade, traced one could not tell where, like those which motes of sunlight can write on a breath of wind. Renato read: "I, Knight Castaldo di Pescogianturco-Longino, tempered this sword sharper than Orlando's. Now you will have no more enemies." They seemed to be verses and the characters were very old.

At this point Renato was overcome by great excitement and slashed the sword down on the knob of one of the andirons as though to challenge the words of his remote ancestor; and the furbished copper knob, a fine piece of craftsmanship, immediately rolled into the flames. So the sword cut through iron with the same ease! Leaving the fireplace and the decapitated andiron, Renato got up and began to wander through the ancient room flourishing the sword and striking it against whatever object came within his reach, at the same time yelling wild exclamations of exultation and grief such as: "Alas, all good fortune is within my grasp! Oh miserable me, now the world is mine, who will be able to resist me now?" And wherever that blade of sun struck, it did not seem to recognize an obstacle and opened up a path; it passed through everything, like the ghost of a blade. Nor did the struck object reveal any fissure unless the balance between the two severed parts was broken and it fell divided to the floor, because of the slant of the slash; and yet even when the slash could not be seen, the sword had in fact cut through, and one felt that all that was needed was a puff of air or the slightest movement for it to split completely.

Thus Renato paced through the room shouting and as he whirled about, everything that was not held upright by its own balance dashed to the floor. In this manner two stone busts of illustrious ancestors which had stood in the spaces between the three doors tumbled to the floor. The backs of several chairs fell with a crash and with a clatter of old iron four suits of armor were lopped off at the waist; the marble hand of a woman which stretched out from a niche was chopped off. The old drapes, cleaved as by lightning, slumped to the floor. Attracted by the racket, the old man who was now the castle's sole servant, appeared on the threshold with a look of astonishment. Renato shouted something at him and the old man immediately withdrew, since his master did not stop twirling the flaming sword.

That night Renato slept on the ancient canopied bed with the naked blade beside him. "This is," he thought, "the good luck I had sensed, this the treasure I was searching for without knowing, this is my great wealth and the happiness which I had expected. This sword can penetrate within the inner particles of every substance, secretly severing them, it can penetrate everything. With this sword I will carry out great exploits; what they will be I do not yet know, but they will certainly be great." And he wanted to fall asleep, but for a long time he could not: the presence of that living sword which shone beside him even in the darkness, filled him with an obscure anguish.

But day after day passed without Renato being able to find a worthy use for his portentous sword. How's that, you'll say, is it really possible that nothing can be done with such a weapon? And yet sometimes it is so. Moreover, one knows very well that the nobler a weapon is, the grander is the use it must be put to: this was not an ordinary sword and it could not be employed in an ordinary undertaking. In this way, waiting from hour to hour for the great exploit and disdaining the minor ones, at the end one also loses the chance to carry out the minor ones and winds up by finding oneself—and let this teach me something—with a handful of dust. What's more, Renato had to admit regretfully, he had no enemies to destroy, nor were there their descendants to be scattered to the four winds; there were no longer any monsters to lay low; so what could the sword be used for? I repeat, it will certainly seem strange to everyone, but just try yourself to imagine a suitable use for this sword, and you will see. On the contrary, rather than defending him from his enemies, Renato's sword itself had become his enemy (and it was to become much more so afterwards!). In fact, not being able, or not knowing how to use it, did not indeed remove the responsibility of possessing it: in truth a tormenting emotion! "Just look," he said to himself, "I hold in my hands a wonderful weapon and I do not know how to employ it." And this thought robbed him of the little peace which had remained to him. "Today," he would say to himself sometimes, getting up on a limpid morning, "today I will do something . . . something wonderful!" But the morning gave way to the afternoon and then to the evening, accompanied by this inane intention. It is true that he would take the sword with him on his walks through the fields and at each step he would decapitate the pure white lilies which swayed in the twilight breeze (faithful image of the tragedy to come!); he had also, as a new test, cleft in half the bodies of two cows which he owned; and in the castle there was no longer a head, an arm, the shoulder of a statue or a morion of armor which had withstood him. But beyond that his imagination failed him. Yes, the sword had almost become his enemy and he would have almost preferred not to have chanced on this heirloom.

And one evening the white young girl came. She was blond, nobly beautiful, supple as a reed, straight and pure as a silvery poplar. She was wearing a dress of heavy white silk that fell to her feet, and a broad belt clasped her thin waist. She looked at him shyly and sweetly.

"What do you want?" Renato frowned when he saw her appear.

"I know very well," she replied timorously, "that you do not want to see me; yet I can no longer live without you, these last days have ended all my doubts and I know that I would rather face a thousand deaths." Renato, who almost never was separated from his living sword, picked it up without thinking from the large oak table where it lay; and he raised its flaming blade between himself and the girl.

"Go away," he replied, "go away from here, leave me. Do you hear me?"

"I will not go," the girl said without retreating, though a little dazzled by the brightness of the blade through which Renato could see her faintly dimmed and distorted image, as in water which has been slightly stirred. "Nothing in the world will make me go now."

"But I do not want to be loved, I do not want to be loved," Renato said, stamping his feet and twirling his sword. And at the same time he was thinking: "Is this perhaps the great exploit?"

"Listen," he continued more gently, "listen to me, my girl. Does not the sun dress the fields with its rays of gold? Do not the birds of the woods sing? Do not the leaves and brooks murmur? Does not the wind blow freely over the ridges of the mountain? What have you to do with me and this owl's nest?"

"The sun," the girl replied, "is soot, the fields are ashes, and all nature is lugubrious and silent if you are not with me, don't you realize that, Renato?"

"Watch out, maiden!" Renato shouted and, seized by a strange intoxication he thought: "This is the great exploit!"

"I have nothing to fear," the girl spoke again, sweetly.

And those were her last words. Renato suddenly raised the weapon, and brought it down on the girl. The blade ran lengthwise through her fragile body without encountering resistance; yet the girl did not fall and, motionless, stared fixedly at her assassin with soft eyes, a smile still hovering at her lips. Her white brow shone like the dawn through a dark windowpane and the distant stars of the night hung above it; nor did one see a trace of the horrible wound. But the sword which Renato still held seemed to have left all its brightness in that lilylike body: the noble weapon had suddenly become as dull as ashes, dark as an extinguished brand, a sad and gloomy weapon indeed. And Renato himself, suddenly abandoned by his exaltation stared with consternation at the motionless girl and did not dare to believe it himself. Flinging the barren weapon far away, he cried: "My God, what have I done!"

Then the girl, though cleft in two, tried to smile at her beloved and to reassure him. And that was enough. Her face started to split open and began slowly to fall apart. A slight, at first almost invisible red line appeared, from the top of her golden hair to her neck and then down between her breasts and along the white silk; and this fissure widened and the blood began to seep out from it, bubbling slightly, especially through her hair. The smile was now a horrible grimace, an ambiguous and frightening sneer; the crack in the fragile body rapidly opened; the girl fell, divided by the implacable sword. Through the fissure the distant stars of night were already glittering gaily; before one could blink one's eye the fragile girl—an unprecedented sight!—fell in two halves to the floor beneath the eyes of her murderer. And only the placid blood joined those scattered limbs.

So it was that the glorious and portentous weapon which Renato should have brandished in defense of the good or at least to gain his happiness, instead was employed to destroy the dearest thing he had on earth.

And who would any longer want to possess this sword which, though as sharp as before, now looked so dead? The man who picked it up cast it into the deepest abyss of the earth in order to save the world from its grievous power. But other men or gods rescued it and it was given to others, through no fault of theirs, by fate. And they dragged it along in their earthly passage, like a cross, and so it will go on causing misfortune.

The Calculation
of Probability

◇◇◇
◇◇◇

Gambler, alone)

At the point I've now reached I no longer have any reason to live and I have no reason to die. But if I don't have any reason to live, isn't that already a reason, perhaps the best, for dying? And on the other hand, if I don't have any reason to die, isn't that already a reason for living, though a feeble one? Eh, if one went on like this God knows where one would end up, for no matter what conclusion one might reach, one would arrive at the truth, that is to say, the lie. . . . No doubt, if I think of the delights of gambling, I have a desire to live. Yet, conversely, if I think I must infallibly lose, as I always have lost, and considering all the consequences of that sad circumstance, I have a desire to die. Or if I think . . . But perhaps this lamentable conclusion is the same for every human pastime? (*Singing in a low voice:*) "Beauty, youth, what are you? Barks floating on the sea of years . . ." Yes, though sometimes even this floating or drifting can prove to be pleasant. Pleasant? Hm . . . At any rate, this reasoning is utterly sterile, and nothing good can come of it. In short, what to do: live or die? Ah well, let other people or another person decide it for me. (*A knock at the door*) Come in!

(*Gambler, Master-Carpenter*)

—Come in, my friend. I sent for you because this beam has been worrying me. Examine it, bang it with your hammer, do what you think best. (*The Master-Carpenter does so.*) Now the question that I wish to put to you is this: will it stand up?

—Will it stand up? But to what?

—What do you mean, to what? Oh yes, that's right, it's a good question. You are an excellent fellow. Well, first of all, would it stand up under a normal load?

—You mean to say under a weight such as it was supposed to support when it was put up many centuries ago? No, certainly not, it's too old and rotted.

—Ah, so it wouldn't stand up!

—Yet, come to think of it, it might. One never knows with these old beams.

—Ah, so it might!

—Yes, but there is a danger. The truth is, it should be replaced as soon as possible.

—No, no, let's not talk of replacing it. To be frank with you, this beam . . . this beam is extremely dear to me.

—Well then, that's another matter. Only I'd advise you to be careful.

—Just a moment, don't go yet. I'd like you to be more precise. So you say that this beam might or might not stand up under a normal load?

—Sure, that's what I told you, and there's nothing more I can say.

—But let's suppose the load isn't normal, eh? What would you say then? If, for instance, it were less than normal?

—Why, then it should be able to stand up. Of course, provided the weight is not concentrated on too small a section or, worse, on a single spot.

—Oh, so in that case the beam would not stand up?

—I don't say positively that it would not, but I believe that it would almost certainly give way.

—Almost certainly. No, you can't get out of it so easily! I want to know whether, by bringing pressure or traction to bear on a single part of this beam, it would give way or stand up. I expect to get a clear answer.

—But I can't give it to you. And in any case, it depends mostly on the intensity of the stress, that is, on the weight itself and the manner in which it is applied.

—I can't make head or tail of all this. Explain yourself. With all the special training courses that they put you workmen through nowadays, you've all begun to talk like college professors.

—You must understand that if, for example, it were a matter of a considerable weight and if one were to let this weight fall from a certain height, the probability of its standing up would be practically reduced to zero.

—Now this is a little clearer, but we are still in the realm of uncertainties. Just to understand each other, let's agree on a certain weight, let's make it one hundred and fifty pounds.

—Oh, but one hundred and fifty pounds is no weight at all for an oak beam, even if it is old and rotted. The beam would certainly stand up, even if the weight were brought to bear on one spot.

—Now, go slow—what if these one hundred and fifty pounds were to be dropped from a height of about one yard?

—Then . . . well, a yard doesn't seem much, but in that case I wouldn't guarantee it—the beam might or might not stand up.

—It might! Good God, we haven't yet got to the point. If that's how matters stand, what you must tell me is this: exactly what is the probability that the beam will bear up, under the aforementioned conditions?

—But these are unreasonable questions. . . . How am I supposed to know the exact degree of probability?

—Come now, try as well as you can to fix on a number.

—But I . . .

—Now, let's go, stop hedging! This is your trade and don't make me lose my temper. So, what is the probability exactly?

—(These rich guys are all half-nuts; luckily our union and C.G.I.L. and the C.N.F. and the C.N.C., and class consciousness, and the evolution of the masses . . .)

—What's this, are you in a daze?

—What is the probability? I'd say very, very high.

—Aha! Very, very high. But how high exactly?

—Well, I can't say exactly . . . that is . . . yes . . . about . . . almost . . . I'd say . . .

—What do you mean, I'd say? Now, my dear fellow, watch your step! Do you affirm, yes or no, that the probability is such-and-such, that is, that the beam has fifty chances in a hundred of standing up?

—Well, yes.

—You affirm it, you certify it, you testify to it, you state it solemnly?

—If you really insist, yes.

—At last. Now just wait a second, I'm not finished. Since you happen to be here, take a glance at this rope.

—I see it. It's rotted and frayed.

—Yes, yes. Now I ask you, what weight do you imagine . . . What am I saying, imagine? What weight do you think this rope can sustain without breaking, incontrovertibly?

—But I couldn't say . . .

—Here we go again. Why can't you say? You must answer with the utmost precision.

—(The best thing is to tell him anything he wants to hear so long as he lets me get out of here.)

—Well?

—At the most, this rope can support one hundred or one hundred and twenty pounds, provided it isn't used at any one time for too long a stretch.

—My good man, I'm not satisfied with your reply: one hundred pounds and one hundred and twenty pounds are not the same thing. Now, then, make up your mind.

—(Holy smoke!) One hundred and twenty pounds.

—And what about one hundred and thirty pounds?

—Yes, maybe.

—Maybe?

—I mean yes, up to one hundred and thirty pounds.

—And could it support one hundred and ninety pounds?

—No, I don't think so.

—You don't think so?

—No, absolutely not.

—So, that's clear. Now, we must set the breaking point of this rope, provided it is not used for too long a time, at approximately one hundred and sixty pounds, right? Which is as much as to say that if it is loaded with one hundred and sixty pounds, there would be a fifty-fifty chance of it breaking or not?

—It should behave just as you say.

—But what if it were subjected to a sudden jerk?

—In that case, the margin of resistance would be diminished.

—How much?

—Logically, in proportion to the length of the active section of the rope, that is, the section under stress or, in other words, to the distance between the point of traction and the point of resistance.

—Now, please, don't start all that doubletalk of yours again. In any case, just to meet you halfway, let's say the active section of the rope is one yard long. So, I repeat, how much would this diminish its margin of resistance?

—Perhaps by twenty pounds.

—Twenty, you say?

—Yes, approximately twenty.

—What is this 'approximately,' my dear man? Now let's sum it up seriatim—you solemnly testify, assert, declare, etc., etc., that this rope, working under the set conditions, has a fifty-fifty chance of supporting a weight of one hundred and forty pounds? And the same goes for this beam, right? In short, that the system formed by this beam and this rope will behave in the same way and lead to the same results?

—(I really have to get out of here.) Yes, I solemnly assert it.

—Go, go, my good man. I thank you, and here are two thousand lire.

(Gambler, alone)

—All right. So now we will make a sliding loop in this rope and, just to be doubly sure, we'll coat it with this laundry soap. Then we'll mount this chair and tie one end of the rope to the beam. That's done. Now we'll place the loop around our neck. There we are. In conclusion, I have a fifty-fifty chance of living or dying. Therefore, let fate decide for me, that's the best solution. Just one thing—in which pocket did I put the string? Ah, here it is. Let's get our hands tied up tightly behind our back, like this. Now everything is in order. In a moment I will kick away the chair and then we'll see. Actually, if this beam breaks I ought to be saved, and yet I still might get my neck broken. But perhaps I won't. It isn't so thick, after all, and there's nothing above it. Besides, this reminds me of the father who said to his son: "To kill oneself is the most idiotic thing one can do; but if one day you can't help it and I'm no longer here to dissuade you, at least promise me that you will hang yourself on this beam and this beam only." When, after his father's death, the day of despair and misery arrived and the son prepared to commit suicide precisely in the way he had been advised, the beam broke and a treasure of gold coins rained down from a hollow within it. So the young man gave up his mad plan. . . . And, in truth, what cannot a rain of gold do, even for the soul? What I'm trying to say is, that treasure apart, this beam might also be hollow, after all. So what's to be done about that? The unforeseen is an element in every human undertaking: should it be me precisely, a gambler, who should bewail such a circumstance? . . . Now then, why delay? It's time to get to work. I shall count up to three, then my foot will firmly push away the chair. So let's do it immediately: one, two . . . and three!

"Night Must Fall"*

◇◇◇
◇◇◇

Merrily I shall then praise you, flute-voiced nightingale,
Because your little mate lives with you in a nest.
—Hoelty

A horn owl is persecuting me. I hear him every night when I return home from a brothel, a literary evening, or, more often, from one of those smoke-laden evenings that drag on forever from café to café, without meaning, and yet with the awkward longing to do something, to focus on something the tremendous energy accumulated during the somnolent day, energy which from time to time substantiates for an instant around an indifferent object, and then withdraws inside us—not just intact, but indeed in a much more violent form it retreats from that object's easy acquiescence, its swift deflating; it with-

* So far as we know this is the title of a play (or drama), about which one could see large advertising posters in all the London subway cars during a certain period. We are not in a position to supply further details; but referring solely to the literal meaning of the phrase, we might remark that the author, not unexpectedly, seems to have given it a reverse interpretation (and perhaps that is why he has fallen in love with it). Almost as if he meant to say: "night must fall, vanish to make way for the day"; or in the same vein: *"il faut que nuit se passe."* In short, these are supposed to be "Lines Written by an Insomniac," like those of Pushkinian fame. (Editor's Note)

draws inside and torments us with ever renewed strength. What matters, I have always thought, is to empty oneself, discharge this energy, any energy, that comes to us from God knows where—how it comes and what it means is none of our business. If only we knew precisely how to get rid of thought, to be unencumbered by it!

He sings in the tall trees of the garden, on which my window opens, even when I invite gamblers to my room and we spend most of the night surrounded by smoke. That is, I don't hear him then; I hear him after they have left, taking away my last cent, and just before dawn, when I am trying to fall asleep. A moment before this I opened the window to air out the room, but the smoke stayed inside, it simply cooled; in there, imprisoned with the nightmare of a mosquito's buzz, I can think at leisure about two women that I would like to have. By the way, I should have said *the* gambler: in effect there is only one, but let us proceed in an orderly fashion.

I suppose that birds, like men, are divided into two schools: those who search for joy and sadness, in short, live, accumulating as many notes as they can and twisting, stretching, rounding them out endlessly; the others, basing themselves on the principle that each note already contains all other possible notes, are content to repeat one of them, not sadly however, and without the slightest feeling of deprivation. On the contrary! They are the most enthusiastic, the purest and at the same time the most serene, albeit the most credulous. This needs some clarification. Every man expects from his words (or word) a great miracle. A recent prophet went so far as to imagine—and even demand (which is what most people reproach him for)—that a word of his should, for example, give rise to a table or a chair, kill the sadness at the bottom of a heart, tear a man out of the ground with all of his roots and lift him up like a wet cat—in a word, alter the world of the senses, mountains, rocks and customs to fit his ideas. This same poet searched desperately all his life long for an idea so simple that the whole world could be happy with it; that is to say, he sought to reduce that idea to a simple word. Textually, he said: "I have an idea, such a great idea that if I could only express it, the whole world would be happy." And what else does this mean if not that he had put his faith in a little word and in nothing but one little word only? Because, if he had wanted to, he would surely have been able to express that blessed idea of his with a lot of words, and he actually tried, with the best of results.

So then, I was saying that birds like my horn owl are more trusting and enthusiastic than flautists. Indeed, the latter, seeing that the great miracle is not forthcoming, lose heart, become skeptical and if they persist (which they cannot help but do), they nevertheless persist by taking off from another point, another note, and put themselves out to declare, explain, paraphrase, catch by surprise. The former, however, do not for a moment lose faith in their brief note and repeat it, repeat it with desperate intensity, each time breathing into it all of their soul. It is curious, for example, to notice how that call of the horn owl never grows old in his throat. It is impossible for a human being to repeat more than twice any deliberate sound, any note that carries a message. The first time is what I shall call the natural alternative, and I do not intend to deal with that here. The second, the meditated or conscious alternative, requires the unconditional involvement of his entire being, the concentration of his entire life upon its highest apex. Beyond that limit even the slightest approximation requires the same effort. There is no need to say consciousness and volition are responsible for this kind of trick: to repeat an intonation or a note, *willing* to do so and being *conscious* of doing so, has always seemed to me the most torturing and stimulating enterprise. Only with one proviso can a human being repeat a word, whatever it may be: the word must wither on his lips. On the other hand, the horn owl always repeats his note as if it were completely new: what portent of strength must his soul contain, to be gathered up and cast away each time through his beak, all night long? But we who listen and know catch our breath each time: each time we undergo with him indescribable suffering, and before we can heave a deep sigh of relief a new ordeal faces him. It seems, in short, that each time the horn owl forgets what he has said a moment earlier, and that he has the time, each time, to die between the notes of his call. And between him and man there is yet another difference, which I referred to before: if a man, even the most trusting among them, were to repeat the same word many times, he would not be able to retain that joyous and serene ring and would, in the end, repeat it with sadness. But, if one thinks this over seriously, it does not mean anything: obviously if man were to die each time and be reborn at the moment of repetition, he too would succeed. Nothing will be gained by pointing out that between a human word and a *Doooit* there is a certain difference: even if, just by the way, I must inform you that I at least have known several men who did repeat *Doooit* quite often and even when it was out of place. Here is why. There used to be a man who was very similar to a horn owl because of his long white beard, his hoary eyebrows, and his round head. But he was not the one who said *Doooit,* a number of others did, mainly young people; and they meant by this to tell him that he resembled a horn owl; at night they would lie in wait at the entrance to dead-end alleys in the village and start calling. It was strange to hear them compete with the real horn owl, although the latter moved a little farther off; still, the moment came when it was no longer possible to distinguish amid all that whistling the real horn owl from the false ones, and the former ended up by diligently participating in the hoax. The old man, I was never able to understand exactly why, did not like to be a horn owl, but on the other hand liked to enjoy the cool evening air in front of his house. Once, with a smile that I would call labored, he let slip: "I have been hearing this call for thirty years!" Another old man from the same village (and this has even less to do with our subject) used to call him "Death" because he was tall and haggard and had something ghostly about him. On summer nights when he took solitary walks through the deserted alleys, one heard that lugubrious cry sound out from an impenetrably dark archway, but from which side it was impossible to say, since the hoaxers remained hid-

den. Fortunately, still in the same village, there was a famous drunkard who, when he was full of wine, called himself "the man"; until one noticed this small detail one could believe that his extraordinarily elevated pronouncements referred to all of humanity and not to himself alone, as was indeed the case. As regards this man, whose tender and pathetic soul has not yet been studied properly, I shall speak on some other occasion, dealing with it as it merits.

Doooit, let's return to that, for this *Doooit* contains all that we need to know. Someone will say: true, those young men were calling out *Doooit,* but this was not their word, nor even a real and proper word, so what sort of miracle did they expect from it? The answer is simple: they expected the old man to throw himself on the ground, writhe in despair, cry and beg them to stop, so that they could then give proof of their generosity, and repent; but the old man only broke out in a silent sweat and this got them even more excited. Furthermore, they took advantage of his poor hearing, which allowed them to repeat the sound effectively, for otherwise, as I said before, only the first *Doooit,* and at most the second, would have been dangerous. On the other hand, those who yelled "Death" really only expected the ghostly man to kill them with a puff of his breath, and they shivered in the darkness of the archways and continued merely to continue shivering.

Anyhow, the *Doooit* of the horn owl is joyful and serene, it presupposes, if I may express myself in this way, blue eyes. And indeed, it is not because of all the reasons that I have presented above that I am interested in this horn owl, the one who persecutes me. It is rather because at other times I've heard the horn owls sing at length in another place. In front of me stretched valleys, and at the horizon tall round hills shaded by the moon. The luminous haze of the oak trees in the valleys was, despite the distance, minutely curled into a porous scallop of light; closer, very close, were trees which suddenly showed leaves of a delicate green and on them, with a quick flutter, the sparrows turned in their sleep. And everywhere, a scent of nettles and moss, a shifting

and settling of minute animals amid the fronds, in short a silence akin to a leaf of watercress. The light was such that a mountain lark mistook the luminescence for that of dawn and began to sing at full voice, unrestrained, with her customary despair, only to collapse exhausted soon after: for the luminescence did not increase, and simply turned green, yellowed and declined. I have often thought about this lark who, afterwards, huddled in the shadow of a furrow and for the first time in her life tasted a wary sleeplessness. There was the bitch, too, who sat down like a sphinx and obstinately pointed the twilight: it was the hour when she began to live intensely. On God knows what, but only then did her immobile eyes become deep and alive. She never failed in that way to call forth in my memory certain types I know who, profiting from my well-known amiability in such circumstances, would come to me with old grievances; one man who would have preferred not to be dead, another was, on the contrary, fed up with too much nonsense and demanded to be dispatched instantly to the nether realm, a third simply insisted that his position be clarified so that he might positively know whether he ought to consider himself alive or dead (he was most likely about fifty, with hairs on his belly), and so on. And it was precisely because of this dog that the horn owl could not be heard right then; it was necessary to wait for one of the gamblers to leave the room.

Yet, in those days, even when I could hear him I avoided listening to him. I must draw attention in substance to a fact that seems very important to me. As a small child, long before I received those nocturnal visits, there were often sunsets and nights that I refused to listen to. To explain what I mean, I will refer to what I said further back about energy (a most inadequate word in this instance): I was afraid of myself. I was afraid that if I let myself go something too beautiful would come of it, something unbearably beautiful, a poem perhaps, or even just an idea that would explain everything and then everything would plunge back into a bottomless ravine. But to remain on the subject of energy, I felt it well up under me in an intolerable

fashion and, obeying a strange instinct for hierarchy and proportion, I pushed it back and wound up by leaving, in order to stay out of the way of opportunity.

"Too much is too much," I may have muttered; to suck up the universe like a raw egg seemed to me bad manners. And, also, I suppose, I felt ashamed, being such a small child, at already being considered (as would happen if the worst came to the worst) a great poet. The fact is actually that when once, for the sake of vertigo, I agreed to let myself be carried away by the procession on Holy Friday (which is sometimes like nights and sunsets), the result was an ugly poem, despite its having been duly written in a state of nearly total unconsciousness. This fact, however, did not put me on the alert at all; I continued to shun becoming a great man. And, personally, I still believe that I could be one today, if only that divine faculty had not withered from lack of exercise. For that's exactly how it is: when I finally considered myself old enough to be a great poet without attracting too much attention, I then realized that, albeit with all necessary caution, I should have made sure to keep fit and that at this point it was too late to do something about it. Well, what I ought to have done we can learn from the horn owl's song: continue to swallow the nights or at least permit myself to speak in their behalf.

The "gambler" is a young man who wears his hat pulled down over his large, very myopic eyes; his gaze, which can be compared to that of a nocturnal bird, is gloomy and suspicious; he is often unshaven. From his aspect one might think of him as a diabolic revolutionist, a man not at all indulgent toward himself and extraordinarily indulgent toward some ironclad idea; or a man only apparently terrifying, whose soul is actually meek beyond measure, who neglects himself and suffers for a softer idea. Something which by all evidence he is not. Because in fact he is not a true gambler, and I call upon each of you to judge the matter.

This man holds me in his power: by an endless series of won

games he has managed to acquire over me an ascendancy which has by now coagulated into an outright natural superiority. There is no point in bothering to recount how this happened; the fact is that he won a series of games at the outset and from there on with each lost game I also lost part of my chance to win in some vague future; winnings ruthlessly pursued losses in order to rob them, until one fine day a stray loss was overtaken as it was trying to rescue the meager legacy of its kind, and was forced ignominiously to relinquish it. In sum, it is mathematically impossible for me to win against the gambler. And yet I often play with him, I hasten to hand over what little money I can scrounge, and I feel terribly ashamed at not being able to do so as frequently as I would like to. What do those many days of humiliation, deprivation and hardship amount to when compared to the ineffable joy of offering my due tribute to this man? By now it seems to me that it would be monstrous, against nature, to deny it to him, and instead, what a feeling of mild well-being it is to feel so exactly right, resting in the furrow of things, part of the order of things, without futile rebellions! The gambler has certainly understood all this, because I see how with his humble and helpful manner he strives to assist me and to remove all obstacles, when it comes to arranging for a game. I have no money and he assures me that *if I should lose* I can pay him at my convenience; he guesses and anticipates all of my wishes; he excites me to wise resignation—that is, to gambling—with adroit, seemingly chance remarks about unhoped-for strokes of luck, felicitous combinations. In a word, he continues in every way to waft the smell of playing-cards all around me. Why do you think he is doing this if not to spare me the pain of losing too little, or the inevitable disillusionment that follows all sterile rebellions? And if indeed he is the figurehead through which fate intends to test me, what fault is it of his? He accepts all my money, down to the last centesimo, as something that is owed him, yes, but without pleasure; if anything, sometimes I feel him cringing behind his eyelids, which he lowers at grave moments, with, I would almost say, shame for the way my resources are ex-

hausted so rapidly. For my own good, he would like to see in me a greater dedication to the august power he represents on earth. He is therefore an incomparable friend, and not exactly a gambler; I have proved, or will prove, that a true gambler must desert parents, friends and everything else in the world.

Anyway, even when the gambler is not buzzing around me, I know all the same that it is impossible for me not to play and not to lose, and clutching to my heart the few banknotes I've been able to scrape together, I deliberately postpone the moment of the game, just as a beloved lover puts off that of the next encounter. "I am able to lose now," I say to myself and, strange but true, I could be content with this warm knowledge and could even, I am about to say, go without losing! Yes, how can one resist certain things? As a proof of which I shall briefly tell this story:

I was at that time living in a large northern city. Autumn had come. Icy winds blew from the north, an opaque mist spread over the city, Sundays followed Sundays with their snowy silence. A party of deaf-mutes arrived at my *pensione*. The old residents had departed one by one, on the sly, and there were evenings when I found myself alone in the common room with the newcomers. Handsome youths with suntanned skins and sharply delineated eyes, lithe girls with luminous manes, old ladies with plump hands, they sat for long tracts of time on the armchairs and their armrests, on the floor, on the tables, conversing vivaciously in their own way. The elderly desk clerk, sitting near the entrance, was sunk deep in the meticulous perusal of his newspaper, while puffs of white fog burst through the door from the street with each gust of the wind, silence fell. I do not like to read books, and therefore I was forced to mingle with that conglomeration of people. Call it silence! What kind of silence was that, alive and animated by the rapid gestures with which those handicapped creatures communicated to each other their most minute thoughts? They understood each other so well and, what's more, their gestures showed so little strain (they nearly looked like normal gesticulations accompanying a normal conversation), so faithfully did their mute lips carve out the words—that I had to admit I was suddenly deafened by it, and each time I struggled against violent though inert terrors. Something, therefore, more akin to an endless nightmare; yet all this has nothing to do with the story.

I was already thinking, in point of fact, that I needed a bit of home, I was already thinking nostalgically of a railroad station at dawn, of the smell of trains, when the French girl arrived. One step back: the fact is that at that time I was going with a short and ugly girl, a compatriot who made me suffer. Why she made me suffer is quickly explained: she knew she was ugly (indeed she considered herself uglier than she actually was) and so she refused to believe in the sincerity of my interest (which in itself was not, as a matter of fact, sincere, but that is something else again) and, consequently, she refused to yield to my entreaties: she was afraid she might forfeit and reveal her ugliness. In short, she made me suffer by her lack of generosity: because she either demanded my interest for its own sake, or in so far as it would have served to transfigure, in my eyes *at least,* that particular ugliness. This being the situation, the French girl arrived with her mother: the mother left a few days later after having settled her in, and the girl remained by herself, to study. She had an aquiline nose, very pronounced and so fleshless as to reveal the cartilage, a huge casque of hair cut in bangs, large, smooth buck teeth, dry, though at the same time restlessly darting, suspicious eyes; on certain rare occasions amid all their perilous flitting, these eyes found it quite difficult to recapture the mute expression which must have been their own. About the rest there is no point in talking; to find some serious defect in her would have been difficult, her breasts were in the proper place like those of all the others, her legs were not crooked, and yet from that whole body, which was exceedingly skinny, emanated a kind of stale stench: mainly, I don't know why, an odor of musty clothes similar to that handed down over the generations by peasant women who are in the habit of wearing three or four flannel petticoats. Aside from this stench (surely altogether imaginary), one could conceive of nothing more amorphous and "independent" than her poor limbs: a woman's leg or breast acquires, so to speak, for the man who observes it, a certain direction, a certain impetus this way or that; nothing of the kind for those legs and breasts. In sum, that body merely had the value of a factual remark; when I induced the girl to confess, at the price of much vehement blushing, that someone had kissed her breasts, I felt no retrospective repugnance or rapture, merely dumb surprise. And I still have not said anything about her cheeks—but on this occasion we shall say jowls: beneath a fat and healthy skin, an indefinable mottled reddishness constantly shone through, which made those cheeks more or less resemble our common mortadella sausage, with the sole difference that regular mortadella cheeks are delicate and rippling, while these revealed an intransigent quality; an intransigence, of course, which gives way all in one piece and must *often* end up, as usual, drowned in a wave of blood. The girl, aware perhaps of these characteristics, accentuated them (if one can say this) with a modest wardrobe based on ginghams and sweaters; which added the final touch to that peculiar kind of sorcery. All these words to say that the French girl was almost a total monster in the face of God and, for a man, the least attractive woman who ever existed. This was the necessary premise.

Now, one night, coming back from a sad evening out, I found her alone in the common room, where, for lack of money, she spent her free time: she pretended to be reading one of her books, but in reality she was watching her surroundings with a suspiciousness that I will not call convulsed but convulsive, and her gaze was at an angle which I thought only priests could achieve. One clearly felt that hers was a false hypocrisy, but precisely because of this the girl became more contemptible; she appeared, let us say, so miserable and lost that no one could possibly resist the temptation to humiliate her and make her more unhappy. I for one began to tell her the usual banalities that are evoked by the least gay moments, which usually contain one part truth, one part deception and, to blend the whole, a vague desire for revenge: a procedure which I might call playing the melancholy fool. Deeply gratified, I noticed that she was listening to me with great intensity, her toad eyes fixed on mine; from this I derived some reason for self-reconciliation, as if having disturbed her were a natural compensation for my not too heavy sorrows. I asked her if one had the right to kill oneself and she obstinately kept trying to prove that no, etc. . . . . It was the time when the night porter donned a huge apron and waited second by second for a particular hour to strike, after which he would declare his utmost regrets at having to turn off the light and beg us to adjourn to our rooms. This he did quite soon, leaving only a very small lamp on in one corner. In that half darkness the girl suddenly knelt on the carpet rug, so as to make use of that dim light, and, resting against an armchair, she scribbled a few words on a slip of paper; then she impulsively handed it to me and, saying goodnight, rushed away. Before she was out of the room I had already read it, and in my entire life I cannot remember having felt more clumsy; even though she was running away, I felt obliged to say something, and this produced the most pitiful mumble. The note read: "Would you like me to become your friend?" Here the story rushes to a climax. Naturally I based my defense on a purported desire not to make her unhappy because of my love, and this finally made me feel ridiculous. I went to see my compatriot; I tried to exploit the incident, by contrasting the generosity of that other ugliness with her lack of generosity; I expected thereby only to use a truth for a base purpose, but, naturally, I made the situation worse. To the bogus question as to what attitude I should take vis-à-vis the French girl, the answer I received, I cannot describe with how much kindness, was that the only thing to do would be (and was) to offer her eternal love; which happened to be rigorously true. In this way I became guilty of blatant dishonesty. In short, dishonesty leading to dishonesty, the fact of feeling guilty toward the French girl, together with fondness, soon made her completely hateful to me. So much so that I very soon saw myself compelled (I will state here, in passing, the only possible basis of moral investigation: happiness—or virtue—appeases itself, guilt always demands more guilt) to subject her to the cruelest of TESTS: I mocked her in public about her virginity and other qualities which I thought were dear to her, I teased her on every occasion and even went so far as to set the night clerk, whose senile virility was easily aroused, in pursuit of her; he in turn had the nerve to paw her one evening in my presence. The last time that I asked her to go out with me, feeling it to be my duty (this was before we broke up) I already watched the way she walked with overt curiosity: she walked flinging her feet inside their heavy boots to left and right, her head and chest in a goring position like a bull, as one sees children do when their heads are too bulky and heavy. This walk achieved its maximum expression on days of sadness. Then the feet actually danced a disordered saraband, and the head grew heavier and fell lower, accurately reflecting the intensity of her sorrow. Since our last conversation was particularly painful to her, I had the good luck to observe her on one of those days when she was in "great form"—and with that the story ends.

> *God, I thought . . . I cannot offer you*
> *prayers but accept at least this word*
> *from an honest heart: I deny you.*
> —Julien Green

At any rate, if this other life, the anti-horn-owl life, prevented me from becoming a great writer, conversely it has taught me several things of capital importance. I will mention one example, while making it clear straightaway that like all the others, it is important solely and precisely as a norm of anti-horn-owlish life. We were saying that I have come to know the only two remedies against pain, grief, melancholy and such-like scourges of mankind: they are chocolate and time; by chocolate I mean any kind of food that is sweet or even, in the less serious cases, not sweet. I'm saying that when one feels sad, chagrined, etc., it is enough to eat a little chocolate and wait a little while for everything to *mathematically* take a turn for the better. It will be said that this is pure illusion; and in that case, tell me this if you can: when this illusion arose in a person for the first time, how did it arise? Thus it is proven that it is an actual and true fact. It will also be said that, in any case, this is nothing new; but it is indeed, and this is what it consists of: as a rule men do not quite believe in that "old stuff," in spite of their proverbs, as indeed is shown by the afore-mentioned argument concerning illusion. And in truth is there any-one who experiences serious pain or regret from cold hands, when he positively knows that all he has to do to warm them is to hold them over the stove? Obviously, cold hands are experienced only by those who cannot obtain a fire. So then, if men only had my faith in the two remedies I have suggested, how could they feel pain any longer, or any-thing like it? What is new is this: that with certain faith, whenever I feel sad, I use either one of the two remedies, and thus, one might say, I am never sad, and pain has lost its grip on me; sustained by this atti-tude, I wish here to pass it on to all mankind for its own good.

Furthermore, this other life has taught me to know men, and also, through a progressive detachment from their way of see-ing things, to know all other animals to some degree. I'm proud of being able to discover the motive behind every one of their actions and affections; it is a tremendous nuisance, I dare say, to know everything about one's fellowmen so completely, and I'm getting to be sick and tired of it. To express oneself so imperfectly, I must point out paren-thetically, truly amounts to offering an undefended flank to the malev-olent who on the basis of extraneous facts will say that my "fellow" is not "man" but "all the other animals"; and unbeknownst to them they will be right—something that, as it always happens, will annoy them immeasurably.

I have learned, lastly, and still for the sake of an example, to know God.

I used to have a small cat whom, because of particular circumstances, I had to bring up away from his mother. The winter came and the cat caught cold, got hoarse; besides, his vigils near the fireplace imprinted large scorched patches on his fur. No wonder! It was the first winter he had to cope with, but those small inconveniences did not stop him from growing up zestful, bursting with good health and limpid-eyed. Since I had promised myself to replace his absent mother in every possible way, I also considered it my duty, when he reached a certain age, to train him for the hunt and to guide his first steps through the pantries and attics. But I immediately realized that there was no need whatsoever for any training in that subject: as soon as the first opportunity arose and a mouse was detected in the pantry, the kitten, set inside there, behaved as if he had found his natural element, refused all advice on the strategy he should follow and the way to lie in ambush and in no time pounced on his prey like lightning. Then I saw that he was lying on one side and was clutching a mouse not much smaller than himself with all four spiked paws; the mouse gave intermittent jerks, and the cat waited, absolutely immobile and without even tightening his grip, for that rebellious will to die out in his arms. His small teeth were gripping with the same intense precision, his eyes were closed and only slightly pinched; seeing him like that one would have thought that he was the one crushed by unbearable pain. And indeed, despite everything, I did not dare to intervene: I unexpectedly recognized the sacred character of that event.

And further:

One day from a very high window I saw a long line of horses who, old now and good for nothing, were being taken to the slaughterhouse. The line passed and I was about to withdraw when a last horse showed up: he had been left behind because he dragged one of his legs; he dragged it piteously, and in order to walk he seemed to lean his muzzle on the fist of the man holding the halter; he also seemed grateful for this help. Each step, however, forced him to caracole and lurch off balance; the asphalt-covered road was not an easy path for his crippled leg. Well, on all sides and from every atom of that horse as he dragged himself along, the city street with its raging vehicles and its stinking mankind seemed to fade grayly into a pale and uniform rustle that washed humbly along the animal's flanks like water cut by a prow. The sky, I assure you, seemed to me no higher or larger than the star-stitched canvas sometimes stretched over the arena of some circus. Only the dusty tubercular trees watched the horse as it went by; all the rest, the body of the rustle, was purulent ophthalmic matter, an indifferent mass of gray bubbling eyes. And yet I was not repulsed by it: can a toad be repulsive? Those eyes too have willed to be as they were.

Do you think I am trying to assert that the horse had won? You are wrong, on the contrary I shout and curse that he has lost. If there is anyone who, inside himself, warms something holy, in the name of this something, let him stop once and for all talking about the sanctity, the sublimity of suffering! I swear to you, on life and for the salvation of your very existence, that there is nothing more revolting, more filthy than suffering! It is not for me to explain with lofty forexamples, do not believe me if you so choose; and when all is said and done it will please me: let all that can perish; and that means all, for nothing is imperishable!

I do not incite anyone to take revenge, but how shall we be able to become better if we continue to be grateful for our ills? It is only to earthly creatures that we must render good for evil. To forgive them would indeed be arrogant, but, in the other instance, it is our sacred duty *at least* to forgive. And we shall not be able to do so unless each one remembers everything, the toad his warts, the leech her murky blood, even the peacock his beautiful feathers, and man all the good he did not possess. . . .

By the way, I am often reproached for paying so much attention to animals. "You'll end up by devoting yourself to the chicken," a friend warned me, using a nice collective singular. Now, apart from the saying of the Hindu sage—"Some attention is deserved"—with all that follows, and without going into excessive explanations, I have just now confessed that the animals are my fellow creatures, so it is no wonder that I associate most easily with them.

To conclude, yes, I will devote myself, and soon too, to the chicken: that I now declare openly on these pages for all who wish to hear it.

And these nocturnal creatures
leave facing us . . .

So come, when May is full, and gaze
with joy upon the beauty of the world . . .
—Hoelty

But the swallows begin to turn on the wires and among the folds of the mild nocturnal warmth, and utter their first chirps, hoarse with sleep and downy; the sky pales, the horn owl has ceased its song . . . it is time to go to sleep.

Or is it time instead to go outside into the pungent air, the pale glow among the trails of shining resin, the aerial swaying of pendulous branches, to meet the sun?

Shadows

Now that thieves' memoirs have become fashionable again, I see no reason why I too should not recount a curious episode of my long and, thanks be to God, fortunate career. Indeed this episode has little to do with that aforesaid career, so meager was the booty which I garnered on that occasion, but, if I'm not mistaken, its interest is not lessened by the fact that it lies elsewhere. In any case, to the facts.

I was young in those blissful days. Blissful, that is, because I was young and for this reason only: in reality I didn't always have something to put in the pot on the fire, I had not yet begun that constant and, in a certain sense, law-protected activity which later assured my well-being and even prosperity, nor had I yet encountered my life's companion, who has been so great a help to me. I was wandering around without a goal, in search of opportunities and, above all, of ideas; and so, one summer night when my hunger was making itself particularly felt (and this condition made me ready for anything) I happened to pass before a large and ancient villa, on a side road several kilometers from the nearest town, which in fact was a small village of our most remote province. And not so much because I hoped or planned anything, but rather out of simple curiosity, I peered through the gate which gave access to a park. What I saw at first made my hair stand on end.

Something had come from a side door of the building which one would have to call a ghost, if one did not want to pass for insane; something, I say, which reproduced point for point the image of these entities dear to the popular imagination; and which before my terrified eyes tottered toward the dense shadows of the park. I tried vainly to sharpen my sight so as to get a clearer view of that large white shape: the night was moonless and cloudy, the villa (with its adjacent areas) was completely dark, so much so that it seemed uninhabited.

I'm not saying that I actually thought I was in the presence of a real ghost, and yet it can be believed that that sight, combined then with my feeling of physical faintness, was such as to dismay me. But fortunately, a moment later, a new and less terrifying apparition gave the situation a more comforting aspect. This was, so to speak, a human shadow; which came out of the very same door, overtook the ghost and began a brief colloquy with it in a muffled voice. Then the shadow went back in, while the other proceeded toward the park. It had not yet arrived there, however, when a crashing shot from behind the villa made me jump. As if that were not enough, the shot was immediately followed by a sharp cry (male), and then a loud and confused hullabaloo. In short, what the devil was taking place in that solitary residence? More than one explanation flitted through my head, and all of them tragic, but at the moment I could not settle on the right one; which in any event was not long in appearing.

I had withdrawn to the shadow of a tree, from where I could follow at my ease the unfolding of events. Thus I saw, quite soon a company of persons, or shadows, cross the park directed to its rear; and just then, to give me an explanation of the enigma, a woman's voice reached me distinctly; somewhat hysterical, distorted, one could not tell whether by laughter or tears. She was saying: "No, no, it's useless, it's useless! Try instead . . . You must show that you are not afraid, and then they might even let you take command, you know. Come on, come on, we'll all go with . . ." Then about two minutes went by, and I heard a trembling voice, a man's this time, which intoned: "In the name of God I order you . . ." (The rest was impossible to hear.)

So the explanation was easy and diverting: these ladies and gentlemen were merely playing a trick on some rather simple-minded friend. They must have led him to believe that the villa was haunted by ghosts, and they were having a good time at his expense. This was confirmed by a pair of ghosts whom I saw at this point go back into the house, at a run and trying to stifle their giggling.

And now, in order to expedite my story, I will say right off that this discovery was enough to transform my generic interest, prompted by mere curiosity, into a more personal and deliberate one. In fact, what better opportunity than this could I have found to practice my profession and as a result bring my hunger to an end? To slip into the house would be the easiest thing in the world, in view of all the confusion, and because the doors were open, everything was dark, and the owners seemed to be slightly batty. I could get through the gate in front of which I was standing without being noticed, I had no doubt about that—if only I could lay my hands on a sheet! Then indeed I would truly be acting under cover.

More shots echoed from the unfathomable rear of the park, answered by one shot from the house. This seemed the favorable moment. And, in short, I glanced quickly at the deserted road, and pulled myself up by the iron grillwork of a large window that opened in the wall a short distance from the gate. From here to the top of the wall was but a step; I found myself on the roof of what seemed to be a lemon shed, from which it was not hard to drop down into the park. And now once again I stopped to reflect. There was, in the first place, this business of the shots, which worried me a bit: I still had not understood clearly at whom or what they were shooting, but the fact is that they were shooting and that caution was necessary. In the second place, though everything I said before was true, if I slipped without further ado into the house, I still ran the risk of finding myself nose to nose with someone who might recognize me, or, worse, not recognize me at all. On the other hand, how could I procure a bed-sheet or something of the kind before entering the house? And yet, as you will hear, if you know how to look and keep your head, op-portunities come flocking to you.

I proceeded cautiously through the park, sheltered by the ancient trees, so as to walk around the house and find out a trifle more about its setting; the details of which my eyes, already accustomed to the thick darkness, could now make out, albeit vaguely. Around me I heard a continuous rustle and pitter-patter of footsteps, so close as to force me at one fine moment to hide hastily behind the corner of a tower or pavilion which stood nearby. Now, from that point I could see the livid rear façade of the villa, and I could also see, somewhat obliquely, an immobile ghost against a large bush, almost at the base of the façade itself. But suddenly at one of the windows appeared a bright shadow, brandishing something that looked like a rifle, quickly joined, with a shout, by another shadow that tried to restrain it. "Let go, let go!" the first shadow shrieked frantically, and from its weapon came a shot, as one saw from the spurt of flame, in the ghost's direc-tion. Yet nothing of what I might have expected ensued: neither cries from the target shot at, nor any reaction whatsoever. The white shape remained where it was without so much as a quiver. Obvi-ously, as was confirmed for me soon afterwards, but as I had imagined anyhow, the ghost, seeing that somebody was out to get him, had fled precipitously through and past the bush, leaving its shroud behind. At any rate, employing the necessary circumspection, I at last got pos-session of the longed-for bedsheet, riddled with holes, if you wish,

since it had been filled with buckshot; but perfectly suited to my pur-
poses. And so here I was ready to enter, even if only fleetingly, the
house and lives of those people. Where for a certain time I played the
part of the mouse, of that animal with its silent and mysterious ram-
blings and circuits, which, unseen listens to our every word, spies on
all of our acts, even the most guarded, and of which no one, were it
not for its jousts and frolics, would so much as suspect the existence.

I went to the first door I found; I was inside. But, having reached
this point and not being, after all, a man of the pen, I renounce trying
to describe in detail the phases and circumstances of my reconnaissance,
and, sacrificing all possible effects, confine myself to reporting the
results. In short, I spied here, listened there, and, when called for, personally ventured on explorations, so that I was quite soon in a position not only to reconstruct the situation perfectly but also to orient
myself in the house and its immediate vicinity. As for the people, after
an hour I had learned to recognize all of them, save for some ghosts
who were roaming about with their heads always covered, and indeed, I could tell one from the other much better than might be believed; for, apart from my eyes' complete habituation to the darkness,
it must be kept in mind that all the doors and windows were flung
open to let in a glimmer of light from the outside. Finally I must
point out, though perhaps there is no need, that despite having gone
in there with the sole aim of stealing, I was kept there longer than
necessary by a sort of invincible curiosity.

So let us sum up. The house was, as I have already said, a large,
ancient house, with an exceedingly complicated arrangement of
rooms, with corridors and passageways, rooms without windows, or
one inside the other, and rooms provided on the contrary with numerous entrances, not always apparent, with changes of level on the
same floor, and huge cellars; and besides this, decorated and furnished
in character, with a profusion of all kinds of curtains, drapes and tap-

estries. In a word, an old provincial manor house; and the most suitable theater for the hoax that was being enacted. Its owners were a Count, who went about almost always followed by his factor or administrator or right-hand man, and the Count's sister. Besides, there were a friend of the house, perhaps a relation, to whom was owed the original idea of the hoax, another friend and relation, a woman friend or distant relation of the sister, and naturally the hoaxed man himself, a small, blondish, fidgety, stout Baron. In all, five men and two women, without counting the male and female ghosts, whose number for obvious reasons I cannot specify, recruited from among the villa's servants and other dependents, such as the caretakers, the farmer and his family, and God knows who else, since a farm was evidently attached to the villa. In case of need, the factor himself could become a ghost. This man and the whole party, including the women, were armed to the teeth, with hunting-rifles, old and new pistols, and all of them kept shooting wildly and purposelessly into the air, at the trees, the open windows, and the invulnerable ghosts, to which I will allude farther on. They were shooting for the fun of it, festively, to deafen and stun the Baron more and more. The Baron was also armed and also shooting, and without bothering his head over the distinctions among the various types of ghosts; but his cartridges were from time to time skillfully "castrated" (that is, in this case, deprived of lead) before being handed to him, and, in general, they tried to direct his attention and fire at objects that would not be harmed. This does not alter the fact that these interventions (as on the occasion reported above, when I had won my shroud) were sometimes tardy—and then one had to keep one's eyes open. For the rest, the entire hoax, considering the complex of circumstances, was not without serious dangers for the persons involved, and therefore seemed more exciting: a gentlemanly hoax. The house was dark for the good reason that ghosts do not show themselves in the light. One may object that it would therefore have sufficed for the Baron to leave it lit or light it again to keep them at bay; but he probably did not want this himself. In other words, his attraction to the horror was, as is wont to happen, stronger than simple fear. Perhaps he had been compelled to impose on himself, almost as a challenge, the elimination of the light, and now, formalistic and petulant spirit that he seemed to be, though fascinated, he took an almost scientific interest in the behavior of those apparitions. Or perhaps he still deluded himself into thinking that he could put his finger on the deception: a delusion, if anything, of the vainest, since the deception was so crude that one had to be, like him, completely hopeless not to see through it. And, lastly, I found matters already arranged and it is not my business to explain how or why they were so arranged. I will merely add that, to avoid mishaps and meet all eventualities, the main fuse had been removed.

Shouting, laughing (but on the sly), shooting, frisking about in a thousand ways; the ghosts appearing, disappearing, slithering away; all those persons skipped freely and capriciously from room to room, upstairs, downstairs, inside and out, in an incessant to-and-fro. The entire house, from the cellars to the attic, together with the park, was the sphere of their exploits, nor was there a room or pavilion one could not enter. For me, the only way that I had to maintain my position was also to behave as a pretty active ghost, and so at times I followed the route of my companions, at times I went off on my own, to see to *my* activities; and either I passed completely unnoticed or, what amounts to the same thing, my presence, when noticed, was everywhere considered natural. If someone addressed me, the circumstances allowed me to reply only with a gesture, or not reply at all.

I started out by visiting the kitchen, where without difficulty I found something to chew on. Immediately after, I set about feeding my pockets, since they too were starved. But these great gentlemen, may God protect them, must have had holes in their hands, along with many other aristocratic propensities, and among the lot of them they kept in the house such a tiny sum that I am ashamed to mention it (it is true that I found a trifle more in the factor's house). I decided to get my hands on the valuables, and I was no luckier there: if they actually had objects of any value, they were certainly wearing them or followed a deplorable custom and kept them buried, useful to no one, in a bank. On the women's dressing tables I found a pair of earrings, two or three little brooches, a bracelet, and a few other paltry jewels, what's more of mediocre alloy, and that was almost all. Overall result: enough to live on for a month, or two at the most. Ah well, nothing to fret about: our profession would be too easy if one always found what one was looking for at the very start. No, it too demands prudence, assiduity, industrious perseverance, fortitude, and I don't know how many other more or less cardinal virtues.

"In the name of God," ("Our savior," a woman suggested) "ah . . . yes, in the name of God our savior, I command you to show yourself fully. And now bend to the right. And now to the left. Now vanish again into hell." ("That's wrong, you've got to say: in the depths of hell, out of which you have risen . . .")

Here was the Baron again, in front of the park wall; encircled by the company, he was giving orders to a ragged and makeshift dummy which someone was maneuvering with a stick from the other side.

"See how it left?"

"Oh, but . . . look, there's another one. There, over there . . ."

But this one did not respond to the exorcisms, perhaps because the manipulator had just left it there, and the Baron discharged into it all the bullets in his huge pistol.

"Oh sure, and what do you think you've accomplished?"

The good man ran toward the house, clutching his face in his hands.

"Listen, come here, honestly now," he stammered a moment later, grabbing by the chest and then tightly embracing his first friend, who, you should know, had conceived the whole thing, "will you swear to me, swear to me on your honor as a gentleman that this is not all a trick, that you're not playing a joke on me, that . . ."

"I swear it," was this man's loud and solemn answer, who seemed to have a rather summary notion of a gentleman's honor, or had been taught by the Jesuits to cross his fingers behind his back, lift his right leg off the ground, and I don't know what else. The Baron almost burst into tears.

This was not the first time that the behavior of Lorenzo (the second friend) and of Marta (the Count's sister) had aroused my curiosity. While in fact this dramatic colloquy was taking place, these two were not paying it the slightest attention and instead were staring at each other intensely, or so it seemed. Or, better, it was the man who was half turned to the woman and was staring at her, while she was looking with an abstracted air at the point of her shoe. The man could have been about forty, and was tall and well built; the woman two or three years older, as could chiefly be gathered from certain weary gestures, since it was also obvious that, dark-haired, supple and with a dazzling, almost phosphorescent complexion, she had remained as fresh as a young girl. But at that point the Count and his faithful factor, both of whom had certainly skipped away to take care of further preparations, noisily returned, cutting short their reverie and my observation.

Other majestic ghosts, full or empty, lingered or slowly paced through all, I repeat, all the rooms of the house; the second kind, the empty ones, had to be switched around frequently so that the Baron, driven by now by the audacity of desperation, should not come too close and find himself holding a bedsheet. I'm talking again about these ghosts, some of which were truly "successful," in order to hark back to the curious impression they made on me, and which, I have every reason to believe, they also made on the Count and his companions. To say it without circumlocution, there in the darkness they sometimes frightened us, too. And, besides, I have forgotten to tell you all the accessories of the *mise en scène,* such as the dragging of chains, the moans, the laments, the thwack of fluttering shrouds, which were lugubrious and bloodcurdling, no doubt about that. Add to this the heart-rending shrieks issuing unexpectedly from the Baron, and our feelings being what they were, you can imagine his.

And so, with these games, the time passed. It was now quite late in the night.

"So will you come, will you?"

In Lorenzo's voice there was an almost frantic urgency. He and Marta, coming into the room where I was, which they thought to be empty, had made me get out of the way by stepping behind a door-curtain. Well, you know, behind the curtain there was obviously a door, flung open like all of them, and so I could easily have gone about my business; but instead I stayed there.

"Will you come?"

"No, I can't . . . I can't."

"But why? Don't you want to tell me, can't you tell me why?"

"Just like that. No, really, Lorenzo, I can't. I . . . I never go out."

"It's not true. You go out often, in your car and even on foot, you go to see your aunts, you do a hundred things in the village. And it would be so easy for you. . . . Come to my house only for half an hour, I swear to you that I won't keep you more than a half hour. There's no one at my house, you know that, I live alone like a dog. Well? Will you come?"

"No . . . no. Besides if my brother . . ."

"Your brother! You never stop talking about him. At your age you can do whatever you wish. Anyway, your brother isn't a fool; even if . . . he must certainly realize that you . . ."

"You don't know him."

"Not again! But what does it matter anyhow? Listen, there's no need for your brother to know. But maybe you don't want to because you think that I . . . No, that's not what I want, Marta, I would just like to have a good talk with you for once, Marta, calmly, without fear.

. . . Or maybe . . . But you see, I'm doing all the talking, as usual. Tell me, so I can understand, say something."

"But I have nothing to say; you know everything, I have already told you everything."

"What did you tell me? All you do is repeat that you can't come to see me, and that you can't do anything else either. If you at least said that you don't want to."

"There, yes, I don't want to."

"But this is false! False in the sight of God, it's a lie, a curse. Listen, can't you for once give way, give way just like that to your feelings, break the obscure tangle you have inside, that tangle of snakes, of cold things which chill your heart, and find a voice, words, words to say to another being, even a fool like me. . . ."

"Lorenzo, don't torment me."

"Listen, Marta, I love you. But perhaps you don't believe it, you aren't able to believe it, even if sometimes you try to. And you call this lack of trust. But it is not simply lack of trust, it is . . . I don't know . . . a more invincible, more tyrannical feeling, more . . . It is that you are cold and proud like the snowy peak of a mountain, selfish like . . . No, what am I saying? You are all these things and so many others much sweeter, much . . . I can no longer look at you without feeling the irresistible need to embrace you, too . . . You are dazzling, and yet you spread warmth. . . . Your slender hands, your teeth, your sparkling lashes . . . Forgive me. It wasn't this that I wanted to say: your silence makes me talk so much! . . . I love you. But you love me too, I know it and I cannot be mistaken, I know it from your eyes, from the quaver of your voice, from everything. And then . . ."

"Lorenzo! Lorenzo, don't talk like this. . . . Anyway, soon you'll go back to the city and won't think of me any more. When are you leaving? Why don't you leave right away?"

"No, Marta, don't act this way. You are martyring yourself, killing yourself, you are clutching your heart with an icy hand to stifle its beating. . . . Is that what you fear? That I might leave, that I might forget you? Or do you really hope for it? But tell me, speak, give me an explanation. Do you fear that one day I will no longer love you while you continue to love me, and your pride already suffers for this thing that does not exist, that could not exist? Or are you afraid? . . . But I want to marry you, I can marry you tomorrow, Marta."

"Oh, Lorenzo, leave me alone, do you want me to beg you on my knees?"

"Come here, Marta, give me your hand. . . ."

"No. Listen; if you hoped . . . If you wanted to arouse these feelings in me, if you had the power to do it, why didn't you do it before? Now it's too late."

"Too late! But what are you saying, why too late?"

"I am old."

"Oh, Marta, stop talking such nonsense."

"But no, it's true, I . . . It's hard for me to say, like everything. There was a time when I could really have been something for a man, for a man like you. . . . Now it's too late, I tell you; it's too late for everything."

"So that's it! You are telling me that you are so ungenerous as not to give me what only you can give because before you could have given me more (let's say that's true); denying the man you love because you can no longer, provided we admit this, give yourself in the full splendor of your beauty, your youth? Oh, this is impossible."

"But I don't love you, Lorenzo. Perhaps I could have loved you then, long ago. Now I no longer can; and I must not."

"There, she's cursing again. You believe, or you say, that you do not love me because you have no intention whatsoever of surrendering to this love. But you should at least try to . . . try to . . . But there she goes again, invoking duty, duties. Duties to whom or to what? Duties at the cost of one's blood, one's life? There are no such duties. I know that you love me, even if you do not know it. Do you want to try once, only for a short time, for barely a moment, to yield to another the power over yourself? Why don't you try it, like that, just to try it? If only you could imagine what a sweet feeling comes from it, what a sense of security, of peace, even if the other person does everything wrong. After all, this isn't what counts, no point in doing things well in the absolute, it's enough to do them, just like that, together; it's enough not to be alone. We two, we are alone. And I no longer want to be, and I don't want you to be either. Alone with our useless intelligence, our complications, our boredom; with our duties, precisely. But if there were two of us, it would be entirely different: everything would have a meaning, even our boredom, and even intelligence, which in this world, as I've said, is the most useless gift, could be of some use to us. . . . You are my cousin, and so you're close to me in the flesh, too. How many things in common this blood relationship has given us! You have always seemed to me warm and familiar, and you, you who are so distant at times, seemed mine already. When I was a boy . . ."

"Hey, you two. Come here, now we're really going to have some fun."

It was the Count who together with his factor was crossing the room, whispering and laughing under his breath. Marta and Lorenzo had barely the time to jump apart.

In the next room awaited some new tomfoolery of the Baron's, who still, and unrelentingly, wanted either to put the ghosts to flight or satiate himself on their sight.

They resumed soon after in another room, into which I had by now purposely followed them. Because of that phosphorescent quality of her skin to which I have already alluded, I could quite clearly make out all of her gestures. And, since this time it had somewhat relented, that rich, vibrant voice, quavering now and then, seemed the voice itself of the dark and ardent province, with its invincible and secret passions, its prides, its infinite complications, its stumblings, its difficulties of expression, its hopeless surrenders, its indomitable and jealous virginities elevated to tokens of superior dignity, with the savage strength of its conventions, which burn up everything and to which everything can be sacrificed, and its trite duties. The enraptured province, I say, where thefe are no "practical and rational" solutions which take into account the rights of man or woman, where inhumanly and nobly one dies for a point of punctilio, and can be lost over a word; where everything matters, where language itself is an echo of less vulgar times.

The varied and incessant noises of the house formed a solid-colored backdrop against which this colloquy stood out. "Why do you still want to throw your life away, Marta?"

"Because I already threw it away . . . then."

"Let's say it's so, now I'm speaking for you without thinking of myself. Tell me, why did you throw it away then?"

"Why! I . . . I don't know. Because I am a fool, of course. Perhaps you're right, because of pride; because I felt or imagined that I was entitled to something else, because there was nobody who touched my heart. . . . And so the time has passed, and now it is too late, I already told you."

"But too late for what, how? You have not wasted your life, all that you have done in all these years has been to accumulate it within you and indeed enrich it, make it ferment; not even a crumb has been lost. All that you have done is to keep it in trust for the man who . . . And even if I am not that man . . . all this immense accumulated strength is ready to restore life to a languishing creature. Is not this the most noble aim? Besides, you haven't many years ahead of you; I know that no one was worthy of you, that I am not now, *but* . . . And would you want to give up, just like that, give up everything, even the most minute, lowest pleasures—the pleasure, for example, that would not involve your pride? Do you want to keep that senseless virginity of yours so preciously? Do you want to give up all things because you can't have everything?"

"All things. It must be everything or nothing. You think it's sense-less."

"Oh, if I knew where to find the man for you, if it meant that I had to engage in mortal struggle with him, I would bring him here to you in my arms. . . ."

She passed her hands over her temples, sinking her fingers into her hair. She said abruptly, with a dull resonance:

"Yes; he is here now, at this very moment. It's you, Lorenzo."

"Marta! Oh, Marta, I knew it, but it's the first time you've said it. Say it again. Come, come closer, give me your hand at last. Say it again."

"Yes . . . and perhaps for the last time. Yes, it is you, but what does this mean?"

"What! What does this mean? It means everything, it means that all becomes simple, that the happiness which we have not had until now . . ."

"Nothing becomes simple. On the contrary everything becomes more difficult, terrible, unbearable."

"Eh, what words! Leave these thoughts behind now, Marta, they do not belong to this moment. Listen, look, I am happy now. You too must be happy, you can't help but be. Marta, cousin, sister, and bride, and mistress and . . . Kiss me."

"Stop, Lorenzo, what are you doing! No, let me go, I don't want to . . . I don't want to."

"Just one kiss, gently, the kiss of a sister."

"No, let me go, have mercy. No . . . no," she concluded, almost with tears in her voice.

She was clinging to him, she was searching for his mouth with hers, which she pulled back at the first grazing touch, then she put her hand over his mouth, digging her elbow into his chest, then re-laxed for a moment and immediately after caught herself, pulling his head toward her and pushing it away almost at the same time, strok-ing his temples, arching her body, trying to escape from him and to

hold him. She was gasping; her voice, even more subdued, repeated:
"No, let me go, have mercy. . . ."

Finally she freed herself with a brusque movement. But immediately after she pulled him close to her, and gripping his face in her hands and bringing hers close to it, said in a suddenly harsh, almost sibilant voice:

"Very well, listen to me, Lorenzo. I . . ." The words she was about to pronounce seemed to cost her an effort. "I love you, I love you more than myself. You wanted to know, you knew it already, and now you know. This is what you wanted from me, that I should tell you in my voice and in these words, and I have done so. But now . . . I love you more than myself, but not more than . . . Anyway, this something which I have within me is invincible, it is imperious, and it demands its victim, its victims. No, let me go, let me speak, and listen carefully. I love you, but I will never be yours. If I were to yield to you once, if I had the weakness, the strength, call it what you will, to yield to you, I would kill you immediately after, I swear it. Mark my words, Lorenzo, my love: I would kill you immediately after. I can't tell you why this is so, why I do not want anyone to say that he has had me. But it is so . . ."

"Psst, hey, come here a moment."

"What's up?"

"It's that . . . Listen, I may be a fool, but . . . I have something to tell you."

"But what is it?"

"How many ghosts are we supposed to have, all told?"

"Well . . . I don't know. Why do you ask me? Oh! did you too . . . ?"

"You know what I mean?"

"Yes, I think I do. Because I must admit that I too . . . But I thought that it was all my imagination."

"Perhaps, in fact it certainly is all imaginary . . . however . . ."

"Filippo knows how many there are. Where the deuce did he go? But watch out; he mustn't be told that . . . You must only say that we think that an intruder, some crook has gotten in here. Of course he won't swallow it, but I mean . . . And don't say anything to the women, for heaven's sake. Ah, here he is. Well, Filippo, we're afraid . . . ahem . . . we have reason to fear that someone has wormed his way in here and . . . and now it would take too long to explain. You're sure you know how many ghosts there are? All right then, we have to count them over again and identify them one by one. Understand?"

"Very well, my lord, it won't be easy under the circumstances, but I'll try. Besides, to tell the truth, I'm not even sure whether some of them haven't left for town tonight. But it won't be difficult to find out from the women. All right, I'm going."

"Marta, I'm frightened."

"Frightened of what, you silly girl?"

"But, you see, for a while now everything in here has been giving me a creepy feeling. And then I happened to overhear something Stefano and Giovanni were saying: they're frightened, too."

"What are you talking about!"

"Yes, yes; they promised each other not to say anything to us, but they told Filippo that they think some crook might have gotten in. The truth is that they're frightened, too."

"I don't understand a word of what you're saying."

"Well, do you want to know? I too have had the same impression. In short, it seems to me there is one extra, I mean one extra ghost."

"But what kind of fantasy is this?"

"No, no, it's really true. I counted carefully. That is, I don't know exactly how many ghosts there are, and so I couldn't really count, but, just like that, by hit or miss, it seems to me . . . In fact I'm absolutely certain. Anyway, couldn't somebody actually get in . . .

someone who wanted to do us harm, I don't know, a murderer, say? Won't you admit that that could easily happen?"

"A murderer? . . . And to kill whom, then? Nobody has enemies among us, all are liked and . . . and loved."

"Just think, he could be here, right here among us, and we would not be aware of anything. . . . And finally, do you want me to tell you? These pranks, I've enjoyed them a lot, but still . . . At bottom I don't like these pranks. You can't fool with ghosts, you never know; these things might really attract them. I wish they'd put on the lights."

So the hoaxers were about to be hoaxed, and by what obscure paths! Yet, among these hoaxers was I myself, who in a certain fashion was hoaxing the hoaxers. An amusing complication (at least so I would hope) for the reader; not for me at that moment. In sum, it was time to think about abandoning the field, and quickly too. And yet it was not an easy thing to accomplish, since not only that damned Filippo but all those who were frightened were now identifying the ghosts, and lying in wait for them, a circumstance that made my pants too tight for comfort. I did not lose hope, however, of getting out of that scrape. By keeping calm and always withdrawing before the advance of those nuts, I would finally come to an unguarded door, and once outside . . . And just then I was helped by an unforeseen and terrible turn of events.

It was almost morning. Despite the sense of malaise which had spread among its occupants, the noises and agitations of the house continued without rest. The shots continued, and the monotonous invocations, the Baron's yelps, the vast movement of shadows. And behold, from some indefinite point of the house's bowels, a shriek suddenly rose. I had heard many shrieks that night, but this shriek had something special about it: it was urgent, it was—how to put it?—true. A shriek of horror. The others too must have perceived that unusual tone, because some of them pushed forward cautiously, while others ran. Then loud shouts from the same direction, calls, finally more shouts, demanding light. And I too instinctively ran in that direction, forgetful of my grave peril.

They couldn't find the fuse. At last the lights flashed out, downright blinding after so much darkness, thus surprising me in the open; and in my haste I had also lost or dropped my bedsheet. Fortunately, they had by then all flowed down the stairs which led into the cellar from the main hallway. Naturally not all the lights had been lit when they had removed the fuse, but the lantern in the hallway had been—there was no way out. And yet I had my reasons for rushing there. I mean to say that I almost imagined, atrociously suspected what I would find. So I had to *see*. And I managed to find an observation post: behind the panel of the heavy door to the cellar, which granted me an ample view of the entire scene. Through the crack between it and the doorjamb, the scene spread out below me, since the stairway continued down a brief ramp after the door.

This cellar was the usual cellar with a vaulted ceiling; ample, wide and well-kept, and hence more disheartening. But a thick cobweb enveloped the lamp attached to the ceiling. And there in that cruel and slightly hallucinatory light, there at my feet lay the corpse of a man: of Lorenzo, who else could it be? He had fallen face down with his jacket gaping wide and pulled down from his shoulders, his hair unnaturally disheveled. A stain of blood, fixed, not spreading and not too large, was in the middle of his back, perhaps a bit to the left. He must have been dead for more than an hour, although I do not know how I deduced that. And if the powder burns I thought I saw on the cloth of his shirt were not a fantasy of mine, he must have been shot pointblank.

In a semicircle around him and facing me were all the characters of this story, with something dusty and at the same time chalky in their consternated and perplexed faces, with their eyelids puckered against the light like those of so many nocturnal animals. There were also all the ghosts, some with their shrouds thrown back, others carrying them on their arms, others yet having thrown them away some-where.

At first they kept silent, then they all began to talk and scurry around at once. Nor did the Baron's behavior fail to live up to its usual standards. He seemed to be violently tossed between the two poles of indignation at the hoax suffered and of horror as well as regret at what had happened; and if he was pretty confused before, you can imagine what he was like now. "But who could have done this?" he was shouting hysterically. "I'm asking you, who did it, how did it happen? Oh, our poor friend. Oh, I'll hate you for the rest of my life. And we've got to do something, let's do something. They did it, one of them . . ." And so on.

And the indomitable Marta was there too, the only one not upset. With a motionless, hard, stony face, with a dark, still look, without a tear, she stared at the rigid body of the man she loved.

Finally they thought of the police. The police—well now; among other things I stood to gain a murder charge at the very least. It was definitely the moment for departure. Besides, they were starting to come upstairs and I certainly could not continue standing there. What's more, it was almost dawn.

The police. And what could the police do in a case like that? Only I knew what had happened, and nobody else could even imagine it. In any event, I vainly perused the newspapers during the days that followed. Perhaps they kept quiet out of respect for the Count and his family. As a rule, you can be sure that these blessed local sheets will never report an accident or anything at all that one has personally witnessed, and sometimes in our profession this silence is irksome.

But I knew, and you will say that I could denounce the crime, indeed that I had the duty to. Ah, my good sirs, if I had gone ahead with these duties, I would not be where I am now. No, not to meddle in other people's affairs has been the basic rule of my life, which has brought me to this tranquil and . . . yes, honored position. From the present story, true enough, you wouldn't say that I don't meddle in other people's affairs, would you? But certainly leaving creatures to their own fate has always seemed to me the most honest and wise rule.

It is true that now you too know. But so much time has passed, and I do not think that there is anything to be feared from your civic enthusiasm. Who knows what has become of those people? Some of them are probably dead. I've heard only about Marta, by chance: she is an old and aristocratic spinster and looks after her property. She still lives in that house, but alone.

But now enough. At a certain point, before, I even started to talk like a poet. It's time to get back to work.